WISHING

FOR

yesterday

A. M. KUSI

Published by A. M. Kusi 2023

amkusinovels@gmail.com

Visit our website at www.amkusi.com

Editor: Lauren Clarke of CREATING ink

Sensitivity Edit: Renita McKinney of A Book A Day

Proofreader: Judy's Proofreading

Cover Design: Regina Wamba of ReginaWamba.com

OTHER BOOKS BY A. M. KUSI

Stepping Into Tomorrow

(Book 1 in The Emerson Family of Shattered Cove)

Risking Forever

(Book 2 in The Emerson Family of Shattered Cove)

A Fallen Star (eBook FREE on all retailers)

(Book 1 in The Shattered Cove Series)

Glass Secrets

(Book 2 in The Shattered Cove Series)

Defying Gravity

(Book 3 in The Shattered Cove Series)

The Lighthouse Inn

(Book 4 in The Shattered Cove series)

His True North

(Book 5 in The Shattered Cove series)

In The Grey

(Book 6 in The Shattered Cove series)

<u>Brave Love</u>

(Book 7 in The Shattered Cove series)

<u>Hope Between Us</u>

(Book 8 in The Shattered Cove series)

<u>Beautiful Collision</u>

(A Shattered Cove Novel)

<u>One Holiday Kiss (eBook FREE on all retailers)</u>

(A Shattered Cove Short Story)

<u>The Orchard Inn Series</u>

(Our first complete steamy romance series.)

For a complete list of all our books, visit:

<u>www.amkusi.com/books</u>

This book is dedicated to all of you in the rainbow spectrum. Keep on showing the world just how beautiful your love is. <3

*"The notion that somehow defining yourself as a man is dependent on,
are you able to put somebody else down instead of lifting them up . . . able
to dominate as opposed to support . . . that is an old view. A view that
thankfully I see a lot of people rejecting."* —Barack Obama

"Maybe the journey isn't so much about becoming anything. Maybe it's about un-becoming everything that isn't really you so you can be who you were meant to be in the first place." —Unknown

GET A FREE SHORT NOVEL

Join our newsletter to get a FREE short novel that's not available on any retailer. Plus updates about new releases, giveaways, pre-orders, sneak peeks, and more.

Visit the website below to join now.

WWW.AMKUSI.COM/NEWSLETTER

TABLE OF CONTENTS

PLAYLIST

"Welcome to Paradise" by Grandson
"So Pissed" by Bohnes
"Care For You" by Ryan Ashley
"Kiss the Boy" by Keiynan Lonsdale
"HIM" by Sam Smith
"Fuck Away the Pain" by Divide the Day
"Die a Little" by YUNGBLUD
"Bad Things" by Noah Davis
"Worst To Me" by Noah Davis
"Peaches & Cream" by Noah Davis
"Be Here For You" by Sam Tinnesz
"Play With Fire" by Sam Tinnesz
"Hate Myself" by NF
"No One Knows Us (feat. Carly Paige)" by BANNERS
"Lost My Mind" by FINNEAS
"Take Me Away" by New Medicine
"Nails" by Call Me Karizma
"Fire on Fire" by Sam Smith

"Dirty Mind" by Boy Epic
"Serotonin" by Call Me Karizma
"Fallen Angel" by Three Days Grace
"Happier" by Ed Sheeran
"It's Raining, It's Pouring" by Anson Seabra
"I Can't Get High" by Royal & the Serpent
"Voices in My Head" by Falling in Reverse
"Falling like the Stars" by James Arthur
"Nervous" by John Legend

1

RICKY

Ricky would always be a bachelor. Relationships were scary as fuck. They forced you to open up parts of yourself that should never see the light of day.

He forced a breath into his lungs. Tiny threads of expectation circled his neck, squeezing tighter with every lovesick look his brothers shared with the women they'd been lucky enough to find love with. Alone in a crowded room, he did his best to look relaxed at the long table surrounded by family and friends. He sipped his vodka and cranberry as he glanced out the window to his left. Big, fat raindrops plopped against the pane from the skies outside as the wind whipped the bare trees at the side of his adoptive parents' farm.

It couldn't have been more opposite to the warmth the farmhouse always held.

Low jazz music bled through the Bluetooth speakers in the dining room as conversations and laughter bounced off the pale walls. The yip of his niece Ariel's new puppy drew his attention to the end of the table where she and Eli sat, sneaking bits of their dinner to the already spoiled black and white mutt, Pepper.

"So, you work with Roman and the bees too?" Itsuki asked Ricky from his right, motioning towards his daughter and Roman.

"Yeah. I own Emerson Apiaries with Roman, and I'm also branching out to take clients at the gym this winter."

"That's interesting. Will you have time to manage all of it? It seems like the bees take a lot of work," Itsuki said.

"Winter's our slow season. Not much to do except bottle and deliver honey until the snow melts—then the real work begins. You'll have to take a few jars home with you when you go," Roman added.

"I would love that. Thank you," Itsuki said.

"Okay, whose turn is it?" His dad's voice rose over the chatter of the rest of the family.

Ricky took another sip of his drink and let his gaze wander around the table. His father sat at the head, his ma beside him as usual. Across from Ricky were Elise and his brother Roman, whispering to each other. Ricky was certain his brother's hand was busy under the table, no doubt responsible for the blush in Elise's cheeks. *Good for him.*

Beside them was Nash, holding the almost one-year-old Alba as she reached for food from her dad's plate and shoved it by the tiny fistful into her mouth. Most of it seemed like it was ending up on his brother's lap. His brand-new sister-in-law, Isabella, leaned on Nash's shoulder, looking up at him like he'd hung the fucking moon. A pulse of jealousy burned Ricky's gut before he shoved it away.

"I'll go," his ma announced, lifting her drink and eyeing Roman with a knowing look. "I'm grateful that I have almost my whole family here with us, and new people to add to that list, despite a rocky start." She eyed Isabella's mother, Catherine, who smiled sheepishly.

Ricky barely held back a snort.

"And for being able to make new friends who will hopefully become family one day soon." His ma winked before tipping her head towards Elise's parents. "For my family, a roof over our heads, and this wonderful food that everyone had a hand in."

Ma sipped from her glass. Everyone took turns going around the table to say what they were most grateful for, as was their family tradition.

"Where is Nova, by the way?" Elise asked.

Good question.

"She said she was picking up her date and would be a little late coming from the airport," his dad answered.

"Nova has a date?" Ricky asked.

His ma's smile was conspiratorial. "Yup. Two kids down, two to go."

Ricky snorted and shook his head. Almost everyone's eyes darted to him, making his skin itch.

He shrugged and sat up a little straighter. "I'm never settling down. You should just be satisfied with your other children and grandchildren."

"Famous last words," Nash teased in his grumpy baritone voice.

"Fudge you." Ricky lifted his middle finger and pretended to scratch his nose.

"That's enough. We have company. At least try to act civilized for a couple hours," Ma chastised.

Ricky tilted his lips and gave her the magic smile that helped him get away with most things. "Aww, Ma, you know it would be a shame to deprive the single ladies—"

The door swung open.

His lungs froze.

All the blood drained from his face. *No. It can't be.* Ricky's heart raced. Sweat broke out on his forehead. Terror seized him in an iron grip. *Nononono. This isn't happening.*

Nova walked farther into the room with a goofy, flushed smile on her face, but next to her was a man Ricky recognized all too quickly despite the two and a half decades that had passed since they'd last been together. *It can't be him.*

The urge to flee rose. He squeezed the arms on the chair, forcing himself to stay put and not draw attention to himself.

Voices melded together, becoming background static. The only thing that got through to Ricky was Nova's boyfriend's name. Everett. Everett fucking Popova. The last time Ricky had seen him had been the worst day of Ricky's life.

His parents got up to greet their new guest. Ricky forced his eyes away from the boy he used to know who'd turned into a man. Ricky studied a dent in the wooden table instead. Every muscle in his body was rigid as a corpse—which was what he'd be if anyone found out how he knew Everett.

"Thanks for having me. I hope I'm not intruding." Everett's deep rumble had a bit of a rasp to it. Ricky's body immediately reacted to it, his hands trembling and his blood rushing through his veins, causing his ears to ring. Hyper-aware of the man, Ricky kept his face turned away, hoping to God Everett didn't recognize him. Ricky was nothing like the fourteen-year-old string bean he'd once been.

Everett and Nova took the empty seats next to Roman and directly across from Ricky.

"You're not intruding at all. Welcome, Everett," his dad said.

"I suppose I should introduce you to everyone, but there's no way you'll remember all their names." Nova laughed.

Ricky's skin was scalding hot. He needed to move out of

their line of sight. He turned as he stood, putting his back to his sister and the man from his past. Instead, Ricky walked to the other end of the table while his sister rattled off names. He bent down and petted the puppy now lazing by his niece's feet.

"So, tell me about yourself, Everett. What do you do?" his ma asked.

Could anyone else hear how hard Ricky's heart was beating? His gaze cut to the exits to the room. Maybe he could make an excuse and leave before he was recognized. But what if Everett figured things out from a photo or something and then told his family how they knew each other? Fuck. This was bad. This was what he'd always feared—that his past would catch up to him and everyone would find out what a scumbag Ricky really was.

You're a good-for-nothing piece of shit. You'll never amount to anything. Little bitch. Not even a real man. Ricky's body tensed, expecting a blow, but it didn't come.

He blinked as Nova said something to their ma.

"It's fine." Everett's voice sunk into his skin like an anchor, pulling Ricky's attention to the face that would haunt his nightmares tonight.

Everett ran a hand through his raven-black hair that contrasted with his pale skin. The strands were longer on top and shorter on the sides, in a fade. His grey-blue eyes glittered with mirth as his smooth lips turned up into an enigmatic smile. "I've been working as a vendor in California for cannabis distributers there."

Fuck, hearing his voice was like taking a hit of a drug. The feeling swirled in his veins, poisoning him slowly from the inside out. His head spun.

"And how did you two meet?" Nash asked.

"Everett and I met at a convention some years ago and

have kept in contact ever since." Nova's voice rose a little higher in pitch. She was hiding something.

"Long-distance relationship, huh?" Roman asked.

Nova rolled her eyes, grabbing a bottle of wine and filling her glass and Everett's. "Mm-hmm. Oh, Elise, I didn't realize your family would be here."

"Yeah, this is my mom, Mai, my father, Itsuki, and my brother, Ren," Elise introduced them.

"Nice to meet you." Nova smiled at them and then guzzled her wine as conversation continued around them.

"Are you feeling okay, Ricky?" Isabella asked.

Ricky flinched at his name as once again, all eyes in the room turned towards him. Hell, Alba even gave him a gummy smile. Why couldn't he turn invisible just this once? He quickly steeled his expression, standing to his full height, and made his way back to his setting, ears ringing. He reached for his drink and chugged it. He'd need some liquid courage to get through this dinner. If Everett said anything, his family would never look at him the same way.

"I'm fine. If I'd known everyone was bringing a date, I would have brought Sophia."

"Who's Sophia?" their mother asked in a hope-filled voice.

"Just one of Ricky's many 'friends.'" Nova smirked.

Everett's eyes locked with Ricky's, and for a moment, Ricky was that teenage boy again, so lost and lonely that he'd trusted another boy with his deepest, darkest secrets. And then life as he knew it had ended.

Everett's eyes widened, recognition clearly dawning. He cleared his throat. "Ric—"

"Hey, man, nice to meet you. Anyone else need more wine?" Ricky scanned everyone's face at the table except Everett's.

"I'll take another scotch." Their dad handed Ricky his glass.

"I'll take a little more of the riesling. Don't forget to save room for dessert, everyone." Isabella motioned to the table brimming with pies, cakes, and cookies.

Ricky forced a laugh, trying to look as unaffected as possible by the ticking time bomb sitting next to his sister. "I'm trying to watch my figure. Wouldn't want to look like your husband," he teased.

Nash chuckled and shook his head. "You think you're so funny."

Ricky picked up his dishes and slipped them under his father's glass, then darted to the kitchen, swerving out of the way of Nash's slap. When all else failed—misdirection, antagonism, and jokes were his failsafe.

He set the dishes on the counter and braced himself against the sink, his chest heaving, faster and faster. Slamming his eyes closed, he forced himself to slow down. Having a panic attack would only draw more attention to himself. Fuck, he didn't want to appear weak.

"Ricardo?" Everett's deep timbre made his knees quake.

Ricky straightened, wiping down his expression until he hoped he looked apathetic.

He turned around.

"It is you. Man, I—"

Ricky clasped his hand over Everett's forearm and dragged him towards the stairs. "We need to talk."

His hand tingled and burned as if Everett was a source of energy. *Must be a panic attack side effect.*

He passed his old room. There was no way he was taking Everett in there. It would make him too vulnerable. Instead, he reached for the doorknob to his parents' office.

Ricky opened the door, tugged Everett in, and pulled it shut before whirling back around on him.

"How the fuck are you here?" Ricky's shoulders rose and fell with heaving breaths as he spoke his thoughts aloud.

Everett blinked as if taken aback. "I—I came with Nova."

Ricky took a step forward, running his gaze from Everett's shiny dress shoes and up the black ironed slacks that perfectly hugged Everett's lean thighs. The cranberry-red dress shirt pulled taut against his chest and had the top two buttons undone, showing off a few dark hairs peeking out.

Ricky was just taking in the guy he used to know—he definitely wasn't checking him out.

Everett shoved his sleeves up his muscular forearms and then settled his hands on his hips. "Ricardo—"

"Don't call me that!" he snapped. "My name is Ricky."

Pain flashed in Everett's nearly grey eyes before they clouded over with what seemed like guilt. His shoulders hunched. "Sorry. I didn't mean anything by it."

"Did you know she was my sister?"

Lines appeared on Everett's forehead. "No. Last I knew, you didn't have a sister—"

"That's just it," Ricky sneered, pointing his finger at Everett as he stepped forward to get in his face. Everett's clean, soapy scent with a dash of something citrusy assaulted his nose, making his mouth water. He shook his head. He reached out for the familiar hum of anger coursing through his veins, staving off the panic, the pain, and the dark desire until everything else was suffocated but rage.

"You don't know me. And whatever you think you do know is wrong. So we've never met before today. Got it?"

Everett's expression morphed into one of pain before his gaze dropped and he nodded. "Sure. If that's what you want."

Fuck, Ricky might have been acting like an asshole, but

this was about survival. This man had the power to ruin everything good in his life that he'd fought so hard and so long for. All of it could be taken away in the blink of an eye.

"Glad we have an understanding." Ricky turned and ran straight into a solid mass of body.

"Oof!" Roman grunted. "Sorry. We didn't know anyone was in here."

Ricky's attention vaulted between Elise's guilty and embarrassed expression and his brother, who was focused on Everett. Questions swirled in his gaze.

"No problem. Nova's date here just got lost. I was making sure he understood what we'd do to him if he hurt our baby sister." Ricky cut Everett a threatening glare. *Keep your mouth shut.*

Hurt shone in Everett's eyes and it fucking tore at Ricky's chest, raking across the scarred flesh of old wounds. They'd been so close once upon a time—and then they had almost died because of Ricky's secret. His heart thumped wildly. Ricky was unable to draw in a full breath. Anxiety set in, spinning through his veins like sticky spiderwebs.

"Better get those drink refills." Ricky pushed past Roman and ran away from the room as his panic attack took over. A rushing sound filled his ears. He took the vape pen from his pocket. Turning it on, he slipped the cartridge into his mouth and drew in a deep breath, filling his lungs and holding the breath before letting it out. He did it three more times until the THC kicked in, calm settling into his bones. His chest fluttered, but he breathed through it.

His bio father, Donald, had been right; Ricky was weak. And if anyone else found out, life as he knew it would be over, and he'd be back where he'd started—alone in a nightmare.

2

EVERETT

Everett's mind was still spinning. His stomach flipped as he returned to Nova's side. Ricardo Benning was now Ricky Emerson. Everett had wondered what had happened to Ricardo after that night—the one that changed everything. *The night I almost got him killed.*

He swallowed the lump of emotion that rose from the memory. The last time he'd seen Ricardo—no, he was Ricky now—his friend's bloodied body had been crumpled on the floor. Ricky's father had been standing over him, fists clenched, eyes lit with a rage Everett had never known.

Nova's arm brushed his, jerking him out of the past. "Everett?"

"I'm sorry, what?"

She smiled at him. "Mom and Dad want to know how we met."

Right. He was here to play the part of the date. A bit ironic for a gay man to be playing the beard for one of his female friends, but Nova had seemed desperate. If a couple of dates to family events gave her a little more peace in her life, why not?

One reason *why not* walked back in the room, the faint herbal aroma of cannabis clinging to the air around him.

Ricky took the seat directly across from him, his eyes directed to the table. Everett's heart clenched, fresh pain seeping through decades-old scars that had never quite healed right.

Someone laughed at the other end of the table. Ricky's gaze crashed into his, cold and devoid of anything other than dark anger—and was that hatred? Everett's stomach tensed. His skin burned both hot and cold.

A not-so-soft blow from Nova's elbow hit his rib cage.

"Uh, sorry, I was just . . . thinking about the first time we met," Everett covered.

"At the conference," Nova supplied.

He smiled at her. Forcing his attention away from the ghost from his past took all his strength. "Right, I was working one of the tables, and Nova here came up with an actual printed list of questions. We ended up talking until everyone started cleaning up and decided to finish the conversation over dinner."

"Was this the one day of the conference I didn't attend?" Nash asked as Everett dug into his dinner.

"Yes," Nova answered. "We exchanged numbers and kept in touch. In fact, without Everett's help, I might not have gotten my business off the ground."

"I doubt that. You're pretty determined when you want something." *Like when you convinced me to be your date.* He winked at her.

Her parents and brothers—all except Ricky—laughed at that statement.

"He knows you, alright," James Emerson teased.

"He certainly does," Renita agreed, her eyes seeming a little hopeful as they volleyed between Everett and Nova.

He didn't feel right lying to anyone. He'd agreed to be Nova's date, but that didn't mean he would be dating her. He was just buying her some time. Ironic that having to pretend to be straight was one of the reasons he'd come to Shattered Cove.

The family continued to tease Nova, giving Everett a few minutes to study Ricky, who was back to studying the table. Ricky looked nothing like the young boy he used to know.

The years had been nothing but gracious to him. His dark hair was hidden behind a backwards baseball cap. His black T-shirt was stretched over his wide chest. Ricky ran a hand over his chiseled jaw peppered with dark scruff. One muscular tattooed arm slung behind him, his long fingers gripping the back of his neck as he relaxed in the chair like he didn't have a care in the world. The colorful Colombian flag of Ricky's heritage complemented his tan skin on his forearm. Everett's arm still burned where Ricky had grabbed him. *Who are you now, Ricardo?*

Everett set his fork down. The Noveas and Aki family resumed conversation, but Nova's brothers and parents seemed to be focused on him. Well, all except the man across from him who couldn't be more disinterested, based on his bored expression. Ricky's apparent apathy was another shot to the stomach. Had what they shared meant so little to him? *He won't ever forgive me.*

"What brings you to Shattered Cove?" Nash asked.

"I was ready for a change of career." *And a new location that wouldn't remind me of my ex.* "My mom lives in a small town outside Concord and my dad is in Bedford. I grew up here in New Hampshire."

Ricky tensed, his arm slipping to his lap, his cheek pulsing the same way it had when they'd been kids and he'd been feeling self-conscious or embarrassed.

"Oh, really?" James asked, glancing at Ricky.

"Yeah."

"Did you want to move back to be closer to family, or was there something else?" Renita asked, once again glancing at Nova before focusing on him with interest.

"What my mother is trying to ask, not too discreetly, is if you moved here to marry me and have babies with me," Nova deadpanned.

"Nova!" Renita chastised.

Ricky snickered, a smile that didn't reach his eyes curving the corner of his mouth. "Nothing like being direct. Didn't you teach us that, Ma?"

Renita shook her head. "What's wrong with wanting my only daughter safe and happy and in love?"

"Nothing, darling." James patted her hand.

Nova's shoulders sunk a little. He could understand her desire to get her mom off her back now. But he didn't want to mislead her family any more than he already had.

"Everett is a friend whom I'm getting to know better, right?" Nova turned towards him.

"Absolutely. And to answer your question, Mrs. Emerson, I'm here for a few reasons. I'm currently working to help New Hampshire legislators hopefully get a little closer to Maine and Vermont's cannabis laws, working towards making it recreationally legal here too. And I will be working with Hope Facility as a counselor and to help with their new program. It's a place for LGBTQ+ youth who are homeless or cared for by the state, as well as a local resource."

"Oh, yes, we're good friends with Aaron, who runs the place with his wife, Brynn," James added.

"That's awesome. Not every family is so accepting of

queer youth." Everett couldn't stop his attention from darting to the man across from him.

Panic flashed in Ricky's gaze before his tan skin reddened. He glared at Everett.

Everett tried to check the emotion that clogged his throat. "A safe place they can go is very much needed. It's nice to see there are people out there who are willing to give them some of the love and care they deserve."

"Amen to that," Renita agreed.

Ricky's chair scraped across the floor as he stood abruptly. "I'm gonna head out. Gotta get ready for my client." He walked over to give his dad a pat on the back and then kissed his adoptive mom's cheek. "Thanks for dinner, Ma."

"You're leaving already?" she asked.

"What about dessert?" Isabella asked.

Ricardo patted his flat stomach. "I thought we went over this. I can't let myself go just because my big brother did."

Nash growled something and handed the baby in his arms to his wife as he stood. "You wanna keep running your mouth? I'll give you something to talk about."

"Not in the house!" Renita yelled. "Can't we have one family holiday meal without you kids acting a fool? We have company. Sit your ass down, Nash."

Nash grumbled but sat back down.

Ricky snickered. "Mama's boy."

Renita narrowed her eyes at him, a warning in her glare. "Something you want to say?"

Ricky shook his head, his smile morphing into something less haughty and more charming. "Nothing but I love you."

Nash scoffed.

"You drive safe and text me when you get to the gym and when you leave," Renita said.

"Of course." He waved to the room. "Have a good night,

everyone. And don't forget the honey jars, Mr. Aki. Roman can show you where they are for you all to take some home."

A few thank-yous came from the other end of the table.

Roman and Elise took that moment to return to the room. Elise looked a little disheveled, making it no secret what they had been up to in the office after Everett had left. Roman was smiling like he'd just won the lottery.

"Don't go yet. We have something to tell you all." Roman beamed.

"What is it?" Renita's voice rose with hope.

"Did she say yes, finally?" Ricky teased.

"Nope." Elise smiled coyly.

"But I did." Roman wrapped his arm around her, pulling her tight against him and kissing her cheek.

"Wait, I'm confused," Nash said.

"Me too," Ren, Elise's brother, added.

Elise reached for Roman's left hand and held it up, showing off the ring on his finger.

"You asked him to marry you?" Mrs. Aki asked, seeming stunned.

"I did."

"My daughter is getting married?" Mrs. Aki clasped her chest.

"This calls for a toast." James got to his feet and disappeared out of the room.

Renita wiped a few tears from her eyes. "Two kids down, two to go." She repeated, eyeing Nova and Everett again. Damn, Nova wasn't kidding about the pressure from her mom.

Everett searched the space Ricardo had been standing in, but he was gone.

Everett swallowed, fighting the urge to run out after him. For twenty-five years he'd wondered what had happened to the boy next door. And now that he'd found him, Ricky seemed to want nothing to do with him.

"How did you propose?" Nova asked, clapping her hands together in excitement.

Elise turned a deep shade of red, her eyes flicking to the floor, and then she picked up her glass and downed what was left with a wince.

"Yes, honey, why don't you tell them how you proposed?" Roman smirked.

"Well, you're really the one that should share since I asked you," she choked out.

"Elise got on her knees and—"

"And asked him to marry me. He said yes, and here we are," Elise said without taking a breath.

"And she asked me first," Roman's daughter, Ariel, piped up from the other end of the table.

"That's right. I did." Elise smiled at her.

"Now you'll get to live with us forever," Ariel added.

Roman kissed Elise's temple. "Forever and ever."

James Emerson returned with a dusty bottle of champagne. "Who wants a glass to cheers?"

* * *

After dinner, they moved on to dessert. Everett smiled and laughed at the conversations going on around him at all the right times, but his mind stayed on the empty seat across from him.

Seeing Ricky again had opened up something that had long been buried. *If only he would talk to me. Then maybe we could both get some closure.*

"I think I better call it a night. Thank you, Mr. and Mrs. Emerson, for having me." Everett stood.

"Oh, we're glad you could join us; you're welcome anytime. And please call me Mama E, like everyone else." Renita pushed her brown and purple-tipped dreadlocks over her shoulder.

"I appreciate it."

Nova stood. "I'll walk you out."

He let her lead the way, grabbing his coat from the hook by the door.

"Thanks again for doing this," Nova whispered.

"You're welcome."

She gave him a hug. "Call me later and we'll meet up, and I'll show you all the cool places in town."

"Will do. Have a good night." He opened the door to a blast of chilly fall air, still damp from the rain, and left.

Everett zipped his jacket closed and headed straight for his rental car, pulling the keys from his pocket.

Someone shoved him forward. He sucked in a quick breath. Everett's chest slammed against the car. *Ugh. What the fuck?* Everett spun around to face his attacker.

Ricky stood there, the indifference from earlier stripped from his expression, the apathetic mask replaced with white-hot fury. "I fucking warned you."

Everett's heart thudded in his ears. Fear snaked around his rib cage and squeezed as Ricky loomed over him, fists clenched at his sides. This wasn't the Ricardo he knew from before—the sensitive boy who'd cry on his shoulder. The one who Everett had shared all his secrets with. That boy was gone. There was nothing soft about Ricky now. He was all hard edges and sharp lines. His broad muscular shoulders seemed impossibly wide as the man stepped closer into Everett's space.

Ricardo never would have even tried to hurt Everett—but Ricky might.

"What the fuck do you think you're doing?" Ricky's deep voice shook with barely contained rage.

Everett opened his mouth to speak, a weight settling on his rib cage, making it hard to breath. He owed so much to the man looming over him. He'd spent decades wishing he could go back and change what had happened.

He drew in a ragged breath, the grief and trauma from that day churning in his stomach, old regret surfacing. "I'm leaving."

Ricky scoffed and pointed back towards the Emersons' huge farmhouse. "You think that shit was funny?"

Confusion swirled in Everett's mind. "I'm not sure—"

"I told you to watch your fucking mouth."

Everett held his hands up, trying to placate him. "I didn't—"

"Don't play dumb. You told them where your family lives. You don't think anyone will put together that I grew up there too? Or the dig you made about not all families being so accepting of queer youth?"

"Oh, shit, you thought I was going to out you?" Everett released a breath as he put the pieces together.

Ricky's eyes narrowed into slits. "I'm not gay!"

Everett stood taller. "Then what the hell are you worried about?"

"Just keep your fucking mouth shut."

Everett frowned, his worry replaced with his own anger. "Last I remember, you liked it when it was open."

He regretted the words the moment they left his mouth.

Ricky's entire body shook with what seemed like a hurricane of emotions. His fists turned white, and his teeth ground so tight, Everett was afraid he'd break a tooth.

"I'm sorry. That was a cheap shot."

Ricky's anger slipped behind a stoic mask.

Everett cleared his throat and continued, "I truly am sorry for upsetting you. I didn't mean to say anything that would make you uncomfortable inside the Emersons'—your family's —home. I just . . . seeing you again after all this time . . . For years I wondered what had happened to you. If you were safe and happy. If you were okay and got the help you needed."

Ricky stared over Everett's shoulder.

"I understand if you hate me for what I did back then. I just . . . I didn't know what else to do." Everett's voice cracked with the well of emotion talking about the past brought up. The helplessness he'd felt. The terror that had gripped every cell of his body.

Ricky's shoulders relaxed the smallest fraction as he met Everett's gaze once more. "I don't hate you."

Everett blinked, hope rising in his belly. "Y-you don't?"

"How could I? You saved my life." Ricky turned and walked away, leaving Everett reeling.

This—this changed everything.

3

─────

RICKY

Ricky hit the bag swaying in front of him. His hands ached and his legs burned with exhaustion, but his mind still wouldn't shut up. Sweat trickled down his forehead, stinging his eyes. He swiped it with his already slick arm, making it worse. Chest heaving, he gripped the bag hanging from the chain to steady it as he caught his breath.

A cool burst of air whispered across his back. He glanced at the person coming through the door. His heart stuttered, his rib cage squeezing, making it even harder to draw breath. His guts twisted.

Everett walked in, running a hand through the sleep-mussed dark tumble of waves on his head. Half-moons of purple hung underneath his eyes as if he'd stayed up all night —like Ricky wasn't the only one who hadn't been able to sleep. *Is it because of me?*

Everett headed straight for the front desk, his grey sweatpants hugging his tight ass. Ricky forced himself to turn around and head over to his gym bag. He picked up a towel and wiped the sweat from his face, arms, and bare chest. He slipped off the tape from his hands before he grabbed the jump rope and continued to punish his body.

Who was Everett Popova now? Was he anything like the boy Ricky remembered? The steady whistle of the rope soothed him as he forced his protesting legs to push further. Pain kept the anxiety at bay.

His attention strayed to the front desk. Everett nodded to the owner and then slipped white earbuds into his ears, heading straight for one of the treadmills. At least Everett hadn't noticed Ricky yet. Twenty-five years had passed without a word from the man, and now Ricky had seen him twice in two days.

Everett started at a slow jog, his lean, muscular arms bent at the elbows, swaying back and forth with his stride. From this angle, Ricky could observe the man from his past. The one who knew his deepest, darkest secrets and who had the power to ruin him with a few words.

But what was he doing here in Shattered Cove? Ricky continued to jump rope. Everett upped the pace, gliding into a run. His hips swayed, powerful legs giving him a smooth gait. A sliver of ink on his broad shoulders peeked out from his muscle shirt. The way he moved was hypnotic. Everett had always been fit, even as a boy, but now—now he was all lean and cut and man.

You like dick? You're nothing but a pussy. Your mother would be ashamed of you—hell, she'd be more disgusted than me, and that's saying something.

Ricky shook his head, trying to rid his biological father's voice from his head. Increasing the speed of the rope, he punished himself. If he felt physical pain, he wouldn't feel it anywhere else, right? He pushed, his legs numb and wobbly from overexertion. Still, he pushed. If he could just go a little further, maybe he could outrun the pain from his past—his shame.

His left leg gave out. He fell hard, smashing his chin onto the floor. Pain exploded in his mouth and knees as the air was knocked out of him. He tried to suck in oxygen but his lungs wouldn't work. Panic strangled Ricky as he shoved up to sitting.

A big, warm hand thudded against his back. Ricky jerked, finally inhaling sweat-tinged air.

"You alright? Your lip's bleeding." Pops, Tidal Gym's owner, patted his back once more.

"I'm fine." Ricky gulped in oxygen, his body trembling.

"You need to get some electrolytes in you. Take it easy." Pops walked away and grabbed a Gatorade from the cooler behind the front desk, then brought it over to him.

Thankfully, Everett's back was still to him, his earbuds obviously drowning out Ricky's misstep.

"Thanks." Ricky twisted the cap off and guzzled half of the drink down, hoping the cool temperature would help calm his racing heart.

Ricky closed his eyes. "Thanks again, Pops. I'll rest here a minute and then take off."

"You sure? You can use the office to take a beat if you need, maybe sneak in a nap on the couch?" Pops offered.

Ricky shook his head. "I'll be fine." He forced a smile he didn't feel. "Quit worrying over me like a mother hen."

Pops eyed him warily. "What time did you get in this morning?"

Fuck, he was onto him. "Not too much earlier than you."

"I got in at four thirty. You've been going hard the whole time. Something wrong?" Pops asked.

Ricky rolled to his knees, thankful for the pain. It helped

ground him. "Needed a good workout. I'm gonna get to the farm."

"After you eat and take care of that lip," Pops insisted.

"Sure thing, Pops." Ricky got to his feet, his knees weak and wobbly like they were filled with both lead and jelly at the same time.

"Don't you start. I got enough attitude from my daughters." Pops shook his head.

"Tell Sunny I'm still waiting to take her to dinner whenever she's ready," Ricky teased.

Pops narrowed his eyes at Ricky. "And you'll stay waiting."

Ricky forced a laugh. "Don't worry, old man. I won't go near your daughters."

Pops opened his mouth to say something but Ricky clapped a hand on his shoulder. "I get it, Pops. I won't pollute your girls."

You good-for-nothing waste of space. Ricky's stomach flipped as bile churned in his gut, his muscles going rigid as if bracing for an attack.

Ricky grabbed his bag, his breath coming faster as he tossed the jump rope inside. He needed to get out of the gym before he embarrassed himself again. Couldn't risk having a panic attack here.

He waved to Pops and headed towards the door. He'd have to shower at home this time. Hard as he tried, he couldn't stop another glance in Everett's direction.

Unfortunate timing, as Everett took that moment to look his way. His full lips parted in surprise a half a second before his brow furrowed in concern. Everett pulled the emergency clasp, stopping his treadmill, his chest heaving. A sheen of sweat glistened on his neck, with more collecting in the hollow of his throat.

The urge to taste him rose out of nowhere. Ricky licked

his lips, the tang of iron filling his mouth. Right, he'd bitten his lip in the fall.

Everett took a step towards him. It was as if the heat of the sun had descended on Ricky.

Was everyone else staring at them? Ricky searched the room. Pops cast him a curious look, and the woman lifting weights peeked at him. Ricky's flesh prickled like tiny fire ants crawled under his skin, biting him along the way. His ears rang as he turned and did what he did best—he ran.

Pushing the door open from the gym, he welcomed the bite of cold the crisp November weather brought. His sweat dried and cooled him down simultaneously as he raced to his truck on unreliable legs. He stumbled right as he reached his vehicle, reaching out to catch himself on the hood. Stinging pain rang up his palms.

Rapid footsteps moved closer behind him.

"Fuck," Ricky swore.

"Are you okay?" Concern soaked Everett's voice.

"I'm fine." Ricky straightened and made his way to the driver's door. He opened it and set his bag on the seat, unzipping the side pocket. He pulled out his vape pen. He needed it to fend off this panic attack.

He pressed the button, slipping the cartridge in his mouth without waiting for it to heat up. He inhaled long and deep and repeated the process, but it wasn't working fast enough.

"Here, try this." Everett handed him a small cartridge from his pocket.

Ricky wiped the half-dried blood from his mouth, eyeing the offering Everett held out to him.

"It's the good stuff. Medical grade," Everett insisted.

Ricky's heart wasn't slowing and his chest rose and fell more rapidly with each passing second as the panic took over.

He took the gift as the offering it was, quickly replacing his cartridge with Everett's. He inhaled long and deep, then held his breath and let it out. He did this twice more before handing it back.

"Thanks." The heady calm from the weed settled over him, starting from behind his eyes and slowly seeping to the rest of his body. His breathing slowed, as did his pulse.

"It's yours. I've got plenty more."

Ricky nodded and tucked it in his bag. "Thanks."

They stood in awkward silence for a moment.

"I—"

"Well—"

Everett chuckled, rubbing the back of his neck self-consciously. "You go first."

"I should go."

Ricky didn't miss the flash of disappointment in Everett's eyes. "You're bleeding. They probably have a first-aid kit in the gym. I could help clean it up for you if you want?"

Ricky's jaw clenched. He shook his head. "I'll be fine. Take care of it when I get home."

"Right, well, I just . . . I missed you all these years. And I'm glad you're okay."

Ricky's body went rigid, heat flaming his cheeks as he said nothing.

Everett sighed. "I just wanted to know if we could be friends again? Now that I'll be living here and we'll be running into each other more . . ."

"And you're dating my sister," Ricky reminded him, forcing a laugh and hoping it sounded less affected than he was. "If my mother has anything to say about it, you'll be my brother-in-law by Easter."

Everett winced. "Yeah, that's not going to happen."

Was Everett leading his sister on? "Why not?"

Everett held up his hands. "Whoa, I didn't mean anything by it. Nova's a great woman."

"And she's dealt with enough assholes taking advantage of her."

"Yeah, I got that. It's not what you think, truly. I meant no disrespect." Everett seemed genuine.

"Then maybe you should spell it out for me."

Everett shook his head. "That's your sister's story to tell, not mine."

Ricky stared at him, but Everett stood his ground. Finally, Ricky nodded. "Fair enough. I'll definitely be talking to her."

"Good." Everett's mouth curved in the smallest tease of a smile.

It was as if every cell in Ricky's body was attuned to that small movement. What would it look like when Everett fully smiled?

"I was looking for someone to teach me some mixed martial arts. Your sister mentioned you might be taking on some clients?" Everett asked.

"I don't think that would be a good idea."

The semblance of a smile disappeared from Everett's face, replaced with disappointment. "Oh, okay. Yeah, of course. I didn't mean to bother you. Have a good day."

As Everett turned and walked back toward the gym, everything inside Ricky pulled him like a magnet towards the man. Ricky was used to disappointing people; it was part of who he was. So why did he become physically sick at the thought of doing the same to Everett? As much as Ricky might be tempted to have a friendship with the man, he couldn't afford to let anyone in as close as he'd once let Everett. The cost of vulnerability like that was far too high. But the man had saved his life—Ricky owed him.

"Ever," he called out without meaning to use the old nickname.

Everett spun around, hope lighting those cool blue eyes. "Yeah?"

"I'm glad you're okay too." Ricky's voice cracked on the last word.

Everett's lips curled into a blinding smile, stealing Ricky's breath. He was the most beautiful man he'd ever seen. Dark hair contrasted with his light skin. Blue eyes with flecks of grey looked like they held entire galaxies within them. Joy and hope—Everett embodied everything Ricky had wanted once upon a time. But those wants had nearly gotten them both killed.

It was better if Ricky stayed as far away from Everett as possible—for both their sakes.

4

———

EVERETT

E verett lifted his cell higher and set it on the console of his rental car. The scent of Pineapple Breeze air freshener cloyed the interior, even though he'd thrown it out yesterday. His mother's bright smile took up half the screen on his phone.

"Oh, it's so good to see your face," she said before pulling the phone far enough away for him to see the background of her kitchen. "John, come say hi. Everett's on the phone."

His stepdad skirted around the table, waving to Everett before looping his hand around Everett's mom's shoulders.

"Hey, kid, how are you doing?"

Everett chuckled to himself. At thirty-eight, he was hardly a kid anymore. "Hey, John, I'm doing pretty good. How's retirement going for ya?"

His stepdad's smile brightened. "Great."

"He's driving me crazy," his mom added.

John turned towards her with an exaggerated expression of shock. "You wound me, my love."

"Don't you have to get to the chess tournament?" she asked.

He kissed her cheek. "I do. I'm heading out now. Hopefully my absence makes you fonder," he teased and waved once more to Everett. "See you for Christmas next month, right?"

"Definitely."

"Have a great day." John waved before ducking out of the way of the camera.

The screen showed the ceiling as his mother's giggle filtered through the speaker and then the wet smack of a kiss. She returned a moment later, a little disheveled. Smoothing her hair, she focused back on Everett.

"So, how was the flight from California?" she asked.

"Long as crossing the country usually takes. I won't miss the six-hour flights, that's for sure. Had just enough time to get my rental car and meet a friend for Thanksgiving dinner with her family." He swallowed hard.

"Oh, well, I'm glad you weren't alone. Wish we could have seen you, but I know you're still getting things settled."

Everett drew in a ragged breath. "You'll never guess who I ran into there."

"Who?"

"Ricardo." Everett shifted on the vinyl seat.

His mom blinked. Her blue eyes widened. "Ricardo Benning?"

Everett nodded.

"Oh my God. Is he . . ."

"He was adopted by a family here. My friend happens to be his sister."

Her shoulders relaxed a few inches. "Oh, that's what we hoped for for him, right? That he'd find somewhere safe and away from that horrible man."

Everett scanned the parking lot of Hope Facility, trying to get a handle on the swirl of emotions this topic always brought up.

"What is it?" his way-too-observant mother asked.

He focused back on her. "He was different."

She laughed. "Of course he's different. He was fourteen when you last saw him. A lifetime has passed."

"Yeah, you're right."

She studied him. "Did you get to talk about what happened?"

Everett shook his head. "He didn't really want to look at me, much less talk."

"Oh, sweetheart. I'm sure seeing you brought up a lot from his past. Much like it did for you, I'm assuming."

"It did. I just . . . I thought he hated me, but he said something that struck me."

"What did he say?" she asked.

"That I saved his life."

"Well, you did." She readily agreed.

Doubt pushed back the relief that had bubbled up at her words. "But it was my fault."

His mother released a long exhale. "Everett, my sweet boy, you've carried this guilt for far too long. You were children, and his father was a grown man. Donald is the only one to blame. You made an impossible choice during a time when there weren't any good ones. And because of your actions, you're both alive—" Her voice caught as she blinked away tears. "It doesn't matter if it's been one day or twenty-five years, I'll never forget the terror of the thought of losing you."

Everett would never forget the horror of that day either. "I'm sorry, Mom."

She shook her head and smiled despite her watery gaze. "Don't you get it? I'm not sorry you did what you did. And it sounds like Ricardo isn't either. So the only one blaming you is you."

Everett tapped his fingers against his jean-clad thigh. "Maybe."

"Ask yourself what's holding you back from letting it go? And then do the work you need to so you can finally heal from this. You've carried this burden long enough."

Maybe if he would talk to me, that would help.

"I'll think on it." He shifted in the car seat and blew out a breath before smiling. "How much do I owe you for the therapy session?"

She chuckled. "You know it's always free for my children."

"Where's Bree?"

"Oh, she's here with her headphones blasting." His mom walked over to the table and turned the camera around. His half sister was bent over a few college textbooks.

His mom tapped her arm to get her attention. Bree looked up at the phone, her brows drawing up in confusion only to be replaced by a big, toothy smile.

She pulled her earbuds from her ears. "Ever!"

"Hey, squirt."

She rolled her eyes. "I'm nineteen. You can come up with a better nickname."

"Nah, you'll always be squirt to me."

"Mom said you're coming for Christmas?"

"Yup. I'll stop by Christmas Eve and stay until noon Christmas, then I'm gonna head over to my dad's," he explained.

"Don't forget my presents." She smirked.

"His presence is gift enough," his mother said.

"Well, I was hoping he'd get me a vape since my mother won't—"

"Absolutely not. You're too young," his mom argued.

Bree stuck out her bottom lip. "You're no fun. I'm an adult now, as you like to remind me."

"Mom's right, squirt. Vaping isn't good for your lungs," Everett interjected.

"See?" his mom added.

"Edibles, however . . ."

Bree's face lit up.

"Everett Daniels Popova—"

"I'll leave you two to your conversation." Everett excused himself, glancing at the building in front of him. "I gotta go into my new job. I'll see you soon."

"Love you, sweetheart." His mom turned the camera back to her.

"I'll text you," Bree yelled.

He chuckled and ended the call, tucking the phone into his pocket. Some things never changed.

Everett opened the door and locked the car behind him before he headed into Hope Facility. The place was a lot bigger than the pictures had made it seem online. He walked through the first set of double doors, through the atrium, and past the next ones leading into a large common room with teens of all ages scattered throughout the space. Some were bent over stacks of comic books; others played board games. The more vocal ones sat before a large TV in the corner, split into four screens, all playing a video game. Cinnamon and the scent of hot chocolate surrounded him like a welcoming hug.

"You must be Everett." A deep voice came from his left.

Everett turned to greet the tall Black man he'd had many conversations with over the phone. "Yes, nice to meet you in person, Aaron."

"Same. Why don't we head over to my office to discuss everything and get the paperwork out of the way? I got your background check results, so we're good to go. We'll get you settled in and then, after the business of the holidays, you can do an official greeting with all the staff and kids. How does that sound?"

"Perfect."

Aaron led the way through the large room towards a hallway. "This is the main gathering room. We use it for events and fundraisers, as well as a sort of common room for the kids."

Someone carrying a big box stepped out from the hall in front of them. Aaron slipped his hands around it, taking its weight. "I told you I'd grab these."

The tiny slip of a woman who'd been behind the cardboard wiped her hands on her jeans with a smile. "It isn't too heavy. I wanted to get the last of the decorations down for the kids to help set it all up tomorrow." Her gaze slid to Everett's. She gave him a timid smile before stepping closer to Aaron.

"Oh, sorry. Everett, this is my wife, Brynn."

"Nice to meet you," Everett greeted her.

"Oh, you're the new hire to help with the expansion and placement project?" she asked.

"Yes, ma'am." Everett couldn't wait to help place more kids in homes where they were loved.

"That's good. These kids need more people fighting for them."

"Absolutely," he agreed.

Aaron adjusted the box in his arms, looking down the hall. "Hey, Sebastian?"

"Yes?"

Everett turned his focus towards the answering voice. A tall, lean man walked towards them. His gaze met Everett's before it dipped down and languidly returned to his face with a slow smirk.

"And who might we have here?" the stranger asked.

"This is Everett. He'll be working on the expansion project with us as well as coming on board as a counselor. Everett, this is Sebastian Wright. He's a pediatric doctor and a volunteer for Hope."

Everett held out his hand to Sebastian. "Nice to meet you."

"Trust me, the pleasure is all mine." Sebastian held his hand a little longer than necessary, erasing any doubt Everett had that he was flirting with him.

"It's nice that you volunteer your services," Everett said.

Sebastian shrugged and waved a hand.

"Would you mind giving Everett a tour while I help Brynn with the rest of the holiday storage?" Aaron asked Sebastian.

"I would love to."

"Does that work for you?" Aaron turned to Everett.

"Sure."

"Great. I'll meet you in my office when you're done." Aaron took off with Brynn, headed towards the main room.

"Well, you've seen the common room. Shall we go this way and loop around?" Sebastian motioned farther down the hall.

"Sounds good." Everett fell in step with Sebastian.

"Are you from New Hampshire?" Sebastian asked.

"Born and raised here near Concord, but I've lived in California for the last fifteen years."

Sebastian whistled. "That's quite the change." He pointed towards the row of doors, gesturing to the offices of the different personnel and group therapy rooms.

"So you're less familiar with the Shattered Cove area?" Sebastian asked.

"Yeah."

"Maybe I could show you around sometime? There's this

place that makes the best pizza, and the beer is served ice cold." Sebastian turned to look at him.

Less than a week in a new town and already being asked on a date?

Sebastian was handsome, in the clean-cut, boy-next-door sort of way.

Ricky's face flashed in Everett's mind. His body heated at just the thought of him, an onslaught of mixed emotions rising too. But Ricky had made it clear he wasn't gay. Whatever they'd shared in childhood could have just been experimentation on Ricky's part, despite how real it had been for Everett. Besides, Ricky had made it clear he didn't want anything to do with Everett.

"Don't feel like you have to say yes. We can go as friends if you want—no pressure," Sebastian added.

"No. Sorry, just got caught up in my head there for a minute. I'd love to meet up sometime."

Straight white teeth flashed as Sebastian smiled, his eyes lighting up. "Great. Can I get your number so we can schedule something?"

Everett pulled out his phone and handed it to Sebastian. "Are you free tomorrow night?"

Sebastian shook his head. "I'm covering shifts for someone at the ER, but I can do Friday night."

Maybe it was time Everett truly let go of the what-if he'd held on to for Ricky. Meeting a gorgeous doctor wasn't a bad start.

"It's a date."

5

RICKY

Ricky reclined in a chair in the corner of his parents' living room with a full belly and a half-full bottle of beer in his hand. It would be a typical Sunday dinner with his family except for the fact that Everett fucking Popova was playing Uno with his niece and nephew at the dining room table with the damned dog sleeping by his feet.

Everett's deep laugh rumbled through the room followed by his niece's giggle. Ricky's tensed, his stomach dipping with a swirl of heat. He clasped the arms of the chair, his knuckles turning white.

Everett had said hello and then given Ricky space. That was exactly what Ricky had wanted—so why did it feel like he was coming out of his skin? Like if anyone looked at him, they'd see the truth?

"He's really good with the kids," Ma said.

Nova stuffed a cookie in her mouth and mumbled something unintelligible.

"You don't have to get all defensive. Everett seems like a

great guy. I'm just happy you found someone like this to start seeing," his mom continued.

Nova's shoulders drooped as she swallowed. "Everett and I are still friends at this point."

His ma turned back to the game happening at the table. "Despite what you think, I don't want you rushing into marriage. I do, however, want you happy and with someone who sees your value." She turned towards Ricky. "What do you think of him?"

Ricky drank the last of his beer, then he wiped his mouth and pushed the footrest back under the chair before standing. "I think he better treat my sister well or he'll find out these muscles do more than look good."

Nova rolled her eyes and snorted.

Ricky headed to the kitchen to grab another beer, passing the dining room where his father and brothers were busy with a game of dominos at the other end of the table to Everett and the kids. Isabella and Elise were chatting over a glass of wine in the kitchen, and they looked up as he entered.

"Sharing any juicy gossip I should know about?" he teased.

"Nope," Isabella answered far too quickly.

"Mm-hmm." He deposited his empty bottle in the recycle bin, opened the fridge, and grabbed another of his favorite Sand Dune IPAs. Popping the top, he leaned against the counter.

The two ladies looked at each other and then sipped their wine in unison. Something was going on there.

"Everett seems like a sweetheart," Elise noted.

Ricky took a drink of his beer instead of answering.

"He's funny," Isabella added.

"And have you seen the view from the back? Nova is one lucky lady." Elise smirked, looking directly at Ricky.

Something ugly and unfamiliar burned in his gut. "Should you be checking out Nova's boyfriend when you're marrying our brother?"

"I can admire a beautiful man or woman. Does the playboy disagree?" she asked, one eyebrow shooting up.

"Honey, I'm not the one you should be asking. I don't deal with constraints like relationships because I don't stop at just looking—where's the fun in that?" He smirked, hoping it hid his true feelings, which were too mixed up for even him to sort.

Isabella shook her head.

Elise tipped hers to the side as if she were studying him. It was unnerving.

No one knows. He tried to assure himself.

"Ricky?" his dad called from the dining room.

Everett looked up, his grey eyes slamming into his with the force of a crashing wave.

"Yeah?" Ricky's voice came out hoarse.

"Bring me another beer, will ya?" his dad asked.

Ricky turned his back on the table, grabbing a new bottle with trembling hands. He squeezed his fingers around the ice-cold glass, needing something to ground him. One look from Everett and his world had shaken off its axis. Anger lit like a fuse inside him, quickly suffocating all his other emotions. Why was he so affected by this man? Why did Everett hold so much power over him? Why did the thought of Nova kissing those full, smooth lips make his guts burn with rage? Guilt weighed down his shoulders like a wet blanket. He should want Nova to be happy. It wasn't like he wanted Ever—Ricky wasn't gay.

He was just worried Nova and Everett would get too close, and Everett would spill their history—Ricky's shame. His family would never look at him the same if they knew.

Paralyzing fear slithered through his veins, winding around him until he couldn't breathe. *You're a sick, disgusting deviant.*

"Son?" His father's voice drew him back to the present. Ricky handed him the drink as everyone at the table but the kids looked at him, questions and concern flashing in their eyes.

"Thanks. You okay?" his dad asked—and James was his father.

"Yeah." Ricky forced a smile. "Just lost in thought."

"That's what that burning smell is," Nash teased.

Ricky needed a distraction—someone to release this pent-up emotion on. Nash had always been willing. He looped his arm around Nash as quickly as he could, putting his brother in a headlock. Nash slapped his arm, standing to his full height. The chair screeched between them and then tumbled to the side.

"Take it outside, boys!" their dad boomed.

Ricky dodged Nash's fist, shoving him while taking out his legs to make his big brother stumble to the ground. Ricky didn't hesitate. He took off to the front door, Nash hot on his heels. He swung it open, but that fraction of a second was just enough for Nash to catch up to him. Nash slammed into Ricky, both of them stumbling over the porch railing into the snow.

The air woodshed out of Ricky. His lungs burned. Adrenaline thrummed in his veins. This is what he lived for—the rush. It made him feel alive—powerful—like nothing could touch him. Nothing else mattered. Not the past, nor the future. Just right now.

Pain exploded in his jaw.

"Little fucker!" Ricky smiled, tasting iron. His lip must have reopened. He shuffled to his feet, out of his brother's reach. He held his hands up in fists as Nash matched his stance. "Getting slow in your old age, big brother."

"I made first contact." Nash smiled.

Ricky shrugged like it didn't faze him. "Lucky shot. I was giving you a minute to recover from the fall."

"Sore loser."

"Old man," Ricky retorted.

Nash swung. Ricky dodged, putting his training to use. They sparred back and forth, trading jabs both verbally and physically until Nash's movements slowed. Ricky went in for the kill. He twisted his body and swung his foot behind Nash's knees, making him fall. Ricky locked his body around Nash's and rolled in the snow so that he was underneath Nash holding him once again in a headlock.

"I feel like we've come full circle." Ricky laughed. "Say, 'Ricky you won,' and I'll let you go."

"Fuck you. Get him, Ro!" Nash yelled.

Ricky's eyes flicked to the porch where everyone but their parents and the kids stood. The tall figure with his hands in his pockets caught Ricky's attention. Everett's lips turned up in amusement, sending a bolt of pride surging through Ricky.

An arm snaked around his neck, cutting off his oxygen. Roman tugged Ricky away from Nash.

"Enough, you two. Jesus, can't we have one family dinner without it turning into a brawl? You're setting a horrible example for the kids." Roman let his hold loosen enough for Ricky to take a breath, but not enough for him to be free.

"Let me go!" Ricky shouted.

"Let Nash go first."

"He needs to concede."

"You wanna stay out here in the cold, wet snow all night?" Roman asked.

"Get off me, fucker," Nash growled.

"Come on, Ricky. It's over. We know you're strong—you remind us every time we see you. Just let him go," Isabella said.

"Okay, but only for you, señorita." Ricky released Nash and rolled away as Roman let go too.

Nash scrambled to his feet. "I'll get you next time."

"I guess that's as close as I'll get to you conceding. I'll take it, cabrón." Ricky laughed.

Isabella fussed over Nash, brushing wet snow from his shoulders before they made their way back inside.

"I don't know why you bait him like that." Roman shook his head and walked inside, looping his arm around Elise and guiding her with him.

Nova shook her head. "You should get some ice on that lip." She turned to Everett. "I'm sorry. My brothers are children in men's bodies."

Everett chuckled, setting Ricky's blood on fire. The adrenaline only added fuel to the longing sparking through his body. *I would have won against both of them if I hadn't been distracted by you.*

Nova pulled a small cigarette box from her pocket. She plucked a joint out and grabbed a lighter. She flicked the top open, lit it, and took a few puffs before passing it to Everett.

Ricky's cold, wet jeans stuck to his legs, leaching any warmth out of his body. But the sight of Everett's lips closing around the end of that joint made every cell blister with lust.

Ricky shook his head. Nash must have hit him harder than he'd thought.

Everett pulled in the drag, held his breath, and then let it out, white smoke billowing from his nose. "This is what you grew?"

Nova nodded.

"It's smooth." Everett took another puff and then offered it to Ricky.

Ricky made no move to take it. The thought of wrapping his lips where Everett's once had been was far too tempting—and that was terrifying.

He spun around, heading towards his house, ignoring Nova's shout. He needed to escape—to get as far as possible from Everett. The man raised too many confusing emotions in him. Tempted him in ways he thought he'd conquered.

I'm not gay. I'm not.

Why was all of this coming to the surface now? Was this a test? He'd beaten this—hadn't he? Or had he just buried it with the rest of his trauma?

Ricky took off at a sprint. Sucking in crisp wintery air, he ran until his legs burned, trying to escape pain of a different kind—of remembering.

6

EVERETT

Everett lifted the paper cup to his lips, taking a sip of the cinnamon-infused hot chocolate with a hint of chili.

"It's good, isn't it?" Nova asked.

He licked his lips as they continued down the street from the Stardust Café. "Delicious."

She smiled up at him and skirted around a woman walking the opposite way on the sidewalk.

"Thanks for coming with me today to look at apartments." He took another sip.

"It was fun. Do you think you'll take the one over Pippa's bookstore?" she asked.

"It was a nice space."

"And you'll have the best coffee in town across the street and access to Shattered Cove's finest choice of old and new books alike right below your living space," she added with a smile.

A crisp wind blew against him. He tugged his wool coat

tighter, careful to avoid the deeper slush on the salted side-walk. "But the apartment complex had access to a gym."

She waved her hand. "Yeah, but you'd have neighbors all around you, and look." She pointed down the street. "Tidal Gym is only a couple blocks that way."

"You're trying hard to sell me this apartment," he teased.

She shrugged. "Pippa's a friend and one of the sweetest women in the world. She needs a good tenant. She said her last one left a few holes in the wall and started a small kitchen fire. You need a good, quiet place to stay, and she needs a responsible tenant who doesn't commit arson—it's a win-win."

He chuckled. "You make a strong case. The Lighthouse Inn is nice, but I want to have my own space again. Be able to cook for myself, you know?"

"Totally." She lifted her hot chocolate to her lips and took a drink.

"So this is Green Park?" He motioned to the large plot of land in the center of town. Most of the trees were bare except a few evergreens. A little farther down, a playground's swings glinted in the sunlight.

"Yes. We hold a lot of town events here. Hope Facility does their annual fundraisers here in the spring, summer, and fall. We even have a winter carnival," she explained, stopping to sit on a bench across from the park.

Everett joined her. They sat in silence, both sipping their drinks.

She tucked a short curl behind her ear. "So . . ."

"So?"

She pressed the tab on the plastic top of her drink. "I was wondering what you're doing for Christmas this year?"

"Are you asking as a friend or someone who needs me to pretend to be her date again?"

She sighed. "I mean both."

"I was going to see my family. Why don't you just tell your mom you're happy single? Or be honest and tell her you're busy sowing your wild oats." He laughed.

She shook her head. "Because my mother would be hopeful every time I brought some guy or girl home. I don't want her to . . . I owe her and Daddy a lot. They saved my life. I could have ended up in a very different place than I am now if not for them. I just don't want to be a disappointment."

Everett wrapped his arm around her and pulled Nova a little closer, kissing her temple. "I've only met your parents a few times, but from what I can tell, there's a lot of love there. I don't think you'd disappoint them by letting them know you just need some space."

"Easier said than done," she deadpanned.

Her phone chimed. She pulled it out and bit her lip.

"Something wrong?"

"No. Just one of my friends."

"Is this one with benefits?" he teased.

She smirked. "Maybe."

He laughed.

"Hey, just because I don't date doesn't mean I'm celibate."

"No judgement from me." He held his hands up.

"So nothing I can say to convince you to come to Christmas?"

He sighed and straightened, hands in his lap. "I've got to go see my family. Plus, I don't want to wear out my welcome with the Emersons."

"Psh. You could never. Seriously, my mom is like the crazy cat lady, only instead of cats, she collects people."

"She has a big heart." He took another drink of his warm hot chocolate.

"Is it Ricky?" she asked.

Everett coughed, choking on his drink.

Nova patted his back. "You okay?"

"Yeah." He cleared his throat.

"So, is it my brother? Did he say something to you?"

"Why would you think that?" He studied the hardware shop across the street, anxiety swirling in his gut.

"He's always staring at you like you ate the last slice of Mom's sweet potato pie—envious and angry."

Everett shrugged, trying to seem apathetic. "I hadn't noticed."

"And how about how he just stormed off when you offered him that joint?" She sat up straight too, studying him closely.

"You'll have to ask your brother."

"Did he say something to you? About you and me dating? I mean, he's overprotective, but never to this level," she pressed.

Everett opened his mouth and closed it. How could he get out of this without lying and betraying Ricky? "He definitely warned me away from harming you. But you'll have to have a conversation with him. I'm sensing a pattern here. You won't talk to your parents—which I understand but don't necessarily agree with. And now your brother. Are you afraid of conflict?"

She scoffed. "Did you see my brothers rolling in the snow? All we have is conflict."

"Yeah, but that's different."

Nova stood, walked over to a trash bin, and tossed her cup in it. "It's getting cold out here. Maybe we should get going."

He shook his head and stood. "We're coming back to this conversation sometime."

"Everett?"

Everett spun around. Sebastian crossed the street from the hardware store.

"Hey." Everett waved.

Sebastian glanced at Nova. "Hey, Nova. How are you doing?"

"Good. I was just showing Everett here your sister-in-law's apartment, hoping he'd rent it out from her." Nova motioned to Everett.

Sebastian looked to him. "Oh yeah?"

Everett stuck one hand in his pocket. "Yeah. It was nice."

"Cool. I was going to apologize again for having to cancel our dinner last Friday," Sebastian said.

Everett waved his hand. "It's really no big deal."

"I'll make it up to you. How about dinner this weekend?"

"Sure."

"I'll text you the details," Sebastian said and turned to Nova. "Nice to see you again."

"Have fun saving lives." She waved.

Sebastian chuckled. "I'll try my best." He gave one last wave and took off the way they'd come.

Nova nudged Everett with her shoulder. "You've been holding back on me."

"What do you mean?"

"You and Sebastian? He's a hottie."

Everett shrugged. "I mean, it would be a little awkward to talk about a potential date with my fake girlfriend, don't you think?"

"No. Not at all. Spill," she demanded.

"We met at Hope Facility. He invited me to dinner. But last Friday, he got called into work. End of story." Everett drank the rest of his hot chocolate and threw away the cup.

"He's a good guy. His brother, Mason, is married to Pippa. Sebastian is great with his nieces and nephew. I see him take them around town sometimes, spoiling them."

Everett couldn't contain his laughter. "You sound like your mother."

Nova's mouth clamped shut as her attention snapped towards him. "I do not." She pressed a hand to her forehead, her eyes widening. "Oh my God, I do. I'm losing it."

"Maybe think about having that chat with her?"

Nova rolled her eyes. "Maybe when hell freezes over. Okay, look, I got to go drop off these cookies to the nursing home."

"Alright. Thanks again for coming with me." He held his arms open for a hug, which she returned.

"Of course. Let me know which apartment you choose. I bet I can even get my brothers to help move you in."

"That won't be necessary." He couldn't imagine Ricky volunteering. "I've already got the name of a good moving company to help unload my stuff once it arrives."

"Okay, well, if you need an extra set of hands or three, let me know." She waved.

He would have walked her to her car, but it was right in front of the bookstore. She'd be safe. Everett turned the opposite way, taking in the sights and sounds of the main hub of Shattered Cove. He really liked the apartment over the bookstore. It would be very different from city life in California, but it could be nice.

Everett continued, passing an alley. A few minutes of walking and the gym came into view. It was easy enough to walk to in good weather, and he could drive in the rain and snow. He headed towards the gym entrance, glancing across the street to the laundromat. He'd have to get his things and come back here—

He crashed into something hard—no *someone*. Everett stumbled back as the person he ran into groaned.

"I'm sorry. I—"

"Jesus fucking Christ! Why are you everywhere I turn?" Ricky blew past him, making a beeline for his truck.

Everett stood frozen as Ricky threw his belongings inside the truck and climbed in. The engine turned over before he peeled out of the parking lot.

"You don't have to be such a dick," Everett mumbled under his breath.

It wasn't like they were close anymore, but Ricky's actions stung just the same. This cold version of Ricky—Everett didn't know how to deal with him. Ricky might say he didn't hate him, but his actions said something else entirely different.

7

———

RICKY

Red and green lights flashed from the Emersons' porch. Ricky's boots thumped on the wooden steps as he made his way up the steps and reached for the doorknob, setting off the motion-activated Black Santa Claus that stood to the side.

"Ho, ho, ho! Have you been good this year?" Santa's recorded voice trilled.

"Not in this fucking lifetime," Ricky mumbled and let himself inside his parents' house. He shut the door, blocking the cold air out, and was immediately swallowed by the spiced warm air from within.

"Good. Now we can open presents." Eli was the first to greet him matter-of-factly.

Ricky toed off his boots and hung up his coat. "Happy holidays to you too, captain."

Eli stared at Ricky's chest, the corner of his mouth quirking up before it straightened again. The kid loved the nickname.

"I got Ariel a book about mermaids. Do you think she'll like it?" Eli asked, twisting his fingers.

Ricky clapped his hand on the boy's back gently. "I think she'll love it more than what I got her."

Eli's attention dropped to Ricky's hands. "You didn't bring any gifts?"

"I dropped them off yesterday."

"Oh." Eli turned and walked out of the mudroom toward the living room, where most of the noise from his family came from.

Ricky took a deep breath, steeling himself for having to spend the day in Everett's presence. He cracked his neck to the side and forced what he hoped was an easy smile

Everyone was seated in the living room. If they added anyone else, they might run out of room to sit. He scanned everyone in the room, his chest tight. But Everett wasn't there. Maybe he was in the bathroom?

"Look who finally decided to grace us with his presence," Nash noted his arrival.

Ricky shrugged and leaned against the wall at the living room entrance. "You're just jealous I don't have a screaming baby to wake me up at the ass crack of dawn."

Nash lifted his daughter, rubbing his nose against hers. "Did you hear what mean Uncle Ricky said about you?"

Baby Alba wiggled out of her father's arms. He set her on the ground, holding her chubby fists as she stood between his thighs.

"See? She couldn't wait to get away from you either," Ricky teased.

Nash grumbled something.

Ariel crashed against Ricky's legs. "Uncle Ricky!"

"Whoa, slow down there, super girl." Ricky pushed off the

wall, picking his niece up and spinning her around. She giggled and clung to his arms.

"She ate a big breakfast, so maybe not so much spinning," Elise warned.

Ricky stopped immediately. "Oh, good call." He set Ariel on her feet.

"Did you get me a present, Uncle Ricky?" Ariel asked.

He made a show of patting down his pockets and coming up empty. "Just kidding. Of course I did. It's already under the tree."

She clapped. "Yay!"

Ricky walked over to the couch and gave his ma a hug and kiss on the cheek. *Mom* was one title he saved for his biological mother, the only other person who'd loved Ricky until she, too, had been taken from him when he'd needed her most. Renita had taken a scared, angry teenager, and over time, she and James had broken through to him. They hadn't just offered him words of affection. The Emersons lived their love and shared it with whomever needed it. Ricky was just a lucky bastard they chose to include despite how much he'd fought against it in the beginning. Somewhere along the line, Renita had become Ma, and James, Dad.

"Merry Christmas, Ma," Ricky said.

"Merry Christmas. Did you want some breakfast? There's plenty left out there."

"I'll probably grab a cinnamon roll if there are any left and some coffee."

"Did you get to the store to get what I need to make ajiaco?" she asked.

"I did. I'll bring it over later so we can make it together." Ricky's smile was filled with genuine warmth. The first holiday he'd spent at the Emersons', Ma had asked him what his favorite dishes were to eat. Ajiaco had been one of his mom's favorites. Making it each year was his way of including her memory with his adoptive family.

"Sounds perfect. But you know I'll be the one actually cooking. You're not allowed near the stove." She winked.

Ricky chuckled and moved on to his dad. "Happy holidays."

"Son." His dad pulled him into a hug and patted his back.

"Can we open presents now?" Nova asked.

"You're worse than the kids with patience," Roman teased.

Nova narrowed her eyes at him and stuck out her tongue.

A few chuckles rose, Ricky's included. He moved to sit next to her but hesitated, casting another look around the room.

"Scared I'll bite?" Nova asked.

"No, just wondering if this spot is reserved for your boyfriend." *Is he here? Or is he coming later?*

Nova waved her hand. "Oh, no. Everett's with his family today."

Ricky sat beside her. "You didn't want to go with him?"

Nova snorted. "Nope."

"Have you met his parents?" Ma asked.

Nova shifted as if uncomfortable. "No. I told you we're just hanging out."

"What about you, Ricky? Are we expecting anyone else at the table today?" Ma asked.

Ricky shook his head. "Just me."

"His harem wouldn't fit at the table, Mom," Nash added not so helpfully.

"What's a harem?" Ariel asked.

Roman choked on his drink, coughing as Elise patted his back firmly.

"Yeah, Nash, what is a harem?" Ricky laughed.

"Uh, it's a . . . ask your dad," Nash said.

"Oh for fudge's sake," Roman sighed.

"A harem is a group of women who all like one man and they share him," Nova supplied helpfully.

Ariel's lips pursed as if she were in deep thought. "Can a group of boys share a girl too?"

Ricky burst out laughing.

"See what you started?" Roman cut a glare at Nash.

"I'm sorry," Nash said between his own deep laughs.

"How about presents? Eli and Ariel, why don't you pass them out to everyone?" Ma interjected, most likely before this could go any more off the rails.

As the kids darted to the tree and retrieved wrapped packages of all sizes and passed them out, Ricky took a moment to breathe. Everett wasn't here. Ricky wouldn't have to worry about his family finding out about his past—at least for today.

Everett was probably at his mom's, enjoying her bacon-wrapped ham and crunchy green bean casserole. *Does she still make it that way?* Ricky had joined them for several Christmas dinners when he'd been younger. They'd even bought him gifts ever since Everett had found out what was going on at home. It wasn't hard to discover—the walls were thin, even in separate houses.

Or maybe Everett was with his dad, enjoying holubtsi—stuffed cabbage—and fish. If things did progress with Nova and Everett, was it possible to keep Ricky's past with Everett a secret?

"Ricky?"

"Hmm?" He jerked his attention to his sister.

"You okay?"

"Yeah, of course. Why?"

"You're staring into space pretty hard." Nova studied him.

He smiled. "I'm remembering this thing this woman I was with last weekend did with her tongue—"

Nova held up her hand. "Enough. I don't need you to flaunt your man-whore ways in front of me."

He chuckled, hopefully seeming more lighthearted than he felt. There was no woman last weekend. In fact, he hadn't actually been with anyone since Everett had come back into his life. Of course, that was just coincidence. It didn't mean anything. Ricky just hadn't needed the release. He was spending a lot more time at the gym, had even picked up a couple clients.

"So, how serious are things with him?" Ricky asked.

"Everett?" she asked as the noise of tearing of paper and excited giggles rose.

"Unless you've got someone else you're seeing?"

She shrugged and looked away. "It's not serious. Open your gifts." She motioned to the stack the kids had placed in front of him. He knew an evasive action when he saw one.

"Don't think you're getting out of answering that."

"I don't know what you're talking about." She pulled a knife from her pocket and used it to cut the tape on one of her boxes.

"Damn, you still carry that thing everywhere?"

"Absolutely. If it's not in my boot, it's on my person." She closed the knife and set it back in her hoodie pocket.

"You like it that much?" Ricky asked.

She nudged him playfully. "You know I do. It's my favorite gift you've given me."

"It's probably a good time to brush up on those self-defense skills too. Text me when you're ready to come down to the gym. Pops gave me a key so we can go whenever."

"I will."

Ricky got up, leaving his gifts until later. He made his way towards the kitchen, the sounds of his family opening presents and their laughter and chatter lessening with each step. He grabbed a clean mug and poured himself some coffee. Leaning against the counter, he took a sip and closed his eyes, remembering his last Christmas with his biological mother.

"Wake up, mijo." His mom's sweet voice wrapped around Ricardo like a warm hug.

Her small hand pressed against him and rocked him. He opened his eyes, blinking up into her dark round ones. "Mom?"

"It's Christmas. Come on. Come see what Santa brought."

Ricardo had stopped believing in Santa when he was eight, but she didn't need to know that. He didn't want to steal any more joy from her than life already had.

Ricardo rolled out of bed, rubbing the sleep from his eyes. He grabbed a sweatshirt and slid on his slippers. The house was as cold as an ice box. Had the electricity been shut off again? He stopped to use the bathroom. Flicking the light switch, he got his answer. What had his father spent the money on this time? Probably gambling again.

Anger boiled in his gut. They'd be better off without his dad. But they had no way to make enough income to live on their own. His mother was fighting for her life. And judging by the dark circles under her eyes, and the hollowness of her frail body, the cancer was winning.

Ricardo shoved the anger down, washing his hands in icy water before rejoining his mom. She held the wall for stability as she made her way through the tiny house, down the steps. He took her hand in his; she was so cool to the touch. Another frisson of worry clattered through him.

He followed her into their sparse living room. His dad had sold anything of value long ago. All that was left was a tattered couch they'd found on the side of the road, and a small TV on a warped fake wood table that leaned to one side.

A spot of green caught his attention. It was more of an evergreen branch than a tree, but it was propped up in the corner, covered in silver tinsel. One candy cane hung from one of the flimsy off-shoots, and a grocery bag lay on the floor underneath it.

Ricardo smiled from ear to ear, forcing excitement when all he felt was disgust and anger at his father. This was what his mother was forced to endure because of that man.

Ricardo was used to wearing masks. The brighter he smiled, the more happiness his mother felt.

"It's for me?" he asked.

"Of course!" She walked over, picked up the bag, and handed it to him.

Ricky opened it gingerly, careful to keep his expression one of joy. He pulled a puffy winter coat out, with only one of the seams torn and a small stain on the front. He swallowed. His gaze flicked to hers. She licked her dry lips.

"Wow, this is amazing." His voice cracked. It had been doing that more lately. Ever said it was normal, that he was becoming a man.

That was good. The sooner he became a man, the sooner he could take care of his mom and not be a burden. He could get her the care she needed. She just needed to hang on a little longer.

"It's perfect. I love it."

Her eyes crinkled at the edges as she smiled and rubbed her boney hands up and down her arms. Fury blistered his gut in a fiery inferno. His mother had no doubt struggled to scrape together enough change to buy this secondhand winter coat for him as a Christmas gift while she pulled her holey sweater closer for warmth her tiny frame couldn't even hold.

"Why don't you wear it for now?" he offered.

She shook her head. "No, this is for you, mijo . . . Do you not like it?"

"Like it? I love it." He put it on despite the guilt eating him up.

Her eyes brimmed with tears. "Good. It fits you well—a little big, but that's good. Gives you room to grow."

"Thank you, Mom."

"Don't forget the candy cane," she reminded him.

"How about we split it? And then get ready to go next door? Everett's mom invited us over for their holiday dinner, remember?"

A loud shout from the other room jerked Ricky from the

memory and back to the present. He sucked in a breath and exhaled, his body trembling. Placing the cup to his lips, he took a sip of his now cold coffee. How long had he spaced out like that?

He blinked a few times and cleared his throat. If he had known that would be the last Christmas he'd spend with his mom, he would have cherished it so much more. She hadn't made it to New Year's. Ricky had had no one but Everett after that. And then, Ricky had ruined that too.

More laughter rose from the living room as someone broke out what sounded like a karaoke machine. Music played, and Nova's off-key voice rose above the others, singing along to the lyrics.

Now he had the Emersons. Without them, Ricky would be alone in this world. There was nothing he could do to jeopardize that.

Everett's light eyes flashed in his mind. He shook his head, trying to rid himself of the image. But he remembered the noises too. The sighs Everett made the first time Ricky watched him jack himself off.

"Fuck." Ricky couldn't think about that. It made those feelings too real. Pretending everything was okay was much safer for everyone.

He couldn't afford reality when his life was built on a fantasy.

8

RICKY

Ricky reached for the vape pen and took a few hits before grabbing his phone. The light was too bright in the darkness of the back of the Uber. Looked like he wasn't too late.

"This the place?" the man asked from the driver's seat.

Ricky peeked out the window to the small bungalow. "Yup. Thanks, man."

The car pulled to a stop. "Sure. Have a good night."

"I always do." Ricky smirked, opening the door and stumbling out. "Whoops. Almost forgot my drinks." He grabbed the half-empty case of beer and shut the door.

The night sky spun above him. It wasn't as easy to see the stars in town as it was from the farm, but a few were still visible.

Laughter spilled out from behind the door of Sebastian's home. Ricky knocked.

"Come in!" Sebastian called from within.

Ricky twisted the knob and pushed the door open. The

scents of pizza, chicken wings, and cigars permeated the space.

He toed off his shoes and walked past the living room to the kitchen. Sebastian's back was to him, and he was standing by another man.

"So, dinner again next week?" Sebastian asked.

Ricky smiled. Good for Seb; he deserved to find someone.

"Yeah, that would be fun."

Ricky froze at the voice that had answered his friend. What was Everett doing here?

"I'll take you into the city to Dark Cove. There's a fusion restaurant there that is to die for," Sebastian added.

Why was Everett agreeing to go out with Sebastian? Were they just friends? Did Everett know Sebastian was gay?

Sebastian turned around, a warm smile on his face. "Good, you brought more beer." Sebastian took the case from Ricky's hands.

Everett's eyes widened on Ricky. "I didn't realize you'd be here."

Sebastian looked between the two of them. "You two know each other?"

"Yeah. Everett's dating my sister," Ricky snapped, anger covering his shock.

Sebastian's brows drew together before he turned to Everett, questions shining in his eyes.

Everett waved his hand. "I'll explain later."

There shouldn't even be a later. Jealousy churned in Ricky's gut and it only made him more angry.

"You know, I think I'll leave you to your poker night. I forgot I've got some work to do." Everett's flimsy excuse grated on Ricky's already frayed nerves.

Ricky should want him to leave. It had been weeks since he'd seen Everett, and the last time they'd been in the same space at the same time, Ricky had quite literally run into him and yelled at him.

"Afraid you'll lose and humiliate yourself at poker?" Ricky pressed.

Everett's mouth dropped open. "No, I'm just—"

"Scared?" Ricky taunted.

Sebastian looked between them. "Uh, are you sure you have to go? The wings just got done and the drunker my colleague downstairs gets, the worse he is at cards."

Everett stared at Ricky for a few moments as if trying to read him. Good fucking luck. *I don't know what the fuck I'm doing either.*

"It's okay. I'll go gentle on you." Ricky grabbed the bottle of vodka from the counter, poured some into a glass, and took a swig, relishing the burn. He walked through the door that led to Sebastian's basement without looking back, a glass in one hand and the vodka bottle in the other.

A familiar face sat at the green felt poker table. Smoke billowed from one end of Dr. Burton's cigar.

"Deal me in." Ricky took the empty spot next to the doctor.

He chugged what was left in his glass and poured another as Sebastian came down, Everett trailing behind him, his hands full of the beer Ricky had brought and a platter of finger foods. He set them at the bar across from the pool table before taking a seat.

Everett's attention burned into Ricky, sinking under his skin making him itch. Hand after hand, Ricky played, winning some, losing others. He emptied glass after glass until the room spun.

Everett got up, grabbed a water bottle, and set it next to Ricky's empty glass before sitting back in his seat.

Ricky scoffed and refilled his glass with vodka.

"Maybe you should eat something," Everett suggested.

"Maybe you should play the game. It's your turn," Ricky retorted.

Doc Burton cleared his throat. "It's actually your turn, Ricky."

"Oh. So it is." Ricky tried to focus on his cards, but his vision swam. He pushed his remaining chips into the pile. "All in."

Everett's jaw pulsed. Good, Ricky wasn't the only one pissed off at this whole situation. Maybe if he was a big enough asshole, Everett would leave his life forever and then Ricky wouldn't have to deal with everything his presence brought up. Something sharp twisted in his rib cage at the thought but he shoved it down with all the other uncomfortable emotions Everett's presence invoked.

"Are you sure you want to do that?" Everett asked.

Ricky stood, the chair grating on the shiny cement floor. "I wouldn't have done it if I wasn't. Are you in or do you fold?"

"I fold," Doc Burton said, tossing his cards facedown on the table.

"Me too," Sebastian said.

Everyone's attention landed on Everett.

He shoved his chips in the middle. "Let's see what you got."

Ricky smirked. "Ladies first."

"Technically, you go first," Doc Burton pointed out to Ricky.

"No, it's okay." Everett tossed his cards on the table.

Sebastian whistled. "Two pair. What do you have, Ricky?"

He dropped his cards faceup and the table went silent.

"You bluffed. Damn," Doc Burton said.

"You got nothing," Sebastian added and shook his head. "Bold move, going all in like that."

"Or dumb as fuck," Everett gritted out.

Ricky shrugged like there wasn't rage boiling just underneath the surface of his calm facade. "There's no reward without risk. Sometimes you gotta take a chance . . . Guess I'm out. Y'all have a good night." Ricky stumbled towards the stairs.

"You got a ride home?" Sebastian asked.

Ricky waved his hand. "I'll get an Uber."

He made his way to Sebastian's bathroom, deciding maybe sitting down to pee was the best with the room swaying like it was. After washing his hands, Ricky splashed some water onto his face. He opened the door and grunted as he was pushed back.

"What the fuck?" He shoved the body away from him.

Everett shut the bathroom door behind him, blocking his way out. "What the hell is wrong with you?"

"Nothing. I'm going home. Why the fuck did you come in here?"

"You can barely walk. You think I'm going to let you get in a car with a stranger who could take advantage of you?"

Ricky scoffed. "Hate to break it to you, buddy, but my innocence was taken a long time ago. Drunk or not, I can take care of myself." He shoved his finger against Everett's chest and winced. Damn, that hurt.

"I guess there's nothing left to rob either because you just lost it all to me." Everett smiled.

"You really took a risk with a two pair."

"Wasn't a risk at all."

"How so?" Ricky asked.

"You still have the same tells."

Ricky froze, his eyes locked with Everett's—the only man who could read him like a book. He was transported back to a time when those eyes had been his only source of comfort.

Like he'd been sucked into a black hole, Ricky was tumbling through a mix of emotions both old and new. Temptation lit his blood, seeking the comfort, the escape Everett offered. What would it be like to just give up control to the one person he could always rely on?

The alcohol had freed him of his inhibitions. Everything was stripped away but a deep-seated need gripping his every molecule. His attention dropped to Everett's smooth lips, and he took a step forward.

"Ricky?" Everett's deep voice rumbled through Ricky, making his knees weak.

Blue eyes locked with his. The urge to dive into those icy pools and escape the prison of his past surged through him with every bated breath.

"Ever," Ricky rasped, leaning in. Everything screamed inside him. He just wanted to silence those voices. Just for one moment in time, he wanted the comfort he'd always found in his best friend.

His belly lurched. He jerked away from Everett, stumbling to his knees before the contents of his stomach were emptied into the toilet.

A warm hand rested on his lower back as he retched. A few moments later, a cool paper towel was wiped over his mouth.

Ricky blinked up through blurry eyes at the angel above him, taking care of him.

"Let's get you home." A strong arm slid under his and around his back, helping Ricky to his feet.

Once again, Ricky had proven himself a mess, and Everett had been there to pick up the pieces.

It seemed some things never changed.

9

EVERETT

Everett opened the passenger-side door, careful not to let the man passed out in his front seat fall out of his car. He reached across Ricky's lap and unbuckled him. Ricky jerked awake, his hands rising as if he were ready to defend himself.

"Hey, it's just me. You're safe," Everett tried to soothe him.

Ricky blinked, seeming confused in the dim light of the car. "Where . . .?"

"I got you home. Come on. Let's get you inside." Everett offered his arm, but Ricky pushed it away, grabbing on to the door instead.

Ricky took a step forward and shut the door, losing his footing on the icy ground. Everett was right there to catch him. Ricky's musky scent wound around him, teasing his senses even though it was tainted with the burn of alcohol.

"I can walk," Ricky mumbled, yanking his arm away.

Everett held on. "I don't think you can."

"I said I can—"

Everett reached over Ricky's shoulder and gripped the

65

back of his jacket, pulling Ricky against his chest so they were nose to nose. "Shut the fuck up, Ricardo. Let me help you get into the house so you don't break your fucking neck."

Ricky blinked slowly, a slight flush covering his tan skin. His eyes darkened, the reflection of the moon the only light in them.

"Fine," Ricky rasped, shooting straight to Everett's cock.

The last thing he needs is to know I'm attracted to him.

"Let's go." Everett's arm dropped from Ricky's neck to his lower back, guiding him up the porch to Ricky's front door.

"Where's your keys?" Everett asked.

Ricky scoffed, "I don't lock my door living way out here in the sticks."

Everett shook his head. "That needs to change." He opened the door and ushered Ricky in.

Ricky leaned heavily on him, despite his earlier protests, and flicked the light on. The feel of Ricky's hard body against Everett's was complete torture. This was as close as Everett could get to the man he'd cared so much about—and it was only because Ricky was so drunk. In the light of day, Ricky would go back to hating him.

"Where's your bedroom?" Everett asked.

"Why?" Ricky tensed.

"Because you need to go to bed."

"Upstairs at the end of the hall." Ricky pointed to their left.

Everett kept his arm around Ricky's waist as they bypassed the kitchen and living room, taking a left towards some stairs. He climbed up the steps behind Ricky; the man's broad shoulders made it impossible for them to walk side by side. Ricky led him to the master suite and flicked the light on, illuminating the space. Dark brown paneling covered the wall across from the door. A queen bed sat in the center covered with big cream-colored fluffy pillows with a dark blue down comforter. A dresser sat to the right with matching end tables on either side of the bed.

Ricky stumbled forward, tripping over his own feet. Everett reached out, steadying him before he could fall.

"Thanks." Ricky's eyes met his.

They stood there. Everett became lost in Ricky's gaze. There was so much Everett wanted to know, so much he wanted to share with Ricky. Would he ever get to? And was it normal for Ricky to get this drunk? How often did he go this far with drinking?

Ricky's gaze dropped to Everett's lips. They'd done that earlier too. It seemed the man wasn't as unaffected by Everett as he wanted to pretend. But why? Why hide it? *Although it seems he thinks I'm actually dating his sister still. Nova and I need to have a chat about that.*

Everett leaned in a fraction of an inch. "Let's get you to bed."

Ricky's eyes flashed with a mix of lust and trepidation. He swallowed; his Adam's apple bobbed. Everett longed to nuzzle against the scruff of Ricky's five o'clock shadow and then nip behind his ear. But he couldn't. He wouldn't take advantage of Ricky when he was vulnerable like this.

Everett led him to the connected bathroom, handed him the mouthwash, and steadied Ricky while he swished and spat into the sink. Everett grabbed a towel off a ring by the tap and wiped Ricky's mouth. He helped Ricky back into the bedroom, over to the bed. Everett tugged down the comforter and blankets.

"Sit down on the mattress," Everett instructed.

Ricky plopped down without hesitation.

Everett bit back a smile. "Good boy."

Ricky's deep brown eyes were eclipsed in black as he tipped his chin to look up at Everett.

Everett bent on one knee, reaching for Ricky's shoes, and took them off one by one. The man's glassy gaze remained on him the whole time. Next, he reached for the hem of Ricky's shirt. A strong hand locked around his wrist.

"What are you doing to me?" Ricky's question came out in a harsh whisper.

"I'm helping you get into bed."

"Why? I've been an asshole to you." Ricky's gaze burned into his.

"Because that's what we do. We help each other, miy lev." He threw the reminder of their childhood back at him.

Ricardo flinched and dropped his hand, leaving a brand of hot electricity tingling in its place.

Everett pulled the shirt over Ricardo's head, tossing it on the ground. Ricky's skin reflected the soft light of the room, highlighting the trail of dark hair peppered over his chest that became thicker and formed a line from his belly button and disappeared into his pants. Ricky's abs flexed. Everett licked his lips, his hands itching to feel every inch of the man before him.

He cleared his throat.

"What about my pants?" Ricky asked.

Everett swallowed. "You want me to take them off too?"

Ricky hesitated, closing his eyes. He bit his lip so hard it looked painful.

Everett pressed his thumb to Ricky's bottom lip, and pulled it out. Ricky's eyes shot open.

"Don't hurt yourself." Everett's voice came out more commanding than he'd intended.

Ricky gave a stiff nod.

Everett reached for Ricky's pants button ever so slowly,

ready to back away if Ricky changed his mind. Ricky was a trained fighter with a lot more muscle than Everett. If he freaked out, Everett wasn't sure he would stand a chance whether Ricky was drunk or not. It was a risk, but something deep inside wouldn't let him walk away from Ricky when he needed him—never again.

Everett undid the button, slid the zipper down. It was impossible not to notice the hard erection pushing against the jean fabric.

Ricky's chest heaved.

"Are you okay?" Everett asked.

Ricky shook his head.

"Do you remember when we first met?" Everett tugged the jeans the rest of the way off and added them to the growing pile of clothing on the ground, leaving Ricky only in black briefs that did nothing to hide just how much he'd grown in other places over the years.

When Ricky didn't answer, Everett pressed against his chest. Ricky lay on the bed without hesitation. Everett grabbed his feet, sliding them up on the mattress, tucking them under the covers. He pulled the blanket up to Ricky's chin.

"You were in your backyard, tossing that old football in the air and catching it. We'd just moved in, and my parents were fighting. Your parents . . ." Everett hesitated. "Well, it seemed we both needed an escape."

Ricky made no outward sign he was listening, his eyes blinking slower and slower with each passing second.

Everett sat on the edge of the bed. "You were my best friend. With me through finding out my parents were getting a divorce, starting a new school."

Ricky's eyes closed, his face relaxed as he passed out.

Everett risked brushing his thumb over the other man's

defined cheekbone. His handsome face didn't even twitch from the contact.

"You were everything to me. My best friend. My first crush. My first kiss. Damn it, Ricardo, I fucking loved you. I know they say kids can't love that young, but what I felt for you—it never completely went away. It's still there. And every time I'm near you . . ." Everett released a sigh. "Something stirs all over again. I know you feel this connection too. So why are you denying it?"

Everett ran a hand through his hair and released a sigh.

"I don't get it. You're friends with gay men, your sister is bisexual, and still, you're so terrified." Everett shook his head, tears stinging his eyes. "Don't let him win, Ricardo. Don't let him steal any more of your life."

Everett took another moment to soak up the view of Ricky sleeping. He was so vulnerable like this, without the reinforced fortress he'd built around himself to keep everyone else out. But Everett saw through it, just like he always had. When you shared your soul with another person, your connection didn't just disappear.

Yet Everett was at a loss as to what to do. It was clear he couldn't have what he wanted from Ricky and get to know each other again, see if they still had something between them. At the very least, he wanted the man to be happy— whether that was with him in his life or not.

"As much as I like taking the lead, the next move is up to you, miy lev."

10

—————

RICKY

Who the hell was playing drums? Ricky blinked his eyes open in the dim room and groaned. He slapped an arm over his face. The noise was coming from inside his pounding head.

What the hell happened last night?

His mouth tasted like ass and was dryer than the Sahara. He rolled over. A scent that most certainly did not belong in his bedroom caught his nose. He froze. Why did it smell like Everett in there?

He jerked up to sitting, searching the bed next to him, chest heaving, then his gaze fell to the floor, to the pile of his clothes.

His memory flashed with images of Everett on his knees, pulling down his pants—

Ricky shoved the blankets down and released a sigh. He still had his briefs on. He didn't feel like he'd had sex. He ran a hand through his hair and tugged until the pain bit into his pounding skull. *What did I do?*

He'd played cards, gone to the bathroom, and then . . .

Everett. Everett had taken him home—had helped him to bed. He turned to the bedside table. A full glass of water sat there next to a note.

Ricky sipped the water, finding two pain pills next to it, and swallowed them down. He lifted the note.

Thought you might need these.

—E

Ricky sighed, guilt crashing into him. He'd been nothing but an asshole to Everett, and even while he was drunk off his ass, the man had been kind to him. Closing his eyes, Ricky reached for the phone charging on the side table. Everett deserved more than Ricky had to give, but the least he could do was pay him back for his kindness.

He unlocked the phone and texted his sister.

Ricky: *Can I have Everett's number? He asked me to take him as a client, and I forgot to ask for it.*

He set the phone aside and crawled out of bed, heading into the bathroom for a quick shower and to brush his teeth. After he was done, he felt a little less like death.

He slid into a pair of sweatpants and a T-shirt before picking up his phone.

Nova: *R U for real?*

Nova: *Hello?*

Nova: *Promise it's really for that? You're not just trying to harass him some more? Everett is my friend and a good guy. He doesn't deserve your overprotective macho bullshit.*

Ricky chuckled and shook his head, clicking on the button to dial his sister.

She picked up on the second ring. "Well?"

"I promise. And you're right, he's a good guy."

"And no macho bullshit?" she pressed.

"What do you take me for?" he asked.

"You. Mister Tough Guy. You punch first and ask questions later." She chuckled. "But not with this guy, okay?"

"I don't always punch first. In fact, I make it a habit of letting them take the first swing—it's self-defense that way."

"Ricky—"

"Okay, it was a joke. Relax. I won't hurt your precious boyfriend."

Nova groaned. "He's not—you know what, fine. I'll give you his number, but you'd better not be an asshole to him. I will come for you, got me? Do I need to remind you about *the incident?*"

Ricky's balls shriveled up at the threat. "You swore you'd destroyed the evidence."

Nova laughed like an evil villain. "I'm the only girl in a house full of brothers. You think I didn't stash that shit somewhere important? I need all the leverage I can get. Be nice, or Mom and Dad will see your hairy ass running from Pastor Morgan's shed with his not-so-innocent daughter moments before it blew up."

"But it was your fault!"

"I'm not the one running from the crime scene with a half-naked girl. It's all about perception anyways, isn't it?" He could hear the smirk in her voice.

"You little snake."

"Be nice to Everett and no one needs to find out the truth."

"You think anyone still cares? That was over fifteen years ago," he argued.

"Pastor Morgan still has the reward paper up at the sheriff's office for any information leading to the suspect who blew it up," Nova deadpanned.

"Fucking small towns," Ricky grumbled.

His sister laughed. "I'll send you his number. Be good."

Good boy. Everett's voice rang in his head. Chills raced up Ricky's spine at the memory of last night.

He was so distracted he didn't notice his sister had ended the call. The phone dinged with a text message.

Ricky copied Everett's number and added him to his contacts.

Ricky: *Thank you for getting me home safe last night.*

He held his breath, staring at the screen. An eternity later, bubbles appeared.

Ever: *You're welcome.*

Ricky swallowed, his hands clammy and trembling as his heart slammed against his rib cage and his stomach roiled, its contents threatening to come up.

Ricky: *Be at the gym at seven tomorrow night if you still want lessons.*

Taking him as a client was the least Ricky could do. He owed Everett more than the man probably realized. That was all this was. Quid pro quo. It had absolutely nothing to do with the fact that Ricky missed having Everett in his life. And it certainly didn't mean he had any feelings for his old friend. This was just Ricky making sure things were even—he didn't like owing anyone anything. Besides, Everett was dating his sister—it wasn't like Ricky was taking a risk.

11

EVERETT

Everett couldn't help checking Ricardo out as the man led him into one of the private rooms at the gym. Mirrors hung on every wall but one, which had a giant plexiglass window facing the hall leading back to the main part of the gym. The floor was covered in some sort of padding.

"It's best if you take your shoes off." Ricky toed his sneakers off by the edge of the door and set his drink next to them.

Everett did the same and turned to face him.

"Come into the center next to me." Ricky motioned in front of him.

Everett did so, casting another look at the mirrors. "Is this where you teach all your students?"

"I just started taking on clients. Pops—he owns the gym— lets me use this room. It helps not having so many distractions when you're first learning."

"Makes sense." Everett nodded. "Nova said you worked with bees. I have to ask how a bee farmer gets into MMA?"

"Asking my sister about me, huh?" Ricky asked, his expression unreadable as he crossed his arms in front of his chest, bare forearms flexing with the movement.

Everett stiffened. "No, actually she volunteered that bit of information, along with the rest of your siblings and your parents' jobs."

Ricky shook his head with a small smile. "I'm just messing with you. Yeah, I'm a beekeeper. But late fall and winter are our slow seasons. Not much to do but bottle honey and make deliveries and build bee equipment."

"Is that how you got into this?" Everett waved to the room around them. "Boredom?"

Ricky's attention darted to the ground and then back to him. The air between them grew heavy. "I just liked the idea of knowing how to defend myself and those I care about."

Because he couldn't do it when they were kids? "That seems like a good reason."

Ricky nodded. "Everyone should know how to defend themselves."

"Well, that's why I'm here. Teach me, Obi-Wan."

Ricky burst into laughter. "Fuck, I forgot you were such a nerd."

Everett shrugged. "Being a nerd pays the bills much better than a jock."

Ricky paused, looking at the mats again.

"Oh, don't tell me you were a jock in high school."

Ricky smirked. "Captain of the football team."

"You must have bulked up after you left. The boy I remember was scrawny and skinny as a string bean." Everett playfully pushed Ricky's shoulder.

The man smiled, and it was the first time he'd done so and it had reached his eyes. "Yeah, I was a little late to the party, but my voice dropped about six months after . . ." Dark clouds edged at the corner of Ricky's gaze, dimming his smile. Ricky looked right at Everett. "Puberty changed a lot of things."

His meaning was clear. Whatever they'd had between them was in the past, and Ricky wanted it dead and buried. Everett forced a smile, pretending that the thought didn't cause stabbing pain in his heart.

"Stand with your feet shoulder width apart. Raise your hands up to the sky and then bring them back down into fists at cheek level, like this." Ricky shifted to mirror his instructions.

Everett copied him.

"Good. This is your fighting stance. You're right-handed, so put your right foot back like this." Ricky slid his foot behind him.

Everett matched him once again. Ricky walked around him and bent down. His hand touched Everett's ankle, and Everett gritted his teeth as a buzz of electricity spiraled out from the man's touch.

"You want to keep your foot at a forty-five-degree angle for more stability."

Everett adjusted his leg.

"Perfect. Bend your knees a little." Ricky moved to stand behind Everett. His hands gripped Everett's shoulders. "Relax. You don't want to squeeze your shoulders or tense your muscles."

Everett breathed out, relaxing his body as he did. All but one muscle seemed to get the memo, but it was hard to control his cock when Ricky was touching him, his spicy, musky scent tainting every breath.

"Let's start with footwork." Ricky went through a series of moves, explaining how to maneuver in the fighting stance so that at no point would he cross his legs. Everett tried to focus on what the man was teaching him, but having a hot instructor with his muscles on display was distracting to say the least. The way Ricky's hips moved with his lithe motion was sensual in a way.

Everett shuffled his feet.

"You got it. Now, let me show you some punches. The first one is a jab." Ricky modeled the move while keeping his opposite hand up near his face.

"It's simple. You extend to do the jab, and always, *always*, keep your other hand up to guard your face. Fighting is just as much about defense as it is offense."

"Like this?" Everett purposely left his arm a little low, needing another touch from Ricky.

"Almost." Wide, strong hands lifted his arm.

Worth it.

"Now, as you're extending it, you're gonna twist it like a corkscrew to keep the shoulder of your punching arm protecting your jaw. And don't have a lazy arm when you pull it back. Quick forward, quick back, like this." Ricky jabbed so speedily Everett would have missed it if not for him repeating the motion twice more.

"Your turn." Ricky gestured for him to have a turn.

Everett did his best, wanting to impress Ricky more than anything.

"Not too bad for a nerd." Ricardo laughed.

"The student will eventually become the master. You better watch it, boy," Everett teased.

Ricky snorted. "Wow, half a lesson and already cocky."

Everett shrugged. "I never promise what I can't deliver."

Ricky's eyes lit up with something that looked an awful lot like lust. "Come on. Next is the cross."

He modeled the move. "So, your hips will pivot this time, but your rear foot stays grounded, pushing against the earth. And you rotate your upper body to do the cross jab." He did it twice more, releasing a hiss of air through his mouth each time.

Fuck, his ass looked tight in those basketball shorts. And those thick thighs rippled with the movement.

"Ever?"

"Hmm?"

"Did you get it or do you need to see it again?" Ricky asked.

"Oh, uh, yeah, maybe one more time." Everett schooled his features.

Ricky went through the motions once more. "Your turn."

Everett took the fighting stance, doing his best to imitate his instructor.

"You want to pivot like this." Ricky's hands dropped to Everett's hips. Everett sucked in a breath.

Everett relaxed enough to allow Ricky to move his body the way he wanted. His skin tingled, and his cock pulsed with arousal.

"You got it now?" Ricky asked.

"Yeah." Everett coughed, hoping his leg would hide his obvious reaction.

"Go for it." Ricky stepped back, releasing him, but his eyes never left Everett's body.

Everett couldn't help but compare himself to the man before him. Everett was lean and tall. He was fit, but nothing like Ricky who looked like he lived at the gym.

"You're getting it," Ricky encouraged him.

"Think I'll be ready for the ring soon?" Everett joked.

Ricky shook his head with a smile. "One step at a time. But you'll get there if you put the work in."

"Oh, I'll put the work in." Everett flirted and then slammed his mouth closed. Was this too much? Would Ricky snap at him again and run away?

His instructor shook his head and pulled off his muscle shirt, leaving him bare chested. So much beautiful skin, this time on full display under the florescent lighting above. Fuck, the man didn't have an ounce of fat on him. Two, four, six— eight—Ricardo had an eight-pack. Christ almighty. Everett's mouth went dry.

Ricky shifted, the deep V of his lower abdomen more defined. "Okay, let's show you a right hook next."

Everett swallowed hard. *This is going to be a lot harder than I'd thought.*

12

RICKY

Ricky swerved just in time to avoid Everett's kick. "That's what I'm talking about. Perfect."

Everett wiped the sweat from his brow, panting. His smile made Ricky's stomach do a somersault.

"I don't think I've worked out this much . . . ever." Everett chuckled.

"You should hydrate," Ricky said.

Everett walked over to their things on the ground and tossed Ricky his Gatorade before grabbing his own water. He tipped it to his mouth and guzzled it down. Everett's prominent Adam's apple bobbed with each swallow. Ricky's abs tensed, and his skin flushed.

Everett lifted the hem of his shirt and wiped the sweat from his face, revealing his flat stomach. Ricky was drawn to the exposed flesh like a magnet. Everett was fit. Dark hair contrasted with his pale skin, looping around his belly button and trailing down to his shorts. Everett tugged his shirt the rest of the way off, his wide shoulders flexing with the movement before his stormy eyes slammed into Ricky's.

Everett's shiny, pink lips turned up. Ricky's heart pounded. He fisted his hands and let them go, trying to release some of the building tension in his body.

It was unnerving to be so close to someone from his past, someone who knew him before. To the one person who'd kept all his secrets and who'd been there for him when no one else had. That was all this was—anxiety. This hyperawareness that moved through Ricky every time Everett was near.

Ricky licked his lips. The urge to run his tongue along the column of Everett's neck and taste him surged up from the depths of somewhere deep inside him.

Ricky unscrewed his drink and drank the contents with trembling hands. "So, when do you want to come again?"

Everett's eyebrow quirked up as he smiled. "Jumping right into the personal questions, huh?"

Ricky choked, coughing as red Gatorade dripped down his chin.

"Slow down." Everett patted his back. Energy thrummed between them. Ricky's skin tingled where they touched.

Ricky wiped his hand across his mouth and put the cap back on, clearing his throat. "Sorry, you caught me off guard there. Usually I'm the one making those jokes."

Everett chuckled. "I can be back as soon as tomorrow."

"You sure? I think you might be sore then. We used a lot of muscles you probably aren't used to working out."

Everett crossed his arms over his chest, his sweat-soaked shirt hanging from his hand. "You can go easy on me."

"That's not my style."

"Oh? You like it rough and fast, huh?" Everett's eyes lit with humor but you couldn't play a player. There was always a hint of truth to any joke—sometimes more.

Ricky shrugged, trying to seem unaffected. He gave his signature smirk. "Maybe I do."

Everett stared at him, the heat of his gaze ramping up the invisible tension between them. "Tomorrow, same time, then?"

"Sure."

"You want to go get a beer after this?" Everett asked.

A beer? Add alcohol to this mess of emotions wrecking and rampaging inside him like a tornado? No fucking thank you.

"I've got other plans," Ricky lied.

Everett nodded, disappointment flashing in his expression. "Oh, yeah, maybe next time."

"Come on. Let's go shower." Ricky picked up his things, opened the door to the hall, and led Everett across to the lockers where Ricky retrieved his toiletry bag.

"You can leave your other stuff here if you want."

Everett added his gym bag to Ricky's locker.

"Code is six-four-two-nine. Feel free to use it when you're here." Ricky headed into the men's shower room.

The sweat dotting his brow had nothing to do with the workout. Ricky swallowed hard. He was about to strip down to nothing in front of Everett. It shouldn't matter. He was just another body like any other in the gym—but it did.

He kept his head down as he grabbed a towel from the rack and removed his clothing, heading straight for the showers without looking back. There wasn't anyone else in here this late in the evening. Unfortunately for him, the gym had open showers, and there was no way to avoid the lean, naked body that took the space across from him. Ricky started the water at the end shower, giving it a minute to warm up before he stepped in, and going for the soap as the warm water rained down on him.

Everett's back was to him. Water swirled down his body, dripping over the twin dimples in his lower back. His plump, juicy ass flexed as Everett reached his arm up, rubbing soap underneath it.

Ricky gritted his teeth, his cock jerking. *I'm not gay. I'm just admiring another man who's worked hard on his body. That's all.*

He turned the knob to cold, the warm water turning to ice.

Everett did the other arm and turned around, his gaze crashing into Ricky's. It took all Ricky's self-control not to look down.

One corner of Everett's mouth quirked up as he soaped his hands, running them around his neck, over his chest, leaving suds in their wake. His fingers slowed to a sensual dance, running over his pecs, down the center of his chest to his stomach. Ricky couldn't look away—it was like a train wreck waiting to happen. This could only end in utter destruction. He shouldn't be looking at his sister's boyfriend this way —or any man for that matter. But he had no control over his body anymore. Primal instinct, something hotter than lust, scorched his veins, paralyzed his muscles until all he could do was watch.

Everett's hand dipped down the deep V of his hips, teasing the trimmed hair at the top of his cock. Fuck, he was big and thick. Veins twisted from the base of his dick towards the head. *He's hard.* Ricky's gaze snapped to Everett's.

With his chest heaving, his heart racing, Ricky bolted from the room, not even bothering to shut off his shower. He needed to get out of there before he undid two and a half decades of work. He couldn't fail now—and not with his sister's boyfriend. Guilt warred with his disgust at himself.

"I'm so fucking weak." He dripped water all the way back to the locker. Not bothering to towel off, he grabbed his clothes from the bag and pulled on material that stuck to his damp skin.

"Ricky." Everett's voice was too close.

Ricky slipped on his shoes, grabbed his things, and ran out the door with Everett calling his name.

Panic gripped him as he sprinted into the cold winter air, sending shivers through him. He raced for his car. Skidding on the ice, he slammed into hard asphalt.

Pain radiated up his side and in his knee, but it had nothing on the squeezing sensation strangling his heart.

"Fuck!" He tried to suck in a breath but it didn't feel like enough. Gripping his chest, he squeezed his eyes closed.

Was he having a heart attack? Ricky curled up into a ball on the icy ground. He stared up at the dark, cloudy sky above. Why did he have to deal with this curse? Why couldn't he be better—stronger?

Because I'm nothing but a failure. I'm weak. His thoughts spiraled into an overwhelming wave of fear and anxiety wrapped up in past memories, crashing into him. He clawed at his chest. *I can't breathe! I'm going to die like this.*

"Ricky!" Everett yelled from across the parking lot.

Hot embarrassment kicked in. *RUN!* The warning blared in his mind like a siren. Ricky forced himself to his feet, opened the door, and shoved his things inside before he climbed behind the wheel. After starting the engine, he peeled out onto the main road between heaving breaths.

He slammed his hand against the steering wheel. "Fuck!" Anger washed over him, easing some of the panic slamming through his rib cage.

That was what he needed—the red haze that took away the pain. He let it seep into him until he vibrated with rage at himself, at his excuse for a sperm donor, at the cancer that had taken his mother from him, and at Everett, for making him feel something he'd long since buried.

He was a man, goddamn it. He was an MMA fighter. He

could bench more than his giant of a brother. He could take down men three times his size. He was not weak anymore—and he'd prove it.

He pulled up his phone as he drove, scrolling through until he found the number he was looking for. It rang a few times before she picked up.

"Ricky?"

"Hey, babe. You up to hang out tonight?" he asked.

"Sure. Did you want to meet up somewhere?"

"I was thinking I could just come over." He needed to fuck a woman—prove to himself he was just as much a man as ever.

"Oh, yeah. Okay."

"I'll see you in ten." Ricky hung up, tossing the phone on the seat next to him.

The screen lit up with an incoming call. Everett's name was displayed. Ricky flipped the radio on, turned the volume all the way up, and stepped on the gas. Maybe if he tried hard enough, he could escape it all—even himself.

13

EVERETT

Everett turned towards the gym entrance. A woman exited, waving towards the man at the front desk who insisted everyone call him Pops. Everett checked his phone once more. Eight o'clock. He checked his messages for the hundredth time.

7:00 p.m. Everett: *Just got to the gym. How far away are you?*

7:20 p.m. Everett: *Did you get held up?*

7:43 p.m. Everett: *Is everything okay?*

What could one more hurt?

Everett: *Just let me know you're okay and not dead in a ditch somewhere. If you don't reply, I'll be forced to call your sister and make sure you're alive and well.*

He sighed and headed for the lockers to grab his things and change back into his jeans.

After he got dressed, his phone buzzed. Everett's hand shot out, his stomach tumbling with nerves as the text flashed.

Miy Lev: *Sorry. Something came up.*

"Bullshit."

Everett: *Okay. How about tomorrow at seven?*

The text bubble appeared and then disappeared. Everett stared at the phone, his heart sinking with every second. Finally, Ricky replied.

Miy Lev: *I don't think that's gonna work. I can recommend someone else at the gym.*

Everett: *Can we talk?*

The text bubble never reappeared. He waited another ten minutes but there was nothing. Everett shook his head and shoved the phone in his pocket. He grabbed his things, walked out of the gym, and climbed into his car. He didn't want to go home alone to his empty apartment. He'd hoped to spend a few hours with his friend and to talk about last night.

"Damnit." Everett turned his new car on and headed towards The Shipwreck. Nova had told him it was the best bar in town to get a cold drink and enjoy some dancing. He wasn't up for the latter, but the former sounded good.

Everett parked and walked into the bar after showing his ID to the bouncer. Blue light illuminated the space from back-lit fish tanks in the walls. A skeleton with a red and white Santa hat sat in one of the chairs by a table, and a ring of flashing holiday lights hung around its rib cage. Distressed shiplap walls made it look like they were truly in the belly of a ship.

He turned towards the wooden bar, finding an empty stool near the center. A woman with tattoos curling around her arms wiped the bar top in front of him.

"What can I get you?" she asked.

"Just a beer is fine. IPA if you have it."

"We have Sand Dune's holiday special brew if you're interested?" she asked.

"Sounds good."

"Charli, Mom's on the phone. Jamison wanted to say goodnight." A man came up to the woman.

She turned, a smile softening her features. "Okay, let me just get this beer." She reached into the fridge and pulled out a bottle. After popping the top, she handed it to Everett.

"Thanks," Everett said.

"No problem. You can settle up with my husband, Finn."

Finn placed his hand over what Everett assumed was a small baby bump. "After that you should relax in the office. I've got this."

"I'm fine—"

"Don't argue. I already put your dinner in there."

She shook her head and smiled up at him. "Fine."

Finn leaned down, whispering something in her ear that made Charli blush before he tapped her ass, and she headed towards what looked to be a back room.

"Do you want to keep a tab open?" Finn asked him.

Everett shook his head. "No, this should be good." He slid his card over to the barkeep.

Finn handed it back and gave him the slip to sign. Everett left a tip and then took a sip of his beer. It was good, with a hint of cranberry. The taste combination shouldn't have worked, but it did.

Someone bumped into him, squishing between him and the patron in the chair next to Everett.

"Sorry. I just need to order a couple drinks," the pretty blonde apologized.

"Sure." Everett leaned farther away, trying to give the two women space as they told Finn their order.

"You'd better give me the dirty details," the brunette said.

"There isn't much to tell. He just called me last night, showed up on my front door. I thought we were going to hook up like usual—he even gave me the normal speech that this was just sex," Blondie said.

"So you slept with him? Was it as good as last time?" her friend asked.

"No. I climbed on his lap and started kissing his neck, and he bolted. Then tonight, he texted me to meet him here."

"What the hell?" the brunette asked.

"Talk about mixed signals."

"You probably intimidate him. Maybe he's ready to put aside his playboy ways and be with you, but it scares him?" her friend suggested.

"Do you think so?"

Finn handed them their drinks. They walked towards one of the tables around the dance floor. Everett tracked them, turning in his seat, and took another drink of his beer.

The brunette sat on her date's lap and the blonde did the same with hers. Everett froze. Ricky's hands landed on the blonde's hips as he laughed at something the other guy said.

They'd been talking about Ricky? He'd gone to her last night after . . . Jealousy speared through him, jealousy that he had no right to.

Ricky had checked him out. They'd flirted, and then he'd freaked out and run into her arms. It stung. Was Ricky bisexual? Or was he in the closet? He'd sworn he wasn't gay, but the way he'd eyed Everett's cock with lust wasn't something a straight man would do. Some part of Everett had hoped Ricky still harbored feelings for him. But the man was scared —of what, Everett didn't exactly know.

Everett should have known better than to fall for a man in the closet again—especially after what had happened with his ex who'd not been willing to come out even when it had put Everett in danger. He'd never let a man use him like that again.

But this was Ricky, his lev. The man he'd fallen in love with before he even knew what love was.

Ricky's laugh carried over the upbeat music pounding through the speakers. Even from here, it sounded hollow. After a lifetime, Everett could tell when Ricky put his mask of pretense on. He was living a lie, and it would destroy him from the inside out. Or maybe that was wishful thinking on Everett's part.

Ricky turned towards the bar, lifting his empty glass and saying something to the blonde on his lap. She got up and he stepped forward, his eyes widening when they met Everett's. The color leached from his face. Ricky reached out his hand to his date, pulling her up against him, his hand grabbing a fistful of her ass like he was trying to prove something. But to whom?

A sick feeling tangled and twisted in Everett's gut—a knowing.

Ricky's father.

Last Everett had heard, that monster was sitting in a prison cell.

14

RICKY

Ricky was losing his ever-loving mind. Every nerve was frayed at the edges, raw. He was hyperaware. Forget a candle burning at both ends—this felt like a fucking dynamite stick waiting to explode.

What's wrong with me? He lay on his bed, running his fingers through his hair and pulling until the pain interrupted the swirling chaos tangling inside him.

Sitting up so his back leaned against the paneled wall, Ricky played over the last two nights. He'd been in a tailspin since running out of that gym. He'd done everything he could to escape this suffocating feeling. Sophie had been more than willing for a booty call.

Shame sunk into his shoulders. He'd never not been able to get it up. And then yesterday, he'd tried again. Had a few drinks, tried to get back into his usual scene. And things were going okay until Everett had texted him, and then he'd seen him at the bar.

Ricky bit his lip and shook his head. "Why can't I get him out of my head?"

Skeletons were supposed to stay buried—and Ricky had locked that shit down tight. His past was six feet under, bound with steel chains, and had been set on fire. That was where it belonged—never to see the light of day.

His phone dinged. A mixture of trepidation and drunken moths swam in his belly as he reached for his cell. He looked at his watch. Seven a.m. Who'd text this early in the morning?

Sophie: *Do you want to get some dinner this week?*

He exhaled through his nose. She knew his rules. He was upfront with all his hookups. No dating—just fucking. And he couldn't even get it up to follow through with the latter. Every time he touched her, it felt wrong. She was too soft. Her perfume was too fruity. She was nothing like—

No. I'm not going there.

Ricky closed out the message and pulled up his favorite porn site. After flicking to one of his favorite videos, he clicked play. He shoved down his sweatpants with his other hand. He gripped his shaft, his eyes on the screen as a dark-haired woman lay, tied to a table, ass in the air.

"You ready for your punishment?" the man in the porno asked.

"Yes," she whimpered.

Ricky slid his hand up and down his shaft.

"Yes, what?" The man slapped her ass.

She cried out. "Yes, sir!"

The Dom squeezed the same ass cheek, massaging over the bright red handprint he'd left. "Good girl. Now, you're gonna take the pain for me like a good sub, aren't you?"

"Yes, sir."

Ricky's cock twitched as the man in the video lined his cock up with her pussy. The camera zoomed in, his tan cock sliding inside her wet hole only a few inches. She whined.

"You want this cock so bad, don't you, button?" the Dom asked.

"Please?"

"You're gonna have to earn it. Take the lashes like a good little pain slut."

"Yes, sir."

"What's your safe word?" the Dom asked.

"Red."

The man thrust his hips, teasing the woman with shallow-angled thrusts.

"Remember, you can't come without my permission. You'll come from the pain I give you before I let you have my cock. Understood, button?"

"Yes, sir."

The camera switched to an angle behind the Dom. His ass flexed as he continued to tease her. Ricky's cock hardened as the cat-o'-nine-tails raised in the air before the Dom brought it down across her back. The leather snapped against her flesh. Ricky's heart raced, blood surging to his fully erect cock.

"You're gonna thank me after each lash," the Dom commanded.

"Thank you!"

Ricky squeezed his cock hard, the bite of pain adding to his building pleasure as he jacked himself off.

The Dom in the video whipped his sub's back over and over. Cries of gratitude fell from her lips. Her body tensed with each impact. The Dom switched between feather-light swipes and hard whips so nothing was predictable. The woman's brown eyes glazed over, her body stilling despite the relentless crack of the cat-o'-nine-tails as she surrendered to the pain.

Ricky's spine tingled, his balls pulling up.

The man turned his face towards the camera slightly. Dark

hair hung over his brows. The similarities between this man and Everett were striking. Aquamarine eyes morphed to grey. The actor's face was replaced by the image of Everett pounding into Ricky.

The slightest hesitation screamed at the edges of Ricky's fantasy, but his impending release was too strong.

Everett's abs flexed with each thrust. His hips drove powerfully as he plowed into Ricky. Delicious pain rained down on Ricky's back as he struggled against the restraints.

Pre-cum dripped down the tip of his cock. His ears rang as he approached the edge of his orgasm.

"Come!" the Dom ordered before driving the full length of his cock into his sub.

Ricky groaned as hot, sticky release shot out of his dick, landing on his belly. He continued to pump, draining himself of every last drop, riding the last pulses of pleasure.

Chest heaving, he slowly came back to the room. The moans and cracks of the whip still played from his phone. He shut it off and looked down at the mess he'd made. Deep shame barreled over him. His stomach tensed as if he'd swallowed thorns, and they were tearing him from the inside out.

He rolled out of bed, going straight to the shower. Stripping down, he was unable to look at himself in the mirror. Ice water rained over his body. He deserved the cold. He was disgusting. An abomination.

With his eyes burning with unshed tears, he cleaned himself as quickly as possible. Numb, he dried off and slipped a fresh pair of sweatpants and a black shirt on. He avoided his bedroom and jogged downstairs to his quiet kitchen.

He'd pretend that he didn't just fantasize about a man fucking him—his sister's boyfriend, no less. Grabbing a banana off the counter, he accidentally hit the pile of mail next to the fruit bowl sending a few pieces scattering on the wood floor. Ricky picked them up, glancing at the letters. His hand froze on the last one.

The sender was an inmate at the state prison in Concord. Donald Benning.

He couldn't breathe, his lungs paralyzed. The paper trembled in his hand. Ricky hadn't heard from his biological father in years. After his stint in jail for what he'd done to Everett and Ricky, his father hadn't been out long before he'd been busted for armed robbery and put back in prison.

How did he find me?

Ricky wanted to burn the letter. But if Donald knew where he lived, was he out? Would he try to come here? Would he tell Ricky's family about what had happened? *Everett's here. What if Donald hurts him—*

Ricky tore the letter open, the envelope falling to the counter.

Hello, son,

You're one hard person to find. Thankfully, I've made a few friends in here with contacts on the outside. They tell me you've got a sweet piece of property over by the seacoast. You're some sort of farmer. That seems fitting—you always did like to play with animals.

The blood drained from Ricky's head. Was that a reference to Everett? Was Donald watching him? Did he know Everett was back in his life?

Ricky forced himself to read the last line.

I look forward to reuniting. We have a lot to talk about. You owe me.
Dad

The words blurred as white-hot rage boiled in Ricky's veins. He crumpled the letter and threw it across the room with a guttural scream.

"Fuck!"

His heart raced, thudding against his rib cage with bruising force. He couldn't breathe.

I need air.

After grabbing his keys, he slipped on his sneakers and raced out the door. The wind cut through his thin T-shirt. Ricky ran for his truck, threw open the door, and climbed in. He turned the engine over, peeled down the driveway, and sped down slippery roads, not knowing where to go but needing to get away.

He slammed his hand against the wheel. "Why! Why can't you just leave me the fuck alone?"

Ricky drove, fishtailing around a corner until he hit the main road leading into town.

Snow-covered trees whipped by. *What if I just steered into one of them, foot all the way to the floor?* The fantasy played out in his mind—the car careening off the road, the freedom in flying before he hit the wall of wooden trunks. Would it be quick?

A car honking pulled him back to reality. Ricky swerved to avoid a collision as he blew through a stop sign. He slowed down, not wanting to hurt anyone else. He parked in a lot and looked up. Back at the gym. It made sense. This was his escape. A way to let out the emotions when he couldn't stuff them down anymore. A way to keep them at bay—only now, those emotions seeped out of him at every crack. Ricky bolted from the car, jogging into the gym and straight into the ring where two fighters tapped gloves as if they'd just finished sparring.

"I got next," he said, tossing his keys on the floor before he took his shirt off, adding it to the small pile.

The two men looked at each other.

The bigger one nodded. "You sure?"

"Let's go." Ricky got in the fighting stance. The guy had at least fifty pounds on him and an extra six inches. He was a giant. But that was what Ricky needed—a challenge. Someone who could beat this feeling out of him.

His opponent matched him, knees bent, hands up. Usually, Ricky would take his time, staying on the defense and studying his opponent. Not today.

Ricky jabbed, following it with a right hook. The giant across from him blocked and then kicked.

Ricky jumped back, avoiding the hit before attacking. Over and over, he punched. His opponent clocked him in the jaw. Ricky jerked back from the force. A slow smile crept up his face.

"You're going easy on me. Come on! I can take it."

"Ricky, maybe you should take a minute?" Pops called from the side of the ring.

Rather than responding, Ricky jabbed again and attacked with a series of moves he hoped would incite his opponent.

It worked. Ricky grunted from the impact of the kick to his center mass, stealing his air as the big guy clipped his jaw. Ricky stumbled to his hands and knees, an iron tang filling his mouth.

He climbed back to his feet, ignoring the pain in his ribs and jaw. Raising his hands to cheekbone level, he nodded once. "Again."

The big guy shook his head. "No, I'm done."

"Come on!"

"Ricky!" Pops yelled. Ricky turned to him to argue when a flicker of movement off to the side caught his attention. *Everett.*

"What are you doing here?" Ricky snarled.

Everett looked between the big guy climbing out of the ring and Ricky. Something akin to sympathy and concern flashed in his gaze. *I don't need your pity!*

"You're done for today, son," Pops said.

Ricky climbed out of the ring. Grabbing his things, he slipped on his shirt and headed for the door.

The winter air did nothing to calm the storm raging inside him. He jogged to his car and tore the door open. A big hand shoved it closed. Ricky reared around, hands up, ready for a fight.

Everett stood chest to chest with him.

"You going to hit me too?" Everett asked.

Ricky's ears rang. Adrenaline pumped through him. His mind screamed. He ground his teeth until they ached.

"Let me go," he gritted out.

"I don't think you're in any shape to drive," Everett said calmly, not budging.

"Why the fuck do you even care!"

"Because that's what we do. We help each other. I'm still here, *miy lev*."

It was the use of his old nickname that did him in. All the anger inside Ricky evaporated, replaced with utter exhaustion. His shoulders finally lowered with a long exhale.

It was ironic that the one man who held the power to break him was the only one who brought him any sense of peace and who would understand Ricky best. Ever was still here despite . . . everything.

Could he really let someone in again? Was it really a risk if Everett already knew his darkest secrets?

It would be different this time. Everett was dating Nova, so Ricky wouldn't cross another line—he was safe from himself.

Ricky sighed. "Get in."

15

RICKY

"Let me drive," Everett insisted.

Ricky frowned. "It's my truck—"

"Get your ass in the passenger seat. You're in no shape to get behind the wheel." Everett plucked the keys from his hand before Ricky could protest further. He should argue, insist—this was his truck after all. He should be the one in the driver's seat, not riding shotgun. But the exhaustion from the morning had already worn on him. He could give up this one piece of control.

Ricky walked around to the passenger side and climbed in. Pops stood by the open door of the gym, a concerned expression on his face.

Ricky waved, hopefully setting the man at ease. Pops gave a curt nod, but didn't move his gaze from them. Ricky shifted in the truck, setting his arm on the middle console. Everett started the engine and shut his door, his hand going to the back of Ricky's headrest while he reversed out of the parking spot. Everett's clean, soapy scent had a hint of orange, and it danced along each breath Ricky took in the cab that seemed infinitely smaller than it had than when he'd been alone.

"Where to?" Everett asked, pulling up to the road. "Left or right?"

"Home." Ricky's voice scraped against his dry throat.

Everett flicked the blinker on and pulled out of the gym's parking lot onto the road. Minutes passed in silence. Ricky angled his head, trying not to make it obvious he was looking at his old—friend.

Everett's long fingers curled around the steering wheel as he made a turn. His right arm settled next to Ricky's on the console that separated them. The heat that bloomed from the connection was too much. Ricky whipped his arm back to his lap.

"I don't bite, you know—unless you ask," Everett teased without looking his way. He gave a deep chuckle that sent a frisson of warmth spiraling through Ricky.

It took all Ricky's strength not to smile. He bit his tongue and turned to look out the window instead for the fifteen minutes it took to reach the outskirts of his family's land.

Everett remained quiet until they pulled onto the dirt road leading to the Emersons' property.

"I think it's cool you and your siblings all live in the same place as the Emersons—your parents—I'm not sure how I should refer to them for you?"

Ricky released a breath, scanning the snow-covered fields they passed. The Emersons owned a lot of land, and they'd put all of it to use in some way or another. Starting with a small patch of initial property and a house, they'd built it from nothing into a legacy. And Ricky had earned no part in it. When they'd offered him a parcel of land, just as they had his siblings, Ricky had fought against the idea at first.

"I didn't want to build here," he confessed.

"Because you don't think you deserve it?" Everett asked, hitting the nail on the head.

How did he do that? Just burst into his life, two and a half decades later, still able to read him like this?

Ricky tensed. He hadn't been this vulnerable with someone since . . . Everett.

"To answer your earlier question, I call them my parents. She's my ma, and James is my dad. But my mom will always be my mom." Ricky exhaled as Everett turned down the road to his home.

Everett nodded, parking in the driveway. "Let me ask you something?"

Ricky shifted in his seat, reaching for the door handle, and waited.

"Do you think Nova deserves her plot of land? Her place in the family?" Everett asked carefully.

"Of course. What kind of question is that?" Ricky snapped his attention to Everett.

"What makes your place here any different than hers? You're both adopted, so what is it?"

"Nova's technically blood-related. She's actually Ma's niece." Ricky was done with this conversation. He climbed out of the truck. Goose bumps pebbled on his exposed arms as he walked up to the front door. Everett's footsteps padded behind him. The warmth of his dark home greeted him—warmth he would have given anything to have when he was a kid.

Ricky walked into the kitchen. He opened the freezer and pulled out a bottle of vodka. Next, he grabbed two glasses and set them on the counter. He poured himself one, then downed the burning liquid in one gulp.

"You want a drink?" He lifted the glass in the air.

Everett shook his head. "It's eleven in the morning."

Ricky shrugged and poured himself another. Everett's

hand wrapped around his shoulder, spinning him, and forcing Ricky to face the man from his past. A dull longing clamored inside him, fighting against the bindings he'd tethered to his thoughts of Everett so long ago. Ricky flinched away. He didn't need anyone. He couldn't let that version of himself see the light of day again.

"What happened today?"

Ricky scoffed, his armor rising. "I was letting off some steam."

Everett stepped forward, stealing the oxygen from the room with his alert gaze. His light blue-grey eyes should have seemed icy, but only warmth radiated from them. Everett's thumb brushed Ricky's bottom lip. Ricky gasped.

"Do you do that a lot?" Everett asked, studying the injury.

"What are you, my therapist now?" Ricky lashed out.

Everett just shrugged, his hands dropping to his pockets. "No, that would be my mother."

Sandy's face flashed in Ricky's mind. Mrs. Popova had been kind to him and his mother when his mother had been alive. "How is your mom?" Ricky asked.

Everett smiled, his handsome face lighting up. "She's great. Remarried to my stepdad, John, and I have a half sister, Bree."

"A sister?"

"She's nineteen and just started college," Everett answered.

"Wow. And your dad?" They had just announced they were getting divorced before everything had happened.

"He doesn't live too far from Concord. He also remarried, but no other siblings on that side unless you count two very spoiled dogs." Everett's laugh slid over Ricky, soothing some of his nerves.

"Glad to hear they're doing good."

"Wanna talk about what upset you earlier?" Everett asked, pinning him in place with his eyes like he knew Ricky was trying to change the subject.

"You sure you're not trying to take your mom's job as a therapist?" Ricky chuckled, but there was no mirth in it.

"Technically I'm a youth counselor now at Hope Facility as part of my job description. That gives me some credit, right?" One side of Everett's mouth turned up.

Right. He worked with queer youth at the center. Why? Was it his way of working through what had happened to them when they'd been two young boys, experimenting with each other?

Ricky poured another drink and swallowed it down before the confession slipped from him. "I think Donald's getting out of jail—or he might already be free. I don't know. He sent me a letter."

Everett stiffened. Gone was the hint of a teasing smile, replaced with a grim set of his jaw. All the warmth in his expression evaporated, a chill taking its place.

"Are you in danger?" Everett asked, his voice a little deeper than normal and sending chills racing down Ricky's spine.

Ricky forced a humorless laugh. The heat of his anger gathered in his chest. He crossed his arms, leaning against the wooden slab of the counter. "I wish the motherfucker would try me. I think he'll find I'm far from the boy I once was."

Ricky lifted the bottle to pour another drink, but Everett's hand stilled him. Everett's touch set a cascade of different emotions loose in him, building stronger with each heartbeat.

Ricky swayed forward a few centimeters, drawn into Everett's pull as he'd always been. Need, desire, and longing all spread through his veins like poison. Memories crashed over him one at a time. The groans Everett made as he came.

The way his eyes widened just before he orgasmed. The feel of his kiss, the taste of his—

"Can we talk about that day? About what happened?" Everett's question was like a bucket of ice water, jolting him from whatever trance he'd been in.

Ricky walked into the living room and sat on the brown leather couch that took up most of the space. He put his feet on the coffee table in front of him. The cushion next to him sunk as Everett joined him.

"I'm taking that as you're not ready," Everett said without any emotion.

"We won't speak of that night, understand? I never want to go back there," Ricky gritted out.

Everett remained quiet for a few moments before he pulled his phone from his pocket. After tapping the screen, he turned it and showed Ricky.

A pretty blonde stuck her tongue out at the camera, holding her hand up in a peace sign.

"That's Bree."

Ricky chuckled. "How is it having a sibling so much younger than you?"

"It's fun. I get to be the cool older brother." Everett smiled and toyed with the corner of the navy throw pillow on the couch. "It must have been an adjustment going from an only child to having three siblings."

Ricky smiled, remembering those early years. "It was a lot noisier. But having a little sister is different than having brothers."

Everett made a noise of agreement. "I might have been worse than John when Bree brought her first boyfriend home for dinner."

Ricky laughed. "I can only imagine. Nova's first boyfriend didn't last until dessert. You'd think it would have been Dad or her three older brothers that would have scared him off, but it was Ma."

"Renita seems like a force to behold," Everett agreed.

Ricky blew out a breath. "She's the most welcoming and loving woman on this earth. But if you cross someone she loves . . . let's just say that Leo comes out full force."

"I'm glad you have them," Everett added quietly. "Things were different with two families. My mom got pregnant with Bree not too long after the divorce. She and John married when Bree was a year old. And my dad met Lorna a couple years later."

"So you have two families." Memories of a younger Everett upset about his parents' divorce flashed in Ricky's mind.

Everett shrugged. "Yeah. I mean, it's great having more people in my family. But it was also hard to find my place. I was sort of stuck in the middle. But my bonus parents are awesome."

"Yeah." Ricky could relate on some level. His place was here now. The Emersons were his family, but he'd always have another lifetime of memories with his biological mother.

"You coming to the New Year's Eve party with Nova?" Ricky asked.

"She invited me." Everett sat a little straighter and cleared his throat.

"Nova's a good person. You should give it a real go with her." *And make it so that what I desire can never be.* "She's just been through a lot with her ex."

Everett turned to face Ricky, his voice careful. "Nova is great. She's just not my person."

The sliver of relief that welled in Ricky's chest was quickly suffocated by guilt. He should want his sister to be happy at any cost. Did this mean Everett and Nova were friends with benefits? It didn't matter. Ricky shouldn't care. He certainly didn't want Everett—no, this confusion was based on their history, nothing more.

"Why not?"

"You really don't know?" Everett's eyes volleyed back and forth between Ricky's, disbelief ringing in his voice. He shifted closer on the couch so that only a couple inches separated them.

Everything inside Ricky screamed at him to get off the sofa—to run away. But exhaustion settled into the marrow of his bones. He was tired of a lifetime of running, of pretending to be something he wasn't.

Everett leaned in. Ricky held his breath, his chest rising and falling faster and faster as his heart drummed like a herd of horses. Everett was decimating his self-control until all that was left was raw need.

Ricky closed his eyes like a coward. But instead of the soft lips he'd expected, warm pressure met his forehead. Ricky's eyes shot open. Everett leaned his forehead against his. Ricky's skin itched, like some part of him was scraping to get through. Terror gripped him, froze his lungs, stopped them from taking another breath. That longing inside built so that it was suffocating. The craving to kiss Everett splintered through the cracks of his self-control. Lust tangled with need, blistering him from the inside out. Everett's hand gripped the back of his neck, searing his skin. Something dark howled from the shadows, the deep recesses of his soul, to be freed.

Everett's hold tightened. A whimper filled the air. Had it come from Ricky?

His every muscle tensed, his hands fisting until his nails bit into his skin. The pain anchored him enough for some of the fog of his lust to disappear. The voices inside his head rose, sharp and insidious.

Homo.

Disgusting.

Your mother would be ashamed of you.

Ricky shoved Everett's body away as he jerked to stand on unstable legs. "What the fuck are you doing?"

Everett flinched. "I—"

"Get the fuck out of my house!"

Everett's gaze ping-ponged between Ricky and the floor. Pain and regret flashed in his expression. Ricky was the cause —he would always be the cause, and it was best he remembered that. All he'd bring was pain and suffering.

Everett stood, his hands bunching at his sides. "I'm sorry. I thought—"

"I said. Get. Out," Ricky fumed.

Everett gave a curt nod, turning towards the front door.

A sliver of guilt streaked through Ricky. "Take my car and go back to the gym. You can leave the keys with Pops."

Everett plucked the keys from the counter where he'd left them and walked to the front door. He didn't have a coat either. Had he left it at the gym when he'd run after Ricky?

Everett stepped onto the porch and turned back to Ricky. "I never stopped, you know?"

He gritted his teeth until they ached, but still, he failed to restrain himself. "Never stopped what?"

"Thinking about you. Wondering where you were. If you were safe." Everett's confession was whispered over the icy wind. "I never stopped caring about you, Ricardo."

Ricky flinched as if Everett's words had been a physical blow.

"That's your mistake. I told you. I'm not him anymore. I can never be him—" Ricky's voice broke.

Everett's gaze morphed into something akin to pity.

"That's heartbreaking, because he's one of my favorite people."

"Well, he's dead. He died that day when—when *he* found us. There's no sense in wishing for yesterday."

Everett gave a resigned nod of his head. Acceptance. Wasn't that what Ricky had wanted? For Everett to leave him be? To pretend like their past didn't exist? So why did Everett's resignation make Ricky feel like he was losing everything good he had left?

"I hope you find your happiness. That someday you'll unlock the cage you keep yourself in," Everett said.

Ricky slammed the door shut, his mind spinning. Heart racing. He dropped to his knees, the wood floor sending a jolt of pain radiating up his bones, jarring his teeth. Pain was good. Pain and anger. They were all he had to keep it together. They'd been his friends for as long as he could remember.

Without the rage and the hurt, without his sarcasm and crude jokes, Ricky was nothing but the scared little boy who couldn't save his mother. The boy who couldn't protect the guy he'd loved all those years ago. He was weak. He was exactly what Donald had said—a mistake.

16

EVERETT

Everett sipped his coffee in the quaint café. The scent of roasted java beans and old books had always been so welcoming whenever he visited his hometown.

"You all settled in your new place?" his dad asked, sipping on his own cappuccino. His Ukrainian accent was thick and his voice was deep.

"For the most part. It's above a bookstore actually." Everett waved his hand toward the built-in shelves all around them.

His dad ran a hand over his long, white beard. His grey eyes, that matched Everett's in color, lit with joy. "It's good to have you so close to home again."

"It's good to be back."

"Are you liking your new job at the center?" Dad asked.

"Yeah. I really am. I think it was a good switch. But I'm also working with a few lawmakers, trying to educate them on the benefits of making cannabis legal here for recreational purposes and making it easier to get medical cards to those who need it."

"Sounds busy. I hope you're making time for some fun in your life." One of his dad's eyebrows quirked.

Everett chuckled. "I've been meeting up with a friend there. And I had a couple dates."

His dad leaned back, relaxing further in the wooden chair of their small table. "What's he like?"

"He's a pediatrician at Shattered Cove Hospital."

His dad nodded. "Wow."

Everett traced the rim of his cup. "We've just gone out a couple times. He's a nice guy—just not . . ." *Ricardo.*

"The spark you're looking for?"

Everett nodded.

"Anything else new?" His dad focused back on his coffee, taking another sip.

Everett shook his head. Silence passed for a beat as his father studied him.

"Mom told you, didn't she?" Everett asked.

His father gave him a sheepish smile. "She might have mentioned something."

"I guess patient-doctor confidentiality doesn't apply with your son?" Everett teased.

"She worries for you—we both do. After Justin—"

Everett stiffened. "Can we not talk about my ex?"

His father held up his hands. "Yak khochesh." *As you wish.*

Everett sighed, taking another sip of his coffee. "As you heard from Mom, I ran into Ricardo Benning. Now he's Ricky Emerson."

His parents might have fought like cats and dogs when they'd been married, but they'd quickly found a way to co-parent. The respect they had for each other had grown as they'd worked to do what was best for Everett, and he would always be grateful for that.

"Ricardo was always a strong name," his father commented, his chest puffing out slightly.

The hair at the base of Everett's neck prickled, like someone was watching him. He turned, surveying the busy café. A woman sitting at a table across from theirs glanced up at him but then focused back on her laptop in front of her. A couple laughed behind him. No one held his gaze.

"Do you want to talk about it?" his father asked.

Everett ran his finger over a ring stain on the wood table between them. "I tried to get close to him again, to be friends, but I don't think he wants anything to do with me."

When his father didn't say anything, Everett looked up.

"You are lying to yourself if you think you only want to be his friend." His father never held anything back. He was blunt to a fault.

"It's a starting point. I don't . . . He seems to only date women now. But sometimes, when it's just the two of us, I can see—longing."

His father nodded. "He was a good boy. But he went through a lot. That kind of thing changes a man. He may not be who you remember him to be."

"It's not . . . He isn't the same. Obviously. I know that. But part of him is still there. I see it in flashes, slipping through the cracks when his guard is lowered."

"And you think you can change his mind—make him open to dating men." The accusation stung.

"This is not the same as what happened with Justin."

His father leaned over the small wooden table, his large hands dwarfing the cup as he curled his fingers around it. "I know Ricardo's always had a special hold on you. A first love . . . They never leave you." His father's eyes grew unfocused, like his mind was far away in the past. "But it doesn't mean it is the only one for you. Sometimes you can love someone and it still doesn't work out—even if they love you back."

Everett shifted in his chair, his father no doubt speaking of his mother.

"I told him I still cared for him all these years," Everett confessed.

His father's eyes widened a fraction before he gave a resigned nod. "I take it things didn't go well?"

Everett ground his teeth. "You could say that."

His father sighed. "You've done all you can—"

"But how do you know that? Maybe if I—"

"Ni." *No.* "I know my son. I know you've tried your hardest. But a relationship cannot survive if only one of you is fighting for love." His father's gaze darkened with his truth.

"I can't just let him go," Everett confessed. The idea of walking away from Ricardo again brought a painful tightness to his chest. He rubbed his sternum.

"He sent you away, did he not? Rejected you?" his father asked.

"But he's in so much pain. I can see it under the mask he wears for everyone else. I know him. He's still a part of me, one that I'd thought died twenty-five years ago when he was ripped away from me." Everett swallowed the ball of emotion that rose as his eyes grew misty.

His father's wide hand landed on his. "You have a big heart, sonechko." *Sun.*

Everett met his father's gaze. "I owe him so much, Tato." *Dad.*

"I think you believe that. And maybe he does too. Maybe he is ashamed of what his father did. A man should never treat his loved ones the way that svolota hurt Ricardo and his mother." His father let out a harsh growl and spat, "Dovbanyy boyahuz." *Fucking coward.* "A father should love his child no matter who they are—or who they love."

"But that wasn't Ricky's fault."

"Ah, but he may not know that yet, sonechko."

Then maybe I could show him.

"I won the lottery with you, son." His father patted his hand and leaned back in his seat.

"Thanks, Tato."

"You deserve someone who is not afraid to show you to the world. Someone who will not ask you to hide the brightest parts of yourself."

Everett let his dad's words sink in. He'd been lucky to have such a strong, loving father. Despite his dad's traditional upbringing in Ukraine, Everett had never doubted his love. At first glance, Andriy Popova was as tough and hard as they came, but underneath the deep, accented voice, and his bulky frame, was the softest heart for those he loved and those in need. *Like someone else I know.* Maybe that was why Everett had so much hope for Ricky. Because Everett understood that what the world saw was never reality. Ricky's angry macho act was just that—an act.

But I can't help him if he doesn't want to be helped. Until he sees he's locked himself in a prison of the past and expectations he'll never be free. Something held the man he loved back. But his father was right. Everett had done all he could, and probably ruined any chance of having a friendship with Ricky at this point because he'd pushed too far too fast. Maybe it was better to give Ricky space despite everything inside Everett that drew him to the man. Perhaps his father was right, and it was not meant to be.

His phone dinged from his pocket. Everett pulled it out.

Nova: *Can you grab a bottle of that delicious wine from that vineyard near Concord while you're there? You're still coming to our NYE party, right?*

He should cancel—stay away from Ricky and give him the space he'd requested. Everett closed his eyes. Ricky's seething face was conjured in his mind as he remembered Ricky kicking him out of the house. But under that anger had been hurt—so much pain. And Everett couldn't help wondering if he'd been the cause of some of it. He'd take it away if he could.

I have to see him one last time at least—to say goodbye. Then I'll give him the space he so desperately desires.

Everett: *I'll be there.*

"I hope you know what you're doing, sonechko," his father said, as if he knew Everett's thoughts.

He didn't. And there was a chance his heart would be torn to pieces again.

But Everett had to take this chance.

"Me too."

17

RICKY

Gold and black streamers were looped around the barn. Balloons littered the floor and were bunched around the floor-to-ceiling beams. Thankfully, most of the kids had tired themselves out and the intermittent popping of said balloons had stopped. Upbeat music bled from the speakers. Warming lamps emitted an orange glow from just beyond the open barn doors. Family and friends gathered, laughing, drinking, and dancing the last night of the year away.

Ricky's hips swayed from side to side, his fingers wrapped around his date's waist. His attention was anywhere but on Sophia. Everett stood in the corner of the barn, a beer in his hand as he animatedly spoke to Nova, Elise, and Isabella about something.

Ricky hadn't expected to see him here—not after he'd kicked Everett out of his house. *After he told me still he cared about me.* But that was crazy. They hadn't been in love—they'd just been experimenting. Two horny boys with their worlds crashing down around them. All they'd had was each other.

Their friendship. *I'm not gay.* So why did he want Everett? Why couldn't he focus on the beautiful woman in his arms?

As the song ended, Ricky lowered his arms and stepped to the side of the dance floor, asking her, "Do you want a drink?"

"Oh, I'm all set. I've got to drive home, unless . . ." She licked her lips letting the suggestion hang between them.

"I think there's some sparkling cider too," he offered.

She blinked as if she hadn't expected that answer. "I'm okay."

"Ricky, can you hold Alba while I dance with my wife?" Nash handed over Ricky's niece without waiting for his reply and headed to the other side of the room to wrap his arms around Isabella, pulling her onto the dance floor.

Ricky smiled at the little bundle in his arms. "Hey, sweet girl. You want to dance with Tio Ricky?"

Nash settled his chin on the top of Isabella's head swaying her as the slow music drifted over the room. She looked up at him, giving him a soft smile. Ricky's giant, grumpy bear of a brother's expression softened as his thick fingers tightened against her waist, pulling Isabella closer before he kissed her with more tenderness than Ricky had thought his brother capable of. Something squeezed inside him.

Why couldn't he find that with a woman?

Because I'm broken.

"You're so good with babies," Sophia said, jerking his attention back to his niece. Alba snuggled against him, the rhythmic sucking of her thumb moving against his neck.

"She's not so bad," he joked, patting Alba's bottom and swaying.

"Ricky, come tell them about Nancy Plotts and the time you filled her car with snow," Nova called loudly across the space.

Ricky tensed as Everett's attention turned to him before

shooting to the dance floor. It was only a brief flicker of a glance, but that one contact had the power of a freight train barreling down the tracks at full speed. Ricky had the sinking feeling that if they ever truly reconnected, it would end in destruction. Everett would be the end of everything Ricky knew.

He barely registered his feet moving across the room, Sophia keeping up at his side.

"All I did was shovel her driveway," Ricky grumbled.

Nova barked out laughter and shook her head, her eyes glassy and bright as she recounted the tale to Elise and Everett. "He shoveled all that snow alright, and put it *in* her car!"

Elise laughed. "What did she do to deserve your wrath?"

Ricky sighed. "She—"

Nova waved her hand again. "I was at a friend's, who happened to live next door to her. She came out while we were in the backyard playing hide-and-seek snowball fight. She started yelling at me, saying she was going to call the police and calling me a thief. My friend came around and we ran inside, telling her parents about the crazy lady next door."

Nova waved her hand dismissively, the cup in her other hand spilling a little on the ground. His little sister didn't drink much, preferring to smoke. So she was a lightweight. The part of the story she left out was the racial slurs the woman had yelled at her for the whole world to hear.

Little Alba whimpered and snuggled closer to him, her breaths evening out as she drifted into sleep despite the noise in the room.

"God, she's cute. Gimme here." Nova opened her arms for the baby.

Ricky pulled away and kissed his niece's cheek. "Nope. I got her to sleep. I get to enjoy the snuggles."

Nova pouted.

"You're good with babies," Elise pointed out.

"That's what I just told him. He'd make a great dad some-day," Sophia added.

Ricky tensed, a sense of longing snapping through him.

"I can see that." Everett's deep voice dragged across Ricky's skin leaving tingles in its wake.

Surprise rose like a helium balloon in Ricky's chest as he stared at Everett.

Why was his every cell attuned to this man?

Nova's laugh was loud and jarring. "He'd have to stop moving through the entire seacoast of women first. Who knows? Maybe he already has some kids. Wouldn't be the first brother to get someone knocked up and not know. Am I right?"

Everett flinched, pointedly focusing on the dance floor like he was trying to escape this situation the only way he politely could. Nova chuckled, but no one else did.

Sophia shifted next to him. What they had was casual, but she didn't deserve to have his sexual history shoved in her face.

Ricky reached out and took Nova's cup. "I think you've had enough."

Her mouth dropped open, her eyes widening. "Excuse me? Who the fuck do you think you are?"

"How about some coffee?" Elise interjected. "Come on." She tugged Nova away from them.

Everett turned to him then, his attention flicking between Ricky and Sophia, his eyes dimming with resignation. Ricky didn't understand why everything inside him wanted to rebel against it.

"Have a good night." Everett nodded and turned without another word, heading through the mass of bodies on the dance floor.

"I'm sorry about my sister. She's drunk," Ricky said, checking on his sleeping niece.

Sophia stepped in front of him. "We all have a past." She smoothed her hand over Alba's back, one corner of her mouth turning up.

"And we're just casually meeting up," Ricky reminded her.

Her brown eyes flicked to him. "Are we still?"

"I was clear that's all I could offer."

She bit her lip. "You were. But you also said it was just sex and no dates, and then you asked me out to the bar and then here but we haven't had sex in months. I wasn't sure if something had changed?"

He shook his head. "It's not something I'm capable of —more."

She exhaled, disappointment bleeding into the space between them as her shoulders lowered. Finally, she nodded.

"I'm sorry if I sent mixed messages."

"I appreciate your honesty." She managed a small smile.

"Do you want to see if there's any dessert left?" Ricky offered.

"No. I think I'll go." She eyed the door.

"You don't have to leave."

"I think I do."

He frowned. "Soph—"

She waved her hand. "I'm fine. Really. But I got my hopes up despite what we agreed, and that's on me."

"I'm sorry." He meant it.

"I'm just sorry you don't think you're capable of more. Because you're a good guy, Ricky Emerson. You'll make someone a really happy someday. Maybe you just haven't found your person yet." She reached up on tiptoes and kissed his cheek.

"Text me when you get home so I know you got there safe," he said.

She gave him another brief smile. "Happy New Year."

"You too."

Sophia walked for the coat wall and grabbed her things before heading out the main door into the darkness. Relief flowed through him. Something lifted from his shoulders. But just as soon, guilt returned. Sophia was a good woman, and he hated that he'd hurt her.

"Three minutes until midnight!" someone yelled.

The music turned down as everyone moved across the floor, finding their partner to ring in the new year with.

"I'll take her. Thanks for getting her to sleep." Isabella reached for Alba.

Ricky carefully transferred the sleeping baby to her mother's arms. A small puddle of drool dampened a spot on his shirt. "No problem."

Isabella joined Nash. Her son, Eli, stood near Ariel and Roman.

Roman wrapped his arms around Elise's waist from behind. After placing a kiss on her temple, he knelt before her. Everyone hushed, and the music stopped altogether.

"Elise, honey, I know you already asked me to marry you," Roman started.

"What are you doing?" she asked.

"But we needed a story we could tell when everyone asks —one that's not X-rated." He winked and Elise's pale skin took on a red flush.

Roman continued, "And you deserve to be asked too. I didn't want to start this next year without telling you, in front of our families and friends, just how much I love you. How I can't wait to wake up to you every morning. And fall asleep with you every night. To know that our life is just getting started, and I promise to strive to be the best version of myself if you'll have me. Marry me?"

She sniffled. "Of course I will. I'm not giving this ring back for anything."

The crowd around them laughed.

"And you're pretty great too," Elise added.

Roman chuckled, rising to his feet and sweeping Elise in his arms. He kissed her.

"Find your partner. Midnight is only fifteen seconds away!" His father's voice rose above the clapping.

Ricky held his breath, searching for Nova and Everett. They stood by the refreshments table, Nova sipping on coffee. Everett leaned against the table, his arms crossed as his lips moved.

"Ten. Nine. Eight—"

Ricky couldn't move. He was glued to the spot, needing to watch with his own eyes. Needing to see why he'd done the right thing, kicking Everett out of his house when everything inside him craved the man's very presence. *He's Nova's.*

"Three. Two. One. Happy New Year!"

Everett leaned in, his back to Ricky as he lowered his head and gave Nova a peck on the lips.

Ricky gasped. Pain sliced through his chest, emotions bleeding from him. Something ugly and possessive reared up inside him. *He was mine first.*

He shook his head, closing his eyes. His hands balled into fists at his sides as he forced air into his lungs, but it was like shards of glass stabbing him with each inhale.

I want him. I want what we had. I want us.

But I can never have that.

That familiar rising darkness rose inside him like a rogue wave, threatening to pull him under and drown him. Ricky's skin burned; sweat broke out on his forehead. When he opened his eyes, Everett was nowhere to be seen.

Nova approached him as the music turned back up.

Ricky's stomach churned with bile. How could he be jealous of his sister? How could he be so selfish?

Nova cleared her throat and eyed him sheepishly. "I'm really sorry about what I said before. I've obviously had too much to drink, but that's no excuse. I didn't mean to scare off your date."

"It was a bitch thing to say in front of Sophia, but not untrue." Ricky owned it.

"Forgive me?" she asked with hopeful eyes.

"Of course." He wrapped his arm around her and pulled her close so they both faced the dance floor.

Ricky cleared his throat. "Where'd your date go?"

"Home."

"He's not spending the night?"

She made a choked sound and then shook her head, guilt flickering in her expression. "Nope."

"What's really going on between you and him?"

She sighed. "He's just a friend. I begged him to be my date for the holidays to get Mom off my back. She's relentless now that Roman and Nash are paired up. I don't know why she's not on your case."

"'Cause I'm a hopeless cause and she knows it." He chuckled, pretending to be far more at ease than he felt, processing her words.

She wasn't really seeing Everett? Relief filled him and then confusion. It shouldn't matter. It wasn't like he wanted to date Everett. He just didn't . . . want anyone else to either. Fuck! It didn't make sense.

"You're not dating him?" Ricky clarified. "You don't like him like that at all?"

Deep, belly-shaking laughter slipped from her lips. "Even if I did, I wouldn't stand a chance."

"Why?" Did she think so little of herself?

"Because I don't have a dick." She chuckled. "Everett's gay."

Ricky blinked, stunned. *I thought he was like me.* Attracted to women but unable to let go what they'd shared as teens.

"Maybe Sebastian will have better luck with him," Nova added.

Ice slid through Ricky's veins. "Sebastian?"

"Yeah. They've gone out a few times. He texted him before he left. I don't—"

Ricky didn't stick around to hear the end of his sister's sentence. He ran outside, the frigid temperature cutting through the long-sleeve shirt he wore. Ricky sprinted to the parking lot like his life depended on it. Something inside him urged him towards Everett. He didn't know why, or what he would say when he caught up with him—he just knew he couldn't let him leave and go to Sebastian.

One car rumbled to life, its lights bright against the white snow. Relief hit Ricky, propelling him faster. The car backed up, turning onto the main driveway that headed towards the road. Ricky jumped over a snow pile. He had to stop that car. Ricky darted onto the road, hands held wide open.

The car slid across snow-covered gravel and lurched to a stop.

Everett climbed out of the driver's seat. "What the hell—"

Ricky was against him before Everett could finish his sentence. "Why didn't you tell me?"

Everett's brows pulled together. Fat white snowflakes drifted from the sky, falling against his inky-black hair. Those grey eyes reflecting the moon, almost glowing.

"Tell you what?" Everett's voice was husky and deep.

"About you and Nova," Ricky gritted out.

Everett blinked. "It wasn't my secret to tell."

Ricky sucked in a breath. Everett's scent filled his lungs like a hit of smoke, seeping into his pores, igniting something primal and needy deep within him. His head spun. Desire like he'd never felt thrummed through his veins. He'd been missing a piece of himself since he was fourteen. Maybe Everett could help him find it. He stood in front of Ricky now, offering a taste of the past—of finding those missing parts. But the risk was so great. To have that piece returned and then the possibility—the likelihood of losing it again? Ricky wasn't sure he could survive it.

Ricky cleared his throat. "I didn't think you'd come after . . ."

Everett searched his eyes. "I almost didn't. But I wanted . . . to say goodbye."

Goodbye? Something sharp pierced Ricky's chest, panic rising within him. *You can't leave when I've just found you.*

Memories tumbled in his mind, one after the other. Every time Everett had been there for him. Their friendship growing, changing, morphing into something bigger—something neither of them had expected. Ever had always been his one constant. And Ricky couldn't help but wish he could go back to that place, even knowing how it would end. He would give anything to return to one of those moments when he was with Everett, safe in his arms, where everything was alright in the world. *My light in the dark.*

"Isn't that what you want, miy lev?" Everett asked.

The frayed ties of self-control holding him back snapped with that nickname. Ricky's lips crashed against Everett's. An explosion rocked through him like he'd swallowed a stick of dynamite. He groaned as Everett's shocked gasp opened his mouth to Ricky. Ricky slid his tongue inside, greedily stealing his taste like a thief. It should have felt wrong, but instead it was so fucking right. Something slipped in place—a sense of rightness. Desire exploded like a volcano inside him, hot and devastating, ruining everything in its path until all that was left was pure, raw need and so much emotion, it stole Ricky's breath.

Everett gripped the back of his neck, clearly recovered from the shock. He kissed him back, and he wasn't gentle. His teeth nipped as he spun them around so that Ricky was against the car. This should have made Ricky panic. He should have shoved Everett away or at the very least taken back control. But he was safe with Everett—he'd always been. Everett was the one person he could just be himself with. The person he could let his guard down around.

Everett's tongue slid into his mouth—taking—as he ground against Ricky.

"Fuck." Ricky couldn't even recognize his own voice. It was so needy and choked with emotion.

"Miy lev, tell me this isn't a dream. Tell me you're really here in my arms," Everett rumbled before kissing him again, like this kiss was more important than air. Like their passionate reunion could all be ripped away in a cruel joke from fate at any second.

Ricky pulled back, staring into the pools of his eyes, hazy with lust. Everett's lips were shiny and swollen from their kiss. The angles of his handsome face were highlighted in the shadows under the moon. He was so beautiful—almost other-worldly. Ricky ached for him like he'd never ached before.

Ricky licked his lips. "Come home with me."

18

____

EVERETT

Everett didn't even blink. He was afraid that if he did, Ricky would disappear. His mind was still spinning. He couldn't have possibly heard what he thought he did from Ricky.

"What?"

"Come home with me."

Fuck. This was real.

"Get in." Everett nodded towards his running vehicle. Ricky took a cursory glance around them before walking to the other side and climbing into the passenger seat. Everett took another gulp of frosty air, trying to calm his racing heart. Disbelief spun into awe. His stomach flipped as he got behind the wheel and shut them both inside.

Everett hit the gas, making the short drive from the barn to Ricky's house. He slid the car into park and shut it off. Silence slowly descended with the darkness.

Everett turned to Ricky, but the man shot out of his seat and onto the driveway, letting in a burst of cold air. Everett got out and followed him up the walkway as Ricky opened the door, switching on the light in the entryway. Everett couldn't look away. The cocky, tough-guy act was gone. In its place was this vulnerable version of a man staring into his eyes with so much need, it made Everett's knees weak. A slight flush rose from Ricky's neck to his cheeks under the moonlight.

Everett couldn't resist reaching out to cup the side of Ricky's face. "If you don't still want this, I can leave at any time."

Ricky's chest rose with a deep breath. He stared back at him. "And if I want you to stay?"

Everett stood taller in the doorway, the icy chill of winter's night behind him and the warmth of Ricky's home in front. "Then I'll do whatever you need. We can talk or not. I can kiss you again or not. But I have to admit, I really fucking want to taste you."

A delicious groan slipped from Ricky's mouth. Everett's hold tightened on his jaw, slipping to his neck.

"Stay," Ricky said just before his lips crashed against Everett's again.

Warm lips caressed his—needy and determined. Their connection sent sparks of arousal shooting off like fireworks in Everett's body.

Holy shit.

He'd never had this much chemistry with someone. Everett pulled Ricky closer. He kicked the door closed and backed Ricky against the wall.

Sucking in a breath, Everett rested his forehead against Ricky's. Holy shit, they were really doing this.

Ricky grabbed his hand and dragged him down the hall. They passed the mostly dark kitchen, save for the small light above the stove, and turned a corner to a set of stairs. Ricky flicked the light on.

Everett's eyes dropped to Ricky's firm ass as he climbed

each step. His cock was hard as steel, his desire soaking into his boxers. Ricky turned the corner at the top of the stairs, leading to his bedroom and switched on the lamp. The small light softly illuminated the room. Everett had been there not so long ago—but this was different.

He stepped forward, eyes locked on Ricky's. He dragged his finger from the hollow of Ricky's throat up the column of his neck. Ricky shivered. *So fucking responsive.* Everett gripped Ricky's face in both hands and melded their lips together. The bristles of Ricky's beard scraped over Everett's chin as he slid his tongue inside his mouth. Heat zipped through Everett's body. He tugged the hem of Ricky's shirt up, slipping his hand over the defined abs that contracted under his touch.

Ricky broke the kiss long enough to pull off his shirt and toss it onto the ground. His muscular body made Everett's mouth go dry. Ricky's biceps flexed as he reached for Everett's jacket. Everett stripped it off along with his shirt.

Ricky let out a small gasp, staring at the lion tattooed over his heart.

"Don't ask me unless you're ready to hear the answer, miy lev." *My lion.*

Ricky's gaze tentatively met his. Indecision swirled in those dark orbs before he leaned forward for a kiss.

Everett collared Ricky's neck with one hand, tugging him until they were chest against chest. Skin against skin. Ricky's calloused hands slid up his back, kneading into the flesh. He wasn't gentle; his fingers dug into Everett's skin like he was afraid to fall and all that was holding him up was Everett.

"Fuck, I want you so bad. But I don't want to ruin this. I don't want to scare you away again," Everett confessed, sinking his teeth into Ricky's neck.

Ricky arched against him, his hard cock rubbing Everett's. A groan tore from Everett's lips.

"I need you." Ricky's voice broke like the confession had cost him.

Everett laid a kiss over the red area. "I'm here. Whatever you need. I got you. Let me make you feel good?"

Ricky's grip tightened on Everett's lower back, his body going rigid. "Yes. Fuck, yes."

Everett gentled his own touch, caressing Ricky's shoulders and arms. He continued smoothing his palm over Ricky's chest and lightly pinched his nipple.

"Fuuuck," Ricky panted.

"That's it, miy lev. Let me hear how much you like it when I take care of you." Everett bent forward to nibble on Ricky's earlobe. His hand wandered lower, tracing the deep *V* of Ricky's hips.

Ricky's hazy eyes rolled up. His mouth slackened as another groan of approval escaped him.

"Can I take these off?" Everett asked, tugging at the button of Ricky's pants.

Ricky blinked slowly. He nodded.

Everett sucked his nipple, varying intensity, dragging his teeth along the hard nub. They both toed off their shoes in a hurry, like Ricky also felt the same urgency. He stripped Ricky's pants and boxers down to the floor. Using his own foot to hold the material in place, he pressed the man's chest. Ricky stepped back, freeing himself from the pants as the back of his legs hit the mattress.

Fuck, his cock was perfect—hard and long with veins swirling along the shaft. A bead of shiny pre-cum dripped from the tip.

Everett ran a finger over it. Ricky's penis jerked. Everett kissed him, urging him onto the bed. Ricky lay down, backing up enough so that Everett had room to climb next to him.

"What about you?" Ricky asked, motioning to Everett's pants.

"You want them off?" he asked.

Ricky nodded again.

"Need those words, miy lev."

"Yes." Ricky gritted his teeth, his eyed glued to Everett's face like something held him back from looking at the rest of him.

Everett dropped his pants, his cock springing free, slapping against his stomach. Ricky's attention stayed riveted on Everett's face, his jaw tight. Everett slid his hand down his torso, taking his cock into his hand. There was something about having another person watch him touch himself that was so fucking hot—and he wanted Ricky to feel desperate for him. Ricky must have thought so too because his control finally snapped. His chest heaved twice before his gaze dropped and widened.

Everett rolled over, gripping Ricky's throat once more. Ricky relaxed, surrendering to his direction so easily. It was truly a gift, the trust they shared—the past and present were all coming together. Would they have a future? There was so much Everett wanted to say. To ask. To bring up. But not now. Not when he finally had Ricky in his arms, his hard, leaking cock sliding against his.

"You feel so good." Everett reached down, sliding his hand around Ricky's shaft.

"Fuck!" Ricky bucked his hips.

"That's it. Fuck my hand. See how slick you are with your own need?" Everett bit down on Ricky's ear, applying a little pressure just to see how he'd react.

Ricky moaned, jerking his hips faster.

"So fucking sexy. Look at you, taking what you want."

"Ever!"

"That's right, baby. It's me here with you, giving you what you need." Everett slid his cock against Ricky's, jerking them both off.

"Holy shit." Ricky mumbled something unintelligible after that. His hips drove harder. Eyes closed tight. "Feels so good."

The smooth hardness of Ricky's cock rubbing against Everett's was almost as delicious as the sweet groans coming from him.

Everett grunted, his dick pulsing with pleasure. Tingles raced down his limbs, gathering at the base of his spine. His balls drew up. "Fuck, I want to taste you so bad."

Ricky gave a choked gasp before his cum shot out of the tip of his cock, spraying ropes of the hot, sticky fluid on both their stomachs. Everett kept pumping, using Ricky's release as lubricant as his own orgasm came crashing over him. Everett's cum mixed with Ricky's. Pleasure coursed through his every nerve ending until he floated in a cloud of ecstasy.

He lay on his back, one arm behind his head as he studied Ricky's relaxed expression.

"That was much better than I remember." Ricky's eyes were still closed, but he gave a tired chuckle.

"Sure was." Everett sat up and went to the bathroom. He grabbed a towel and cleaned himself up before running one under hot water and bringing it back to Ricky. He dragged the wet cloth down Ricky's abs. They flexed as Ricky's eyes opened, still glassy with pleasure.

Ricky reached for the material. "I can—"

Everett shook his head. "No. Let me take care of you."

Ricky stared at him for another moment before he relaxed back onto the bed. Everett threw the towel with the dirty clothes on the floor and pulled the covers down so Ricky could roll over into them. He slid on the mattress behind him, wrapping his arms around Ricky and holding him tight against his chest.

Everett kissed along Ricky's jaw. "You okay?"

Ricky turned over, snuggling into Everett's chest, and nodded.

Everett caressed Ricky's arm. "We're gonna have to work on you using your words."

Ricky didn't respond. Everett's stomach dipped. Was this too much, too fast? But Ricky was still there, still touching him. Letting Everett hold him. That was something Everett wouldn't take for granted.

Ricky's breathing evened out as he drifted into sleep. Everett savored each moment he was close to the man he'd always cared for. But this time felt different. This affection he'd held for Ricky all these years wasn't the same as the emotion that stirred in his chest now. These were different—deeper. He could fall in love with Ricky—maybe he was halfway there already. *But what if he doesn't love me back? Could I survive that?*

Everett stared at his lover's sleeping face, trying to memorize every detail.

Everett had never been good with unknowns. But for Ricky, he'd do whatever it took to show him they were meant to be in each other's lives. He'd be patient. This couldn't be the end. This was just the beginning.

19

RICKY

Ricky rolled over, slowly coming awake. He snuggled into the pillow and inhaled. Sweet orange filled his nose. His eyes shot open. Memories of last night played through his head like a movie. He closed his eyes and tensed, waiting for the guilt to come crashing down on him—but it never came.

He peeked around the room. *Empty.* He released the breath he'd been holding and a new ache bloomed in his chest at the rumpled space next to him. A part of him felt abandoned, wishing the man who'd always been there, who knew the real Ricardo, had stayed. Another piece of him was relieved. He didn't have to face what he'd done. What he'd let Everett do to him.

Ricky ran a hand through his tousled curls. The floor of the hallway creaked. The door opened, and with it, the smell of bacon and coffee floated in. Everett walked inside, his hair messy like he hadn't bothered to brush it since rolling out of bed. He studied Ricky as his mouth curved up into a handsome, crooked smile.

"Good morning. Thought you could use some sustenance after last night." Everett carried a tray which held two coffees and two plates with bacon and eggs. He set it on the bedside table before handing a coffee to Ricky. "I don't know if you take your coffee differently now. We can trade if you want?"

Ricky accepted the steaming mug and took a sip. The earthy coffee melded perfectly with just enough sweetener and cream. Everett had remembered. Something tightened in his chest. "It's perfect."

Everett's smile widened as he sat next to Ricky on the bed, their elbows grazing. The scent of citrus wafted over with his closeness. Ricky tensed, focusing on his coffee, and took another sip. Anxious moths tumbled in his gut at the possible repercussions of what they'd done.

What if someone had seen them last night in the parking lot? *Fuck. How could I be so stupid?* If someone had seen, they'd think Ricky was gay. They wouldn't understand. This wasn't —he wasn't—

"Is that a problem?" Everett's hand landed on Ricky's knee, bringing him back to the present.

Ricky startled. Everett's attentive gaze burned the side of his face.

"What?" Ricky asked.

"That I borrowed a pair of your sweatpants?" Everett motioned to the navy bottoms he wore.

That's fucking hot. Ricky wanted to beat his chest in pride. He'd never been a possessive type of guy with anyone he'd dated. Not that they were dating.

"You seem tense." Everett's free hand glided behind Ricky, gently massaging his shoulders.

His touch was like catnip. It would be so easy to relax into it, to fall back into what they'd shared before. The friendship and connection he'd longed for ever since. The kind of care he'd never found with anyone else. Ricky definitely wasn't—

"I'm not gay," Ricky said.

Everett froze. Two breaths passed before his hand dropped back to his lap. "Do you fool around with all your guy friends?"

"No!" Ricky shifted to face Everett. "Never. You're the only guy I've ever . . ."

"Let jerk you off?"

Ricky ground his teeth and nodded.

"Kissed?" Everett asked, his voice taking on a deeper tone.

Ricky swallowed, his focus dropping to Everett's lips. "Yes."

Everett was quiet for a few moments, as if he were deep in thought. "Do you not want me to touch you again?"

"That isn't what I want. But . . ."

Everett motioned back and forth between them. "What is this to you?"

"This is . . . us. This is how we've always been. You've got my back, and I've got yours. We're friends." Ricky shook his head. "I don't know what the fuck we are. But what I do know is that for the first time in a lifetime, I feel like something is right."

"You want this to happen again?" Everett clarified, dragging his finger up Ricky's wrist to the crease of his elbow on the inside of his arm.

Ricky shivered. His voice caught in his throat. If he didn't say it out loud, it wasn't real. If he wasn't actively making the choice to say yes, it didn't mean he wanted another man to touch him, right?

Everett gently pinched the bottom of Ricky's chin between his fingers, turning his face towards him. "I'm going to need those words, miy lev."

Ricky swallowed and then nodded.

Everett tsked. "Say it. Tell me you want me to touch you again."

"I—I do," Ricky whispered.

"You want me to kiss these lips again?" Everett brushed his thumb over Ricky's lips, and they instantly parted.

"Yes." His chest heaved as his cock hardened.

Everett leaned in, his mouth coasting over the sensitive parts of Ricky's ears as he whispered, "You want me to make you come again?"

Ricky closed his eyes. His whole body shuddered like a live wire, totally attuned to the man sitting next to him. "Fuck yes."

"You used your words. Good boy."

Those two words slammed into Ricky like a tsunami. *Holy fuck.* Why did it feel so good? Did that make him less of a man?

"You know what good boys get?" Everett asked.

"What?" He fucking needed to find out.

"They get their cock sucked." Everett took both their coffees and set them on the tray before pulling down the blankets enough for Ricky's already hard dick to spring free.

The idea of Everett going down on him eased his apprehension some. If he was getting a blow job, then he was the one in control, right?

Wrong.

Everett pushed his chest so Ricky lay back on the pillow.

"Watch me slip my lips over your cock. Don't take your eyes off me while I lick your cum. And most definitely don't orgasm until I tell you. If you listen, you'll be rewarded. Understand?" Everett asked.

"Yes." Ricky's voice came out hoarse.

Everett moved Ricky's heels up towards his ass and spread

his legs, putting his cock on display. Everett's hot breath coasted over the tip of his dick. It jerked. "Fuck."

"Watch me," Everett said before his tongue lapped at the bead of pre-cum. He gripped Ricky's balls, rolling them in his hand as he licked and teased the thick vein running down Ricky's shaft. His mouth descended over the tip, sucking gently as he took Ricky into his mouth inch by inch.

Ricky was hypnotized by the image below. The flex of Everett's shoulders as his head bobbed up and down on Ricky's cock. The pleasure rippling from the hot mouth on his most sensitive places as one hand worked his balls and massaged down his taint. The other hand reached up and pinched his nipple, adding a little pain to the mix that had his hips jerking. Everett shoved his hips down and sucked harder.

"Fuck! I'm gonna—"

Everett popped him out of his mouth and licked the thick vein again. His orgasm receded.

"You bastard," Ricky groaned.

Everett's eyes lit with satisfaction as his lips curled into a cocky smile. "Your orgasm is mine. I get to choose when you come. And only good boys who listen get their cum swallowed."

Ricky groaned, lost in the torturous pleasure tingling through every cell. "Please?"

"What was that?"

"Please?" Ricky repeated.

Everett licked his lips, his gaze eclipsing so that only a ring of silvery grey remained. "I like it when you beg. Say it again."

"Please? Please make me come?" Ricky didn't hesitate, his need growing by the second.

Desire coursed through him. Need coated his every panted breath. Lust burned through him like a flash fire—white hot and unstoppable. Everett's mouth slicked over and over his cock. Everett's tongue flicking the tip of Ricky's dick had his eyes rolling back in his head. He whimpered, using all his self-control to hold himself back.

Higher and higher, his need built as Everett dug something out of his pocket before he sucked Ricky's cock once more, taking it all the way to the back of his throat.

Ricky moaned. "I can't hold it off. Feels too good. Fuck—your mouth." Ricky thrust his hips, his body begging for release. "Please, let me come. Ever—"

"That's it, baby. Just a little longer. Trust me, okay? And I'll make you come harder than ever before," Everett said as something slick and cold slicked around his asshole, massaging.

Ricky gasped. The forbidden act only added fuel to his already raging fire.

"Do you trust me?" Everett continued drawing steady circles with his finger while he teased the tip of Ricky's cock.

"Y-yes."

Everett could have asked for the deed to his house and Ricky would have signed on the dotted line—he was that desperate to come.

The tip of Everett's finger slipped inside his asshole.

"Mmmghhh." Ricky's head lolled back.

"That's it. Just breathe." Everett pulled his finger out for a moment before returning with more lube, this time pushing in deeper. He shifted in and out in small movements as Ricky's legs tensed, his abs flexing. Everett sucked the tip of Ricky's cock, grazing his teeth over the sensitive flesh as his finger fucked Ricky's ass.

"Fuck, Ever. I can't hold back much longer." He panted. "Too good."

"Yes you can." Everett's finger continued moving in and out. "Relax for me."

Ricky released a breath. Pleasure overrode all his other senses. He didn't have to worry about anything at all but holding off this orgasm. There was something so freeing about riding the edge, surrendering his body to Everett. Trusting that he was safe enough to let go of everything and just be. A wave of pleasure rippled through him, holding firm before the crest of an orgasm. Fuck, who knew so much pleasure could be had without coming?

"That's it. Just like that. So perfect. Fuck, you're so sexy like this. Splayed out so I can feast on your cock and play with your ass," Everett said.

Everett's praise fell on him like rain in a desert wasteland. Ricky moaned. He'd do anything for more of it. He was lost in this hazy state of need—of surrender. His mind emptied, his worries and hesitation gone. Nothing else existed but the two of them. Only Everett's humming that vibrated over his cock, making Ricky's balls tighter than a drum. Everett's slick finger pumping in and out of Ricky's asshole, getting a little deeper each time. The overwhelming need for more. More pleasure. More commands. More praise.

Sweat beaded on Ricky's forehead as he kept his gaze locked on the man who'd become his whole world.

Everett licked the head of Ricky's cock. "Look at you, taking everything I have to give you and denying yourself of what you want most—just for me. That's so fucking hot."

Ricky's eyes rolled up. Everett's dirty words slid down his body like icy-hot tiny explosions adding to his high. It took everything in him to focus back on Everett.

"Good fucking boy. Now, say my name and come." Everett sucked Ricky's cock, his head bobbing faster and faster.

Everett curled his finger inside Ricky's asshole, hitting

something that had Ricky's hips jerking off the bed as his vision went black. Ecstasy exploded through his every nerve ending, sending shocks of pleasure rippling through him. His muscles tensed.

"Ever!"

Instead of one orgasm, this felt like a hundred all rolled into one. Like a star bursting within, destroying everything he thought he knew and overriding it with such an intense euphoria that he hadn't known existed.

Everett swallowed around his cock, lapping up his cum.

Ricky pushed his head back into the pillow, his chest heaving as he relaxed into a puddle of utter bliss.

Everett crawled up on the bed next to Ricky, wrapping his arms around him and tugging Ricky against his chest. Ricky went without protest, snuggling against Everett's pec. It was nice to just let someone take care of him for once.

"That was . . ."

"That was us," Everett finished for him.

Ricky blinked open his heavy eyelids. The bulge in Everett's pants was impossible to miss. His hand moved down Everett's stomach and then stopped. Something held him back.

"It's okay," Everett said, as if reading his mind.

"I want to make you feel good too. It's only fair," Ricky added. That was what this was, right? Two friends exchanging pleasure and comfort?

"This isn't tit for tat." Everett caressed his back. "We don't have to do anything you're not ready for."

"I just let you . . . you know. I should get you off. It's not like it would be the first time."

Everett sighed. "*Should* has nothing to do with this—with us. I don't want you doing anything just because you think you owe me. I want you to want to. And if you don't, then I'll deal with it."

Ricky took a few deep breaths, processing what Everett said before he replied, "I do want to. I just . . . It's hard when it's my . . . choice." That was harder to say out loud than he'd thought it would be.

"So you like when I take control?" Everett asked, his voice deceptively casual.

"It's not—I mean, no, of course not, but . . . I don't know. Maybe. Sometimes."

"That cleared it up." Everett chuckled and kissed his forehead. "How about we take a shower and then I'll heat up our coffee and breakfast?"

"What about your boner?" Ricky asked.

"I'll take care of it, or I can ignore it." He shrugged.

Ricky's cock stiffened again. "You should take care of it."

"Now?"

"Yes."

"You want to watch me come?" Everett asked. Something about the question sounded vulnerable.

"I do."

Everett's hand slid down under his sweatpants and he pulled his cock out. Fuck, he was big and hard. His long fingers wrapped around the shaft, moving up and down. His abs flexed as his cock jerked. Shiny pre-cum dripped from the top, and Ricky had the strongest urge to lean in and taste him. He froze.

"It's so sexy when you watch me fuck my hand," Everett said.

"It's hot to see. Makes me hard again, which should be fucking impossible after *that* orgasm."

"Mmm. The way you moaned when your dick hit the back of my throat . . ." Everett's gaze grew hazy.

"You liked that?"

Everett panted, his fist moving faster. "Yes."

Ricky tilted his head to take Everett's nipple in his mouth and sucked, scraping his teeth over the sensitive flesh.

Everett's hips lifted from the bed to fuck his hand harder. His pre-cum acted as lube, his hand making a slapping, sliding sound as he jerked off. He groaned. "Feels so good, miy lev."

Ricky preened at the compliment. Some of his hesitation fading, he wrapped his hand around Everett's, and they jerked Everett off together.

"Fuck, I'm coming," Everett moaned.

Ricky gently bit Everett's nipple and sucked harder while his hand slipped down to massage Everett's balls.

Everett shouted as hot cum spurted out of his cock onto both their stomachs. His hand slowed as a few more ropes of cum seeped out, running down his fingers. Ricky turned his face towards Everett's, their eyes meeting for a brief moment before Everett kissed him. Ricky's tongue slipped between Everett's parted lips. This kiss wasn't hungry with lust like the ones before. It was slow and sensual. Intimate and life-changing. Kissing Everett was everything Ricky never knew he needed. That was both terrifying and amazing.

Ricky pulled back, not quite ready to face everything this man stirred up inside him. "I guess we both really need that shower now."

Everett smiled. "Come on. I'll make sure you get clean."

"What does that mean?" Ricky rolled out of bed, Everett following.

"It means I can help with all those hard-to-reach places."

"I won't argue with that."

Ricky started the shower while Everett took the sweatpants off. He climbed in before Everett, standing under the spray of hot water. His eyes shot open as Everett brushed a soapy sponge over his shoulders.

"You don't have to—"

"I want to. Unless you're too uncomfortable?" Everett asked.

"No, it's not that. I can take care of myself."

"But you don't have to this time. Let me." Everett soaped his back, then moved slowly down his arms and then to his backside. He parted Ricky's ass cheeks, cleaning, but it wasn't sexual. The soft, sensual touch with warm, soapy water brought a new wave of relaxation, and with it, emotion that clogged Ricky's throat. It had been a lifetime since he'd had someone treat him with such tender care. To be touched with such loving caresses made his knees tremble and his eyes burn.

He shouldn't want this. But how could he turn away from Everett? The man who had always known what he'd needed and given it freely to him. Everett deserved someone better. But Ricky was a selfish bastard. He couldn't let him go—not yet. Not when he'd just found him again. He didn't know what this was between them. It wasn't just friendship. It was more— but it was something he'd never encountered before. An emotion and relationship without a name. All he knew was he couldn't stop it. He didn't want to. He would be selfish just this once. He'd take what Everett offered and savor every moment, every sweet caress and gentle touch that made his body burn alive with a desire and need he'd never known—at least for now.

20

RICKY

Ricky opened the door to the honey shop and led Everett inside. Nerves twisted his stomach into knots. What would Everett think of his business? Would he be impressed?

"So this is where the magic happens at Emerson Apiaries," Everett said. His gaze roamed over the room, starting from the stack of boxes with empty jars on the right to the bottled stacks on the left that Ricky had to deliver this weekend.

"What's that big tank for?" Everett motioned to the stainless steel bottling cylinder on the big table.

Ricky walked over, setting his palm over the handle at the base. "This is how we bottle the honey."

"Wow. Okay, walk me through the process. You get the honey from beehives, right?" Everett asked.

"Yes. And then we unload them from the trucks. Behind that door is the loading dock." Ricky pointed to the sliding door across from them.

"Do any bees come back with you?"

"Of course. We try to leave as many as possible behind, but during the summer and early fall when we extract, this place is buzzing with them," Ricky explained.

"Don't you get stung?"

"Absolutely. Honey bee stings don't hurt as much as a wasp sting, and they can only do it once and then they die. There are actually studies on the medical benefits of bee stings for inflammation," Ricky answered.

Everett cocked his head to the side, his lips tilting up. "Look at you, Mr. Bee Farmer the Scientist."

Ricky laughed. "Hardly. And I'm a beekeeper, not farmer."

Everett held up his hand. "Sorry. Mr. Beekeeper. What exactly do you do to extract the honey?"

Ricky gestured to a door on the left-hand side of the room. "Come find out."

Everett followed Ricky in, the scent of beeswax and honey clinging to the spacious room. Ricky set his hand on one piece of machinery. "We stack the beehives here on the floor, usually on a pallet. Then we take the frames out one by one." He turned around, looking for something to use as an example. A stack of old mostly empty hives in the corner caught his eye. He grabbed the rectangular frame from inside one hive and brought it back. "These will be filled with honeycomb. We need to scrape each side to open the comb and spin the honey out. So, we set it here and this machine pushes it through, doing just that. We have a handy wire tool, like a comb, to get whatever was missed. Then we pick it off and stack it vertically in this." Ricky pointed to the wide cylinder that came waist high.

"And the honey drips down to the bottom?" Everett asked, peeking into the round tank.

"Yes, but when it's on, it spins fast. All the honey gets

pulled out and drips down to a tube attached, leading it to the clarifier."

"Which is?"

"Come on. I'll show you." Ricky led Everett to the bottom floor. He bypassed barrels of honey and turned into a smaller room, standing next to the stainless steel rectangle with a few dividers inside.

"It's empty now, but the honey comes down here through the tube. Fills up the clarifier. This will heat it enough to be bottled. Some beekeepers heat it more so that it doesn't crystalize as easily—which is when the honey gets harder. But heating it leeches it of many of the benefits of raw honey."

"That's cool. Sounds like you know your stuff," Everett said.

Ricky shrugged. "Little bit. Come on, I'll get you some to take home—er, wherever you're staying."

"I took the apartment above The Oyster Bookstore."

"Oh. That's cool. Do you like it?" Ricky tried to sound casual as he walked up the short set of stairs to the boxes of bottled honey at the entrance to the shop. He picked up a jar shaped like a bear and handed it to him.

"It's good for now. It's just me, so a studio works fine. Not too far to visit family. Close to the beach. Town seems nice. But the locals are what sold it for me."

Ricky swallowed. "Yeah?"

"Maybe one in particular." Everett's elbow grazed Ricky's.

He swallowed down his nerves and met Everett's gaze. "Tell me about him."

Everett's eyes glittered as he smirked. "Oh, he's sexy as fuck."

"Yeah?"

"But he knows it, and it shows," Everett teased.

Ricky snorted and shook his head, crossing his arms over his chest. He leaned against the counter behind him.

"He's protective of those he loves. And he's loyal." Everett took a step closer. "He's got me tied up in knots."

"Why?" Ricky asked.

"Because he's scared and that makes him unpredictable."

Ricky looked away. Everett set the honey on the counter behind Ricky and gripped his chin, forcing Ricky to face him once again as Everett leaned in so close that his exhale coasted over Ricky's lips.

"But you know what I like most about him?"

"What?"

"He's the only one who's ever known every part of me. The only one I can truly be myself with. No matter how much time has passed between us, it feels like that hasn't changed." Everett's voice hitched.

Each word was like a shot straight to Ricky's chest, causing him to come a little more undone.

Everett smiled. "And don't get me started on how fucking hot he is when he's begging me to make him come."

Ricky laughed, Everett's deep rumble joining him. The laughter faded as they stared into one another's eyes. Something eased inside Ricky at the freedom being alone with Everett brought him. His shoulders felt a little lighter. The voices in his head that screamed about what a failure and pervert he was were silenced. Everett was his safe place. It seemed so quick, but this wasn't a new discovery—this was a reunion. *This is us.* And they didn't need a label. This was how they'd always been. Two sides of the same coin.

Everett leaned in, stopping as his lips barely brushed Ricky's, like he needed Ricky to meet him partway. Ricky gave in, playfully biting Everett's bottom lip.

Everett groaned as Ricky gripped the base of his neck and

he deepened the kiss. Fuck, he tasted too goddamned sweet with an earthy hint of coffee. Everett's clean-shaven face was pressed against his own. The sensation of Everett's other hand sliding down to his ass made his cock surge with blood. A rush of endorphins spread through his body like a damn bursting, making him feel alive—high and floaty—like nothing could touch them. He'd never felt this way with anyone.

An excited little muffled voice slipped through the closed door. He jerked away from Everett, shoving Everett back just as his niece entered the honey shop, her father only a few steps behind.

"Uncle Ricky! Daddy says I can help decorate the honey bears for the gift baskets Elise is making." Ariel beamed.

"That's awesome," Ricky said.

Roman walked in, his eyes volleying between Everett and Ricky. "Hey, I didn't see your truck. I wondered whose car that was."

"Is Everett going to help too?" Ariel asked.

"No. Everett was driving to see Nova and passed me walking back to get my truck. He offered me a ride and wanted to see the honey house, so I gave him a tour. Nova's probably hungover after last night anyways," Ricky quickly lied.

"Yeah, might want to give her until the afternoon—even then you're risking your life," Roman agreed.

Everett gave Roman a stiff smile. "I'll be sure to remember that."

"Daddy, I have to go potty," Ariel whispered as she tugged her dad's hand.

"Let's go, then." He led her up the stairs to the extracting room, the door still ajar as they walked out of sight.

Ricky released the breath he'd been holding. "Fuck, that was close."

Everett stood like a statue, hurt bleeding in the space between them.

"What's wrong?" Ricky peeked over his shoulder to make sure they were still alone.

"That. That's what's wrong."

Ricky turned to him, confused. "What? You're pissed I didn't want my brother and niece to see me—" He looked back to the doorway before whispering, "Sucking face? I told you I'm not fucking gay."

Everett's cheeks pulsed. "What's so wrong with a man loving another man?"

"Nothing!" Ricky rubbed a frustrated hand over his face.

"Then why do you say it like it's the most detestable and shameful thing?"

"Let's talk about this outside." Ricky didn't wait for a response before leaving the honey house, grabbing the jar of honey from the counter.

The door closed behind him as Everett followed. "Explain this to me, because I'm trying really fucking hard to understand your hesitation."

"I'm not . . . I told you this can't be anything more than us. I'm not gay."

You perverted little deviant.

Ricky's shoulders drew up, tense and rigid as if he were preparing for a fight.

You're a disgrace. An abomination.

Your mother would be disgusted.

Ricky bit his lip, fighting for something to ground him. The tang of blood pulled him back into his body. *Why can't I escape my past?*

Everett sighed and shook his head before he took a step towards his car. Fear of Everett walking out of his life for good drowned out the terror of being discovered. He didn't have an answer; he just knew he couldn't let Everett go.

Ricky took his arm and tugged. "Please stop."

"Why? It's obvious you don't want me here."

"I do. I do—it's just complicated," Ricky said.

"So un-complicate it for me." Everett crossed his arms over his chest.

"I don't want this to end." *Not yet.* The idea of going back to life without Everett now that he'd found him, gotten a taste of what they could share, seemed empty. "Please, just give me some time to figure things out."

Everett stared at him, as if struggling with the decision.

Ricky cleared his throat. "Last night was amazing."

Everett's upper lip twitched. "This morning wasn't bad either."

Ricky chuckled. "That too."

"So you want more of that, but you don't want anyone to know?" Everett clarified.

"Yes."

"You don't know what you're asking of me." Everett tipped his head up to the sunny blue sky.

An icy wind blew through the snow-covered trees. Ricky tucked one hand into his pocket for warmth. "You said you'd do anything for me last night. This is what I need."

Everett looked at him. "I don't like lying—"

"You didn't seem to have a problem going along with Nova while she paraded you around like her boyfriend." Ricky was still a little sour about that.

"That isn't fair. I offered to be her date for the holidays. I made it clear there was nothing serious between us to your parents and told them we were friends. Whatever Nova said was on her. I was helping a friend out and it snowballed into something else. Which is why I told her I was done after New Year's Eve."

Ricky held his breath. Was that a no?

"However . . ." Everett said.

Ricky exhaled.

"I understand I can't pull you out of the closet. You have to be ready to come out for yourself."

"I'm not ga—"

Everett held his hand up. "Gay, bi-curious, bisexual, pansexual, whatever. The fact is, I learned the hard way I can't do that."

A shadow passed over Everett, pain flashing in his eyes and turning them to ice. What was that about?

"I don't want to lose you. I just found you again. But this is a big ask." Everett sighed and rubbed the back of his neck. "You need to take time to figure out whatever you need to figure out. I did mean what I said. I'd do anything for you."

"I'll figure it out."

"I need some time to think about it," Everett said.

Ricky's chest tightened. "Ever—"

The door to the honey shop opened, causing them both to look. Ariel came prancing out, Roman a few steps behind with an armful of boxes.

"Did you give him some honey to take?" Roman asked.

Ricky offered the honey jar to Everett. "Yeah. Here you go."

Everett grabbed the jar, his fingers wrapping around Ricky's and lingering there as he slowly pulled it towards him.

With their eyes locked, Ricky tried to communicate everything he couldn't say aloud with his family standing ten feet from him.

Ricky cleared his throat as Everett took the honey jar. "Have a good day."

"You too." Everett's focus dropped to Ricky's lips as he licked his own. Did Everett want to kiss him goodbye as much as Ricky wanted to kiss him?

Fear wrapped around his chest and tightened with each lingering second. The stronger the pull towards Everett, the tighter the ropes cinched.

"Thanks for the honey." Everett waved to Roman.

"You're welcome," Roman replied.

"Have fun decorating." Everett smiled at Ariel.

"Drive safe." Ricky's throat felt as if he'd swallowed gravel.

Everett met his gaze once more and gave him a nod before climbing into his car. He started the engine and drove away without another look.

Ricky watched Everett's car turn left out of the driveway and head back towards the main road. He'd had an amazing night and morning. They'd been having fun together until Roman had arrived. Then everything had changed. *But he agreed to think about it.*

So why did it feel like Ricky had lost?

21

EVERETT

Everett sat behind a dozen rows of teens in the main room at Hope Facility. Aaron Ridley, the founder and owner, stood before the kids, sharing the story of his trans sister and how she'd been the inspiration for the center. Everett's pocket vibrated. He pulled out his phone as discreetly as possibly, which wasn't hard from the back row.

Miy Lev: *Are you up for a workout tonight at seven?*

Everett's thumb hovered over the reply button. He'd had a good twenty-four hours to process everything. He'd just gotten out of a relationship with someone in the closet, and that hadn't ended well to say the least. Everett had promised himself he'd only date men who were out. But this was Ricky, his lev. At least Everett's ex had acknowledged he liked men to Everett—Ricky couldn't even do that. Ricky thought Everett was the exception. Why was he holding himself back from living life as his truest self? His adoptive family seemed more than accepting. Nova was bisexual, and Everett was pretty sure that wasn't a secret. So what had Ricky hesitating?

"Mr. Everett Popova is here to share his story with you all.

I know a few of you have seen him around the last few weeks. He's joined our family as a counselor. Please give our official warm welcome to Mr. Popova." Aaron clapped and several of the kids joined in as well as a few other staff.

Everett stood, sliding his phone back in his pocket without answering. He waved to the rows of teens, making his way to where Aaron stood in the front.

Aaron shook his hand and clapped him on the back. "Welcome to the family."

"Thanks for having me." Everett addressed the many faces staring back at him, some disinterested, others wide-eyed and curious.

"Wow, I thought I'd been intimidated standing in a room full of lawmakers, but you've got them beat by a landslide," Everett joked.

A few laughs drifted from the crowd.

"My name is Everett. You can call me that or Mr. Everett, Mr. Popova—whatever's easier for you."

"Can we give you a nickname?" one of the kids in the middle asked, pulling his hoodie up a little higher on his head.

"I'm willing to accept suggestions." Everett smiled. "Now, I know you're probably asking yourself, what could an old man like me have to say that could help you where you're at in this journey we call life?"

"You're not *that* old," one of the kids said.

"Yeah, Mrs. Marge has you beat," another snickered.

"I heard that, Billy Nottingham. See if you get an extra piece of chocolate cake next time." Marge, the chef for the whole facility, joked.

"I didn't mean it in a bad way. With age comes wisdom, right? You're the wisest of us all, Mrs. Marge," Billy quickly corrected.

Marge gave him an unimpressed look and shook her head as one corner of her mouth turned up.

"Billy's right on one account—with age does come wisdom. But that's most likely because we're old enough to have made a lot of mistakes and gained a lot of experience that's shaped the way we view the world." Everett looked around, making sure to scan every face. These were kids who could benefit from the mistakes he'd made. If his story could save one kid from going through similar difficulties, then sharing would be worth it.

"I had a friend when I was younger. We were best friends. We lived right next door to each other. My parents fought all the time. His dad was mean, but especially when he drank. It started as a friendship, but there was always something different about—" Damn, he'd almost said Ricky's name. "Him. We'd both leave our houses to escape the wrath and the rage. All we had was each other.

"We grew closer, physically. I was bigger than him; puberty had come early. So I protected him from kids at school who had a problem with him for whatever reason." Everett took a deep breath, the emotion from that time as fresh then as it was the day everything had happened.

"One day, we were in his room. He'd just gone through losing his mom."

Everett slipped his arm around Ricardo's shoulder. "I'm sorry."

"Why couldn't it have been my dad? Or me? Why did she have to die?" Ricardo's shoulders heaved with a sob.

Everett had no idea how to answer that question. Why were good people taken early and scumbags like Ricardo's father left to torment others on this earth?

"I don't have anyone else," Ricardo said.

"You've got me." Everett pulled him into his chest and held on tight. "I'm always here for you, miy lev. Always. No matter what."

Ricardo pulled back enough to look in Everett's eyes. His friend's gaze was watery and bloodshot and filled with so much visceral pain, Everett felt it in his own heart. "You swear it?"

"Promise."

Everett closed his eyes at the image in his mind of his best friend crying in his arms as Everett held him and leaned in for a kiss to comfort Ricky before all hell broke loose. Tension weaved into his body. His knees bent slightly as if preparing to fight the monster in his memories. His stomach knotted as his lungs constricted.

"What happened?" a young teen at the front asked, leaning forward.

Everett blinked his eyes open, trying to shake off the feelings from that day that still clung to him.

"His father became violent after finding us and I . . . got away. I went to my parents. My mom called the police while my dad ran over there. My friend was loaded onto an ambulance, unconscious. And his dad was arrested. During the questioning, I told them what had provoked the father—that he'd seen us kissing. That was how I came out to my parents."

"Damn, man," Billy said.

"Was your friend okay?" the girl asked.

"For many years, I didn't know what had happened to him. But I found out recently that he's doing well. He got out of there and was adopted by a good family." Everett cleared his throat. "I told you this to let you know, I've seen firsthand that coming out, or being outed to your parents or caretakers, can be a huge risk. And I understand that some of you've had similar experiences, and that's one reason you live here at Hope Facility. If you ever want to talk about it, my door is open."

"What did your parents say when they found out?" someone from the back asked.

Everett smiled. "It was the one thing my parents didn't fight about. They both agreed they loved me as I am. I got lucky with them."

"Is your friend happy?" Billy asked.

"I—I think . . . I think he's much happier than he was. But just like all of us, he's on his own journey to find out who he is and live life as his authentic self."

"I'd be scared if I were him. You never know if people will abandon you just for being you, for liking what you like, loving who you love." The girl from the front spoke again, dragging her finger over the edge of her metal folding chair.

"Have any of you ever felt that way and want to share?" Everett asked.

A moment of silence passed before a girl from the back raised her hand.

"Yes, go ahead." Everett encouraged her.

"I'm Bailey. My mom kicked me out when she found me and my girlfriend together. She said I had two choices: living on the streets, or conversion therapy."

Everett shook his head. He'd heard horror stories of those abusive practices. "I'm sorry."

The girl shrugged. "I chose therapy because I was fifteen. How was I supposed to live on my own? My girlfriend's parents sat beside mine in church, so it wasn't like they'd have been better about it. I couldn't ask to stay there and risk them doing the same to my girlfriend or worse. It was hell. And I spent another year barely seeing my girlfriend and pretending to be the perfect straight daughter." She cleared her throat. "I ended up in the hospital and finally told someone what was happening. They slipped me a Hope Facility brochure, and after I was released, I told my mom I couldn't do it anymore. That denying my true self made me want to die. I asked her if that's what she really wanted?" Her voice choked with emotion. The girl next to her wrapped her arm around her and hugged her.

"She told me I was better off dead than continuing to live a life of sin," the young lady finished.

Brynn, Aaron's wife, who'd been standing off to the side, got up and moved to sit by the girl. Brynn wrapped her arm around the girl and whispered what no doubt were comforting words.

"Thank you for being brave enough to share your truth and your story. I know many in this room can relate. We're in this together, whether you come from understanding and supportive parents or from a tougher situation. My door is open and I'm so grateful to be able to be a part of this amazing place and do what I can to help support you all." Everett searched the faces around the room as Aaron walked back to his side.

"Thanks again." Aaron turned to address the teens while Everett made his way to his own seat.

His stomach rolled at the knowledge that so many of these kids had experienced trauma. *Just like Ricky.* Though Ricky had never seemed to find a supportive place like this to help him through his struggles. He'd stuffed it down, pretending that part of him didn't exist. Maybe that was why he worked so hard to seem tough, to never show weakness—perhaps that was his idea of what masculinity was. Maybe if he knew for certain that his family would love and support him no matter what, he could get the courage to come out?

Everett's mind worked as his stomach flipped with a mix of excitement and nerves. Ricky had never told a single soul about what they'd shared. He'd never gotten any support. He'd never had anyone who would listen and accept him in a safe space. Maybe Everett could be the one to show him. Perhaps with some time—that was what Ricky had asked for, after all—Ricky would see that the benefits of being his true self would outweigh the risks of coming out.

Determination lit inside Everett. He just needed to show Ricky how good life could be if they were together. This was nothing like Everett's situation with his ex—Justin had had no plans of coming out. Everett could give Ricky some time. Maybe this was Everett's chance to save Ricky—this time from himself.

22

RICKY

Sweat dripped down Ricky's temple. Everett's legs locked around his waist.

"Hang them on my hips." Ricky rested his hands on Everett's thighs as he lowered them. "Good, now scooch closer to me so you get better control."

Everett did as he instructed and smirked as Ricky's cock rubbed against his.

Ricky's gaze darted around the near empty gym. One of Pops's daughters wiped down equipment in the far corner while a young guy flexed in one of the mirrors, taking a selfie.

"Like this?" Everett teased his hips forward again, causing all of Ricky's blood to move south.

"Yeah." His voice came out husky as he tried to keep his body in check.

"I'm beginning to see why you like this sport so much." Everett waggled his eyebrows up and down playfully.

Ricky chuckled. "Come on. You want to learn how to do an arm bar or what?"

Everett held up his hands with a sly smile. "Sorry. Continue, Jedi master."

"For fuck's sake." Ricky shook his head, trying to hide his grin. His skin heated. Adrenaline rushed through his veins at touching Everett like this in public where anyone could see and assume they were just two guys working out together.

"Penny for your thoughts?" Everett asked, jarring Ricky back to the task at hand.

"Nothing. Alright, so if I go to hit you like this . . ." Ricky extended his arm in a slow-motion punch. "You should block with the same side I punched with to guard your skull."

Everett brought his right hand to the top of his head, his arm blocking the rest of his face.

"Great. Now use your other arm to cross over and grab my punching arm. Tuck it against your chest and swoop your other arm up over my neck, and pull me against you while you lock your arms around my neck." Ricky walked him through the movements. "Good. Let's try it again."

Ricky lightly jabbed with his left hand. Everett blocked with his right arm and moved through the next steps fluidly. Everett's grip turned from lax to firm. Ricky's face was crammed into Everett's neck. A fresh burst of musk with citrus filled his nose. Everett's scent was quickly becoming his favorite.

"Admit it. You just want an excuse to rub your dick on me." Everett's breath coasted over his ear, his deep voice rumbly.

Ricky tugged away, but Everett held firm. Ricky's cock jerked, arousal heating his blood.

Everett squeezed his legs tighter, his erection rubbing against Ricky's and only adding to his building desire.

"Looks like someone likes to be restrained." Everett bucked his hips again.

I guess so. But that made him weak, right? Being the one not in control made him submissive, didn't it?

His stomach rolled as shame killed his erection. He used his skills to duck his head and twist out of Everett's hold. *See? I'm still in control.* He'd only played at being overpowered. They both knew Ricky was the better fighter.

"You need some air?" Everett asked, concern creasing the edges of his eyes.

"No." Ricky snapped to his feet. "Just tired. Maybe we can pick up some other time?"

"Sure." Everett got up and walked over to the corner of the mat, grabbed their waters, and handed one to Ricky.

"Thanks." Ricky unscrewed it and took a big gulp, trying to buy himself some time and calm the anxiety snaking through his veins.

Everett put a hand on his shoulder. "You sure you're okay?"

Ricky walked towards the shower. "Yeah, just tired. I need a shower to perk up. How was your day at Hope?"

"Good. I got my formal introduction today and got to talk to the kids as a group." Everett followed him.

They got their shower supplies and stripped naked. Ricky glanced around the room, making sure no one else was in there with them before he allowed himself to look at Everett's toned body. Everett's skin glistened with sweat. His dark smattering of chest hair stuck to his flesh. His stomach flexed, making his cock jerk. Ricky's mouth watered. His own dick stirred to life again.

"You want a picture for when you're alone in your bed tonight?" Everett asked with a knowing smirk.

Fuck. Anyone could hear. He could lose clients if they knew about Ricky and Everett. *And what would Pops think?*

Ricky jerked his attention to the locker as he stuffed his

clothes inside. "So, you're like a therapist? That seems like a big jump from the cannabis industry."

"Consulting was my main job in California but I've volunteered at queer youth centers all over for years. I actually went back to university for a second degree in social work and psychology. I'm more of a mentor than a therapist though," Everett explained, setting his soap on the shelf by the shower and then he turned it on.

Ricky started his own shower, letting it warm up before stepping in. He closed his eyes as the hot water rained over his head, slipping down his shoulders to the rest of his body. He blinked, trying to clear some of the moisture from his vision as he wiped a hand over his face. His mouth went dry. Everett had soaped up his hands and was washing his dick first. His fingers were wrapped around his long cock, stroking up and down. Ricky froze. Everett's eyes were locked on his, dark and heavy with lust.

Ricky's hands flexed, itching to grab his own dick at the sight. Steam rose, adding a layer of privacy to the spacious tiled room. Tension wove tightly through the misty air.

"You're making me so fucking hot, staring at me like that." Everett's husky voice was like an aphrodisiac.

Desire and need built, wrapping around Ricky like a velvet rope, teasing and erotic.

"Touch yourself," Everett said.

Ricky's hand moved down his stomach, wrapped around his cock. He bit back a groan.

Everett jerked himself off a little faster. "That's it. Make yourself come while you look in my eyes."

Ricky squeezed his dick a little harder as he obeyed, giving in to the lust pumping through his veins.

"That's it. Stroke yourself. Imagine it's my hand," Everett added.

Ricky's eyes grew heavy as Everett's words penetrated the fog of lust.

"You're so damn sexy like this. Doing what I say. Jerking yourself off as you watch me. Your body is perfection. And those tattoos—fuck. Just looking at you is gonna make me come," Everett groaned.

Ricky's hand didn't falter, the excitement of danger as Everett approached only added to his pleasure. This was risky—but so fucking hot. Ricky's cock pulsed, his balls drawing up. He was close.

"What do you need, miy lev? Tell me," Everett pressed, moving from his shower closer to Ricky's.

Panting, Ricky chased his orgasm. He was right on the edge—almost there—

Everett's hand landed on his ass. Ricky jumped out of the shower.

"What the fuck are you doing?!" Ricky whisper-yelled, flicking his gaze around the room to make sure they were still alone. He released a breath when he found the door still closed. Anyone could walk in at any second. It was one thing to catch someone jacking off; it was another entirely to find him doing it with another guy touching him.

Ricky turned back to Everett, whose face was now carefully blank. His friend turned around and headed back to his shower, rinsing himself off in silence.

Ricky stood on the tile floor, water dripping off him into a puddle at his feet. He couldn't help but be torn. It was clear he'd hurt Everett by his small freak-out. But they'd gone over this. No one could know. Ricky could lose everything.

Everett turned his water off and collected his shower things before quickly making his way back to the lockers.

Ricky sighed, rinsed himself off, and followed. Everett had his towel wrapped around his hips as he pulled a fresh shirt over his head. He slipped his sweatpants on underneath and then untied the towel, tossing it in the dirty bin before heading towards the exit.

"Ever, wait."

Everett paused, holding his breath.

"I'm sorry. I didn't mean to hurt you. I just . . ."

Everett turned around and swallowed, his Adam's apple bobbing. "No, you told me your boundaries and I pushed too far. I'm the one who's sorry. It's hard for me to . . ." Everett blew out a breath. "I'll try to read the situation better next time."

Ricky should probably apologize too. He was the broken one. He was the one with the issues. Why did Ever want to stay around him at all? "It's fine. I just . . ."

"Need time," Everett finished for him.

Ricky had meant he'd needed time with Everett before he moved on. He was stealing his attention and affection like a thief. But how could he let Everett go now? After finding him again? After all they'd shared?

Maybe he could be better for Everett. He couldn't give Ever everything he needed, but Ricky wanted to try. As long as no one found out, what was the harm?

"Thank you for understanding," Ricky said.

Everett nodded.

"I'll talk to you later?" Ricky asked.

"Yeah. Sounds good." Everett took a step forward and then stopped, his hand tightening on the strap of his gym bag as if he were holding himself back. "See you later." He spun around and left Ricky alone.

Ricky sighed as he grabbed a towel and dried himself off. This was going to be a lot harder than he'd thought. Ricky was playing with fire.

But what was life without a little danger?

23

RICKY

Ricky set down the last box in the full van and shut the back doors. He jogged into the honey house and looked around one more time, making sure he had everything needed for the delivery.

Ding

Ricky pulled out his phone. *Oh.* His heart sank. *Not Everett.*

Nova: *Do you still have that handgun?*

Ricky's brows drew together.

Ricky: *In a lock box. Why? Did the FBI contact you again? Did something happen?*

A bubble appeared as Ricky held his breath.

Nova: *No. I was just thinking about taking some shooting lessons. I figured you might have some good pointers?*

Ricky breathed out a sigh of relief.

Ricky: *Sure. Save your cans. I'll take you to the back pasture and teach you there.*

Nova: *Perfect.*

Ricky tapped out of the message thread with his sister and

opened the one with Everett. They'd exchanged only a few words since Ricky had freaked out at the gym yesterday.

Ever: *You get home okay?*

Ricky: *Yeah.*

Ricky: *I'm sorry about last night.*

Ever: *Nothing to be sorry about. It was my fault. I pushed too fast.*

Ricky's thumb hovered over the reply button. He'd struggled with what to say back but, in the end, never sent a thing. He'd waited for Ever to reach out again, but maybe he was waiting for Ricky to make the first move because of what happened?

Ricky squeezed the back of his neck. "What do I do?" His gaze flicked out the window towards the van. He had a long day of deliveries ahead. Maybe . . .

Ricky tapped the reply button.

Ricky: *You free today?*

He held his breath, waiting for those text dots to appear. Nothing happened for a full minute and his heart sank. Ricky had never been this excited or on edge to see someone.

He sighed, sliding his cell into his back pocket as he grabbed his keys and headed for the van. It wasn't until he pulled into a parking spot in front of the café, directly across the street from Everett's apartment that his phone dinged with a message.

Ever: *All day.*

Ricky: *I'm across the street at the café in the white van. Wanna go on a road trip to Concord? I've got a few stops to make on the way.*

Ever: *You giving away free candy and abducting children?*

Ricky: *Delivering honey, actually.*

Ever: *Give me fifteen minutes.*

Ricky pocketed his phone and jogged into the café. Remy greeted him from behind the counter. "Good morning to you. What's got you all smiles? Or should I ask?"

Ricky laughed. He hadn't realized he was smiling. "Just a good day is all."

"Mm-hmm." Remy gave him a knowing look. "The usual?"

"Actually, I'd like an extra coffee too. Black. And maybe a couple lavender cookies and apple crumble muffins."

"Coming right up."

Ricky waited while Remy got his drinks ready. After he paid, she slid a bag of baked goods across the counter. He picked them up and walked outside to the truck. Balancing the cups in each hand and the bag of goodies under his arm, he struggled to open the door.

"I got it," Ever said, appearing by his side. He reached for the door handle and pulled it open.

"Thanks." Ricky climbed in, setting his items down in the console as Ever walked to the passenger side.

Ever set a grocery bag by his feet. "Thanks for the coffee."

"You take it black, right?" Ricky asked.

"Yeah. Unlike some people, I grew out of my drown-the-coffee-in-sugar-and-cream phase," he teased.

"It tastes better this way."

Ever smiled and buckled in.

Ricky nodded towards the bag at his feet before pulling out on Main Street. "What's in the bag?"

"Supplies." Everett reached down and plucked a few items out. "I got us the standard road-trip snacks like chips and candy bars. And I couldn't resist grabbing a few Monster drinks."

Ricky shook his head. "Those things are lethal."

"Remember when we each drank five that one night?" Everett asked as Ricky drove them out of town.

"Your mom thought we'd done drugs." Ricky laughed.

"You were shaking and your eye was twitching." Everett

shook his head with a big smile. "After that, they were banned in our house and she forbade me from drinking them again. So, don't tell her."

"My lips are sealed." Ricky dragged his fingers across his mouth like he was zipping them shut.

"Oh, I also got us Blue Shark gummies and Warheads."

"I haven't had those in . . ."

"Me either." Ever's gaze burned the side of Ricky's face. "Eating them made me think of you."

Ricky swallowed and focused on the road. The impact of what Everett said hit him full force. Ricky had meant something to Everett—just as much as Everett had meant to him. *I'm not in this alone. I never was with Ever.*

"Ricar—er, Ricky?" Everett asked, reaching out to take his hand on the console before he pulled his arm back like he'd been burned.

Guilt crashed over Ricky. He'd done this—created this tension between them. Made Everett hesitant, which was never the kind of man he'd been before. Everett was always so sure of himself—that was one of the things Ricky liked about him.

Ricky grabbed Everett's hand and gave it a squeeze. "You can call me Ricardo if you want. I don't care what you call me. And when it's just us in private—you can touch me however you want to."

Everett released a long breath and flipped his palm, weaving his fingers through Ricky's, holding his hand. "So . . . where exactly are we going?"

"I have a couple mom-and-pop shops to drop off orders to along the way, and then a bigger store in Concord. I thought we could get lunch while we're there."

"Sounds good. My dad lives in the area. There's an

awesome café with the best sandwiches. You interested?" Everett asked.

"Sure."

"Awesome." Everett picked up his coffee and took a sip. "So, tell me how you got into beekeeping."

"It was Roman's idea actually."

"Yeah?"

"Well, sort of. We went mudding one day, ended up tearing up a neighbor's field and ruining a few hives after knocking them over."

"Ouch."

"Yeah. Well, we worked for the beekeeper to make up for what we'd destroyed, and Roman loved it. I didn't mind it at all. You get used to the bees and the occasional stings. My favorite part is working in the wood shop though, building the equipment in the winter. And keeping the books."

"Looks like you make a good team if your business is able to support your brother's family and you." Everett motioned to the boxes in the back as Ricky turned onto a different road.

Snow-white landscape whizzed by. The only color was the green clusters of evergreens. "We do okay. If we expand anymore, we'll need to hire some full-time help, at least for the spring and summer."

"I'd like to see what you do someday. But I'll definitely need a bee suit. I'm not as brave as you when it comes to stinging insects." Everett chuckled.

"It's not as bad as you think. You'll have to come out this summer with me." Ricky swallowed. Would Everett be there in the summer? He had to be.

"I will." Everett's thumb rubbed gentle circles over Ricky's hand.

The connection sent a vibration up Ricky's arm, pumping

through his bloodstream until a kind of buoyant happiness filled Ricky's chest like a warm balloon.

"What about you? What got you into the business you're in?"

"I started smoking weed in college." Everett held up his hands. "I know, I was a late bloomer when it came to experimenting."

Ricky shrugged. "I think that's common for college kids."

"My roommate was really into growing. He taught me a lot. And it helped with the—with my panic attacks and . . ." Everett's grip tensed. "I used to get nightmares. It helped me sleep without the dreams."

"What were your nightmares about?"

"You."

Ricky sucked in a breath, trying his hardest to focus on the road. "I'm so fucking sorry."

Everett dropped his hand only to grip the back of Ricky's neck. "Listen, you have absolutely nothing to be sorry about. You and I did nothing wrong together."

Ricky's stomach hardened as he pulled his eyes away from the road to glance at Everett. Grey-blue eyes, filled with so much passion, stared back at him.

"I wish I could believe that," Ricky rasped, focusing back on the road.

Everett dropped his hand, threading his fingers through Ricky's. "I guess I'll just have to do my best to convince you, then."

Ricky swallowed, his eyes burning with emotion. Warm gratitude filled his rib cage that Ever had fought so hard for him, for his friendship and understanding. Ricky regretted that he couldn't be the man Ever wanted—at least not right then. Determination glowed inside him like a fiery ember, sparking back to life. *I need him in my life. Whatever it takes.*

"It would be easier for you to leave me and find your happiness. Someone who can be what you need," Ricky said, his throat dry as gravel.

Everett nodded. "Easier? Probably."

Ricky's heart sank.

"Good thing I've never been one to take the easy route. I much prefer complicated and maybe even a little dangerous. Nothing worth keeping is ever *easy*. And I intend to keep you as long as you'll let me, miy lev." Ever lifted Ricky's hand to his lips and pressed a kiss there.

Ricky was speechless. It was like Everett had reached into his chest and pulled out his beating heart, leaving him completely vulnerable. Instead of feeling panicked and having the urge to flee, Ricky relaxed his shoulders. For once, he was completely safe with someone. The freedom that his trust in Everett enabled him to have was heady.

"I want to try." *For you.*

Everett turned towards the window. "You said we're going to Concord, right?"

"Yeah."

"Anyone know you here?" Everett asked.

"No."

"Do you have to rush back to Shattered Cove?"

Ricky shook his head. "I've got nothing going on until dinner at Mom and Dad's tomorrow. Why?"

Everett turned towards him. "Do you trust me?"

Ricky had the feeling that whatever his answer was would change everything. "With my life."

"I won't ever betray that privilege," Everett promised.

Ricky relaxed in his seat. The open road was before him. The man he'd come to care about was by his side like he was always meant to be there. And perhaps he was, because for the first time in Ricky's adult life, he felt whole. Like there had been an Ever-sized piece missing in him this whole time, and he was just figuring it out. The voices in his head were silent. The weight had been lifted from his shoulders like Everett had taken some of it.

Ricky wasn't sure what label to give Ever—he was more than a friend. Lover didn't fit—they were more than casual fuck buddies. Was there a word for someone who was more? For someone who knew your very soul? For a man who was quickly becoming Ricky's everything?

24

EVERETT

Everett picked up the steaming cups of coffee from the counter at the café and weaved through the busy lunch crowd, searching for his date.

Ricky sat with his back towards the wall in the corner, facing the door. His dark, curly hair was mostly hidden under a baseball cap. He was the sexiest guy in the room. Hell, probably the best-looking man Everett had seen. With muscles for days that didn't just look pretty, Ricky knew how to use every inch of his body and turn it into a weapon if his sparring at the gym was any indication.

Ricky's eyes crashed into Everett's before a small smile turned up one side of his mouth. That made Everett's knees weak as he snapped out of gawking and headed over to their table. He set the drinks down.

"Thanks," Ricky said.

Everett took the seat across from him. "The woman at the counter said she'd bring out our sandwiches when they were ready."

Ricky took a sip of his coffee and scanned the room. If his shoulders were any higher, they'd touch his ears.

"You okay?"

Ricky's attention snapped back to him. "Yeah I just . . ." He looked around again.

Everett's heart sank. Rejection bubbled up inside him. Did Ricky not even want to be seen with him?

"Relax, Ricky. No one here knows you. Even if they recognize me—which probably won't happen—they won't alert the newspapers." Everett stared at his coffee.

A warm hand nudged his. The steady thrum of energy he'd come to expect from Ricky's touch tingled up his arm.

"Ever?"

"What?"

"Look at me."

Everett dragged his gaze along Ricky's button-up plaid shirt, lingering a moment on the dip of his throat before meeting his eyes.

"It's not that."

"What is it, then?" Everett asked.

Ricky scanned the room again and shook his head. "It just feels like someone's watching me. I don't know." He rubbed the back of his neck.

Everett took a quick look around the room. The few tables nearby were full of groups chatting. Several people sat alone, working on their laptops. The line for the counter still stretched to the door. But he didn't catch anyone's eye.

He turned back to Ricky. "Do you think you're being extra sensitive because this is your first time out with a guy you've had sex with?"

Ricky's jaw pulsed as he glanced around the room once more. He leaned forward, his voice dropping to a whisper. "We haven't."

"Haven't what?"

"Had sex." Ricky's skin took on a reddish hue of a blush.

"I guess that depends on your definition of sex."

One of Ricky's eyebrows rose skeptically. "I think everyone can agree penetration is the definition of sex."

Everett shrugged. "For most people—mainly heterosexual people. Only one hole counts for them." He laughed. "But that doesn't take into account all the other people out there who don't enjoy or can't have penetrative sex. What about sides?"

"Sides?" Ricky asked, confusion whirling in his expression.

"Tops, bottoms, and then there's sides," Everett hinted.

"What exactly do—" Ricky glanced around them and lowered his voice even more. "Sides do?"

"Non-penetrative stuff."

Ricky swallowed, his focus back on his coffee.

"Here you go, handsome." The woman from the café set down two plates in front of them.

Ricky sat back, giving her a smile. "Thanks."

"Yes, thank you," Everett added.

"You're welcome. Enjoy." She left them.

Ricky stared at his sandwich a few moments more before glancing around again.

"If this is too much, we don't have to stay. We can get these to go and get back to the van."

Ricky was silent for two beats and then straightened and shook his head. "No. Let's eat. You're right—no one knows me here. I must just be letting it get to my head." He rubbed the back of his neck again like it was bothering him. "Maybe it's just me freaking out."

Everett moved his foot under the table so his knee pressed against Ricky's. Ricky looked up.

"I told you I wouldn't push," Everett said. "This will only

work with communication. So if it's too much and passes your comfort zone, I can back off. I want this to be fun for you."

"I appreciate it. And I am—enjoying our time together." Ricky picked up his sandwich and took a bite.

They ate in silence for a few minutes. Ricky wiped his mouth and pushed his empty plate a few inches away before taking another drink of his coffee. Ricky's hand landed next to Everett's, his finger tracing a line over the top of his hand. Everett's brows drew together.

"I've been thinking a lot about what you said," Ricky said.

"About?"

"That no one here knows me. And I can't stop wondering . . ."

Everett swallowed, fighting the urge to thread his fingers through Ricky's, needing to touch him but not wanting to push him too far. "Wondering what?"

"What it would be like to let go for one day. To be . . . the me I am with just you but . . . out here."

Everett's jaw slackened as he blinked twice in disbelief. "Out here, like in a city, hours from Shattered Cove? Or out like out of the closet?"

Ricky stiffened, his finger pausing. "Like in the city here. I'm not—" He leaned forward. "I'm not gay. I've never been attracted to another man."

"Never? Not even, like, Henry Cavill?" Everett asked, partly teasing but mostly curious.

Ricky rolled his eyes. "He doesn't count."

"Um . . . why not?"

"Because he's like your doppelgänger. Still counts as you."

Everett burst out laughing. A few people turned their heads, scowling at his disruption.

"Sorry, but exactly how many other *exceptions* do you have?"

"I mean, that's it, mostly."

"Mostly? Oh, come on. I need to hear more."

Ricky mumbled something under his breath.

"I'm sorry. I didn't quite catch that?" Everett bit back a smile.

Ricky sighed and leaned forward again as if he didn't want anyone else to hear. "Johnny."

"Johnny who?"

"Depp."

A beat passed. "Captain Jack Sparrow? You got a thing for pirates?"

Ricky laughed and shook his head. "I got a thing for guys who remind me of you."

Everett stopped short. Ricky was still smiling, but vulnerability flashed in his eyes. Everett's stomach flipped. "So we're really doing this? While we're here in Concord? Being . . . us?"

Ricky opened his mouth to speak.

"Everett! Oh my God, I thought that was you." Another voice pulled his attention away.

Bryan walked over to their table, his arm linked through his husband's, Chris's.

Everett stood and shook his hand before doing the same with Chris. "Hey, guys. How are you?"

"Good. We just stopped in for a bite before we go back to the shelter. I didn't know you were back in town." Bryan peeked around his shoulder at Ricky before giving Everett a knowing smile. "Oh, and not alone, I see."

Everett turned to Ricky. "Ricky, this is my friend Bryan and his partner, Chris. Guys, this is Ricky."

Ricky stood and held out his hand to shake theirs. "Nice to meet you."

Bryan looked between them. "Are you busy tonight?"

"Oh, yes. You have to come," Chris added.

"Come where?" Ricky asked.

"To the bar, of course. It's been ages since we've seen you and caught up," Chris said, looking at Everett.

"I'm not sure. We're just in town for the day," Everett said, looking to Ricky. There was no way he'd be ready for a gay bar—would he?

"How can you say no to a face like this?" Chris held Bryan's jaw in his hand, squeezing his cheeks slightly. "I need to know the secret, because it would save me a fortune." He laughed.

Chris shook his head, pulling his husband's hand away before he smiled innocently at him. "Oh, come on. You love the new plants."

"I love that you love them. That's entirely a different thing," Bryan teased.

Chris rolled his eyes, turning back to Everett and Ricky. "Ignore him. He's just pent up from missing his last boxing session."

"You box?" Ricky asked.

Bryan nodded. "Yeah. Not professionally or anything. I've done a few circuits. But now it's more for fun."

"No way. I'm into MMA," Ricky said.

"Cool. Maybe we could spar sometime? If you're gonna be sticking around?" Bryan asked.

Ricky glanced at Everett. "We were just gonna stay the day, but maybe next time we could plan something?"

Everett swallowed, trying to hide his surprise. His stomach flipped like he'd reached the top of a very high roller coaster.

"Definitely," Bryan said.

"So, you won't stay for one drink tonight? You could crash at our house if you want?" Chris asked.

Ricky looked to him. Everett tipped his head to the side. *Do you want to stay?*

"Well, we'll be at The Queen at seven if you want to join. At least we'll start there. Do you have the *Friends Finder* app?"

"Yeah," Everett said.

"Great, well, we'd love to see you. If not, we'll catch you next time. Have a wonderful afternoon." Bryan waved good-bye. Chris smiled and they left together.

Everett sat back in his seat, Ricky across from him, his leg bouncing under the table. Had that interaction made Ricky uncomfortable? Ricky hadn't wanted anyone to see them after all.

"You okay?" Everett asked.

Ricky hesitated and then nodded. "Yeah. Just in my head."

"We don't have to go. We can walk around town and then head back if you want."

"And if . . . if I want to go?"

Everett paused. "Then we can go. But you do know it's a gay bar, right?"

"So, no one would care, then? We'd be just another couple —uh, couple of guys, right?" That red flush was back on Ricky's cheeks.

"Correct. You'd be just another color in the rainbow," he teased, trying to break the tension.

A hint of a smile curled Ricky's lips. "And will I have to worry about other guys trying to . . . hit on me?"

Everett leaned forward this time, his hand slipping under the table to land right above Ricky's knee, stilling the anxious jiggling. "No, you won't. Because I'll be glued to your side, making it clear you're taken. And I've never been one to share something once it's mine."

Ricky's lips parted, his chest rising and falling faster as his eyes dilated. So the possessive side of Everett turned Ricky on? And here he'd been holding back, afraid he'd scare Ricky away. Everett slipped that little piece of information away for later.

"You're sure this is what you want?" Everett confirmed.

Ricky nodded. "I think—yes. It is. I want . . . one day of seeing what it's like. Where no one knows me."

A shadow of doubt niggled at Everett. But maybe that was just fear of losing Ricky when he'd just gotten him. He didn't want to push and have him running away again. But if Ricky said he was ready to try, Everett was all in.

"Okay."

Ricky's eyes brightened with a mix of nervous excitement. "Really?"

"Absolutely."

"What should we do until then?" Ricky asked.

Everett smiled. This was his chance to show Ricky just how good things could be with them. He wouldn't waste a single second. "I have a few ideas."

25

RICKY

"You suck so bad," Ricky said.

"That's not what you said the other night." Everett smirked at him from the end of the pinball machine. "That's also not what the scoreboard says."

Ricky chuckled. He'd had the last few hours to relax into this thing between them. The two beers he'd had at dinner had helped—and the fact that no one knew them here at the bar arcade, nor out on the street. It was a chance to enjoy each other's company without worrying someone he knew would see them and make assumptions.

"I guess that makes me the winner. We never did settle on a prize." Everett tapped his chin, his eyes glittering with mischief.

He was so much like the boy Ricky had known. Ricky's stomach tilted and flipped. "Oh, no."

"What?" Everett asked.

"I know that look."

One half of Everett's mouth lifted in a smile. "All this talk about sucking gave me some ideas."

"I bet it did." Ricky couldn't hide his own smile despite the curl of anxiety that snaked around in his gut. *I'm really doing this.* "Just like old times."

Everett laughed. "Yeah, but now that we're older and wiser, maybe we could come up with a better prize?"

Ricky scoffed. "We both know there isn't much better than a blow job."

"Then maybe you're not as experienced as you think." Everett gave him a knowing wink.

Ricky swallowed. The blood in his body conflicted, some going to his cheeks for a blush and the other his cock, making it hard as steel.

Ricky took a deep breath, looking at his phone to buy some time, but he didn't actually take note of it. He was too focused on preparing himself for the guilt that would crash into him. When it didn't, he looked up.

Everett was studying him. His voice was gentle, but firm. "You don't have to do anything you don't want to. That goes for losing competitions too."

Ricky nodded, scanning the few other patrons gathered around the TV watching a game. Others were scattered around different arcade games.

"I know." And he did. No matter what, he was always safe with Everett. He could be his true self.

"Is it almost seven?" Everett asked.

Ricky looked down at his phone again and then pocketed it. "Just past."

"Guess we should head over if you're ready. It's a short walk from here."

Ricky grabbed his jacket from the table they'd occupied for dinner. He slipped it on while Everett did the same. They left the bar and headed down the street. The bitter chill in the air made their breath fog in front of them.

Everett pulled out his vape pen and took a couple puffs before offering it to Ricky. Ricky accepted, taking a few hits before handing it back. They passed a few couples and other people walking the opposite way on the sidewalk before turning down another street. Bass thumped as they grew closer to a tall, black-brick building. Gold lettering on a black background displayed "The Queen" in fancy font. Two rainbow flags bookended a Black Lives Matter and trans pride flag.

Ricky's forehead broke out in a sweat despite the cold night. Though the weed helped dull his anxiety, Ricky stopped abruptly. Someone cursed behind him and skirted around him, nudging his shoulder.

Everett turned, worry creasing his expression. "You okay?"

"Yeah I just . . . forgot."

"Forgot what?" Everett asked, his worry morphing to confusion.

"What it was like to be with you. To have you looking out for me."

Everett stepped closer, moving to the side of the concrete to let passersby go around. He grazed his hand over Ricky's jaw before settling it on his shoulder like he needed to touch him but knew a display of affection out there on the street might be too much for Ricky. It only made Ricky's knees weaker. His resolve slipped, and he placed his hand over Everett's.

"I'll always have your back. You and me, remember? That's all that matters. If this is too much, we don't have to go in," Everett said.

Ricky shook his head. Everett didn't understand. He thought he was trying to back out of this. "No, that's not what I mean. You knew this would bring up anxiety for me. You tried to help before it was even a problem. You always were good at anticipating my needs. That isn't something that I'm used to. It just took me by surprise."

Everett's expression softened. The corner of his lips turned down. "That's a fucking shame. On one hand, the possessive, selfish bastard inside me is glad no one got to know this side of you. But the other bigger part is consumed with anger that you felt for one moment there was something wrong with you that you have to hide."

Ricky swallowed, a mix of emotions welling in his chest.

"You get to be anyone you want in there." Everett pointed over his shoulder towards the gay bar. "You'll be accepted for being gay, dressing up in drag—"

Ricky snorted.

"Or coming in with nothing but a leather speedo and harness with glow sticks. In fact, it's encouraged." Everett smiled. "But I hope you'll take this opportunity to be your true self—whoever that Ricky is. Because I think he's pretty amazing."

Each word was like an arrow piercing through the shell of armor Ricky had constructed to keep himself safe, landing in his heart. He'd never be the same. Not after running into Everett again. Not after tasting his lips. Nor the intimate moments they'd shared. Ricky was irrevocably changed forever. He couldn't go back if he wanted to. The only way was forward.

Ricky scanned the street once more out of habit. *Am I really going to do this?* He met Everett's patient gaze. A lock of dark hair hung over Everett's forehead, breaking up the line of his eyebrow. He was so handsome—fucking beautiful.

Ricky backed away so Everett's hand fell from his shoulder before Everett threaded his fingers through Ricky's. Everett squeezed. "You sure about this?"

"The only thing I'm sure about is you," Ricky confessed,

leaving the confines of the cage he'd built for himself to be vulnerable with the other man.

Everett's eyes shone like tears had welled up in them. He cleared his throat, pulling Everett's hand as they bypassed a hotel and walked into the bar.

The bouncer at the door let them in. Music thudded louder as they entered a second set of doors. The inside décor didn't match the dark exterior. Inside was bright. The walls were a royal blue with gold accents. Booths were lined with blue velvet seats and white and gold marble tables. There was a stage to the left with two golden poles running all the way to the high, mirrored ceiling.

"Do you want to start with a drink?" Everett motioned to the right where a small line formed around the shiny blue bar top.

"Vodka, please." Ricky pulled out his wallet.

"I got it." Everett held up his hand.

"Let me," Ricky insisted, handing over the cash.

The song switched. Something upbeat and sensual bled through the speakers. A group of people danced on the floor in the center of the room. Men draped their arms around other men. A woman kissed her partner in one of the booths. Another two people flirted and laughed at the bar.

Everett didn't let Ricky's hand go as he led him to the bartender and ordered their drinks. Normally, Ricky was the one to take charge during dates. He opened doors, ordered drinks, took the lead. Not that this was a date with Everett. But it was nice to let someone else take the reins for once.

Ricky took another look around. Two men standing farther down the bar affectionately chatted away, laughing every now and then. Their wedding rings glinted in the flashing lights. They couldn't keep their hands off each other.

It was clear they loved one another. What was so wrong with that?

Nothing.

Ricky had never had a problem with gay men. What would it be like to be that way with Everett? To be free to kiss him in public? To date him?

"Here you go." Everett handed him a vodka cranberry.

"Thanks." Ricky downed half of it in one gulp.

The alcohol burned the back of his throat, sinking into his gut. Warmth spread out, blooming like a flower in his veins. The back of his eyes tingled from the THC, making Ricky's head fuzzy and relaxed.

"Thirsty?" Everett asked.

Ricky downed the rest of his drink without answering, setting his empty glass on the counter. He wiped his mouth with the back of his hand. "Can we take our coats off?"

Everett hesitated a moment, scanning Ricky before he nodded. He took his hand again, leading him through the growing crowd towards the booths.

Two hands raised from a booth near the back, waving in the air. Everett's friends from earlier smiled at them. Everett flicked a glance to Ricky as if asking if this was okay. Ricky inclined his head. They walked over to the two men.

"I'm so glad you could come." Bryan motioned to the other side of the booth.

Ricky took his coat off and slid in, setting his jacket on the bench. Everett handed him his coat to join the pile.

"Glad we could too," Everett said.

"I was just begging Bryan here to dance with me. You two want to join?" Chris asked.

"I think we'll stay here for a bit," Everett answered.

"Suit yourself. Next round of drinks is on us," Bryan said, standing. He held his hand out for Chris.

They left the table, moving to the dance floor.

"You don't like to dance?" Ricky asked.

"I love it. Just didn't think you'd be ready for that."

Just one more act of thoughtfulness that made Everett impossible to not fall for. Shit, that was what this was. Ricky was falling for Everett. The thought should have terrified him—and it did. But for once, he didn't care. Who would be hurt if he gave in like he wanted to with Everett? No one. His mother was gone; she would never know. His father couldn't hurt him again. So why was he resisting something so fucking perfect between them?

He'd searched decades for someone who could make him feel a fraction of the emotions Everett brought out in him. No one else had come close. He'd told Everett he would try—and now was the time.

His palms itched. His legs bounced under the table with frantic energy. He needed to move. To make a choice. *It's now or never.*

He turned to face Everett. The man's sexy, chiseled features were highlighted by the shadows and blinking lights. There was no judgment from Everett—only patience. He was willing to take what Ricky could give and demand no more. But Ricky wanted to push his boundaries. Wanted to please Everett. He just wanted a goddamned opportunity to see what could be—and this was his chance.

"I'm ready. I want to dance with you," Ricky said.

Everett didn't hesitate. He got out from the booth. Ricky followed. Everett cupped his jaw, staring into his very soul. "If it's too much—"

"It's not."

"Okay. But if it is, don't run. Just tell me."

Ricky nodded.

Everett pulled him towards the dance floor, weaving in

between writhing bodies until they were in the center—just a couple more figures lost in a sea of dancing. Bass reverberated through the speakers, vibrating up his feet. Lights flashed, reflecting off the mirrored ceiling.

How does this work with two men? Where do I put my hands?

Everett gripped Ricky's hips, pulling him against his taut body. Chills rushed through Ricky. His palms landed on Everett's shoulders as they moved to the beat. Everett's touch was intoxicating, spinning Ricky higher and higher in his lust-fueled haze. Everett's thigh slipped between Ricky's as his hips swerved, and writhed, causing their jean-clad cocks to rub against one another.

Ricky's groan was swallowed by the music. Adrenaline pumped through his veins. He was dancing with a man in front of other people. He was letting Everett touch him in public like a lover.

Ricky scanned the crowd. No one looked their way. No one cared. He was just another face in a crowd. And it was so fucking freeing. Excitement swirled through him, a sense of free-falling. The rush—it was unlike any other.

Ricky let the music flow through him as he gave in to the beat, surrendering everything that was left for this one moment where he was completely himself—not holding anything back.

"There's nothing fucking hotter than a man who knows how to use his body, and has the confidence to back it up." Everett's rough voice rose in his ear as his hand slid down to the top of Ricky's ass. His hand flexed like he was holding himself back.

Ricky twined his hips, digging his fingers into Everett's shoulders. His chest heaved, staring into the fathomless depth of Everett's darkened orbs. How far could Ricky push before Everett snapped and gave in to this tension?

"You keep looking at me like that and I'm gonna kiss you in front of all these people. Let them know you're mine." Everett licked his lips.

"Fuck. You're gonna make me come in my pants." Ricky grinded against him.

Everett leaned in so that his lips hovered right over Ricky's ear, crushing their bodies even closer together. "You have no fucking idea what you're doing to me."

"Show me."

They danced, their bodies molding to one another like they were made for this. Lust and trust wound together and released a cyclone of building desire.

"What exactly do you want from me?" Everett rasped.

"I'm asking for you—all of you. Don't hold back. And I won't either."

Everett's groan rose above the music before he sunk his face into Ricky's neck. His exhale tickled Ricky's oversensitive flesh. Everett scraped his teeth over Ricky's pulse point. Ricky's cock flexed at the bite of pain.

Everett gripped the back of Ricky's head, staring at him. Bodies moved all around them, blurring into the background. Nothing else existed but Everett and Ricky.

"I'm trying to go slow. To give you time and space. But if this is your one night to see what it would be like—to completely let go—you should know the other side of me." Everett's chest heaved.

"Show me. Give me all of you," Ricky said.

"If I'm too much—"

"I'll tell you."

"You better." Everett didn't give Ricky a chance to respond. His lips crashed against his, rough and possessive.

Ricky lit up like a Christmas tree. Need thrummed through his every cell. Adrenaline mixed with the substances in his body, humming through his veins. But nothing compared to the overwhelming pleasure being this close to Everett brought. It was like everything was exactly how it was supposed to be in the world. Like Ricky had always been meant to end up here, locked tight in Ever's arms, making out with him on a dance floor. An invisible cord threaded out from his heart, winding around them and cinching tight. It tethered him to the man in front of him. Nothing would be the same after this.

I can't go back.

Everett's tongue slipped through the seam of his lips— taking. And Ricky loved every minute of it. He kissed Everett back, hiking his leg a little higher, using all his strength to hold on to the man.

Everett's hand slipped the rest of the way down his ass, grasping a handful as he thrusted his hips. The teeth of Ricky's pants zipper cut into his own cock. Pain and pleasure melded together in a heady mix.

Ricky pulled back. Everett framed his face with both hands like a man possessed, yet he was searching Ricky's face like he expected Ricky to stop this. To say it was too much.

It wasn't fucking close to enough.

"Let's get a room at the hotel next door."

26

RICKY

Ricky's heart pounded like a freight train. He was sure Everett could hear it as they approached the hotel room door. He drew in a breath, his chest tight. His skin taut with awareness. Everett slipped the key card into the door. The light barely flashed green before a big hand grabbed his, tugging him inside.

Ricky crashed against Everett in a tangle of lips and teeth and tongue. This wasn't like any kiss they'd shared before. It was rough and raw—so full of need Ricky could taste it in each swipe of Everett's sweet tongue. Ricky met his frantic energy with his full force.

He clawed at Everett's clothes, not caring when a few buttons popped off. He needed to get Ever naked. Feel his skin against his own.

Need choked him. Strong, capable hands freed him of his own shirt, tossing it on the floor. Everett bit Ricky's bottom lip harder than usual. Every nerve ending inside Ricky lit up, firing alive and stilling all at the same time. Peace wound around him, thick and heady like a fog. He groaned and tipped his head to the side.

Everett's fingers deftly undid the button of Ricky's jeans and opened them enough to slide his hand inside as he kissed Ricky's neck.

"Fuck—Ever—"

Everett's teeth grazed over the sensitive flesh before sucking on the same spot he'd bitten earlier in the bar. Ricky's eyes rolled up as his knees buckled. He gripped Everett's shoulders for stability.

Everett pulled away. Cool air replaced the warmth of his body. A feeling of loss shot through Ricky.

"Fuck, I can't wait." Everett cursed and dropped to his knees, shoving Ricky's pants the rest of the way down his legs.

He didn't have time to step out from his jeans before Everett's mouth enveloped him. Light eyes filled with so much heat locked with Ricky's as his cock slid in and out of Everett's hot, wet mouth.

"Ever!" Ricky gasped. "Your mouth feels so good."

Everett dragged his teeth over the tip. Ricky bucked his hips, reaching down to grab hold of Everett's hair.

"That's it, baby. Take what you need," Everett encouraged. "And make it hurt."

Ricky blinked down at him and then thrust.

Everett hummed around his cock. Pleasure coursed through him like a dam bursting, filling every part of him with boiling lust. His cock slid to the back of Everett's throat. Ever swallowed.

"Fuck! You're gonna make me come."

Everett's hot mouth sucked him back down with a vengeance, working him until he was right at the edge.

A string of unintelligible words and groans fell from

Ricky's lips. His mind spun, caught up in a cyclone of ecstasy as he drove his hips deeper.

Everett licked his tip. "You taste so fucking good. But you don't get to come right now."

Ricky blinked his eyes open. *When did I close them?*

Everett stood in front of him, pulling his shoes and the rest of his clothes off, and tossing them in the pile with Ricky's.

Ricky drank him in—really let himself look this time, savoring every inch of lean muscle.

Everett backed farther into the room and sat on the bed. His erection bobbed with his movements.

"Come here." Everett patted the white comforter he sat on.

Ricky stepped out of his shoes and pants before he walked forward, exposed and filled with desire at the same time. He sat down, leaning in immediately to kiss Everett. Ricky palmed Everett's thigh. Electric arousal jolted through him. He jerked his hand away.

"Nervous?" Everett asked.

Ricky shrugged.

"Answer me." Everett's voice deepened.

"A little."

"We don't have to do anything you don't want to do. This is for you." Everett smiled. "And me. Fuck, you're a fantasy come to life."

Satisfaction whirled in his rib cage. "I want to. I want to experience this with you. I just . . ."

You perverted little—

"Don't." Everett's voice cut through the noise in his head, quieting his father's voice.

"Don't what?"

"Go wherever you were. Overthink this. Stay here with me." Everett slid his hand up Ricky's chest, collaring his neck and squeezing just enough that Ricky perked up, his every cell attuned to Everett's lips. His knees would have buckled again if he'd been standing.

What did it mean that he liked when Everett took control?

"Tell me what you're thinking."

Ricky sighed and closed his eyes.

"Don't hide from me, miy lev." Everett's words were gentle though his hand held firm.

Ricky kept his eyes closed as he confessed his raw truths. "I like when you're in control and that . . . makes me uncomfortable."

"You think it makes you weak?"

Ricky nodded.

"Why?"

Ricky opened his eyes. "Because a man should always be strong. In control."

"Who says?" Everett asked, no judgment in his tone.

Ricky's brows drew together. "Most of society."

Everett nodded. "Do you think I'm weak?"

"No." Ricky shook his head.

"I've given up that control. I've bottomed. I've sucked your dick. Isn't that, by your definition, making me weak or less than a man?"

"No. You're not—it doesn't count for you."

"Why? Because I'm gay? That gives me a pass?" Everett laughed but there was no mirth in it as his hand fell to his lap. "By society's rules that also makes me less than a man. I'm a queen, an abomination of nature to some."

Ricky winced at the truth in his words. "I know it doesn't make sense."

"Explain it to me. What are these qualifications of being a man?"

Ricky looked around the sparse hotel room. This was not how this night was supposed to go.

"Talk to me," Everett pressed.

"I can't be weak again."

"What is weak to you?"

"Giving in to emotion."

"All humans have emotions. It's a literal part of our makeup and what helps keep us safe and alive. In order to be a 'man,' you're saying we all need to pretend like none of that exists—except anger, right?"

Ricky shifted on the bed. "I don't know how to put it into words. I just know there are things I should do and things I shouldn't."

"Why, though? What are you afraid of?"

Ricky paced around the room. "I don't know, okay? I never took time to think about it and make a list."

"If you ever took the time to examine such a list, I think it might be helpful. You might see that all the traits you try to shove away have nothing to do with being a man and every-thing with not being like a woman."

Ricky snapped his attention to Everett. "What?"

"Any man who subscribes to this notion, believes that being a man means never being emotional unless it's anger. Never submitting in any aspect of life because whose job is it to submit? The women, right? So gay men are the equivalent of a pervert or a woman, according to them. That's why our insults are always feminine. Bitch, bastard, pussy, cunt—they all invoke the same bullshit assumption that women are weak and a real man would be nothing like a woman."

Ricky shook his head. "No, I—"

"I know you don't dislike women. I know you loved your mother. I can see how you feel about Nova and Mrs. Emerson. But you've internalized all the shit Donald taught you."

"This has nothing to do with that fucker."

Everett held his palms up. "Who else are you trying to prove yourself too?"

"To—this—fuck!" Ricky's hands trembled. *Am I trying to prove myself to someone?* "He told me my mother would have hated me if she knew I felt the way I did about you."

"He lied."

Ricky closed his eyes. It sounded too good to be true. He wished he could believe it.

"Your mother loved you."

"She did. But she was also really religious."

"Or your father saw a point of vulnerability and exploited it because he's the worst kind of asshole."

Ricky sat back on the bed with a sigh. "There was a couple who once lived across the street from us before you moved next door. Two men with a son a year older than me."

Everett's warm hand slipped into Ricky's in silent support.

"They came over and introduced themselves. When the man mentioned he was married to the other man, I was confused. I had no idea two men could get married. Never seen it anywhere in my life. I looked at my mom and her usual friendly demeanor changed to the same stiff disposition she had whenever we heard my dad's car pull into the driveway."

Everett's thumb rubbed up and down Ricky's hand. "Did anything else happen?"

"She waved goodbye politely. When we got in the house, she told me in no uncertain terms to not play with their son."

Everett released a deep breath. "I'm sorry. That had to be confusing. Maybe she had her reasons though? Maybe she knew your dad would find out and give you a hard time about it."

Ricky's lungs seized. Surely not. That couldn't be why . . . could it? But his mother hadn't harbored a hateful bone in her body. She'd always been focused on the good in people—that was part of the problem with her and Donald. No matter what that man did to her, she stayed, partly in fear and partly due to her inability to go out and support them while she was sick. But even before her diagnosis, she'd stayed despite the beatings, the neglect, the infidelity, and the alcoholism.

"Do you think so?" Ricky asked, afraid to hope.

"I do. Your mom loved you. I don't think you being with a man would have changed that . . . but, either way, she's gone. You can't keep living in this self-imposed prison. She wouldn't want that for you."

Ricky nodded.

"Do you want me to draw you a bath? Or start the shower?" Everett asked, his patient gaze searching his.

Ricky sucked in a fortifying breath and let it out. "I want you to show me what it would be like."

"You have to be more specific than that."

"To be yours."

Everett slid his hand around him and hugged him tight against his chest. "If you were mine, I'd hold you. I'd make sure you were really okay. And let you know that we didn't have to do anything physical. We can just lie here, watch some shitty TV, smoke some good weed, and relax."

"And if I was yours, I would want you to kiss me and touch me, and show me everything I've been missing out on since you were taken from my life."

Twin grey orbs darkened—a lunar eclipse of lust swallowing up any doubt they were not on the same page. "You want that?"

"I want everything you're willing to give me."

Everett's mouth slanted over his. Smooth lips teased his own apart. Everett's hot tongue slid into his mouth. Ricky sucked, eliciting a groan from his lover.

This wasn't like before—their deep hunger had been tamped down and melded into something hot and sensual. Deepening the kiss, Ever climbed over Ricky, urging him onto his back. They crawled up the bed, never breaking the kiss. Everett's hands were everywhere at once. Roaming palms smoothed down Ricky's shoulders and over his hips. Ever grounded his cock against Ricky's. Blood rushed, making Ricky's ears ring. His dick was hard and aching.

"So fucking perfect," Everett said, kissing him gently before climbing off the bed. He picked up his jeans and pulled out a couple packets from his pocket and discarded the pants once again.

The bed sunk under Everett's weight as he settled between Ricky's spread legs.

"If you were mine, I'd use this lube to jerk you off." Everett dropped a condom wrapper on the bed before tearing the other packet with his teeth.

He squeezed out some of the clear liquid and smoothed the lube over Ricky's cock as well as his own.

Ricky hissed at the contact, ultra-sensitive and ready to combust.

"Don't you fucking come until I tell you." Everett's half-lidded eyes glazed over in pleasure. His lips parted with a breathy moan as he enveloped both of them with his hand.

Ricky sat up enough to slide his hand down, cupping Everett's balls.

Everett gasped. "Fuck, you're gonna make me come."

"That's what I want," Ricky confessed as a wave of certainty crashed over him.

Ricky wanted to bring Everett just a fraction of the pleasure he'd given him. To make him come so undone, they wouldn't be sure where one ended and the other began.

"I'd rather come inside you," Everett said, something desperate in his tone.

Ricky flushed as white-hot heat speared him. His ass clenched in anticipation. The thought of Everett fucking him, coming inside him had more pre-cum dripping down the tip of his dick.

"Do it," Ricky gasped.

"You want me to fuck you?"

"Fuck me like I'm yours." Ricky slid his fingers through Everett's hair, dragging him down to capture his lips while his other hand worked his lover's cock.

A warm, wet finger circled Ricky's asshole. He clenched involuntarily.

"Just relax. I got you." Everett's voice was like a balm for Ricky's anxiety.

One finger teased the rim around and around as he sucked Ricky's tongue. Lost in the pleasure and anticipation, Ricky's muscles clenched, and wanton need erased the rest of his inhibitions. Everett slid his finger slowly inside. In and out, he worked Ricky's ass.

"Breathe." Everett pumped his fist over Ricky's dick and added another lubed finger, stretching him farther.

Pleasure cascaded in a waterfall of tingly sensation from the tip of Ricky's head down to his toes. Need coursed through him. "Ever!"

"You're doing so good. Taking my fingers like that. You're so fucking sexy." Everett added a third.

Ricky's hips thrust off the bed. Whimpers and moans fell from his lips like he was a man possessed. His eyes rolled up. "Please."

"Please what?" Everett asked.

"More."

"You want my cock, don't you, miy lev? You want me to

fuck you like you're mine." The wrapper to the condom crinkled as Everett opened it. He slid the latex on and then the fat head of Everett's penis lined up with Ricky's asshole. Ricky released a deep breath, trying to relax his muscles.

Everett squirted more lube on his cock, rocking his hips so the tip moved in and out, teasing Ricky to no end.

Ricky gasped. A sliver of discomfort at the tightness pulsed through him as a burn started. There was no way Everett was going to fit.

"Relax, baby. You're doing so good." Everett kissed his mouth. His hand still slowly jacked Ricky off.

Pleasure once again overrode every thought. Ricky sucked in ragged breaths. There was no going back after this.

"Shhh, just breathe with me." Everett gripped the back of Ricky's head, forcing him to look in his eyes as his chest expanded with an inhale. Ricky matched his breaths with Everett's, inhaling and exhaling in sync. Everett didn't move, holding his tip just inside the opening of Ricky's asshole.

"That's it. You're doing so good. Just keep breathing like that. This is the hard part, and then it's gonna feel so good." Everett rocked his hips, slow but firm.

A sliver of pain had Ricky wanting to clench, but he forced himself to relax and breathe through it.

Everett's cock slid in, giving him a satisfied, full feeling.

"That's it, baby. You did it," Everett praised, thrusting his hips gently in and out, driving Ricky higher and higher. Every drive of his hips hit a spot just a couple inches in, sending pulses of pleasure rippling through him.

"Ungh." Ricky panted, clinging to Everett's shoulders as he stared into his eyes. "Fuck. That feels so good."

"Good. Think you can take a little more?" Everett asked.

Ricky nodded, reminding his body to relax through the sensations building in his groin. Everett thrust his hips a little harder, his attentive gaze locked on Ricky the whole time. Ricky's erect cock grazed Everett's stomach, Everett's soft skin teasing the leaking tip.

"You like it?" Everett asked with a little more bass in his voice.

"Yes." Ricky's blunt nails dug into Everett's shoulders as he fought off his orgasm.

"You asked me to make you mine." Everett brushed his thumb over Ricky's jaw. He drove his hips forward, claiming another couple inches. "That's it. You're almost there." Everett pulled out a little before driving deeper.

"Fuck, fuck, fuck." Ricky tensed, the impending orgasm growing in strength. He wouldn't be able to hold it off for long.

Everett thrust forward gently, holding Ricky's legs out until he was fully seated inside Ricky. Chest heaving, Ricky gave a groan of pleasure as Everett's balls slapped against his ass.

Ever licked his lips. "If you were mine, I'd tell you how fucking perfect you are, laid out under me like this. Taking everything I have to give to you."

"So do it. Make me yours." Ricky grasped Everett's arm that held one of his legs up.

"Unh." Ricky grunted. "You feel so good."

Everett smirked. "Thing is, Ricardo, you're already mine."

He squeezed his hand around Ricky's cock, jerking him harder and faster, matching the pace with his thrusts. Ricky couldn't breathe; he couldn't speak. All he could do was experience the onslaught of pleasure. Connecting like this, in a way they'd never done before, woke up a part of him that had never seen the light of day.

Me.

This is me.

This is us.

Ricky reached up, holding on to Everett's shoulders as the man fucked him closer and closer to his pleasure.

"I'm hanging on by a fucking thread. Come for me, whenever you're ready. Come all over us," Everett commanded.

Ricky grabbed Everett's face, kissing him hard as tingles rushed down his spine, gathering in a yearning mess of pressure, building and building before he exploded—shattering into a million pieces. There was no way he could be put back together the same way ever again. Something within him had changed forever. Ricky came so hard, his vision darkened. Hot spurts of his cum sprayed over both their stomachs.

Everett's movements became stiff as he jerked above Ricky. His face contorted into an expression of pleasured agony. Everett's mouth swallowed Ricky's shout. More of Everett's weight settled on Ricky as his cock pulsed in Ricky's ass.

Slowly, carefully, Everett drew out. Ricky winced at the loss. Everett rolled off him, using a tissue to take care of the condom and throw it in the waste bin. He lay next to Ricky, chest heaving as he spread out his arm. Ricky snuggled into him, the slickness of his cum drying on his abs.

Everett gripped his chin, tilting it to kiss him ever so gently. His forehead rested against Ricky's.

"You've always been mine, miy lev. And I've always been yours."

The conviction in Everett's words hit Ricky like a freight train. He opened his mouth and closed it.

After all, he couldn't argue with the truth.

27

———

EVERETT

Everett slipped back inside the hotel room, balancing a coffee in each hand and with a bag of breakfast sandwiches hanging from his teeth. The room still smelled of sex. He loved it. He'd had the urge to skip to the café down the street but had managed to refrain from doing so —barely. The smile on his face was uncontainable. Ricky Emerson was *his*. Everett couldn't possibly feel any more joy than he did.

Everett slid back into bed, setting his coffee down on the side table and then dropping the bag of sandwiches in his lap before he trailed his finger over Ricky's forehead, moving one of his dark brown curls out of the way.

Ricky blinked his eyes open and groaned before shutting them. "What time is it?"

"Nine. We still have two whole hours before checkout."

"Then I can go back to sleep." Ricky grabbed his pillow and burrowed deeper into the sheets.

Everett chuckled and moved Ricky's coffee in front of his face.

Ricky sniffed and opened his eyes again. "Is that coffee?"

"Just the way you like it."

Ricky groggily sat up, rubbing his eyes, and leaned back against the headboard before reaching for the drink and taking a sip. "Thank you."

Everett motioned to the bag in his lap. "I got breakfast sandwiches too. Egg and sausage or bacon and egg."

"You spoil me." Ricky smirked, taking another sip.

"You're so easy to spoil." Everett leaned over and kissed the side of Ricky's mouth.

Ricky's dark eyes flicked to Everett, back to his coffee, and then to Everett once more.

"What?"

"Nothing." Ricky drank again.

"Ask."

Ricky swallowed. "Is it always like that?"

"Sex?" Wait, Nova had gone on and on about Ricky's sexual history with women around the seacoast. He wasn't a virgin. "You mean with a man?"

Ricky nodded.

"I have to say, being intimate with you is better than any other sexual encounter I've had in my life."

"Because it's us," Ricky added with a cocky quirk of his lips.

"I think so. Speaking of, I'm clean. I got tested a month and a half ago. And I hadn't been with anyone for months before that," Everett said.

"Me too."

"Then we're good."

Ricky shifted on the bed. "Is it normal to be a little sore after?"

The corner of Everett's mouth tipped up. "Yeah. I tried to

go gentle. A little soreness is normal. But if it lasts or gets worse, let me know, okay?"

"Okay . . . do you normally . . . are you usually . . ."

"I've had my dick in your ass. I think we're safely in the you-can-ask-me-anything phase of this relationship," Everett teased.

Ricky snorted, a slight blush rising to his cheeks. "Do you always top?"

"Mainly, but not always. I'm a vers, which is to say I'm versatile. Whatever fits the mood, I guess."

Ricky nodded wordlessly.

"Do you have to rush back to Shattered Cove today? There are still some things I'd like to show you. But it would mean a little more travel and getting home late."

"Things? Like how to suck your cock?" Ricky laughed.

Everett joined him. "That does sound mighty appealing, but I meant places. There are some fun wintery things to do in the area if you're up for it."

"I'm free. I texted my mom and let her know I wouldn't make it for family dinner tonight."

Excitement bubbled up in Everett's chest. "Awesome. Give me a few minutes to make some reservations and we're good to go." Everett grabbed his phone from the table. He opened the lock screen and tapped the right app. A few more clicks and he set his cell back on the table.

"Done?" Ricky asked, placing his cup on the table on the other side of the bed.

"Yeah. But we don't have to rush. First thing is brunch at eleven thirty down the street." Everett grabbed his coffee and took a drink.

Ricky smirked. "So we have time for another round?"

Everett's smile was back full force. "I think I can be persuaded."

"I'll have to work on my oral argument, then." Ricky leaned in, kissing Everett.

Fuuuuck. Would he ever get used to this? When Ricky was in his arms, it felt like the missing piece of the puzzle of Everett's life had been found. Life had pulled them apart, but maybe fate had brought them back together.

28

RICKY

Ricky's stomach lurched to his throat as a fresh cloud of snow dropped from the evergreen trees above. The buzz of the snowmobile's engine partially drowned out his yelp of excitement. Everett's arms tightened around his waist.

"You okay?" Ricky yelled to be heard over the engine and the helmets.

"Didn't know you'd turned into such a daredevil," Everett shouted back.

Another snowmobile zoomed past them with Everett's friends onboard, yelling and waving as they went.

"Come on. We're almost there." Everett pointed to the spot where the trail split.

Ricky cranked the gas and Everett's hold around his stomach tightened even more. Everett's strong thighs pressed against the outside of Ricky's. The notable bulge against his ass was unmistakable. Adrenaline mixed with lust. Moments from their morning flashed in his mind. Everett's hot mouth on him, cleaning up in the shower . . .

"Fuck it." Ricky braked, bringing the snowmobile to a stop.

"What's wrong?" Everett asked.

Ricky got off and waved Everett forward. "Thought you'd like to have a turn driving."

Everett tipped his head, his helmet flashing in the fading sunlight that dappled the snow-covered forest.

"Why are you smirking?" Everett asked skeptically.

"You can't see my fucking face. How do you know I'm smirking?" Ricky laughed, adjusting his helmet.

"Because I know you." Everett slid forward, gripping the handlebars.

"Yeah, you do." Ricky climbed on the back, wrapping his arms around Everett's body. His cock nestled against Everett's ass this time.

Everett pressed the gas and continued driving them down the wooded path. Ricky waited a few minutes, letting Everett settle in and acclimate to the trail before he tore off his gloves and stuck them in his pockets. His hands slipped under Everett's coat to the snow pants that buttoned at Everett's waist.

The snowmobile jerked to the side before righting.

"What are you doing?" Everett asked.

Ricky leaned in, undoing Everett's jeans inside the snow gear, and slipped his hand inside them to palm Everett's dick.

"I'm gonna make you come while you drive us through the woods. So you better be quick or your friends might get to see you in an entirely different light." Ricky smiled to himself as he worked Everett's erection in his hand, getting it harder with each stroke.

Ricky braced one hand on Everett's chest for balance and squeezed his thighs against Everett's.

"Fuck." Everett's head tipped back for only a moment

before he straightened, keeping the snowmobile at an even pace down the trail.

"That's it, Ever. You feel how hard you are? I guess you like a little danger too. How does it feel? Pretty good, judging by the amount of cum dripping out of your cock." Ricky jerked him slowly at first, pumping him with the intention of teasing Everett out of his mind.

Everett hit the gas, the snowmobile gaining speed. Ricky switched up his pace too, his hand fucking Everett harder and faster.

The vehicle slowed as Everett's chest heaved. Ricky ground his cock against Everett's ass as he slowed his jerks.

Everett growled. "You're driving me crazy."

"You control the speed. You want it rough and fast? You better hit the gas, baby."

Everett gunned it. Ricky held on tighter, fighting back a smile as excitement and hunger for more urged him on. How far could he push Everett? When would he snap?

Ricky pumped his fist, the smooth, velvety texture of Everett's big cock a contrast to his calloused hands.

Momentum pulled Ricky forward, mashing his body even closer with Everett's as the snowmobile lurched to a stop. Everett was off and grabbing Ricky by his coat, hauling him to his knees before Ricky could blink.

"You're a bad fucking boy, Ricky."

"Maybe you should punish me, then," Ricky goaded, staring at Everett's cock jutting out from his open pants.

"Maybe you should finish what you started."

Ricky swallowed. His own cock pulsed at the idea. He wanted to taste Everett, drive Everett as wild as he'd driven Ricky.

Ricky unsnapped his helmet and tossed it on the ground.

Everett reached for his own helmet.

"No—"

Everett tipped his head to the side in question.

"Leave it on."

"You want this?" Everett asked.

"I want to suck your cock more than I want to breathe right now."

"Good. Because you won't be breathing unless I let you." Everett gripped the back of Ricky's head, lining his cock with his lips.

Ricky licked the tip, the sweet, salty mix of pre-cum exploding on his taste buds like the most potent aphrodisiac. Fuck, he tasted good. Ricky lapped at the tip, dragging his tongue over the vein that ran to the base of the shaft and cupped Everett's balls with his hand, massaging.

Everett groaned as he rocked his hips. Ricky opened wide, sucking down every inch of Everett's cock. He focused above, a part of him wishing he'd told Everett to take the helmet off so he could see exactly what he was doing to him. Another part was even more turned on by the forbidden element the helmet added. Ricky could be sucking anyone off. It could be a stranger he'd run into. But it wasn't. It was Everett fucking Popova under that helmet. And he was the only man Ricky had ever gotten down on his knees for.

Ricky hummed around the cock in his mouth as Everett's grip on his hair tightened. Pinpricks of pain needled his scalp, only adding to the rightness of the moment. Everett thrust his hips deeper, hitting the back of Ricky's throat.

"If you feel like you're gonna gag, try swallowing around my cock. Relax your throat," Everett guided him.

Ricky took a deep breath through his nose and did as his lover instructed. Everett pulled back and then pushed back in, this time making it even farther, blocking Ricky's airway. Everett didn't move back. Instead, he pushed deeper, hitting so deep Ricky was sure the man's dick was halfway to his stomach.

Ricky's lungs burned, needing oxygen. One hand continued to work Everett's balls as his other gripped onto his thigh.

"That's it. You take my cock so well. So obedient, down on your knees like this, at my mercy." Everett pulled back and Ricky sucked in a lungful of fresh oxygen before Everett began fucking his mouth, slow but deep. Ricky fought off the urge to gag, trying to swallow.

"Fuck. Your throat is so tight. You're gonna make me come."

Tingles of excitement and arousal surged through Ricky. He wanted that. He wanted to make Everett happy. Bring him pleasure. Make him come harder than he ever had before. Make this a memory he'd never forget.

Ricky was overwhelmed with emotion. Tears blurred his vision. He slammed his eyes closed, keeping them at bay.

Everett continued to use his mouth. In. Out. Breathe. In. Out. Breathe. Over and over Everett's cock slid in, building up speed. Ricky's teeth grazed the tip as Everett pulled all the way out before driving his hips forward again.

A moan fell from Everett's lips. Grunts and groans filled the snowy forest. There was something so magical about connecting physically in such a serene place.

Everett grunted. "Fuck, I'm coming. And you're gonna swallow every drop. Finish what you started."

Ricky wiggled his tongue on the underside of Everett's shaft as he continued to fuck his mouth. Everett's cock jerked before sweet, hot cum came spurting out into Ricky's mouth. He swallowed it down, licking greedily, lapping up everything.

Everett tugged him back by the hair. Ricky released his cock with an audible *pop*.

He was pulled to his feet at the same time that Everett took off his helmet and let it drop to the ground.

"Good fucking boy." Everett slammed his mouth over Ricky's in a hungry kiss.

Ricky grabbed the back of his head, grasping on to Everett like he was trying to hold on to this moment.

The buzz of another engine drifted from the distance, breaking their connection. Everett's lips were swollen and shiny, his eyes glassy with satisfaction. His hair was sweaty and tousled from the helmet. His pants were still undone. He looked like a sex god.

Everett zipped his pants back up as the vehicle got closer. He was put together a moment before Bryan drove over to them.

"You okay?" Bryan asked, looking them up and down.

"Yeah, just took a quick break," Everett answered.

Bryan looked between them before a small knowing smile appeared on his face. "Right. Well, Chris has the fire going and the grill fired up. Dinner will be ready in about fifteen. See you soon." Bryan waved and got back on his snowmobile, driving in a circle before heading back the way he'd come.

Everett turned to Ricky. "That was hot."

Ricky laughed. "It certainly was."

"I want to return the favor."

"We don't want to keep your friends waiting. Besides, I'm starving. And if we're keeping score, you've given me more orgasms. That's just for you." Ricky grabbed his helmet off the ground along with Everett's and handed it to him.

Everett took it. "I'm not keeping score. I just like to make you come."

"Makes two of us, then." Ricky hopped on the front, starting the snowmobile.

Everett climbed on behind him, wrapping his strong arms around Ricky's waist. "But later . . ."

"Later is definitely a possibility." Ricky laughed as he drove them out of the woods and through a field before turning towards the log cabin they'd started their snowmobile adventure at.

They parked next to Bryan and Chris's other snowmobile, removing their helmets as Chris came onto the porch.

"Thought you two got lost." Chris smirked.

"Leave them alone." Bryan playfully pushed Chris's shoulder.

Chris laughed. "Alright. Come on. The bratwursts are just coming off the grill. And I've got two cold beers with your names on them, or some hot coffee with Irish cream. Pick your poison."

"It all sounds good to me." Everett turned back as if to check on Ricky.

"I'll take you up on that beer." Ricky walked up the steps.

A roaring fire glowed from a stone and concrete fire pit surrounded by a comfy-looking C-shaped patio couch.

"Can I help with anything?" Ricky asked.

Chris shook his head. "Oh, no. Have a seat. Beer's in the snow off the side there. Hot coffee on the counter inside. All the food fixings are here except—"

"Brats are here too." Bryan carried a tray of freshly grilled sausages over to the long built-in counter on the side of the porch.

"Wow. You really went all out for us. Thanks, man," Everett said.

Bryan waved him off. "Pshhh, please. You just gave us an excuse to have a winter barbecue. It's been too long since we've had company. Help yourself. There's sautéed onions and peppers, and buns for the sausages. A few other things too."

Chris grabbed a few paper plates and handed one to Bryan and another to Ricky, and extended one towards Everett.

Ricky grabbed it instead. "I got it."

"Sure." Chris headed over to the food.

"I'll get the food if you want to grab me a beer?" Ricky asked.

"Definitely." Everett turned to the back of the porch, reaching into the snow for their drinks.

Ricky filled two plates with their meals and brought them back, taking the seat next to Everett. Bryan and Chris sat opposite them on the couch, the fire between them.

Satisfied groans filled the air.

"Damn, this is good," Ricky complimented the boys.

"The bratwursts are from the farm down the road. They raise their own pigs and meat stock." Chris pointed in the distance.

"Ricky's family does a little of that too." Everett glanced at him before taking another big bite of his dinner.

"Oh really?" Bryan asked.

"Yeah. My parents run a farm in Shattered Cove."

"Do you also work the farm?" Chris asked.

Bryan elbowed him in the gut.

Chris laughed.

"What?" Ricky asked.

"Ignore my husband. He has a thing for shirtless farmers." Bryan's expression changed like he was trying to look unimpressed, but the small tilt of his lips gave his true affection away.

"We all have our fantasies, don't we?" Chris took a sip of his coffee.

"True," Everett agreed.

Ricky perked up and squeezed Everett's knee. "What's yours?"

Everett licked his lips and set his beer down on the tabletop built around the edge of the fire pit. "Well, I must admit I have a thing for beekeepers, or maybe just one in particular."

A flutter of nervous excitement spun around Ricky's belly.

"Oh, is that what you do? You keep bees?" Chris asked, setting his hand on his husband's thigh.

"Yeah, me and my brother," Ricky answered.

"Oh, you must have a good relationship with him, then. Working with family can be the best or worst thing depending on the people and the day." Bryan laughed and sat back in the seat, lifting his arm to wrap around Chris.

Ricky laughed too. "That's very true. Nah, he's a good guy. We tussle like any brothers but I know he has my back no matter what."

Ricky swallowed as the two men across from him carried on the conversation, poking and teasing one another. Everett sat relaxed next to him, empty dinner plate in his lap. Would Roman and his family back Ricky up if he wanted to date Everett though? The glimmer of hope that glowed at the thought was chased by the familiar fear of the last time someone found out. Donald's hatred. The pain of his fists and steel-toe boots.

A warm arm wrapped around him, pulling Ricky closer. He blinked, trying to clear the painful fog of memories that had descended.

Everett leaned over and kissed his cheek. "You okay?"

Ricky flicked a glance to the other men on the porch as the last of the sunlight faded over the blue snowcapped mountains in the distance. They were kissing and whispering to each other without a care in the world who saw them, just as they had been at the café. Out and proud. *Will I ever be able to do that? Can I give that to Everett?*

He turned back to the man next to him who was waiting patiently for an answer.

"Am I okay?" He shook his head. "I don't know what I am anymore. I just know that this is the only place in the world I want to be at this moment. With you. Wherever you are."

Everett leaned in, kissing him gently before pressing his forehead against his. "I love you, miy lev. And I don't need you to say it back. I just need you to know, I'm in this for you if that's what you want."

Ricky pulled back, needing to see the conviction and depth of feeling in Everett's gaze. Everett's honesty slammed through him, weaving around every jagged piece, licking over old scars and new alike with devastating and unflinching love. Everett had meant every word.

Ricky wanted to say the words back—because they were true. Ricky was falling in love with Everett—or maybe he'd always been. But could he really give Everett what he needed? He wanted to. And he'd try—he'd come so far already, hadn't he? He could do this. For Everett, he'd do anything.

Instead of replying, Ricky leaned in and kissed Everett again, letting his body do the talking.

Everett deserved more than promises he wasn't sure he was capable of keeping—despite how much he wanted to.

After all, words without action were meaningless.

29

RICKY

icky jogged up the steps to Everett's apartment with a spring in his step. He knocked.

The door opened and Everett smiled back at him. "Hey, handsome. How was the workout with your client?"

"It was good." Ricky flicked a glance down the steps to the snowy sidewalk. Someone passed by but didn't linger.

When he focused back on Everett, it was impossible not to see the hurt flash in his eyes. Ricky was doing a shitty job at whatever this was between them. But he had to figure this out before confronting his family. They deserved that at least.

He lifted the bags of takeout in his hand by way of apology. "I brought dinner."

"Smells like my favorite." Everett stepped aside.

"Because it is." Ricky entered the apartment and slipped off his shoes.

He leaned in and kissed Everett in greeting. He might not have been perfect, but he could give Everett this.

Ricky padded to the kitchen and set the bags on the counter.

Everett opened a cupboard and pulled out two plates. "Beer? Or vodka?"

"I think it's a beer kind of night."

Everett plucked two from the refrigerator and popped the tops. He grabbed two forks before setting it all at the small table by the window in the tiny kitchen.

Ricky opened the food and dished out their plates before carrying them over to take a seat across from Everett. They moved in sync, a dance they'd come to know pretty well these last couple weeks since their weekend away.

"Thanks for getting dinner," Everett said, digging his fork into some pork lo mein.

"You're welcome." Ricky grabbed a crab rangoon and bit into it. The creamy filling spilled out on his tongue. "Mmmm."

"Good?"

"Not as good as your cream filling." Ricky winked.

Everett barked out a laugh and shook his head.

They ate for a few minutes before Everett asked, "I was thinking about trying out Atlantis for dinner this week. I kind of miss Atlas's cooking from when I stayed at the Lighthouse Inn."

"He's a great chef. All the pasta is house-made, fresh. And his vodka sauce is to die for," Ricky said before stuffing another bite of food in his mouth.

"So you're okay if I make reservations for Friday?"

"Sure. I can fend for myself for one night. It's not like I haven't before." Other than Sunday dinners with his family, he'd spent just about every night with Everett since they'd gone to Concord.

"I meant a reservation for the two of us." Everett set his fork down.

The sliver of panic that threaded through Ricky just added to his guilt. He was holding Everett back. What if he was never able to push past this fear?

"Guys have dinner as friends all the time, if that's what you're worried about. I don't see how it's different than going to the gym together." Everett lifted the beer to his lips and took a sip.

Ricky wiped his hands on a napkin and blew out a breath.

"Let's talk about this. Can you tell me what you're thinking right now? No judgment," Everett pressed.

"I don't want to hurt you, and I know I am. I want to be the guy that goes out in public and doesn't give a shit who's around when we spend time together . . ."

"But . . ."

Ricky sniffed and stared into the patient eyes across from him. "But my whole body locks up at the thought." He pressed his hand to his chest. "My chest gets tight and my heart races. I feel panicked."

Everett reached out to take his other hand from its spot resting on the table. "Thank you for sharing that with me."

Ricky scoffed.

"What?" Everett asked, the hard lines of his brows pulled down in question.

"How can you be so understanding?"

Everett took another drink of his beer before answering, "My last boyfriend was in the closet too."

Ricky tamped down the burst of jealousy that burned in his gut. It wasn't like he hadn't been with other people. He'd never been the jealous sort—not until Everett.

"We saw each other only in private. And it stayed that way for almost a year. I know better than most that for someone to come out, it has to be because they want to for themselves." He shrugged. "I was just hoping that he'd want that too."

Ricky squeezed Everett's hand, trying to lend some comfort to what was obviously a sore subject for Everett.

You don't know what you're asking of me. Everett's words from that day outside the honey store replayed in Ricky's head.

"You're not with him now, so I'm guessing it didn't work out the way you'd hoped?"

Everett shook his head. His eyes dropped to his plate. "I finally convinced him to come out with me at night to see a movie. We went to a late showing. Afterwards, we walked to the parking garage. When we got to the car—" Everett's eyes glazed over like he was far away, reliving what had happened. He swallowed.

Ricky held his breath, waiting on pins and needles for the rest of the story.

"I hugged him and thanked him for coming out with me." Everett sat up and cleared his throat like he was uncomfortable. "The next thing I know, I'm shoved away from him and fell on my ass. He yelled, 'Get off me, faggot.' And I was honestly too shocked to realize what was going on."

Ricky's hand fisted in his lap as anger roiled in his belly at how Everett had been treated. Yet Ricky hadn't been the most receptive to Everett in the beginning either. *I was an asshole too.*

"Apparently, there were a few guys in the car park watching us that I hadn't seen. They came over and started shouting at me, asking my boyfriend if he was okay. And then my ex told them he didn't even know me, that I was some random guy who'd followed him to his car."

"What the fuck?" Ricky growled.

Everett pulled his hand out from under his with a wince.

"Sorry," Ricky apologized.

Everett shook his head. "It's okay."

"Tell me you dumped his ass right there and then, spreading all his dirty laundry out," Ricky said.

Everett laughed but there was no humor in it. "Couldn't quite speak after that, with being jumped by two full-grown men plus my ex."

Ricky stood abruptly, needing to move before the rage poured out of him. His chair scraped against the wood floor. "Fucking assholes."

"Ricky—"

"I want to hunt them down and beat them all to shit for you," Ricky fumed.

Everett moved to stand in front of him, grasping Ricky's hands in his own. "I'm okay."

"Yeah, but you might not have been. What if—" *What if they'd killed him? Taken Everett before I got a chance to see him again? To share this with him again?*

A warm hand cupped the side of his jaw, forcing Ricky's attention to Everett's face. "Hey, miy lev, it's over. I'm here, safe and sound. I had a few broken bones and some other injuries but the security at the parking garage saw what happened on their cameras and rushed out to help me."

"So there was video evidence? Those assholes are in jail?" Ricky asked.

"Yes."

Ricky released a breath he hadn't realized he was holding before hugging Everett tight. "I almost lost you before I found you again."

Everett kissed his shoulder. "But you didn't."

"Is that why you wanted to take MMA lessons? To learn how to defend yourself?"

Everett nodded. "Did you think it was to spend more time with you?"

Ricky shrugged as he broke the hug. "Yeah."

"Well, that was a bonus."

"And I was horrible to you when you first came back." *I'm an idiot too.*

"I understand why. Just like I understood why my ex did what he did."

Ricky opened his mouth to argue.

Everett held up a hand. "I didn't say what he did was okay or excusable. I just meant I understand his motivation after taking some time to heal from the situation. I'm sure he's beating himself up way more than I ever could. Hiding who you are eats you up inside. You can never be truly happy unless you live your life as your true authentic self."

Ricky drank in Everett's words. Had he been happy in his life? Sure, there had been moments with his family when he'd felt it. And when he and Everett were alone, Ricky was on top of the world. But maybe there was more out there.

Everett brushed his hand over the back of his neck. "I swore to myself I wouldn't ever date someone in the closet again."

Ricky's heart jumped. Anxiety snaked up his limbs.

"But then I reunited with you and . . . I've been thinking a lot. I don't . . . I don't ever want you to come out for me. That would be wrong of me to ask."

Ricky opened his mouth to say something—anything to keep Everett from ending this.

Everett lifted his hand again. "Just hear me out." He pressed the same palm to Ricky's chest. "I meant it when I said I never stopped caring about you. And right now, this is enough because you've shown growth. I can't promise it will always be because I don't know. And I will let you know if my needs change. But regardless, you should decide what's best for you and live the truth that's yours."

Ricky didn't feel quite at ease as he had earlier, but this

was something. Everett had been honest with where he was at and the least Ricky could do was the same.

"I—I'm trying. I really am. I think with time I can get there."

"It's your journey. So consider any pressure you felt on my end gone. Okay? I realize I might have been pushing a little too much. But it's because I'm so fucking happy with you. I don't want anything to ruin this. I can see a life with you, miy lev." Everett kissed Ricky's lips, soft and sweet. "Maybe even a lifetime. Perhaps a dog and a couple of kids running around."

Ricky stopped breathing.

Everett chuckled, his chest bouncing off Ricky's. "Calm down. I don't mean today—or anytime soon. I'm just trying to let you know I can see a long-term future with you. If you're in this and you want it too."

Ricky closed his eyes. He could see it. Coming home late from the fields in the summer and having Everett there. They'd have dinner on the back deck, dance under the moonlight before going upstairs to make love. *When have I ever used those words?* Normally it was pure fucking. But that didn't quite fit the intimate moments he shared with Everett. Maybe someday a little girl or boy with Everett's beautiful eyes would run around and play with his other nieces and nephew.

He opened his eyes and looked at Everett. "I want you."

Everett smiled. "I'm all yours."

"And I'm not ashamed of you. I need you to know that. This has nothing to do with you and everything to do with me." *Because I'm ashamed of me.*

"Thank you for saying that. I needed to hear it," Everett confessed.

He always seemed so mature and thoughtful. Like not much bothered him. But Ricky didn't miss the flash of pain in Everett's eyes when he did something to keep their relationship a secret. And now he understood why it cut so deep. And he fucking hated himself for putting Everett in this position.

Maybe he'd be better off without me. There was no maybe about it. But Ricky was too fucking selfish to let him go. *Not when I just found him again.*

Everett wasn't giving up on him—so Ricky wouldn't either. He'd try his hardest to figure this out. He could be brave for Ever.

"What did I do to deserve you?" Ricky asked.

Everett's thumb brushed over his lips. "You were you."

"Cocky and hilarious?" Ricky smirked.

Everett kissed him gently. "Cocky? Yes." *Kiss.* "Protective of those you love." *Kiss.* "Intelligent." *Kiss.* "And you have the most beautiful heart, despite your attempts to pretend otherwise. I see it." Everett slanted his mouth over Ricky's. Arousal swirled inside Ricky, lighting him up. Yearning mixed with affection. Need compounded. His heart was flayed open for one terrifying moment, and then he felt euphoric. He was safe with Everett. Everett had seen his worst moments and still he was there—loving Ricky.

"You forgot hung like a fucking horse," Ricky rasped.

Everett's smile lit up his whole face. "Shame on me. That should have been first on the list."

"Obviously," Ricky teased.

"I must have forgotten. Maybe you could show me again, make sure it's cemented in my brain." Everett's smile turned sly.

Ricky sighed dramatically. "I guess there's no other choice. I'll have to make an impression you'll never forget again." He kissed Everett one more time, slipping his tongue inside Everett's mouth.

The hot feel of Everett's tongue tangling with his made his knees weak. Ricky sucked. Everett groaned. And when Ricky pulled away to catch his breath, Everett's gaze was dark and hungry with the same lust that flowed through Ricky's veins.

"Come on. Let's add a few more things to that list." Ricky took Everett's hand and led him to the bedroom where they could shut out the real world and all its problems—for a little while anyway.

30

RICKY

Ricky opened the door for Hope Facility. He'd been here a few times for fundraisers, but never on his own. Nerves had his hands trembling. He gripped the bags of takeout tighter. *Would they take one look at him and know he was attracted to Everett?* He nodded to Marge, one of the many adults present in the common room.

"Hey, sweetie. You looking for someone in particular?" she asked, wiping down a spill of hot cocoa on one of the tables.

Ricky scanned the room. Teens and tweens of all ages puttered about at different tables all set up with different activities such as art, board games, and video games.

"Yeah, Everett Popova. Do you know which way is his office?"

Marge smiled and looked him over once before answering. "Yeah, he's down the hall there." She pointed towards the back of the room. "Fifth door on your right."

"Thank you."

"No problem."

Ricky walked through the room, heading straight for the

hallway, part of him hoping to not run into anyone else, the other part feeling guilty. But this was him trying. Baby steps, right? But would that be enough? *Can I ever be open about how I feel for Everett?*

A plaque hung over Everett's cracked door with his name on it and a few colorful flyers, including his schedule at Hope. Ricky raised his hand and knocked.

"Come in," Everett called.

Ricky stepped in, holding the takeout and drinks he'd brought. Everett's tired eyes lit up and a smile split his face as Ricky closed the door behind him.

"Hey, I didn't expect to see you here." Everett stood, coming around his desk to give Ricky a hug.

Ricky leaned into Everett, inhaling his scent for a hit of calm.

Everett released him and looked to the to-go containers. "What's this?"

"You mentioned last night how busy work has been and how you'd missed lunch. I didn't want that to happen again."

"That was thoughtful of you. Thanks."

Ricky's chest swelled with pride. He wanted to take care of Everett like the man had done for him. "No problem. I thought maybe I could join you?"

Everett sat in one of the two chairs facing his desk rather than his original seat, clearing some of the paperwork out of the way.

"Of course. Sorry, everything's been crazy. We have so many kids who need a home, and although we have some foster volunteers, the background checks are rigorous, which takes time, and then I've got to make sure it's not only safe but a good fit for each kid."

"Are you the only one on this project?" Ricky asked, setting the food on the table along with the drinks before tossing the bag into a trash bin in the corner. He sat next to Everett.

"No. Aaron is as well and one other person. But it's a lot of paperwork, and many interviews with the potential foster family and the kids."

"Understandable. Seems like they couldn't have picked someone better than you for this. I know how much you care about these teens." Ricky reached out and set his hand on Everett's knee.

"I really do." Everett ran a hand through his already disheveled hair, like he'd been doing it all day. The tired rings under his eyes showed how much this had affected his sleep this week. Ricky wished there was something more he could do to support Ever.

"Eat." Ricky stood. After walking behind Everett's chair, he gently massaged the base of his neck and shoulders.

Everett relaxed with a pleasured groan. Ricky's eyes flicked to the closed door.

"Oh my God, you're good at this," Everett said.

Ricky smiled and kissed the top of his head. "Just relax and eat your lunch. You need a break to recharge so you can go back to saving the world, one queer teen at a time."

Everett chuckled. "Thank you."

"I wish there was something more I could do to help."

"This is more than enough. Unless you want to sign up for some volunteer hours? We can always use more hands on deck."

Ricky thought about it. Could he get involved there? Even though he felt like an imposter?

Everett patted his hand. "It's okay. No pressure."

Ricky cleared his throat and dug his thumbs into a knot at the base of Everett's neck.

Everett hissed and leaned his head to the side.

"I'm just not sure how I could be of help here, you know?"

"Marge can always use a few more hands in the kitchen."

Ricky burst out laughing. "Sometimes I forget how much you don't know about me."

"What do you mean?" Everett asked around a mouthful of a sandwich.

"I have been forbidden from kitchens and anything to do with fire. The only exception is when Ma makes ajiaco for me. I help cut up stuff and get the ingredients, but she does the actual cooking." Ricky sat next to Everett once more.

"Why?"

"Let's just say, there have been a few fires."

"A few?" Everett's eyebrows rose.

Ricky shrugged. "It's a weakness of mine."

"I think you just haven't had the right teacher."

Ricky laughed. "Many have tried."

Everett smiled and shook his head before taking the last bite of his sandwich. Ricky dug into his.

They finished up their lunch and Ricky cleaned up.

"This was nice," Everett said, some color back in his cheeks.

Ricky walked over to him, combing his fingers through Everett's messy hair, smoothing it out. "It was."

"Thanks for lunch and the massage."

"You're welcome. We'll finish the massage tonight. I'll get dinner and meet you at your apartment where you can relax and let me take care of everything." Ricky leaned in for a kiss at the corner of Everett's mouth.

"I look forward to it," Everett said as he stepped away.

A knock sounded. Ricky stiffened, his attention darting to the door. Thankfully, it was still closed. Whoever was on the other side was waiting for permission to enter.

Ricky turned back to Everett.

"Give me a minute," Everett called to whoever was outside. He stepped closer to Ricky.

Ricky's heart thudded in his chest.

"I see you trying, and I appreciate that," Everett said before reaching for the door and opening it.

A teen girl stood in the hall, clasping and unclasping her hands together.

"Hey, Mr. P. I—I can come back." She glanced at Ricky and then to her scuffed Converse shoes.

"No need, Bailey. My friend was just leaving," Everett said.

Bailey stepped inside, taking the seat Ricky had occupied before. Ricky moved to the hallway, casting one last look at the young girl. There was something about her. Something in her dark eyes that Ricky recognized.

"Thanks for stopping by," Everett said.

Ricky nodded. "Yeah. No problem. I'll see ya later."

He turned and walked back towards the common room. He looked at the space with new eyes. He'd always known what Hope Facility's purpose was. But something felt different. As he headed toward the front door, fragments of the kids' conversations reached him. Some were laughing. Some were ribbing each other. More still were talking about normal things—sports, the latest TV show they'd seen. These were kids just like any other. So young, full of life, and unique. Yet they all had the same thing in common. They were unwanted by their birth families because of who they were. Emotion clogged Ricky's throat. He knew how that felt. These kids were all braver than him in some ways—in a lot of ways. They deserved someone to love and care for them like he'd found in the Emersons. For someone to accept them the way they were born. He wanted to know Bailey's story.

"Hey, Ricky. What are you doing here?" Aaron's voice had him turning away from the group of kids.

"Uh, I was just bringing a friend lunch but . . ."

"But?" Aaron asked.

"Are all these kids looking for placement?"

Aaron faced the kids and nodded towards the hall Ricky had just come from. "Why don't we talk about it in my office?"

"Okay." Ricky followed him down the hall and into the room.

It wasn't like he could foster someone himself, right? But maybe he could help make a difference. He could take a note from Everett's book and use his past for good.

Maybe Ricky could even learn something.

31

EVERETT

The bitter February wind whipped against Everett as he made his way from Hope Facility to his car. He balanced his messenger bag on his shoulder as he reached into his pocket for the keys. A folded piece of paper stuck under his windshield wiper flapped in the breeze.

What is that? Had one of the kids left him a note?

Everett plucked it off and unlocked the car before climbing inside. His breath came out like a puff of smoke in the chilly vehicle. He slid the key in and started the car, getting the heat blasting before he opened it.

Perverts burn in hell!

Everett stared at the hateful words scribbled across the page. His stomach churned. What if one of the kids at Hope had found this? He crumpled it in his fist and tossed it into the side of his door with the other trash.

His phone rang from his pocket. He pulled it out while the car heated up. He smiled and clicked answer, setting the phone on his dashboard.

"Hey, Mom."

"Hello, sweetie. How—what's wrong?" Lines appeared on her forehead and at the corners of her eyes, just as they did every time she was concerned.

Everett sighed and shook his head. "How do you do that?"

"What?"

"I was smiling. How did you know anything was the matter?"

She waved her hand dismissively. "Because I'm your mother. I birthed you. Got to see every expression that little face made. Don't you think I know when something is up?"

He chuckled. "It's nothing I can't handle. Did you need something? I was about to head home."

"Oh, no. I just wanted to catch up and see how your day was going. And find out if you had any plans to visit now that you're only a drive away instead of a flight?"

"Sure. I can come one of the weekends this month?"

His mother walked through the kitchen, staring off-screen to what Everett knew from experience was the calendar on her wall.

"I have something going on every weekend this month. And I want to be able to see you when you come, make a day of it. How about a weekday?"

"I'm really busy with a project still. I shouldn't take time off."

"As long as you're taking some time for yourself. Remember even superheroes need time to fill their cups."

"Mom," he grumbled. He was the farthest thing from a superhero.

"How about later next month in February? Or March?"

"I'll text you some dates."

"Sounds good. Love you."

"Love you too, Mom."

"Bye." She waved and he ended the call.

Everett set his phone on the console but it rang again.

Nova was calling. He clicked answer and put it on speaker-phone as he shifted into drive.

"Hello?"

"Hey, Everett. How are you doing?"

"Fantastic. You?"

"Uh, well, I know this is last minute, but . . ."

A puff of air left his nose as he shook his head once and pulled out onto the road. "Nova, is this about another pretend boyfriend date?"

"Not exactly. I wanted to know if you'd come to family dinner," she said.

"As your date?" he asked.

"Okay, fine, yes. I'll get you some of the good stuff as repayment—as much as you want. Pretty please?" Nova pleaded.

"Bribery will only get you so far." He laughed, taking a right turn towards town.

"How far will it get me this time?"

Everett rolled over the possibility in his head. He'd thought he would be spending tonight by himself while Ricky went to be with his family. But maybe this way they could spend time together still. Besides, who wouldn't want to have dinner with the Emersons? They were entertaining and interesting as all get out. "I'm not a liar, Nova. I didn't realize your family would think we were seriously dating when I agreed the first time."

"Then don't say you're my date. I've told them it's not serious and we're mostly friends."

"Mostly, huh?"

She sighed. "I'm a terrible friend, aren't I? Oh, shit. I

didn't even think that I'm basically putting you back in the closet. And you just moved to town. If my family saw you with another guy—oh, Everett. I'm sorry. I really was only thinking of myself."

"I agreed, after all—this isn't just on you. But I think it's time we make it clear we're only friends."

"Yeah . . . so that means you're coming?"

"Let me double-check something, but I think I can make it—"

"Yes!"

"I didn't say yes. Let me check and get back to you."

"Alriiiight. But put me out of my misery and let me know soon, okay?"

"So demanding when you're the one asking the favor," he teased.

"Well, you've been a lifesaver. And I owe you, big."

"I'll keep that in mind." He smiled. "Okay, let me get you your answer."

"Okay. Bye!"

"Goodbye," he replied before she hung up.

"Call *miy lev*."

His phone dialed Ricky and rang twice before Ricky answered. "Hey."

"Hey, I know you're busy tonight with your family's dinner. But Nova just called and asked if I would come as her guest. I told her I was done with the farce of us being together, and she needed to make it clear we were just friends . . . Is that okay with you?"

Ricky was silent for a few moments before he said, "Sure. I guess I'll see you at dinner."

"Are you certain you're okay with this? You don't sound happy."

"It's fine."

"Okay, so I guess I'll see you tonight after all."

"Guess so. Look, I gotta go."

"Okay. I—"

The phone call ended.

"Guess I'll see you later," Everett sighed.

Something was definitely off with Ricky. Now he really wanted to see him and make sure everything was okay.

Everett texted Nova back that he was coming when he stopped at the store for a bottle of wine to bring, before heading to the Emersons' farmland. Maybe he could steal away a few moments with Ricky.

* * *

Everett raised his hand to knock, but the door was whipped open. However, his welcoming committee didn't include the Emerson he wanted to see the most.

Nova beamed at him like she'd won the lottery. "Oh, thank the goddess. Get in here." She tugged him in and shut the door behind them. He handed her the bottle of wine and slid off his coat, leaving his shoes stacked neatly by the door.

"Okay, so I told Mom we were not together anymore, but we're still friends. And I broke up with you, for the record, because that way she won't dislike you."

"Gee, thanks."

"It's the least I could do," she said, missing his sarcasm. "Ooh, this looks good." She eyed the label of the wine he'd brought.

"It's for your mother. You know, so I can impress her and have her help to convince the woman I love to take me back because I'm such a pitiful lovesick fool," he teased.

Nova stared at him for a beat. "Oh, that's good. You're a genius." She pointed at him and then headed towards the dining room where laughter and conversation were coming from.

"I take it sarcasm isn't a form of communication you understand when it's used against you." He walked towards the living room. "Funny, because that's usually how you communicate most of the time. So that makes me believe you're being deliberately obtuse."

"Big words for a man I just broke up with," Nova teased.

Everett chuckled as they rounded the corner. The entire Emerson family was spread around the large farmhouse table.

Mrs. Emerson smiled at him brightly and waved. "Welcome back."

He grabbed the wine from Nova and held it out to Renita. "Thanks for having me."

"Oh, so polite. And you bring your host a gift? A man like you won't be single for long." Renita winked at him before looking at Nova.

Some sort of silent conversation went on between them. Everett took the opportunity to find Ricky. He sat beside his nephew, Eli, with a beer in his hand. His eyes were bloodshot and his hair a little ruffled, like he'd been running his hand through it over and over. Was he a little paler than usual, or was that just Everett's imagination?

"You're just in time. Dinner's ready," Mr. Emerson said, getting to his feet.

The rest of the siblings and their partners rose and made their way to the kitchen.

"I'll get your plate, honey. You stay here and rest those feet." Mr. Emerson kissed Renita's cheek. She smiled affectionately. The love she and James shared was palpable.

"Are your feet bothering you?" Everett asked.

She waved her hand dismissively. "Everything hurts when

you get to be my age. Don't worry about me. Go get your food. And, Everett?"

"Yes, ma'am?"

She leaned in. "Don't let my daughter scare you away. You're welcome anytime."

"Thanks, Mrs. Emerson."

"I thought I told you to call me Renita or Mama E?"

"Sorry. Habits are hard to break." He smiled and glanced at Ricky, who was downing the rest of his beer before he stood.

"Go get you some food. You're too thin. Need to get some meat on those bones," Renita said.

"On my way." Everett rushed after Ricky into the kitchen, but Roman was talking to him.

"Save room for dessert. Mom made her German chocolate cake from scratch, and trust me, it would be a mortal sin not to try some," Nova said to Everett before heading back into the dining room.

Ricky's brothers greeted him and their partners said hello as he filled his plate with a little of everything and brought it back to the table.

When Ricky entered a few moments later, he chose a different seat to the one he'd been in before—it seemed to be the farthest from Everett at the table. Was he afraid that if they sat too close, someone would know they were together? Everett tried to ignore the bite of pain that stabbed through his chest. It wasn't like he had leprosy. He'd agreed to not let anyone know they were together, but it didn't mean he had to be treated like he was an outcast. They'd been making so much progress over the last month.

Everyone dug into their dinner. Conversations melded together. Someone would inevitably try and drag Ricky into the conversation, and he'd be his usual cocky self, teasing and instigating arguments with his siblings. Flirting shamelessly with Elise and Isabella.

It was obviously to get a rise out of his brothers, but it still didn't sit well with Everett. *Was this what I signed up for?* Ricky was clearly reacting to the stress by overcompensating. Maybe if he knew how accepting his family would be to someone who was gay, he'd relax a little?

Everett turned to Renita and James. "This food is delicious. Don't tell my mom I said this, but your mashed potatoes are perfection."

Renita smiled and James laughed.

"Your secret is safe with us," James said.

"Be sure to take some leftovers home with you," Renita added.

"I will. Thank you." He took another bite before continuing. "How long have you lived here?"

"Oh, let's see." James sat back in his chair and scratched his chin and turned to his wife. "We bought the first fifty acres when Nash was, what? Five?"

Renita nodded. "Yes. This old farmhouse needed a lot of work even back then."

"It's truly beautiful," Everett complimented.

"It's home. At one time, it didn't feel so big though." James chuckled.

"I bet—not with four kids darting around," Everett said.

"Four energetic teenagers with emotions running amuck. Lordy, the noise level." Renita shook her head.

"I bet it's a lot quieter now," Everett commented nonchalantly.

"Sometimes it's too quiet. But that's what our visiting grandbabies are for." Renita motioned to the kids around the table.

"Have you ever considered taking another child in?

Maybe a teen?" Everett's voice rose over the rest of the conversation at the table.

He hoped Ricky would tune in to his parents' response.

Renita narrowed her eyes at him. "You mean like a teen from Hope Facility?"

Everett laughed. "You caught me. I'm involved in their placement program. And I'm always on the lookout for loving and accepting families like yours to help place the youth with."

He glanced at Ricky, who was staring daggers at him.

"Well, we do have a few spare rooms," James mused, taking another bite of his dinner.

Renita sighed. "We do. But don't you think we're too old?"

Everett shook his head. "Not at all."

"I'm not sure we'd qualify, with everything going on with the investigation," James added.

Nova had filled Everett in about Nash's missing ex-fiancée, whose body had been discovered on their property, and the connection she had with the serial killer—she knew another victim.

"I could look into it if you're interested. We're looking to place them with families that will show them love and support while they grapple with being queer and getting an education after their families have disowned them. Or sometimes the state has removed them due to an unsafe environment at home," Everett explained.

Renita and James looked at each other.

"I think it's something to consider. Might be nice to have a few more kids running around here. Maybe Eli would like having someone closer to his age on the farm."

"Ariel is my friend," Eli said, joining the conversation.

"Don't you think you have enough to deal with, Mom?" Nova asked.

Everett blinked. He'd thought for sure Nova would support this idea. It would give Renita a much-needed distraction from Nova's dating life.

Renita narrowed her eyes at Nova. "I am perfectly capable of deciding what I can and can't handle."

"Of course," Nova answered too quickly.

What was going on between the mother and daughter?

Renita broke the stare-off with Nova and turned to Everett. "Let us think about it and we'll get back to you."

"Sounds good—"

Ricky's chair screeched as he fled from the room.

Everyone's attention darted to the hall where he'd disappeared.

"What's got into him?" Roman asked.

"Did you put Ex-Lax in his coffee again?" Nash asked Nova.

She held up her hands innocently. "No. I haven't done that since the last time he hid in my house and scared the crap out of me."

"Hmm." Renita hummed worriedly as the front door opened and slammed shut.

Everett forced himself not to run out right after him. Ricky wouldn't want that. But Everett had to know he was okay.

"Excuse me. I think I left my phone in the car and I was waiting on a text from my mom."

"Oh, you have a close relationship with your mother?" Renita asked.

Everett smiled as he stood. "Yeah. Save me a piece of that cake that Nova couldn't shut up about if I'm not back in time." He forced his feet to stay at a walk until he rounded the corner. He ran to his shoes, not bothering to lace them as he grabbed his coat and jogged to the porch, pulling the door closed behind him. He searched the snow-covered driveway. Ricky's car was still there.

"Where are you?"

He walked down towards the cars, scanning the area around them. A single set of footprints let through the fresh layer of powder leading towards the barn.

Everett breathed a sigh of relief. He'd found Ricky.

32

RICKY

White noise. That was all Ricky could hear as blood whooshed through his ears. His chest burned as it fought against invisible strings of anxiety tied tighter than a drum when he tried to suck in a breath. It wasn't enough. Was there air in here? *I'm going to suffocate alone in this barn and no one will know.* He clutched his chest. His heart beat so fast it hurt.

Ricky's mind spun, guilt and confusion swirling around like mud, muddling his mind. He stumbled forward. The smell of animal manure and hay in the building was muted by the panic building in his body like a volcano ready to erupt.

Maybe it will kill me this time. Maybe everyone would be better off without me. Everett would be safe.

Ricky took out his phone, pulling up the text he'd received just before Everett had arrived for dinner with his family. With trembling hands, Ricky lifted the phone to read the text from the unknown number again.

I guess you didn't learn your lesson. Can't wait to see you in person and finish that conversation we started all those years ago before we were interrupted. Maybe I'll pay that fairy a visit too. I'll make sure to thank him properly for showing me what an abomination was living under my roof. Such a disappointment.

Everett could be in danger because of Ricky—again. Donald knew where he was. He would see Everett if he hadn't already. Had that been him at the café in Concord? How had he gotten Ricky's number? He needed to keep Ever safe. *But how can I do that when being with him paints a target on both our backs?*

The bitter winter air cut through the thermal long-sleeve he wore, but it didn't even phase him. He pulled the material farther from his chest as if that was the reason he couldn't get a full breath in.

Ricky tripped over a notch in the floor, skidding to his knees. The phone went sliding across the floor. Pain sliced up his legs and hands before he rolled to the side and brought his knees up, letting his head hang between them.

Everything seemed to be spinning around him. All his senses were muddled by the basic need to breathe. It was like he was in a thick fog or deep underwater. Pressure crushed him from all sides.

A warm hand slipped behind his shoulders.

Ricky jerked his head up, his every muscle rigid. The only thing worse than dealing with this panic attack was having someone see him like this.

Everett's eyes were shadowed with concern. His full lips formed a straight line. "Breathe, miy lev. Just breathe."

"I'm." He attempted another lungful. "Trying."

Everett rubbed firm, smooth circles around his back as his other hand cupped the side of Ricky's face, turning Ricky to face him. Ricky's attention flicked to the closed barn door. No one would see them together like this. Some of the tension eased, but guilt quickly took its place.

"Focus on me. What do you see?" Everett's deep voice pulled his attention back.

My everything. "Grey. Your eyes are grey like the moon."

The corner of Everett's mouth flicked up before it straightened out again. "I didn't know you were so poetic."

Ricky chuffed, his chest still heaving.

"What do you hear?" Everett asked.

"You, your voice."

"What else?"

Ricky listened. "The animals."

"Now what do you smell?"

"Also, the animals." Ricky smiled for a moment. "And you. Your cologne. Like soap and oranges."

"Good thing I showered today." Everett smiled too, but it didn't reach his eyes. "What can you feel?"

"Embarrassed."

Two severe lines formed right above Everett's nose as his brows drew together. "Why?"

"Because of you seeing me like this," Ricky confessed, swallowing down the thick ball of emotion rising in his throat.

Everett dragged his thumb over Ricky's cheek. It came away shiny. Shit, he was crying too? Ricky slammed his eyes closed.

"Don't do that."

"Do what?" Ricky asked.

"Hide from me like you have anything to be ashamed of."

"But I do. I have so much to be ashamed of." His eyes burned with more tears.

Everett gripped the back of Ricky's neck. "Look at me."

Ricky blinked his eyes open, forcing himself to face the man he'd let down more than anyone else. Everett's eyes shone with unshed tears.

Ricky's heart squeezed. He'd done this. Caused Everett to hurt. "I'm so fucking sorry."

"Don't you get it? You don't have anything to apologize for. I'm here because I'm worried about you."

"Panic attacks. I get them . . . a lot. Although they've slowed down a bit recently."

"Do you get any help for them?"

"That's what the weed is for."

"I meant do you see someone for them?"

"Like therapy?" Ricky shook his head. "Nah. I just need to . . . get over it."

Everett's jaw pulsed. "Is this another 'real men don't have panic attacks or go to therapy' line of bullshit?"

Ricky shrugged.

Everett sighed, rubbing his hand down his face. He seemed to be mulling over something as he stared at Ricky and then shook his head. Ricky's stomach sunk. This was where Everett would realize Ricky wasn't worth it and leave.

"I'm sorry if what I said in there caused this."

Ricky stiffened. Everett was apologizing? "Why did you bring that up?"

"I thought you'd see that your parents would be supportive of you being with a man if you knew they were going to take a queer teen in. I thought it would show you that it was okay to come out in your own time. I'm sorry if it had the opposite effect. I really was only trying to help," Everett explained.

He'd just been trying to help. But that was what had gotten him almost killed last time. Ricky couldn't risk it again.

Can't wait to see you in person and finish that conversation we started all those years ago before we were interrupted. Maybe I'll pay that fairy a visit too.

Donald's message flashed in his mind. The idea that he was watching Ricky, that he could go after Everett—

"I can't do this." Ricky pulled away, rolling to his knees before standing with a wince. Maybe if Ricky stayed away from Everett, Donald wouldn't go after Ever. Here Ricky was, bringing more danger and stress to Everett's life once again.

I can't do that to him again.

Ricky couldn't deal with Donald and all the old fears he triggered along with everything that came with the present and Everett now.

What if he went after Ever to get to me?

I can't be responsible for him getting hurt again—or worse. The image of Ever's broken fourteen-year-old body flashed in his mind. He fisted his hands as he was thrown back in time to the fear, and the rage of that night.

"Do what?" Everett stood.

"Look at me!" Ricky motioned to himself. "You bringing up the subject put me in a full panic attack. You deserve better than this. I thought I could do it—but I don't think I can."

"Can I ask where this panic is coming from? What about this scares you so much? What's the worst thing that would happen if you came out?"

"They would leave me!" *And you could be hurt.*

Everett bit his lip. "You truly believe if you told your family you were dating me, James and Renita would turn their back on you?"

"No. Yes. Maybe. A part of me does. Fuck, this is so confusing." Ricky held his head and shook it as if that would clear some of the fog.

"Have they ever done anything to suggest they would not be accepting?" Everett asked carefully.

"No."

"Then why—"

"Because my own blood family rejected me. The very man who was supposed to love me, who helped bring me into this world. He'd rather see me dead than be with you," Ricky snapped. He'd rather see both of them dead.

The line from the first letter Donald sent months ago flashed in his mind.

You owe me.

Everett stared at him a few moments in silence. "You're afraid they will abandon you."

"Everyone else did. My mother died. I never saw you again—"

Everett flinched.

"Fuck." Ricky's shoulders sunk with yet more guilt. "I didn't mean it like that. I know you were also a kid, you didn't have a choice—"

"But you're right. Maybe I could have fought harder. Came looking for you sooner at the very least."

Ricky shook his head. "It wouldn't have changed anything." *Because we're back here again.*

"Don't say that."

"It's true. If I can't even get through a dinner with my family when this topic was brought up as a full-grown adult, how the fuck do you think a teenage or early twenties version of me would have handled it?"

Everett nudged some fallen hay with his shoe. "I can't help but wish for yesterday, to go back in time and do things differently. Make this right."

"There was no other path. You saved my life by leaving me and going for help. Leaving was the only way I survived."

"Still," Everett insisted, "you're right. The past is behind us. We can only move forward."

"That's just it. I'm telling you, I don't think I can be the man you need. I want to—fuck—I want that so bad."

"What are you saying?"

"This." Ricky motioned between them. "It's not fair to you—"

Everett stepped forward, grasping Ricky's hand and pulling it against his chest. "Don't say that. If you need to slow down, we can do that. If you don't want me to hang out with your family for a while, I can do that too. But don't pull away. Don't let Donald take this from you. I know this is right. The love I have for you is pure and good. I just wish you'd let yourself accept it. Fuck." Everett shook his head as the tears dripped down his face. "I hate seeing you in this much pain. He's got you so fucked up, and he isn't even here."

"Daddy issues." Ricky shrugged, trying to feign indifference despite how accurately Everett's words hit the nail on the head.

"Don't do that. Not with me," Everett said.

"That's what I'm trying to tell you, Ever. I can't do this with you. I can't be the man you need."

Everett pulled him against his chest, hugging him tightly. His mouth coasted over Ricky's ear. "It's not about what I need. It's about you having the freedom to be the man you are, have the life you were meant to live. To be free. I just wish you could see that. If you need space, I'll give it to you. But I'm not going anywhere."

"You should." *He'd be safer that way—they both would.*

Everett pulled away enough to look Ricky in the eyes. "I see through this." He pressed Ricky's hand over Everett's chest, the lion tattoo hidden beneath the layer of clothing. His heart thumped. "You've forgotten who you are, miy lev. But I haven't. You're fierce and brave. Loyal and full of so much love. Donald tried to take that from you, tried to make you doubt yourself. To take everything good and soft in you and turn you just as hard as him. But it's all lies. You're still there despite his attempts. You're so good. I wish you could see what I see when I look at you."

Everett kissed Ricky, soft and sensual, their lips melding together as if they'd been designed to fit. Ricky wanted to give in, more than anything. To drag Everett to his house, make love to him, and crawl back into their bubble where they could shut the world out. The temptation was powerful. But that was selfish of him. He'd be risking Everett's life. His father had been a big motherfucker. Even if Ricky could take him physically now, Everett wasn't good enough to defend himself yet. And what if Donald brought a gun like he did to the robbery? The stress of worrying about his father and coming out was too great.

Everett pulled away, as if sensing his hesitation, and searched his eyes. After a weighted moment, Everett's shoulders sunk before he nodded once. "I've caused you hurt, and for that I am so fucking sorry."

Everett's words confirmed what Ricky already knew. Everett was too good for him. He deserved better.

Ricky shook his head. "Maybe we should take it as a sign that despite what we want, we can never be . . . us."

"Just give it time—"

"Can you stop? You can't save everyone!"

Everett blinked. "I'm not trying to."

"Are you sure? Maybe that's what this is between us. We're just reliving this trauma from being kids. Perhaps you think you can save me again." Ricky shook his head. "But you can't."

Everett stumbled back a step as if Ricky's words had been a sledgehammer. Everett's full lips turned down into a frown, his eyes shining with so much pain it bled through the space between them. "That's—no. That's not at all what this is. You can't really believe that—"

"Maybe I do." Nothing but the sound of their breathing and a few animals scuffling around in hay filled the barn as they stared at each other. "I wish I could be the man you need."

Everett nodded, his jaw pulsing before his eyes closed. A beat passed and then his eyes opened, filled with so much hopelessness it gutted Ricky. "The thing is, I know you can be that man. I never asked for perfection. Only progress."

"Ever—"

"I'll make my excuses to Nova and your family." Everett stared at the stray pieces of hay on the barn floor.

"You don't have to do that—"

"I do." Everett's attention was like the force of gravity as he met Ricky's gaze—sucking him in and pinning Ricky in place. "Because the only thing I want more in this world than to have you love me back the way I love you is to make sure you're protected and happy. If you will be more at peace without me . . ." Everett's voice trembled. "There's nothing I can do to change that."

"Ever—"

Everett met his gaze, hope flickering in his eyes.

"I want you to be happy too. That's why we can't continue this."

"This? Being a relationship?"

Ricky shifted uncomfortably. "Our . . . us. What we are. It's only getting your hopes up. I thought I could do this. I wanted to. But I just proved it's physically impossible."

Everett swallowed, his Adam's apple bobbing before he wiped his face, his hurt expression morphing to resolve. "I hope you find your happiness."

And I want you to be safe and free to be who you are without having to look over your shoulder all the time.

Ricky wanted to take it back. He wanted to rewind time

and linger in the morning before when they'd woken in each other's arms. When he'd been at peace and loved and whole. But his mouth stayed shut. He couldn't risk it. There was too much at stake. His family, Everett's safety—his heart. It was better for everyone if Ricky pulled away. So he didn't say anything as Everett headed for the barn door. He didn't stop him when he walked out. Ricky gritted his teeth and forced his feet to stay in place until the sound of Everett's car faded down the driveway.

Even then, Ricky remained paralyzed—only this time with regret.

What the fuck was I thinking?

He'd hurt Everett when all the man had tried to do was love him. And Ricky had torn out his own heart in the process. He was lost in a bleeding mess of his own making—and Ricky only had himself to blame.

He should have known better. The last time he'd followed his heart, he'd ended up a bruised and broken mess.

So why had he thought this time would turn out any different?

33

———————

EVERETT

Everett stared out the big window overlooking Main Street. Big, fat snowflakes drifted down, slowly covering the parked cars below. Headlights reflected off the wet asphalt as drivers made their way to their Valentine's activities.

Everett ran his fingers through his hair with a sigh. Maybe he'd order pizza for dinner. *Is Ricky out tonight?* Everett shook his head, fighting the roll of nausea that weighed down his stomach. It had been a lonely week. Every time something good had happened at work, there'd been a moment when he'd gotten excited to share his news with Ricky, but then he'd remembered.

Maybe we should take it as a sign that despite what we want, we can never be . . . us. Ricky's words came back to haunt him.

The man he loved couldn't even admit they'd been in a relationship to Everett himself. And what did it say about Everett, choosing men who were not available in the way he needed them to be? *Am I trying to save him in some fucked-up repeat of our past? I'm sure my mother would have something to say about that.*

But he didn't want to talk to her or anyone about him and Ricky. It hurt too much.

Knock. Knock.

Everett turned towards the door. Who could that be? Flutters of nervous anticipation filled his belly. He moved forward, hope bubbling up. Could it be Ricky? Everett didn't bother with the peephole and opened the door.

The smile on his face immediately dissolved. "Nova?"

"Don't look so excited to see me," she deadpanned and held up plastic bags. "I brought takeout, ice cream, edibles, and chocolate. You have popcorn, right?"

"Uh, yes. I do. What are you doing here?"

"Actually, my family thinks I'm on a romantic dinner away with my new boyfriend out of state. So I need somewhere to disappear to for the night. And a little bird told me Sebastian is working on call in the ER tonight. So I knew you were free. No sense in both of us spending Valentine's alone." She raised the bags higher as if offering them up.

Everett stepped aside, taking one of the containers. "I don't know if I'll be good company tonight." He shut the door behind her and followed her into the kitchen.

"What's wrong?" She pulled out the contents of the bag, spreading the goodies on the small kitchen island.

Everett sighed, opened a plastic container of her homemade cookies, and took a bite of one. "I'm in love with someone, but I don't think they are capable of loving me back the way I need. And it sucks because he's the most amazing person. He's capable of so much more than he knows."

"Sebastian?" Nova asked, opening a drawer and grabbing a fork.

"No. He and I are just friends."

Nova took a bite of the spicy noodles, chewed, and swallowed before she spoke. "Some people are hard to shake. You give them so much of you, thinking you are on the same page. Both sharing, working towards the same goal. Then one day, you look around and realize you were alone the whole time. The relationship was one-sided, and you'd been gaslit to ignore the red flags." She stared ahead, as if her mind was far off. Blinking, she cleared her throat. "You're a great guy. And even though you were only temporarily my date, I can say you were a pretty decent boyfriend."

"Gee, thanks."

She chuckled. "But in all seriousness, a relationship takes two. Two people committed to the same goals. Life experience has taught me if someone wants to be with you, they will walk through fire just for one more moment at your side."

"Fire, huh?" Ricky wouldn't even hold his hand in public. That should have been a red flag, but it was different when Everett understood the reason behind it. Ricky had been traumatized. He'd internalized so much.

Or maybe I was making excuses because I wanted us to work so badly. Fuck, maybe I do have a savior complex.

Nova shrugged. "That's why I'm still single. I want fire. I want someone who isn't afraid of the deepest, darkest parts of my soul. Someone who knows that fire intimately, looks it in the face, and laughs with dirt under his or her fingernails from clawing their way out."

Everett's brows rose as he blew out through his mouth. "That's quite the image."

"No, that's life. Shit happens. I need to know that when the trouble comes, I have someone at my back with experience. Someone who will truly see me and not hesitate to do what's necessary to keep what we have protected." Nova pushed the food around in the takeout container. "But I guess that's why my boyfriends are all fake or made up. That doesn't exist for me."

"Like soulmates?" he asked.

She twisted more noodles around the fork. "Maybe."

"And you think you and Brooks were soulmates? And now that he's gone, you've lost your chance? Do you believe there's only one person out there for us?" Her brothers had found love after loss, so why didn't Nova think that was possible for her?

She shook her head. "No. I'm not talking about Brooks." Her voice changed when she said his name. Hurt bled through, but it was tinged with a bitterness Everett hadn't heard before.

She must have noticed the questions in his eyes because she waved him off. "I thought we were meant to be. I was head over heels in love. I would have done anything for that man. And I did, for a long time—too long. Maybe if I hadn't been so concerned with being what he wanted so much, I would have seen the signs. My ex-fiancé was not who he seemed to be." She sniffed. "And when I found out the truth, everything changed. I won't trust so easily next time."

"I'm sorry."

Nova blinked as if coming out of a memory back to the present. "Enough about me. This is supposed to be a happy holiday, so I propose we eat and take some edibles and watch a sappy love story where at least someone gets a happy ending."

"Why not horror or action? Skip over the love part entirely?"

She tapped her lip. "Hmm. How about one of each? We can start with horror, but if I get scared, you're gonna have to deal with me sleeping on your couch with all the lights on."

He laughed. "Okay, deal. But I can take the couch and you can have the bed."

"Even better. Such a gentleman. And I know we're not

gonna talk about our love life anymore, because we don't want to be downers. However, I must say, whoever this idiot was who let you go didn't deserve you. You have a lot to offer and you're an amazing human being with the biggest, kindest heart. He's a fool if he doesn't see what was in front of him." She got up and walked over to Everett, then wrapped her arms around him in a hug.

He squeezed her back. "Thanks."

She pulled away. "You can thank me by getting out that good weed I know you have stashed in here somewhere. We can't be sad when we're high." She winked.

He laughed. "Alright. You get the movie going, I'll get the bong."

"Now you're speaking my language." Nova picked up a handful of snacks and moved them onto the coffee table in the living room.

Everett went to his bedroom and pulled out the supplies they'd need. He set everything up before offering Nova the first hit.

The bubbling noise of the water preluded the puff of smoke she released. "Wow. That's smooth."

"It's medical grade, so go easy on it." He took the bong from her and set up his own hit. "So, how is the Emerson . . . uh . . ."

"What?"

"I was going to say clan, but I don't think that's right."

She giggled. "Probably not."

"How's your family?" *How's Ricky?*

"Fine. Mom's been on my case more than usual, hence the made-up date." Nova picked up the remote, scrolling through the movie choices.

He opened his mouth to ask about her brothers.

"Oh! I love this one. Though I probably won't sleep in the

dark for a good month after watching it." She pressed play and snuggled into the couch, taking one of her cookies with cannabis butter mixed in.

Everett grabbed one of the takeout containers, digging in as the opening credits rolled. He wanted to know how Ricky was doing, but maybe it was for the best that he didn't know. It would tear him up even more to find out Ricky was happy without him.

Guilt over that selfish thought immediately clouded over him. He didn't want Ricky to be miserable. Not really.

Everett rubbed a hand over his chest, but nothing took the ache away. Not the company, nor the weed.

The only thing Everett wanted was the one thing he couldn't have.

34

RICKY

Ricky's muscles ached. His legs moved as if they were filled with lead. His heart was in worse shape than his body after one intense workout too many—which was saying something. Walking to his car from the gym, he pivoted to go around a big puddle of slushy water. Pain lanced up his calf.

"Shit." He grimaced and limped towards his truck. "I guess I overdid it." He tossed his gym bag in the cab, but he wasn't ready to go home.

He'd spent the day at the gym, trying to escape thoughts of Everett. He'd tried that all week in different ways. Getting high made him hyper-focused on Everett. Drinking made him an emotional mess. He was distracted at work and had accidentally bottled two hundred and fifty of the wrong size honey bears. Something had to give eventually, right?

He slammed the truck door closed. He needed air. Ricky turned and moved towards the sidewalk, favoring one leg as he headed towards the main part of town. He couldn't stop or everything would come crashing down on him.

Pink and red sparkly hearts glittered in store shop windows.

"Fuck." He'd forgotten today was Valentine's Day.

Was Everett out with Sebastian? Or someone else? He passed storefronts, keeping his focus glued to the sidewalk. Bitter February air turned his nose cold, creating a cloud with each exhale. The tips of his ears were surely red because he'd lost feeling in them. He should have grabbed a hat. But what was the point? He wanted to be numb. Perhaps then the pain would stop.

A bell rang ahead of him. The door to The Stardust Café opened and a couple filed out, dopey smiles on their faces and hearts in their eyes as they linked arms and walked past him with a cake box in hand. No one blinked an eye at the two men making their way towards their next destination. *I want that.*

His focus snapped across the street to Everett's apartment. The light flickered from one of the windows, like the TV was on. Was he spending Valentine's Day alone in his apartment? Ricky's chest tightened. The thought of Everett with someone else made his blood boil, but the idea that he was alone made Ricky feel like the biggest asshole in the world. *I can't have him. I'm no good for him.*

Ricky should leave him alone. Let Everett find someone who could give him what he needed. To keep him safe.

Ricky took a step towards the crosswalk and then froze. What was he doing? He spun around and walked into Remy's café instead. The warm coffee- and peppermint-scented air enveloped him. It was too hot after being in the cold. He shrugged off his coat and looped it over his arm as he got in line behind a couple of teens holding hands. He'd truly picked the worst day to walk around town.

They ordered and moved out of the way. Ricky stepped

up to the counter. Remy had her back turned to him but her daughter, Lyra, stepped forward.

"Hey, Uncle Ricky."

"Hello, my favorite niece."

She smiled and shook her head.

"Aren't you a bit young to be working?" he teased.

"I'm almost fourteen." She rolled her eyes. "Mom said I could work weekends and holidays to save for my car."

"Planning ahead. I like it." He nodded and spoke loud enough for Remy to hear. "Just like her mama."

Remy turned around and smiled. "No complaints here."

"What can I get for you?" Lyra asked.

"A coffee with cream and sugar to go." He scanned the bakery case. Maybe something sweet would perk him up. "You got chocolates?"

"Yeah, Mom said there's a local who's starting a new business. Mom offered to carry some of their specialty chocolates to help get the word out. Do you want some? They're really good."

"Sure. Give me one of the big boxes."

Lyra opened the case and pulled out a sleek black box with a magenta ribbon tied around it and set it on the counter. Remy stepped up to the counter with his coffee in hand.

"Thanks." He took the cup from Remy and turned to Lyra. "What do I owe you?"

Lyra tapped the screen and turned it around. Ricky pulled out his credit card and paid, adding a hefty tip for his niece's car fund.

"Thanks, Uncle Ricky."

"You're welcome. Say hi to your brother for me." Ricky waved and collected his chocolates in the other hand. He sipped the drink and walked outside. The cold bit through his navy henley as he stared across the street at Everett's windows. Running away obviously wasn't working for him.

Maybe if he saw that Everett was okay, he'd feel better. *Or maybe I'm grasping at straws here.*

He couldn't continue this way.

Ricky took a sip of his coffee as passersby walked around him. He was frozen. Unable to walk away. Everything inside him pulled him towards Everett's apartment like a magnet. A part of him wished Everett had never come back into his life. Because now, he couldn't imagine his world without Everett in it.

"Fuck it." Ricky checked both ways and jogged across the street. He took one more sip of his coffee and then tossed it in the trash. Everett deserved to know about the text and that he might be in danger because of Ricky yet again. Going over there to see him had absolutely nothing to do with needing to see his face and make sure he was okay. Nothing at all.

Taking a deep breath, he walked up the steps to Everett's apartment above the bookstore. Anxiety swarmed his stomach like a hive of angry bees—buzzing and frantic. His heart raced, blood rushing through his ears as he neared the door. He swallowed. He'd come this far.

I just need to make sure he's okay.

Ricky raised his hand and knocked once. The small noise in the covered stairway sounded more like a boom. Anticipation mixed with anxiety tumbling in his guts.

The door creaked, like someone was standing on the other side. Another moment later, the knob twisted and Everett's bloodshot eyes met his.

"Ricky—" Everett turned to glance behind him before focusing back on Ricky and pulling the door tighter against his own body, as if he were hiding something.

The blood drained from Ricky's face. Did Everett have company? Had he moved on already?

"What are you doing here?" Everett asked.

"I . . ." *I miss you. It feels like a chunk of me is gone without you this past week. I think I love you too.* Rather than saying any of that out loud, he stared dumbly at Everett.

Everett's eyes dimmed as he nodded and started to shut the door.

Ricky's hand shot out, holding it open. "I missed you."

His skin burned like hot lava had been poured on him, red and raw. Open and vulnerable, he waited with bated breath for Everett's response.

"I miss you too."

The sigh of relief that left Ricky's chest was like a weight lifted from him. "Can we talk? I brought gourmet chocolates." He lifted the box.

Everett hesitated, glancing behind him and then to Ricky. "I don't think that's a good idea."

"Oh." Ricky's stomach sank like it was filled with rocks. "I see."

Everett had company. Was it Sebastian?

"I'm sorry. I shouldn't have come." Ricky swallowed and turned.

Everett's hand caught his arm. Warm, electric energy shot up his limb at the contact. Ricky savored the bittersweet feeling. It might be the last time he got to be this close to Everett.

"It's not what you think. Nova stopped by with food and weed and wanted to watch a movie. She fell asleep ten minutes in, and she's on my couch," Everett explained.

"Oh." Ricky could breathe again. Relief poured through him.

"We're friends, and your mom's been on her case about her dating life."

"Yeah, Ma's just worried about her. Nova used to be different before Brooks. I think Ma just wants her to find her happiness like Nash and Roman have," Ricky explained.

"And you?" Everett asked cautiously.

Ricky shook his head. "There's no chance for me."

Everett's jaw pulsed. "I see."

"You don't though. There's no chance for me because I gave my heart to my best friend when I was fourteen. Recently, I found out he's still got it," Ricky confessed, holding his breath as he waited for Everett's reply.

It was the truth. And it was time Ricky faced it himself.

"What are you saying?" Everett asked.

"I'd like to talk. Is that something you . . ."

"When?" Everett asked.

Now. "Tomorrow?"

"Okay."

"My house at six?" Ricky proposed.

"I'll be there," Everett said.

Ricky couldn't hold back his smile if he tried. Hope built inside him. "Come hungry."

"Alright."

"Goodbye, Ever."

"It's not goodbye, miy lev. Not with us." Everett slipped back inside his apartment, shutting the door.

Ricky let out a long exhale. The walk back down the stairs was much lighter than the trek up them had been.

It was time Ricky faced the facts.

He was in love with Everett Popova. The question was, what was he going to do about it?

35

EVERETT

Everett ignored the rapid thudding of his heart as he got out of his car. Black trees underscored the dark sky like spiky shadows. The only light came from the porch, spilling out into the winter night, glinting off tiny ice crystals in the snow. Everett fisted his hand as he lifted it. Before he could knock, the door opened.

Ricky stood on the other side. There was a wary expression on his haggard face. It was like looking at a snapshot of the lost, lonely boy Everett knew decades ago. Ricky was probably just as nervous as Everett.

"Hey," Everett said.

"Hey." Ricky moved aside, letting Everett in.

Everett toed off his shoes.

"Can I take your coat?" Ricky offered.

Everett slipped it off his shoulders and hung it on the hook on the wall. "I got it."

"Right." Ricky glanced towards the kitchen. "Do you want a drink?"

"Maybe something hot."

"I got coffee, cocoa, tea?"

"Cocoa would be nice."

Ricky led him to the kitchen. Everett took a seat at the bar while Ricky quietly got to work heating water and preparing cups. Silence stretched between them, anticipation and nerves winding Everett tighter and tighter.

Glasses clinked together and Ricky cursed. His hands trembled as he filled the mug with water. Everett couldn't sit still any longer. He got up and walked behind Ricky. Carefully, he placed his hand over Ricky's, steadying him.

Ricky turned his face away, but his body relaxed, giving in to Everett's direction as he finished pouring the water and set the kettle back on the stove.

"Ricky?"

Ricky still wouldn't face him.

"Miy lev, please?"

Ricky's chest rose and fell before he turned around. His watery, bloodshot eyes speared Everett's heart. Everything in him demanded he make it better—take away the pain.

"What is it?" Everett asked.

Ricky shook his head, forcing a fake smile as he met Everett's gaze. But his grin wobbled and then disappeared altogether, like he didn't have the energy to pretend anymore. "You broke me."

Everett flinched, dropping his arms. The last thing he wanted to do was hurt Ricky any more than he already had.

"Before you came back, I thought I was okay, going through life with shallow relationships and focusing on my family. But I can't go back to that. I've tried." His voice broke.

"I'm sorry I brought this all up for you again," Everett said, unsure of how to fix things. Maybe there was no repairing what they'd lost.

Ricky shook his head. "There you go again, taking all the blame for my fuckups."

"I—"

Ricky held up his hand. Silence blanketed the small kitchen.

"When I'm with you . . ." Ricky pressed a hand to his heart. "It's like you woke up some part of me I didn't think I was capable of feeling. And it scares the shit out of me . . . but it's right. I know in my gut that you're my person. That what we have between us is more. But I'm having a hard time convincing the part of me from the past that you won't—" Ricky swallowed as if needing time to get a handle on his emotions.

Everett risked a step closer, coming almost eye to eye with Ricky. "I won't what?"

Ricky searched Everett's eyes. He must have found what he was looking for because he answered, "Leave."

Ricky was afraid that Everett would abandon him? *I did once before.* He might have been a kid when they were separated, but he could have come looking for him when he was older.

"I'm so fucking sorry."

Ricky let out a humorless laugh. "Don't you get it? It's not your fault. It's mine. It's my fucked-up head that won't let me —" Ricky smashed his hand over his face.

Everett took Ricky's wrist, pulling Ricky's palm over Everett's heart. "Do you feel that?"

"Yeah."

"It beats for you. Despite all the shit that's been thrown our way. Through the difficulties we've had recently. You're who my heart wants. Who maybe it's always wanted. We just got a little lost along the way."

Ricky blinked slowly. "But we found our way back together."

Everett collared the base of Ricky's neck, moving closer so their faces were only inches apart. "Fucking right we did. And if you think I will let anyone or anything get between us again, then you don't know me at all. Short of you telling me you're completely done and you want me to stay away, I told you, you own my every fucking heartbeat."

"I wish I didn't."

Everett's breath caught in his lungs. Fear turned his stomach into solid stone, sinking it like a lead weight.

Ricky's eyes volleyed between his. "I wish I didn't own it so you could be free to be with someone who could hold your hand walking down the street without worrying what people would think. Someone who could kiss you whenever he wanted without fear of someone thinking less of him."

"You think that's something queer people don't deal with on an everyday basis? Do you know all the stories I could tell you of the couples assaulted for simply spending time with the person they love? All you have to do is look at the news," Everett said.

"Do you worry about that?" Ricky asked.

"Sometimes. I used to a lot more. Especially after everything that happened with us and then with my ex. How could I not be?"

"But you're out."

"Being out doesn't mean you're not still afraid of what others might do to you. For me, it meant choosing my happiness—love over hate. I got to a point where I knew I couldn't let fear control my life or take away my joy."

"So you think I just need to get to that point too?" Ricky asked, hope lighting his voice.

"Are you saying you want to come out?"

Ricky's lips pursed. "You're really the only man I've ever wanted. After I moved here, I kept my distance from other guys—unless my brothers were there. It took a while for me to be comfortable enough around them too. But they didn't really give me a choice."

Everett chuckled. "I bet they didn't."

"From the moment I was dropped off, Roman and Nash showed me my bedroom. Gave me the lowdown in school. Protected me—they just accepted me. It took me a little longer to come around."

"It takes time to build trust, especially when that trust had been broken by those you cared about the most," Everett added.

Ricky leaned against the wooden counter behind him. "I thought if I could get the right girl on my arm, I would fit in better. So I did everything I could to be that guy that everyone liked. The life of the party. Captain of the football team. And it worked . . . for a while."

"Did it make you happy?" Everett asked, genuinely curious.

"In a way. It distracted me. I had fun. But something was always missing. I could never be who I truly was with anyone else." Ricky blew out a breath. "I couldn't let people in. I don't know . . . if I'm capable of that. But you—you were already there. So when you came back, I knew that letting you in again and losing you would ruin me."

"Miy lev—"

"No. I need to say this. Get it all out." Ricky cleared his throat. "I was terrified that even by you talking about gay teens with my family, or them seeing us in the same room, they would suspect something. Elise has already made comments to me, comparing me to her gay best friend. A part of me still believes I'll lose my family if they find out. I know they're not that sort of people, but I don't want to risk it and have things forever be changed between us. That's not something I can take back. But that wasn't the whole reason I tried to end things that day."

"What's the real reason?" Everett asked.

Ricky blew out a breath. "I got a text from my dad. He's out, and he threatened me and you in the text. He's not done with me. And having you with me puts you in danger all over again."

Anger welled in Everett's veins, scorching him from the inside out. "He contacted you again? You need to tell the police."

Ricky shook his head. "What are they going to do—give me a protection order? A piece of paper won't stop Donald from coming after me—or you, to get to me."

"You were trying to protect me." It all made sense now. Why Ricky had been off on the phone call and at the Emersons' dinner that night.

"I come with risks. And I freak out when the topic of being gay is brought up with my family. I'm a fucking mess."

"But you're my mess. And I love every scuffed and dented piece of you," Everett reminded him.

Ricky's shoulders sagged. "I don't see how it's fair of me to ask for you to be with me. To put up with all this shit. I can't even come out to my family, for Christ's sake."

Everett took a deep breath and let it out. *It makes sense why he'd feel that way.*

"I see where you're coming from. And I hope you understand I'm really not trying to force you out."

"I know that. And I appreciate it, but I can't help feeling like it isn't fair to you," Ricky said.

"I've been thinking about what you said about me having a savior complex." Everett blew out a breath.

Ricky shifted on his feet. "I was angry and scared. I shouldn't have—"

"I don't think you were off base. I . . . maybe I need to do some work on myself too. I never thought trying to help someone could be negative."

Ricky opened his mouth, but Everett held up his hand. "Just hear me out."

Ricky nodded.

"A big part of my volunteer work started because of our experience. And I carried a lot of regrets with me because of that. Maybe subconsciously I chose this career path to rewrite our own history in the only way I could."

"It doesn't have to be a bad thing." Ricky dragged his thumb over Everett's jaw. "You just have to understand nothing you can do will fix what happened—believe me, I've tried. And you can't keep giving pieces of yourself to others in order to try and save them at the cost of what's good for you —even to me."

"It feels wrong not to give someone you love every piece of you," Everett confessed. An ache built in his chest.

Ricky tilted his forehead against Everett's and stayed there for two breaths. "You remind me of my cousin Remy."

Everett pulled away, confused. Remy? From the café? "How so?"

"Her and Mikel didn't have an easy road of things. He was her first love, and despite his struggles with drugs and alcohol, she gave him everything and then some. It only enabled his addiction."

"You think I'm enabling?" Everett asked, sincerely wanting to know the answer.

"I think if you keep putting everyone else before your own needs, you'll have nothing left. And even if you love someone with everything in you, it's not always enough."

Ricky's gaze darkened as if he was thinking of someone specific.

"Like your mom?" Everett chanced.

Ricky swallowed. "I don't want to be like him and take advantage of you."

"I haven't ever thought of you that way. You're the farthest thing from that monster," Everett argued.

Ricky tipped his head thoughtfully. "But his blood runs through my veins. And I could be a user like him. I think I have been in a lot of ways, actually. That scares me. But I want to be better. For you. And for me."

A burst of pride filled Everett's chest. "And so you shall, miy lev."

"I want to come out. I think I just need a little help to get there."

"Have you thought about therapy?"

Ricky groaned.

"It's not weak to get help for the difficulties you face. It takes a real man to take on that responsibility and do that painful work. It takes a lot of strength to look inwards and admit that something needs to change and then work on bettering yourself," Everett said.

The corner of Ricky's mouth turned up. "Spoken like the son of a therapist."

Everett pushed Ricky's shoulder playfully. "Come on."

"Yeah, okay. I do want to try and deserve you." Ricky was still smiling, but his words held so much truth to them, and it hit Everett square in the chest.

Everett threaded his fingers through the hair at the back of Ricky's head, forcing him to look in his eyes. "Don't do that."

"What?" Ricky asked, pupils dilating.

"Put yourself down. You deserve good things. Happiness,

love, and acceptance. You deserve a space that's safe to be yourself."

"Then I deserve you."

Emotion clogged Everett's throat. He swallowed it down and dragged his thumb over Ricky's jaw. "Where do we go from here?"

"The bedroom?" Ricky smirked.

Everett laughed, his whole body lighting up with humor. Ricky licked his lips, arousal swirling in his dark brown orbs.

"I need to know the boundaries and your expectations," Everett said.

"Give me two months. We stay on the low in Shattered Cove and with my family. That will give me time to build up to it and prepare myself for whatever the outcome may be." Ricky trembled slightly.

Everett pressed his lips to Ricky's cheek. "Your family will love you no matter what."

Ricky blew out a breath. "I fucking hope so . . . You're not worried about Donald?"

"We're not the young boys we once were. We're not helpless. If Donald wants to try something, I believe we will have an entirely different outcome this time."

"You're sure?" Ricky asked.

"I'm sure about you. You said two months?"

Ricky nodded. "Can you give that to me?"

"Will you go to therapy too?"

Ricky hesitated.

"Please?"

"Okay. Maybe you can help me find one that will be well . . . suited?" Ricky asked.

"Of course. I'm here for you in any way you need."

"What if I need your body on mine?" Ricky asked.

Everett nuzzled his neck and inhaled his heady scent

before peppering kisses over the exposed skin. Ricky shuddered.

"I'd say, get your sexy ass upstairs. Last one to the room gets to come last." Everett didn't wait for his words to sink in before he was off, darting up the stairs towards Ricky's room. A hand wrapped around his leg and pulled. Everett lost his footing and went down with a thud as Ricky pushed past him.

"You thought you could cheat." Ricky laughed.

Everett got back up, taking a few more steps before he launched himself at Ricky's back, sending them both sprawling across the floor of the hallway. The bedroom door was just a few feet away. Ricky tried to crawl out from under him, but Everett looped his arms and legs around Ricky in a hold that he'd learned from their time at the gym.

"What do you think? Has the student become the master?" Everett teased, his erection grinding into Ricky's ass.

Ricky laughed, out of breath. "You still haven't made it to the door."

"But I will—"

Ricky slipped out of his hold, flipping them over so he was on top, a triumphant smile on his handsome face. "Or you won't."

"It's gonna be fun to wipe that cocky look off your face." Everett lifted himself up enough to kiss Ricky, their lips tangling, teeth nipping.

He wasn't gentle. He gave every piece of himself in that kiss. Heart thudding against heart, with nothing but their clothes separating them, the men kissed like they'd become each other's only source of oxygen. Everett couldn't get enough of Ricky's taste or touch. He needed more.

Ricky groaned and rocked his hips forward. Everett took advantage of the opening and rolled them so that he was on top, their heads just inside the bedroom door. He pulled away, looking down at Ricky below him, panting for breath.

"Looks like it's a tie. What now?" Ricky asked.

"Now we come at the same time." Everett pulled the bottom of Ricky's shirt over his head. Smooth, tanned muscles filled his vision. Everett stood, removing his own henley. Ricky got to his feet, taking off his pants and boxers at once, and then his socks were last to go. He stood naked, his hands at his side.

"Ever." Ricky's voice was a plea.

"Say you're mine."

Ricky met his gaze with a fierceness that Everett hadn't witnessed yet from him. "I've always been yours."

"Show me."

Ricky leaned forward, his lips brushing over Everett's lips in the briefest kiss before getting on his knees. Warm hands opened the button on Everett's jeans, tugging them down to his ankles along with his boxers. Everett's cock stood erect, straight and so fucking ready for whatever Ricky was going to do next.

Ricky's focus homed in on the tiny bead of cum on the tip. He licked his lips. Everett's muscles contracted with that tiny movement. Fuck, he was so far gone.

Ricky tilted his head, looking up at him. "You're the only man I've ever gotten on my knees for. The only one who owns every piece of me—even the parts that scare the shit out of me. I'd do anything for you." Honesty shone in Ricky's eyes. He hadn't said the words yet, but this was Ricky showing that he loved Everett—and what was more, Ricky trusted Everett enough to give him this gift.

Everett tapped the lion tattoo over his heart. "You've always had mine too, miy lev."

Ricky's attention dropped to the ink imbedded in Everett's

skin and then flicked back to his face. He parted his lips, but instead of speaking, he leaned forward and sucked Everett's length into his mouth.

Everett groaned as he rocked his hips, moving in and out of Ricky's hot, wet, mouth. "Fuck, baby. You feel so good. So sexy taking my cock like this."

Ricky hummed around Everett, taking him deeper as he massaged his balls. Everett fought the urge to roll his eyes back, not wanting to miss a moment of his boyfriend sucking him off.

In and out, Everett moved, easing into a faster rhythm. He was careful to make sure it wasn't too much for Ricky. But the man sucked him down enthusiastically, gripping his ass and pulling him deeper.

"You like it when I use your throat, huh?"

Ricky hummed in agreement.

White spots appeared in Everett's vision. Pleasure rippled through him, gathering in the base of his cock.

"You're gonna make me come," he warned.

Ricky only sucked harder.

"Fuck, baby. I want to come with you."

Ricky eased off with an audible *pop*. "I want you to come in my mouth."

Everett took his hand, helping him to his feet. "Then get on the bed."

Ricky moved, lying down on the mattress.

Everett stepped out of his bottoms and climbed on top of him so they were in the sixty-nine position. He sucked Ricky's cock like a man starved. Everett wanted Ricky to feel as desperate with pleasure as he was. He worked the cock in his mouth, matching the same pace as Ricky until they moved as one. In. Out. Over and over in a reckless cycle of ecstasy.

He spread Ricky's leg wider, freeing more room for his

hand to tease Ricky's balls and taint. Ricky's ass clenched and he groaned, sending electric prickles of heady arousal tumbling through Everett.

"I know you're close, baby. Hold off just a little longer." Everett replaced his mouth with his hand. He wanted to wring every last drop of pleasure from the man he loved.

"You're so fucking good at this." Everett licked up the cum dripping from the tip of Ricky's cock.

"Now come." Everett sucked Ricky's dick and slapped his ass hard, digging his fingers in and squeezing, adding that bite of pain his man seemed to love so much.

Ricky's hips jerked forward, seeking his release. His dick pulsed in Everett's mouth before hot cum shot into the back of his throat, forcing him to swallow it down. Ricky's release triggered Everett's own orgasm. Euphoria threaded through his every nerve, lighting them with the burning power of an entire galaxy of stars. Ecstasy warmed Everett's veins and relaxed his muscles as Ricky's hot tongue lapped from the base of his cock to the tip and gave one last suck, draining him of all he had.

Breathless, Everett rolled over and climbed to the top of the bed, lying next to Ricky.

Ricky's chest heaved as he crawled into Everett's arms. "That was—"

Everett cut him off with a kiss. His taste melded with Ricky's. It was the hottest fucking kiss ever—with languid strokes of his tongue and delicate nips of Ricky's teeth. Everett basked in the sensual connection.

"I love you," Everett said.

And just maybe, his love would be enough to get them through what lay ahead.

EVERETT

"Who let that man in my kitchen?" Nova asked.

Everett chuckled as his attention volleyed between his friend and the man who'd spent all night in his arms. "Why is everyone so opposed to Ricky cooking?"

An amused smile curved Ricky's lips as he chopped onions.

Nova walked over to the counter and set down a couple pounds of ground sausage wrapped in butcher paper. "Cooking is not something my brother is capable of. Setting my house on fire is more like it."

"That was one time, and it wasn't your house—just the stove." Ricky argued, tossing the chopped onions into hot oil in the stock pan.

Nova crossed her arms over her chest. "My overhead fan was melted and had to be replaced."

Ricky glanced at Everett. "She exaggerates."

Everett's smile grew at the siblings' antics. It couldn't be as bad as they were making it seem.

Nova let out a frustrated growl. "Seriously, why are you even over here? I figured you'd come once all the work was done with the rest of the family."

Ricky's body tensed, and he flicked an anxious glance towards Everett.

"I asked him if he wanted to learn how to make borscht too," Everett answered.

Nova narrowed her gaze on her brother. "Since when do you want to learn how to cook?"

"You wanted me to give him a chance." Ricky shrugged.

She turned to Everett. "Many have tried to teach him and many have failed. Are you truly up to the task?"

Everett laughed and handed Ricky the spatula. "I think I can handle it."

Nova studied them a minute before exhaling. "Alright." She moved behind them, opening a cupboard and pulling out a fire extinguisher.

"I hardly think that's necessary." Everett shook his head.

"Trust me, you'll understand by the end of this," Nova said with surety.

"I feel like I should be offended on your behalf. Your sister has so little faith in you," Everett said, pointing to the pot. "Stir that so it cooks evenly and then chop up more cabbage."

Ricky stirred the contents in the pot. "I don't blame her, really."

"Excuse me? Whose friend are you, anyways?" Nova smacked Everett's shoulder playfully before leaning her back against the counter in her kitchen.

Everett looked at Ricky, giving him a secret smile only they would understand. "He's not so bad once you get around his prickly shell."

Nova snorted, breaking the moment. "Okay, but I hold you personally responsible for my kitchen."

"Understood." Everett added sliced butter, cabbage, celery, and minced garlic to the pot before giving it a stir.

"Perfect. Do you have the broth?" Everett searched the supplies spread out over the counter.

"Shoot. I knew I forgot something. I'll be right back." She stopped and pointed to Everett. "Don't take your eyes off Ricky and the stove."

Everett blew out through his nose and shook his head. "I won't."

Nova placed two fingers near her eyes and then pointed at Ricky in a silent warning before she left.

"She can be intense." Everett chuckled.

"You have no idea." Ricky laughed.

"Are you really as bad as she seems to think?"

"I mean, it's not like I do it on purpose." Ricky turned to him, his back against the counter. His muscular arms crossed over his chest, his shirt riding up to show his defined biceps. "I just happen to have horrible luck when it comes to cooking."

A single pec flexed upwards and then the other.

"Did you just—"

"You were checking me out, so I thought I'd give you something to look at."

Everett laughed. "Well, your sister did say to not take my eyes off you."

Ricky stepped forward, eating up the space between them. He glanced towards the entrance before leaning in so his breath coasted over Everett's mouth. "I can't stop thinking about this morning."

A mirage of sexy images filled Everett's head. "Oh yeah?"

Ricky pressed his lips against Everett's. "Maybe tonight we can have a repeat?" It'd be the start of a second week in a row spending the night together since calling their truce.

"You can bet on it." Everett checked the front door,

making sure it was still closed before he grabbed the front of Ricky's shirt and dragged him against his own chest. Everett's teeth nipped his lover's soft lips. Ricky's rough beard slid over Everett's clean-shaven face. A groan rumbled, and Everett wasn't sure if it had come from Ricky or himself.

"Fire! Fire!" The smoke alarm blared and then screeched.

The two men jumped apart. Everett's gaze flew to the stove. A small thread of smoke danced upwards from the pot.

Ricky jumped into action first, grabbing a tea towel to pick up the pot and pulling it away from the stove. The end of the towel caught on the gas flame, igniting the end. Everett pulled it from Ricky's hand, tossed it into the sink beside them, and turned the water on.

The acrid scent of smoke clung to the air. Ricky ran to the sliding door next to the kitchen and opened it, the alarm still blaring.

They turned to each other, their chests heaving.

"That one wasn't my fault," Ricky said before they both burst into laughter.

"What the fuck?" Nova screeched as she came into the house carrying two mason jars filled with golden liquid.

"It wasn't my fault," Ricky repeated through his fit of laughter.

Nova set the jars down and turned to Everett. "I told you not to take your eyes off of him." She grabbed another tea towel from the drawer and climbed on the counter to wave it by the alarm.

A moment later, the blaring ceased.

"It was my fault. And truly, there wasn't even much of an issue. We forgot to stir the veggies and a little smoke set off your screaming alarm. I didn't know fire alarms could even say stuff. I thought they only did that annoying beeping noise," Everett said.

"Yeah, well, after the last incident, I had a better system installed and it's hyper-sensitive. Even toast sets it off sometimes," Nova explained.

"See? It's not even a big deal," Ricky added.

Nova narrowed her eyes at him. "You burned my favorite hand towel!" She held up the singed and sopping fabric from the sink.

"I'll buy you a new one," Everett promised.

"Fine. But *he's* not allowed anywhere near the stove anymore. Got it?" Nova asked.

Everett bit back his smile. "Got it." He moved to the pot, inspecting the damage. "Only the bottom layer is burned. I think if we transfer the rest to another pot, it's salvageable and we won't have to start all over."

"It'll give it a little smoky flavor." Ricky smirked.

"You're lucky I love you," Nova said.

They got to work putting the kitchen back in order. Everett moved from the stove to the cutting board as Nova poured a jar of broth into a new saucepan.

A small finger wrapped around Everett's pinky, where it rested by his side. It took a conscious effort not to draw attention to himself as he glanced at Ricky.

Ricky gave him another secret smile. "Maybe I could do with a few more lessons."

"I think I know someone who might be up for the task," Everett said.

"I don't think we could afford someone like that," Nova teased. "Ricky's as bad at cooking as I am at relationships."

"Or maybe you haven't found the right partner," Everett said, motioning to the jar of diced tomatoes. "We'll need that in there too."

"Or maybe I'm better off alone. It doesn't seem to be

doing Ricky any harm." Nova's tongue poked out the side of her cheek as she opened the jar.

"Maybe I'm not as alone as you think." Ricky didn't look up from the cutting board.

Everett held his breath. Of all his siblings, Ricky's bisexual sister would be the most understanding. Would he tell her first?

"Excuse me? What does that mean?" Nova walked over to Ricky and slung her arm over his shoulder.

Ricky smirked. "It means that maybe you shouldn't shut yourself off completely to love, dear sister. You never know when it might show up."

Ricky's brown eyes only flicked to Everett for a second before he focused back on the fresh dill he was dicing.

"What?!" Nova screamed, hurting Everett's ears. He winced.

"Jesus, take it down a few octaves," Ricky grumbled.

"You can't say something like that and then not tell me anything," Nova argued.

Ricky's cocky smirk was back, his eyes lighting with mirth. "I just did."

"Rickyyyyyyy."

"Novaaaaa."

She crossed her arms over her chest and huffed. "You're no fun."

Hope expanded in Everett's chest. Ricky had come so close to coming out to his sister. Each day, the man he loved showed Everett that he'd meant what he'd said. He was trying. Today was a win.

"Everett, tell him how unfair he's being," Nova said.

"You're so whiny today. What's gotten into you?" Ricky asked.

"Don't try and change the subject." Nova stirred the pot.

Everett couldn't hold back his laugh. "A bit of the pot calling the kettle black, aren't we?"

"You know what? I think I liked it better when you hated each other." Nova shook her head but smiled. "Fine. Keep your secrets. I'll get them eventually."

Ricky walked over and looped his arm over his sister's shoulders, tugging her close, his tall frame towering over her. "What's got you grumpier than Nash today?"

She sighed and leaned into him as if her strength to fight had left her. "You know how you run into someone from your past and think, maybe this time can be different? Better?"

Ricky's jaw pulsed. A sliver of panic lit his dark eyes as he flicked a wary gaze to Everett. The corner of his mouth curved up for the briefest moment. "I may have some experience in that department."

Everett's heart soared. In some small way, Ricky had acknowledged them.

Nova snorted. "Yeah, well, I guess that was bound to happen to you—hey!"

Ricky playfully ruffled her hair.

Nova's eyes narrowed as she shoved him away. "Don't you dare touch my hair!" She smoothed her curls into place and huffed at her brother.

Everett couldn't hold back the smile at the siblings' antics. "So, this reunion with your ex didn't go well, I take it?"

"How does a man make it to almost thirty and not know where the clit is?" Nova asked.

Ricky's face soured. "Can we not talk about your clit, please?"

A devious smile split her face, and her eyes lit with mischief. "Would you prefer *pleasure button*?"

"That's even worse!" Ricky darted to the other side of the

kitchen counter as if distance could save him the embarrassment from this conversation.

"How about bean? Devil's doorbell?" Nova followed him around the kitchen as he ran away from her. "Would you prefer happy button? Jewel sounds flashy. Oh! Love bud! That one makes me want to barf, personally."

"Who comes up with these euphemisms anyways?" Ricky asked.

"Some old white man with too much time on his hands and no people skills. Or those extra-annoying couples with the cutesy names for each other. I had a friend once that named all her boyfriends' cocks." Nova laughed.

"Oh God, please tell me you're not going to share them?" Ricky asked.

"I think your brother is embarrassed enough for the three of us," Everett pointed out.

"It's almost too easy to make him squirm," Nova agreed.

"Almost as if you were using humor to deflect and distract us from the real question we asked," Ricky deadpanned.

Nova shook her head.

Everett laughed. "You two have so much in common, it's hilarious."

"I'm nothing like him."

"It's okay, sis. I am pretty awesome," Ricky added.

"Soooo?" Everett asked Nova.

She crossed her arms over her chest. "So we hooked up, it sucked, but now he thinks he can, like, call me all the time, and so I blocked his number because he wasn't taking the hint—"

"The hint being, you ghosting him?" Everett clarified.

She rolled her eyes. "Yes, me not responding to his messages or numerous calls. So I blocked him and now just have to deal with the awkwardness when I go into town and hope I don't run into him."

"He lives here?" Ricky asked.

"I thought he was back visiting family. Apparently, he moved back in with his parents because he lost money in a business venture. But don't worry—he's got another idea I got to hear allllll about. He's looking for investors for some kind of gaming seat with a flushable toilet attached." Nova made a gagging sound.

"How do you find these guys?" Ricky asked, his nose scrunched up, adorably confused.

She sighed. "I had a moment of weakness and he was there, and he might be an idiot but he was pretty to look at." She opened the fridge. "Does anyone want a drink?"

"I'll take a beer if you have it," Everett answered.

"Me too." Ricky's elbow touched Everett's with each slice through the fresh greenery. The fresh scent of herbs helped to overpower what was left of the smoke in the room.

The two men shared a look.

I'm proud of you. Everett hoped Ricky could read it on his face.

Ricky leaned in, his shoulder brushing Everett's as he whispered, "Thank you."

Everett wished he could lean just a couple inches farther and kiss his boyfriend. But that would come—and soon. There was no rush.

Not when they had the rest of their lives to look forward to.

37

RICKY

Ricky pushed the dolly forward, creating another stack of empty bee boxes. Roman lifted the staple gun over the fresh row of new frames and glanced at him.

"Oh, thanks. I'm just about done here." Roman brought the tool down. A click of air released as each staple found its home in the rectangular honey frames.

The hum of the generator became background noise. Ricky made his way to a stack of boxes in the corner of the wood shop right past Nash, leaning against the wooden counter and eating an apple.

"Maybe we should open the door and let the fresh air in. It's pretty warm today," Ricky suggested, picking up a box and carrying it to the side of Roman's work space. He opened the box and pulled out the thin wax inserts before sliding them into the freshly made frames that Roman had built and then added them to the empty hives.

"I'll do it." Nash lifted the garage door they had attached

to the other side of the wood shop, making it easy to load their equipment into the truck bed from outside.

Fresh air filled the room, mixing with the scent of pine and sawdust. Notes of spring danced on the late March breeze.

"Thank fuck winter is coming to an end," Nash said in his grumbly voice. "I need to get back out on the water."

"It will be nice to get to the bee yards and see how they survived the winter," Roman agreed.

Ricky's phone dinged. He set the wax inserts down and pulled it out.

Ever: *Thanks for lunch. That was sweet of you. It means dinner is on me.*

Ricky: *I look forward to it. Maybe we can fit in a sparring session at the gym after my therapy?*

Ever: *You wrapping that sweaty, shirtless, sexy-AF body around me for an hour? Sounds like the best kind of foreplay.*

"Earth to Ricardooooo." Nash snapped his fingers near Ricky's ear.

Ricky startled, dropping the phone. He snatched it up, his heart racing. Had his brother seen who he'd been texting?

Nash laughed and Roman shook his head.

"What is up with you lately? You've been so distracted," Roman said.

"You think he's got a girl?" Nash asked.

Roman turned around, crossing his arms over his chest. Bits of sawdust coated his long-sleeve shirt. "Let's see. He's on his phone much more often. And I rarely see his car at his house at night."

"And don't forget that dopey-as-fuck smile on his ugly mug." Nash smirked.

"Assholes," Ricky said, getting back to work.

Nash's bulky arm wrapped around Ricky's shoulders. "You got a secret that you want to share, little brother?"

"Nope." Ricky shrugged him off.

"Come on. Is it Sophie?" Roman asked.

"There's no woman." *Because I'm in love with a man.* Sweat dotted Ricky's brow.

"You're acting awfully suspicious." Roman eyed him skeptically.

"Don't you two have anything better to do than bust my balls?" Ricky asked.

"Can we not talk about your balls?" Nova's voice had all three brothers turning to the door as she walked in.

"Jealous we have them?" Ricky asked. *Deflect.*

Nova scrunched her face in disgust. "Eww. No."

Ricky forced a laugh.

"I much prefer pussy these days," Nova replied.

Everything inside Ricky came to a screeching halt.

Roman didn't even blink.

Nash tipped his head to the side. "Since when?"

She rolled her eyes. "Wow. I knew you were self-centered, but not blind."

Nash stiffened and turned to Roman, as if he'd have an explanation.

"You don't remember her and Alicia dated in high school?" Roman asked.

"I thought they were friends," Nash answered.

Ricky was still processing this. The phone in his pocket dinged, but he ignored it.

Nash narrowed his gaze on Nova. "You were friends with my wife in high school too."

"Relax, if I'd done anything at all with your wife, she or I would have told you. But would it really make a difference?"

Nash shook his head. "No. I love Bella with every piece of me."

She nodded. "Good." Nova stepped forward and whispered, "But if you do ever wonder where she learned that thing with her tongue—"

"That's not even funny to joke about," Roman intervened.

Nova shrugged and eyed Ricky. "Surprised this one didn't beat me to it."

"See? Even she's noticed you've been off." Nash focused back on Ricky.

His siblings' attention burned his face.

"Is everything okay?" Roman asked.

"Christ, you three need to give it up. I'm busy and enjoying my life. Is that a crime?" Ricky snapped.

"We just want you to be happy." Nova stepped forward, wrapping her arms around Ricky.

He relaxed into his sister's embrace and smoothed his hand over her back. "I am happy." *More than ever.* His brothers hadn't batted an eye at Nova's bisexuality. There was hope. But would it be different for him because he was a man?

Nova cleared her throat. "Well, I came over to give you all an update."

"About the missing and murdered women?" Ricky asked. One of those women happened to be Nash's ex-fiancée.

"The FBI has kept in touch. Something just doesn't feel right. How could I not only know two of the victims but have lived with them?"

"In the foster house you were at before Mom and Dad found you?" Roman asked.

She nodded. "I did a search of the other girls that I was there with. All but one responded. She hadn't posted in a while on her social media. But she lives in Maine. So I went to check out her place—"

"You what?" Nash barked.

"You went alone?" Roman snapped.

"What the fuck were you thinking?" Ricky asked.

Nova took a deep breath, pulling away to stand on her own. "I only went to Portland. It wasn't far—"

"Someone is out there kidnapping and murdering women you used to know and you go looking for trouble, alone and defenseless," Roman said, mirroring Ricky's thoughts.

"You make it sound like I'm some helpless damsel in distress. I have my knife. And I know self-defense; you taught me." She narrowed her eyes at Ricky.

Nash fisted his hands at his sides. "Don't ever do something that reckless again. I'll go with you."

"Guys, seriously. It was an apartment complex in bright daylight. A sweet old lady lived next door. I was in no danger," Nova explained.

Roman's cheek pulsed. Nash grumbled low. But Ricky was still trying to wrap his mind around the fact that his sister had put herself at risk like that.

"What did you find?" Nash asked.

"There was an eviction notice taped to her door and piles of mail. Looks like she's been gone for some time. So, I called the FBI—see? I'm not an idiot," she huffed.

"And?"

Nova shifted, toeing the ground with her black Docs. "It looks like she's a missing person now too."

His brothers let out a string of curses.

"You could have painted yourself a target if you aren't one already," Ricky said.

"And if I hadn't gone, no one would have known Hannah was missing. Now at least she has people looking for her." Nova's eyes glittered with determination.

"You shouldn't have gone," Roman scolded.

Nova stepped up to him, pointing her finger at his chest despite the fact that he towered over her five-foot frame. "You have no idea what it's like to have no one to rely on. To know that if you walked out the door and never came back, no one would even notice."

Roman swallowed. "I'm sorry. That's not something I'd wish on anyone. But you can't be the one sticking your neck out. Let the FBI handle it."

"He's right." Nash pulled Nova's attention away. "I want to find Anastasia's killer just as much as you do, if not more. But you can't put yourself at any more risk. If this psycho is going after women from that house, you are likely a target too."

"You shouldn't leave the farm alone," Roman added.

Nova's mouth dropped open like she was about to protest.

"You should let us know when and where you are at all times," Ricky agreed.

"You too?" She looked at him as if he'd betrayed her.

"This could be life or death. You leave, you tell one of us where you're going," Roman said.

"And we might tag along," Nash added.

"No." Nova shook her head and crossed her arms over her chest.

Ricky reached out, pulling his sister into a hug. He kissed the top of her head. "We just want you to be safe."

She pushed away from him. "I know, but, guys, this is overboard. There is no sign that I'm a target. The killer brought a letter onto our property, or don't you remember?" She stared at Nash. "If he wanted to kill me, he could have."

"Okay, fair point. But I still don't like it," Ricky said. "It means he knows where you live and how to access our property without being seen."

"How about I be careful, and if I get any more ideas

about visiting pretty apartment complexes by myself, I take someone along?" Nova suggested.

"How about we tell Mom and Dad what's going on?" Roman asked.

She whirled on him. "Don't you fucking dare," she huffed. "This is exactly why I keep shit to myself. You all want to be tattletales and tell Mom and Dad everything. What are you? Ten?"

"You let us know where you're going or we tell them." Roman didn't budge.

"We could get her a tracker like the one Eli wears," Nash suggested.

"You've lost your fucking mind if you think I'm going to let you chip me like a damn animal," Nova fumed.

"It's a device you wear, not an implant," Nash deadpanned.

Nova let out a frustrated growl.

"How many other girls were in the house with you?" Ricky asked.

"Six, not including me."

"Two are dead, and one is missing." Roman scratched his beard and shifted on his feet. "I don't like it."

"I wish we knew what evidence they had. Bently said they've cut him off from the case after the second body was found out of state."

"Were these girls—uh, women—were they all victims of . . ." Ricky trailed off.

All the brothers knew a little of Nova's history, but one topic of conversation that had always been off-limits was her stint in the foster system.

Nova's brown skin took on a paler sheen. She blinked, opening and shutting her mouth twice.

Ricky slid his hand into hers. He knew the look of panic intimately. "You don't have to talk about this now."

"What if it's him? Our foster dad?" Anxiety bled through Nova's voice.

"Why would he come after you after all this time?" Roman asked.

"Did he go to jail?" Ricky asked. He'd had peace knowing his father was rotting in prison. *Though that may not be the case anymore.*

"For a little while. He's been out for years." Nova's tone was dull.

The phone in Ricky's pocket took that opportunity to ring. He didn't miss the way Nova jumped. She was scared, whether she wanted to admit it or not.

"Sorry." He pulled out the phone. Ever's name flashed on the screen.

"That's okay. You can take it," Nova said. "I just wanted to update you all and I have."

"It's okay. I can call them back later."

"He just doesn't want to answer in front of us because it's his secret girlfriend," Nash teased.

Nova brightened. "Your girlfriend? Answer it!"

She reached for the phone, but he swiveled around, his heart in his throat. He wasn't ready for them to see whom he was speaking to. Nova flailed her arms, but she was too short to reach. Instead she knocked his arm and his thumb slid to the answer button.

Shit. Now he had no choice. He put the phone to his ear, clicking the volume low so his siblings wouldn't overhear Everett's voice.

"Hello?"

"Hey. Wanted to check in since you didn't answer the text about dinner. Everything okay?" Everett asked.

"Yeah, it's fine. My brothers and sister decided to drop in."

Nova stood on tippy-toes, as if straining to hear. Ricky shoved her towards Roman and walked farther away.

"Oh, so that means you can't talk right now?" Everett asked.

Ricky breathed out a sigh. "Right."

"So you have to keep a totally straight face while I go into detail about how good it felt to fuck you last night?" Everett's voice grew husky.

"Jesus."

Everett chuckled on the other end of the line. "Is my cum still leaking out of your ass?"

Ricky let out a strangled gasp.

"Maybe you're quiet because you're remembering just how good it felt to have my lips around your cock, sucking every last drop out?"

Images of their sexual escapades during the last month since they'd reunited played over in Ricky's head. The blood rushed to his cock, but the last thing he needed was a boner with his siblings present.

"Pizza sounds good. I gotta go."

Everett's laughter still rang in Ricky's ear as he ended the call. He turned around and all three of his siblings stared at him with matching smiles on their faces.

"What?"

"He's flustered," Nova pointed out.

"Ricky's never flustered," Roman joined in.

"I am not." Even Ricky knew it was a lie as the words slipped past his lips.

Nash walked over and clapped him on the back. "Just remember, the falling part is scary, but the love part makes it all worth it."

Ricky stood speechless as his brother walked out of the wood shop, tossing his apple core in the bin on the way out.

Would his brothers be so supportive if they knew he was in love with a man though? He turned to Nova as Roman got back to work. Maybe he was stressing out for no reason. Perhaps him being bisexual wouldn't change anything between them. But Nova was blood-related to the Emersons, and he wasn't.

"Oh, I got your mail in my box." Nova reached into her back pocket and pulled out an envelope.

"Thanks." He took it. "But don't think I forgot what we were talking about before my call."

"Your lover that makes you flustered, you mean?" she teased.

"Just watch your back and be careful. Call me and I'll go with you when you go out—especially at night."

Nova rolled her eyes. "You gonna tell me who has you tied up in knots?"

"Not on your life." He smiled.

"At least tell me if I know her?"

He shook his head.

"Don't you want to make sure I haven't made out with her? If she's a local, there's a good chance—"

"You're not getting anything out of me. Now get out of here so I can get some actual work done." Ricky shooed her out the door.

"This isn't the end of this conversation." She pouted, heading out the door.

Ricky shook his head, a goofy smile no doubt on his face. He turned back to the counter, tossing the envelope on it.

He could do this. Maybe he'd start with telling his sister. She might be the most understanding.

Ricky took a deep breath. It was time he pushed past his

discomfort and took the first step towards the life he wanted with Everett. He was halfway through the two-month time frame, and though he felt he was making progress, the thought of coming out didn't get any easier.

Ever deserved to hear just how much Ricky loved him, but not while he hid him away like a dirty little secret.

Their relationship deserved the sun over the shadows because their love was just as powerful. Life had tried to pull them apart, but fate had brought them back together.

And Ricky wouldn't waste another minute reclaiming what they should have had all along. He'd fight the devil himself if needed. Donald's letter flashed in his mind. He wouldn't let fear of his father come between them again. Ricky would protect Everett this time.

He wasn't the same young man he'd been when Donald had left him beaten and bloody on the floor. He was a trained fighter. And Donald would never lay a hand on anyone he loved ever again.

"Come at me, motherfucker."

38

———

RICKY

Ricky passed the vape pen to Everett, lying in bed next to him. Everett took a few hits, releasing the herb-scented smoke into the small bedroom in Everett's studio apartment.

"My mom called me again. Wanted to know if I could come up for a visit in a couple weeks," Everett said, handing over the pen.

Ricky took it, pressing the button and bringing it to his mouth for a hit. "Oh yeah?" he asked on an exhale.

"Mm-hmm. Do you have any deliveries to make that way anytime soon?"

Ricky took another draw, filling his lungs with vapor, and blew it out again. "Nope."

"Oh." Everett pinched the fabric of the comforter, plucking invisible lint from the material.

"Ask me."

Everett glanced at him and then smoothed out the blanket. "You said two months. I won't pressure you. We've got one down and one to go."

"Ask me." Ricky took another hit.

"Do you want to come with me?" Everett asked.

"Yes."

Everett turned towards him, adjusting his head on the pillow. "Really? You don't have to—"

"Yes, really. Your family already knows our past. And I would like to see your mom again. Your parents saved my life as much as you did . . . I think I'm ready." *And I don't want to let you down.* "Baby steps might be good anyways. We'll start with your family and go from there. Maybe even see if your friends want to meet up at the bar after?"

The gratitude and pride shining in Everett's eyes were nearly blinding. "If it's too much, we can leave early."

"No, we can't. If it's too much, I'll take a walk and you can spend time with your family."

"You're sure?" Everett asked.

"Do you want me to change my mind?" Ricky chuckled.

"No. But I don't want to pressure you either."

"I'm ready. I know this won't be easy, and I'll probably fuck up, but I want this—with you." Ricky took one more deep inhale of weed.

He rolled over in bed, blowing out the cloud of smoke as he set the vape pen on the bedside table. He leaned against Everett's arm, snuggling into his chest. The cannabis sank into his bloodstream, creating a warm, floaty buzz through his veins. He sunk farther into Everett's body, fully aware of every inch of his lover's body against his. The smooth warmth of Everett's long fingers gently smoothing over his arm brought him an even deeper sense of calm. This was heaven. Tilting his head to stare into Everett's glassy eyes, Ricky couldn't believe he was really there. Even after all these months, it still blew his mind that Everett was back. That Ricky was in bed with the boy from his past, now the man of his future. It wouldn't be an easy journey, but Everett was worth it all. Ricky's heart squeezed.

"What's up?" Everett asked.

"Just thinking."

"Care to share with the class?" One corner of Everett's mouth turned up.

The urge to make it a full-blown smile hit Ricky hard. "I didn't know you were into role-play. I'm guessing you'd be the professor in this scenario?"

Infectious laughter tumbled out of Everett. Those pale orbs sparkled with humor. Ricky's breath caught in his chest.

"You're the most beautiful thing I've ever seen," Ricky blurted.

Everett's smile gentled. His humor morphed into something affectionate.

"I didn't—fuck, I just meant—"

Everett kissed him, silencing his struggle. "Thank you. I think you're pretty damned beautiful myself."

"Should we be using words like beautiful when we're both guys?" Ricky asked, settling back on Everett's arm.

Everett's gaze roamed around the bedroom of his studio apartment, as if he were contemplating Ricky's question. "I think we should be free to use whatever words we want with each other as long as both of us are comfortable with them. Beautiful means possessing certain qualities that give great pleasure or satisfaction to see, think about, hear, or experience with any of our senses." Everett brushed his lips over Ricky's forehead. As he pulled away, Everett's mouth split with a gorgeous smile. "I'd say you tick the boxes for each and every one of those."

"Look at you, Professor Popova, knowing definitions and shit," Ricky teased.

Everett chuckled. "You certainly bring me pleasure to observe."

Ricky licked his lips. "Yeah?" The image of Everett watching as Ricky jacked himself off flitted through his head, his cock waking up at the idea.

"Especially when you're asleep."

Huh? Well, that hadn't gone the way Ricky had thought it would.

Everett laughed again. "I can see that isn't what you'd thought I was going to say."

"Why when I'm asleep?"

"Does that creep you out?" Everett asked, clearly amused.

"It might, depending on your answer."

Everett rolled over, pressing Ricky onto his back until they were face to face. Ricky's cock was fully awake now and ready for a repeat of the previous night.

Everett dragged his knuckles down Ricky's cheek. "When you're asleep in my bed, relaxed and lost in dreams, it takes my breath away. To see you here, in my space, trusting me enough with all of you—yes, it's fucking beautiful. It's something I'll never take for granted."

Ricky's mouth went dry. His heart thudded. Could Everett feel what he did to Ricky?

"And your laugh."

"What?"

"You laugh in your sleep."

"No I don't. Someone would have told me." Wouldn't they?

"Thought you didn't do overnights?" Everett smirked.

"My brothers or Nova would have said something."

"I'll try and record it next time for you." Everett kissed him. "Do you want to hear all the other ways that make you beautiful to me?"

Ricky melted into the mattress. "Go on. My ego desperately needs a boost."

Everett snickered but went on. "The way your skin feels against mine, like two opposing forces that were always meant to crash together, creating something bigger than either of us could be on our own. Our attraction unstoppable by even the most determined force."

Ricky's teasing smile faded. He swallowed down the welling emotion.

Everett kissed up his jaw, and his lips coasted over Ricky's ear. "The way your voice sounds when you're crying out in pleasure. Your groans like an erotic symphony for only me. Knowing that I brought that out of you—fuck—it's beyond beautiful."

Ricky panted. Need and love and gratitude whirled inside him like a tornado, pulling the last strings of his self-control loose.

I love you. Ricky kissed him, letting his body do the talking. Their lips caressed each other. Their tongues tasted and savored. He took his time, trying to burn this memory into his every synapse.

Everett rolled his hips, his cock rubbing against Ricky's. Skin against skin. Nothing separated them; they were still naked from the night before.

Awareness and anticipation slid through his veins like an avalanche, gaining speed with each gentle kiss and rough nip. Something loosened in Ricky's chest, languid and open. He wanted . . . more. *I want everything.*

"You know what I think is most beautiful about you?" Everett asked, supporting his weight on his arms on either side of Ricky's head.

"What?" Ricky's chest heaved as he blinked up at the man who had given him so much already.

Everett tapped Ricky's chest. "Your heart. Who you are and how much you care for the people around you. How soft you are—"

"I'm not—"

"Don't ruin this moment with your macho bullshit. You can be soft and be a man. You can own your feelings and your sensitive pieces without compromising your masculinity. You can be both. A man and nurturing—like you are with your nieces and nephew."

Ricky stared at Everett, unsure of what to say.

Everett continued, "It takes a lot of strength to be vulnerable, and you've given me that. And by far, that is the best gift I've ever received, and I will cherish it until my last breath."

"Ever . . ." Ricky fought against the emotion rioting in his chest.

"I'm here."

And Everett was and always had been. From the beginning. Through the worst moments of Ricky's life. Still, despite the shit show of their reunion. Everett was right there, waiting patiently, despite the baggage Ricky brought with him.

"I know. You've always been with me even when you weren't. You changed my life in a million ways. I don't know how I will ever repay you," Ricky said.

Everett shook his head. "You don't owe me anything. All I want is you and for you to be happy."

"You make me happy." Ricky kissed him again, pouring everything he felt into the dance of his lips against Everett's. "I just want you."

"Then have me." Everett rolled his hips again, spinning Ricky higher and higher.

But Ricky wasn't worried this time. He'd never fall again with Everett by his side. He was safe, and loved, and so fucking happy it leaked from his pores.

He wanted a life with Everett. To share a bed and a home. They could be a family. The slightest bit of hesitation reared its ugly head, fear of what he'd have to face to attain that future. But he pushed those ugly feelings away. He wouldn't let his past dictate his tomorrow. Not this time.

His skin burned with a lust fire he'd never experienced as Everett grinded against him. Ricky's hands roamed, coasting over the warm flesh of his lover, their bodies twisting as their mouths fused together. Ricky wasn't sure where he ended and Everett began. Hot, sweet tantric breaths intertwined between heady kisses. Ricky bent and trailed his mouth over Everett's neck, licking his salty flesh. Everett's deep groan only intensified the burning need inside Ricky.

"I don't know how you do it," Ricky mused, sliding his arm down to dig his blunt nails into Everett's firm ass.

"Do what?" A lock of dark hair hung over Everett's eye.

Ricky tucked it behind his ear before meeting his gaze. "Make me come so undone."

Everett's smile was filled with joy and a hint of cockiness. "You haven't seen anything yet, baby."

"Oh, I hope that's a promise."

"You can bet your life on it." Everett captured his mouth once more, palming Ricky's cock before running his fingers around his balls.

Ricky couldn't hold back the pleasured groan rumbling in his chest.

Here in bed together, the world fell away and they could just be, floating in a cloud of sensual bliss and soft caresses. The rough scrape of Everett's unshaven face against the dip of Ricky's neck sent a shudder ricocheting inside his body.

Everett leaned over to the table beside the bed, grabbed the lube, and squirted some on his hand.

The cool brush of Everett's slick finger over Ricky's asshole was a carnal contradiction to the heat burning Ricky from the inside out. Everett added more lube, easing his finger into Ricky's ass little by little, circling the rim and pushing in gently.

Need twisted violently in Ricky's chest, stealing Ricky's breath. Some part of him was unlocked, exposing the deepest, most hidden parts of his soul. The overwhelming desire to submit to Everett, to let go of everything and trust that the man he loved would protect and care for him, crashed through Ricky. He wanted to give Everett this.

Pleasure snapped and spiraled as Everett worked Ricky's ass, adding a second finger, his other hand wrapping around the base of his own cock, jerking himself.

"Fuck, that's so hot," Ricky groaned.

"Not as hot as your hole squeezing around me. Knowing that in a moment you'll take my cock like the good boy you are. You want that extra credit, don't you?" Everett slid a third finger inside, fucking him gently with his fingers.

So they were adding role-play to this? Abso-fucking-lutely. "I'll do anything for your big cock, Professor."

Everett smiled, and it lit up his whole face as he squirted more lube onto his cock, jerking himself with it. He lined his hips with Ricky's.

The tip of his dick inched into Ricky's ass. Ricky tensed at the tightness and slight burn.

"Relax, baby. Breathe."

Ricky's body tuned into Everett's voice, letting it guide him deeper into this space where his sole purpose was to obey Everett's every command. To let go and just take whatever his lover gave him.

"That's it. Fuck, you're perfect. Look at you, taking my

cock. It's the sexiest fucking sight." Everett grunted, driving his dick deeper, his hands locking Ricky's hips into place.

Ricky groaned in pleasure. The burning disappeared as Everett slid in the rest of the way, filling him completely.

"It's so good. So, *so* fucking good," Ricky gasped.

"Hold on, miy lev. I'm gonna make it unforgettable," Everett promised, his voice husky and deep.

Everett drove his hips in and out. It wasn't soft or slow, but needy and savage. Ricky wasn't climbing up a peak, but being propelled with such a force, he was rocketed towards a new plane of ecstasy he'd never known and wasn't sure he could ever come back from.

He came in a kaleidoscope of colors bursting in his vision. The world as he knew it shifted and broke apart until he had no choice but to surrender to its madness.

"Fuck, I'm coming! Ever!" Ricky's orgasm tore through him. Ropes of hot cum marked his stomach, making a wet sound as Everett continued to fuck him, chasing his own release. His thrusts became jerky and uneven as his face morphed into an expression of strained bliss.

"Show me I'm yours," Ricky pleaded.

"Ricardo!" Everett drove his hips twice more and then pulled out, painting his cum across Ricky's abs.

Hazy half-lidded eyes landed on Ricky. "So fucking beautiful."

And maybe beauty wasn't some pretty thing wrapped in a bow. Maybe beauty could be messy and slicked with sweat. It was the dirt underneath the fingernails of those who had fought tooth and nail for their freedom. It was the scars of the past, healed and decorated with new ink, redefining them. The jagged, gnarled warrior's stripes in a new light—proof of bravery. Perhaps beauty truly was in the eye of the beholder. Because there wasn't anything more beautiful than the man hovering above Ricky, marked with his cum, and the knowledge that they shared something that they'd never share with another. This feeling went beyond love to something incomprehensible. Words were not enough to contain the emotion that decimated life as Ricky knew it. He was forever changed —there would be no going back.

39

RICKY

A shiver crawled up Ricky's spine as he exited the car. Sunlight sparkled on bits of melting snow. A consistent slick of water dripped from the eaves of the houses in the quiet suburban neighborhood he'd parked in.

"You ready?" Everett asked, coming to stand next to him, his shoulder brushing against Ricky's.

After taking a final deep breath, Ricky blew out until his lungs were empty and then slipped his hand into Everett's. "Yeah. Let's do this."

The lines between Everett's brows had been there since he'd picked Ricky up this morning, and they'd only deepened since they'd pulled into his mom's driveway.

"We need a code word," Everett said.

Ricky quirked an eyebrow. "What?"

"If it gets to be too much. You say the word, and I'll come up with an excuse why we have to leave."

Ricky's chest tightened as it filled with gratitude for the man standing next to him. He squeezed Everett's hand reassuringly and smiled. "Thank you."

"That doesn't sound like a good code word. We'd use it too much naturally." Everett tipped his head to the side, the corner of his mouth kicking up.

Ricky playfully nudged their shoulders together. "No, thank *you* for doing this. For being so patient with me and my anxiety. For understanding and not taking it personally when I . . . lose my shit."

Everett cupped Ricky's face in both hands, moving to stand in front of him. "You're worth it."

Ricky tried to turn away but Everett held on.

"Don't hide from me." Everett's eyes glittered with so much affection, it socked Ricky in the chest, and his knees wobbled. But he didn't fall—because Everett was there to support him.

"There doesn't seem to be a point. You always see through me, down to my very soul."

Everett leaned in, kissing him lightly. His next words coasted over Ricky's lips. "Because we share the same one, miy lev."

Ricky's eyes widened. Everett saying he loved Ricky was one thing, but soulmates? That familiar curl of anxiety coiled within him. Shock gave way to excitement tinged in fear. Because what if it was all taken from Ricky again?

"Now, let's go inside. I know my mom is already at the window, but I'm not sure how much self-restraint she has to not come out and bombard you with questions and hugging. There will be lots of hugging. I warned you about that, right?"

"No, but I remember your mom." Ricky smiled. "Let's not keep her waiting any longer."

"No code word?" Everett asked.

Ricky shook his head. "No. I know it may seem weird, but your family knew me then. They know about you and me. It doesn't feel as . . . intimidating as being around my family."

He turned to Everett. "And I trust you. I know no matter what, you have my back."

Everett slid his hand into Ricky's once more and intertwined their fingers. "Alright. Let's do this."

They walked up the steps as the front door opened, and Everett's mom walked out with a bright, welcoming smile. "I was about to come out and get you myself!" She didn't wait for them to make it to the door—rather, she met them on the top step and immediately wrapped her arms around Ricky.

He hugged her back, struggling to suck in air in her tight hold. He glanced at Everett, who chuckled and mouthed, *"I told you so."*

Sandy pulled back, gripping his biceps. "Oh, let me look at you." She had tears in her eyes. "You're so handsome and tall. You barely look like the same boy at all."

He laughed. "Twenty-plus years and puberty will do that for a kid. But you don't look like you've aged a day."

She waved her hand. "Oh, you've become a charmer too."
If you only knew.

Sandy sniffed and looked between Everett and Ricky. "Thank you so much for coming to see us. I know it probably brought up a lot of different feelings. And we want to respect that. But we are so happy to welcome you to our home. We missed you and worried about you. Everett tells me you're a beekeeper now?"

"Yes, ma'am."

"Well, come on in where it's warm. There are a few people in there who can't wait to see you and meet you." She hugged Everett.

"I thought it was just us?" Everett asked, flicking a worried glance towards Ricky.

"It is. But your dad really wanted to stop in and see Ricardo—I hope that's okay? He said he wouldn't stay long.

But he brought Lorna too. That's it." Sandy's gaze volleyed between the two of them in question.

"It's fine." Ricky cleared his throat. "I'd love to see Mr. Popova."

"Alright, come on in." She headed into the house.

Ricky stepped forward to follow her, but Everett tugged his arm in place. Ricky turned to him in question.

"You sure this is okay still?" Everett asked.

Ricky gave him what he hoped was a reassuring smile. "Yeah. I have a few things I've always wanted to say to your dad. Now I'll get the chance."

"Okay."

Ricky leaned forward and kissed his cheek. "Come on, let's go see if we can steal some homemade rolls before dinner and have your mom chase us out of the kitchen with her dish rag like old times."

Everett laughed as they entered the house. Sandy stood in the foyer, holding hands with Everett's stepdad.

The man held out his hand to shake Ricky's. "Welcome to our home. I'm John. Everett and Sandy have told me a lot about you. It's nice to finally meet you."

"Nice to meet you too."

"And this is Squirt, the sister that I told you about." Everett wrapped his arm around the tall girl off to the side of his mom.

Bree elbowed him in the gut. Everett clutched his stomach and gave her a little more space but smiled mischievously.

"My name is Bree. And I swear, if you don't stop calling me that, I will find a way to end you." She narrowed her eyes at her brother before turning to Ricky. She smiled. "I do have to say, you've got good taste, brother."

"I know." He smiled but cast Ricky a cautious glance as if wondering if being so open was okay.

Ricky hated that this was what Everett had to deal with because of him—second-guessing everything he did or said when they were around other people. "I'm the lucky one."

Everett swallowed, staring at him as a wave of emotion bled in the space between them.

"Okay, does anyone want a drink? I've got wine, tea, coffee, beer, or John could run out to the store if we need anything else."

"A beer would be good," Ricky answered.

"Same," Everett said.

"I'll grab the drinks. Why don't you two head into the living room?" John said before he headed farther into the house. Everett led the way, Ricky, Bree, and Sandy all following as they passed through the foyer and into the main hall with high ceilings. Stairs wound up to another level on the right. French doors remained open on the left as they passed what looked to be a study with built-in bookshelves and a desk. They passed a formal dining room, the kitchen, and a few closed doors, and then made it to a spacious living room with a roaring fire. A giant U-shaped white couch sat on a colorful woven rug in front of it. But it was the older man sitting next to an unfamiliar woman sitting on the sofa that made Ricky's stomach flip.

As they entered, Andriy Popova stood, along with his wife. The tall, burly Ukrainian man that had seemed like a giant to fourteen-year-old Ricky was still very much the same. More lines had appeared at the corner of his eyes, and his hair was greyer, more white than black.

"I hope it is okay that we came?" Andriy asked, his eastern European accent still as heavy as Ricky remembered.

"Of course. I'm glad you did, Mr. Popova."

Everett's dad shook his head and held out his hand. "You're a man now. You can call me Andriy."

Ricky held out his hand to shake, but Andriy pulled him into a bear hug and clapped his back. "I'm happy to see you are well. And with my son, no less."

Ricky sucked in a breath as he was released. He searched the man's eyes for insincerity but only found honesty. A weight he hadn't realized he'd been carrying lifted. A part of him had wondered if Sandy and Andriy would still blame him for what Donald had done to Everett.

"It's good to see you too." Ricky's voice was thick with emotion.

A voice cleared behind Andriy. He shifted and the woman behind him came forward. "This is my wife, Lorna. Lorna, this is Ricardo."

"He goes by Ricky now," Everett said.

"It's fine. You knew me as Ricardo, and that's okay."

"Are you sure? We don't mind," Sandy insisted.

"I'm sure," Ricky answered.

"It's so nice to meet you." Lorna smiled.

"I hate to go, but I've got to check on dinner," Sandy announced. "Bree, could you help?"

"Sure."

"I'd love to lend a hand if you need it," Lorna offered.

"Of course. You're always welcome." Sandy hooked her arm through Lorna's and the women left.

Everett took a seat on the couch, and Ricky joined him. Andriy reclaimed his spot as John came in and handed beers out before disappearing again.

Ricky took a sip of his drink and set it on the coffee table in front of them.

"So, how is the new job going? Still loving it?" Andriy asked Everett.

"Is it still new when I've been there for months?" Everett chuckled. "It's good. I love what I'm doing at Hope Facility.

They have a great work culture, and I can see the impact it's making with the teens that attend. I just wish there wasn't a reason for my position—having so many queer youth in need of a good home."

Andriy shook his head and blew out his mouth as he leaned back on the couch, his thick fingers folding over his stomach. "They should not have become parents if they weren't ready to love their kids no matter who they are or who they love."

"Sorry to interrupt, but Mom needs help getting something from the attic and John ran out for more beer," Bree said.

Everett turned to Ricky, a question in his expression.

"Go for it. I'll be fine," Ricky assured him.

"Be right back." Everett got up and left with his sister.

Ricky reached for his beer and took another sip, staring into the fireplace across from him. This was his chance. He cleared his throat and turned towards Andriy.

"You make him happy," Andriy said.

"What?"

"You make my boy happy. It's like a piece of him had been missing all these years since you were taken away." Andriy took a sip from the mug on the table and set it back. "He was happy enough. But something was always absent. Now that spark is back. I think it is you he was missing."

"I missed him too," Ricky confessed. "And I never got the chance, when everything happened, to thank you. A lot of people would have turned their heads the other way, figured it was none of their business. But you didn't. And I'll be forever grateful for that. You saved my life."

Andriy shrugged like it was no big deal. "I did what anyone should do when someone is being hurt. No adult should lay their hands on any child. He was no man." Andriy's face pinched as if he were disgusted.

"I would understand if you or Sandy blamed me for Ever getting hurt." Ricky held his breath.

Andriy sat forward, elbows on his knees as he leveled the weight of his stare on Ricky. "We had nothing to blame you for. That was on Donald."

"But I kissed him—that's why—"

"*Ni.* You did nothing wrong. I will admit I was surprised you two were . . . well, that you had feelings, and were more than friends. But that didn't change anything. My son is my son no matter who he loves. No matter what. And he's a good man. He's a good judge of character of people—most of the time." Andriy smiled. "I'm glad you two found one another again."

"Me too."

Andriy nodded. "Everett tells me you're in a good place now. With a good family?"

"Yes. My ma and dad are the best."

"This is good news. I'm glad to hear it. And I wanted you to know you are welcome anytime in my and Lorna's home."

Ricky's throat clogged with emotion. He swallowed hard. "Thank you. I appreciate that."

"Hey, Mom said dinner's ready." Everett walked in, running his eyes down Ricky as if checking to make sure he was okay in the ten minutes Everett had been gone.

"We don't want to keep her waiting." Andriy stood, taking his cup with him.

Ricky grabbed his and Everett's beers and handed one to Ever.

Everett took it and held back as his father exited the room. "You okay?"

Ricky filled his lungs with fresh oxygen and exhaled. "Yeah, I'm better than okay."

Everett nodded but something hesitant flashed in his gaze.

"Did you get whatever your mom needed?"

Everett's gaze dropped to the floor. "Yup."

"Are *you* okay?" Ricky asked.

"I got you by my side and a wonderful meal ahead with my family. I'm great."

"You're sure?"

Everett sighed. "I'm sure."

Ricky hated the idea that Everett was uneasy for his sake.

Ricky slid his arm around Everett's waist. "Let's go eat some good food, then."

There was something freeing about being in a room full of people who didn't bat an eye that he was with their son as a date. About the fact that Everett had his back, but so did Sandy and Andriy. Despite everything, Everett's parents were welcoming him into their family like they'd done years ago. It was comforting that some things didn't change.

Ricky peeked at Everett as they walked through the house towards the dining room with the clank of dishes, and conversation got louder the closer they got. Everett had always been constant in Ricky's life, as kids and now as adults. As best friends and lovers. He had nothing to worry about with Everett. The trust they'd built had a solid foundation.

Ricky was safe with Everett, always and forever. This was the man he wanted to spend the rest of his life with. And he'd prove it when they got back to Shattered Cove.

40

RICKY

Sweat dripped down Ricky's temple, but it was nothing compared to the heat he and Everett created as they grinded on the dance floor. Delicious friction teased his cock to the point of pain. Nothing but denim separated them as they moved to the sultry upbeat song playing loudly over the speakers. Colorful lights flickered over the crowd of writhing bodies like rainbow rain. As the artist sang about all the bad things he wanted to do with his boyfriend, Ricky couldn't help but plan out their night in his head. They could tumble into the hotel room. Maybe Everett would let Ricky tie him to the bed. Or maybe Ricky would take control this time? He smiled with all the wicked ideas that came to mind.

Everett spun around as the song came to a close. His lips were wet when they met Ricky's. He smelled of sweat and a hint of citrus. It was intoxicating—Ricky wanted more. He gripped the back of Everett's neck, pulling him closer as he slid his tongue inside his boyfriend's mouth.

Everett's chest rumbled, vibrating against Ricky's, his fingers digging into his waist.

Ricky pulled back, breathless. Everett's eyes glittered with a mix of arousal and pure happiness that mirrored Ricky's own. Everett's skin flushed, his cheeks pink.

"I love you," Ricky confessed as the music switched to something slower. "So much it scares me sometimes."

Everett's eyes widened before the biggest smile split his face. He cupped Ricky's face and kissed him once more. "Then I can be brave for you when you need it. Because you've had a piece of my heart since we were fourteen, fumbling through our first kiss. But now—now you have all of it."

Ricky grinned. Emotion clogged his throat as he stared at the man who'd blasted through every wall he'd erected. The man who had sacrificed so much to show up in the way Ricky needed.

They swayed slowly to the music, foreheads pressed against one another. Finally, he let all his guards down. It was terrifying to open yourself up and be this vulnerable. But Everett had never given Ricky a reason to doubt him.

"When we get back tomorrow, at family dinner, I'm going to tell them." The words left him with surety wrapped in a ribbon of anxiety. It would be the scariest thing he'd ever done, but this was who he was.

As the song continued, the singer spoke words directly from Ricky's soul. About a man not needing to be ashamed of who he was for loving another man. This was exactly who Ricky was meant to love—every molecule in his body agreed. Everett was it for him. He was his boyfriend, partner, and maybe they'd be parents one day. He wouldn't risk telling his family unless he was sure.

"I never thought I'd have this, you know?" Ricky asked.

Everett pulled back to look in his eyes. "Have what? Love?"

Ricky nodded. "Didn't think I was capable of it. Because the only boy I ever came close to feeling something deep for was you. And after everything happened, I felt hollow—like I didn't have a heart anymore. It died that day—Donald beat it out of me."

Everett leaned in, his fingers threading into the hair at the back of Ricky's head. He made a fist and tugged, leaving no doubt who was in control. "Oh, miy lev. No one could take that from you unless you gave it. I think your heart just got a little bruised and broken along the way, so you hid it behind your walls."

Ricky licked his lips. "I think I was waiting for the right person to scale them—not break them down. I've seen enough violence in my life. I needed patience and understanding."

"You needed the right person." Everett searched Ricky's eyes.

"I needed you. Years ago, I gifted my heart to you, and you kept it safe. Protected it all this time. So, now I can be whole."

Everett's eyes glistened as the song faded to an end. The lyrics urged Ricky to kiss the boy in front of him.

"I'll always keep your heart safe, miy lev."

"And that's why I love you so much." Ricky smiled.

Everett grinned as something techno thudded through the speakers. "Say it again."

"I, Ricardo Emerson, love you with everything in me. No matter what we're gonna face in the future, I know I wouldn't want anyone else by my side. I trust you." Ricky kissed Everett once more.

"Damn, you two are gonna set the whole place on fire," Chris yelled over the music.

Ricky and Everett pulled apart and laughed.

"I was rather enjoying the show." Bryan waggled his eyebrows up and down playfully.

His boyfriend swatted his arm. "I just bet you were."

Everett turned towards his friends. "Let's go out for a smoke and cool down. This is not my favorite music."

Ricky laughed as they made their way back to their coats. They headed out the door and walked to the side of the building just inside a dim alley. Couples passed by a few feet from where they stood on the main sidewalk. One overhead streetlamp lit the space by the dumpsters. The faint smell of garbage hung in the air. Light bled out from the big window looking into the bar.

Ricky pulled out his vape pen, warming it up as his feet crunched in the dirty snow at the very edge of the alley.

Bryan pulled out a joint and passed it to his boyfriend. They lit up while Ricky took a few puffs of his pen and passed it to Everett. Smoke curled in the air, floating up to the cloudy dark sky. The temp wasn't as cold as it had been a few weeks ago, a sure sign spring was coming sooner than later.

"I'm glad you guys could meet up with us again," Bryan said.

"Yeah. Maybe one of these days we'll have to come to Shattered Cove and you can show us around," Chris suggested.

Everett's gaze flicked to Ricky like he was unsure if he should accept.

Ricky wrapped his arm around Everett and pulled him close. "That sounds like a great idea. We have a guesthouse on the property we use for wedding parties. I'll check, but I'm sure you two could stay there."

"Ohhh, a guesthouse? Fancy. That sounds wonderful. We'll plan it." Chris smiled and took another hit.

With the pungent scent of weed, laughing friends, and the

high of finding the kind of love Ricky hadn't thought was possible, Ricky turned to Everett.

"Thank you." Everett leaned in and kissed him softly.

"Fucking faggots!"

A wall of white-hot anger locked around Ricky. He jerked away from Everett, searching for the source of the voice.

His feet were moving before he thought better of it, despite the arm pulling him back. A guy with a disgusted expression shook his head and turned away.

"The fuck did you just say?" Ricky asked.

The guy stopped and turned towards him. "I said you're all a bunch of fairies. Are you dumb too? Should I talk slower so you can understand?"

Everett gripped his arm tighter, tugging him back. "Ricky, don't—"

Ricky jerked away, approaching the man. His hands were fisted at his side, and he was ready for a fight if it came to that. "No. This asshole needs to apologize to you and your friends."

The man puffed his chest out, proud and confident as if not realizing just how much unmatched he was to Ricky. Still, he snarled, "It will be a cold day in hell when I apologize to a cock sucker."

Ricky moved but Everett was faster, putting himself between the asshole and Ricky.

Everett faced Ricky, pressing his shoulders as if trying to urge him back. "Just ignore him. He's not worth it."

The asshole snickered. "That's right. Listen to your boyfriend like a good little bitch—"

Ricky's fist connected with the man's jaw. Rage boiled his veins. Everything screamed inside him, pulling him a million directions, but anger won out.

A red haze covered his vision.

Faggot.

Such a pussy.

Weak.

Ricky's fist rose and fell over and over. The satisfying crunch of bone splintered under his fist. Warm blood splattered his arm.

I'm not helpless. Not this time.

Someone grabbed him from behind, like a vise, unmovable. Ricky spun around, twisting his body in motions that had become second nature. He raised his fist to the newcomer.

"NO!" Everett grabbed him and shoved him against the wall. "Stop! It's over."

The burly newcomer kept a wary eye on him, the streetlight highlighting the name of the bar on his shirt.

Ricky blinked as everything came back in focus. A crowd of people stood around them, staring as another big bouncer with a matching shirt from the bar picked the asshole off the ground.

"He broke my fucking nose!" the asshole wailed.

"Get out of here," the bouncer barked to him and then turned to Ricky. "You wait a few minutes until he's gone, and you get out of here too. We don't condone fighting in or around this establishment."

Ricky gave a nod, letting him know he understood as he flexed his cut knuckles. The asshole walked away casting him one more glance filled with so much rage. "Fucking pussies."

Ricky tried to push forward, but Everett held him in place. "Don't."

"Okay, everyone. Show's over. Go on." One of the bouncers shooed everyone away.

"You guys better go. No reason to ruin your night too," Everett said to his friends.

Chris and Bryan both studied Ricky.

"You sure? We can stay if you need help," Bryan said.

Did they think he was a danger to Everett? *Fuck.* A sliver of pain speared his chest.

"I'm fine. You guys have a good night." Everett's voice left no room for argument as he stared Ricky down, still pinning him to the wall.

Bryan and Chris reluctantly made their way back into the bar with one of the bouncers.

"What the hell is your problem?" Everett seethed.

Ricky had never seen Everett this mad. "You think this is my fault? He called—"

Everett turned his face towards the dark alley and closed his eyes like he was counting to ten. The streetlight illuminated a dark red gash by his eye, one that was quickly swelling and bruising.

"You got hurt." Ricky pinched Everett's chin between his fingers gently, turning Everett's face to get a better look.

This is my fault. He got hurt because of me. Again.

"It's nothing." Everett pulled away.

"Did I do this?" Ricky was horrified at the thought.

"No. I caught an elbow to the eye from the man you attacked. You realize he could press charges? You swung first."

A wisp of relief sank into his bones that he hadn't been the cause of Everett's injury. But this whole mess had started because he and Everett had shared a kiss on the street.

"I'm going back inside, but I have my eye on you." The bouncer warned them before heading back into the bar.

Everett wiped a hand over his face and sighed. "You have to let shit like what that idiot said go. It's gonna happen— more often than you think. People are gonna say stupid, igno- rant, and hateful vitriol. You gotta ignore them and live your life. The best revenge is our happiness."

Everything in Ricky pushed back against that idea. "So

I'm just supposed to lie there and take it when some douchebag says horrible things about the man I love?"

"Don't do that."

"What?" Ricky asked, his hackles raised.

"Make this about you protecting me."

"But—"

"I wasn't in danger. I'm a grown-ass gay man who's been out since I was a teenager. You don't think I've dealt with a hundred of those guys? Fuck, I'm still finding notes on my car telling me I'm either going to burn in hell or calling me a pervert."

"What? Someone is leaving notes on your car and you didn't even tell me?" That red haze crept up at the edge of Ricky's vision once more. Could it be Donald? Was someone after Everett because of Ricky?

Panic seized his chest, winding around him like a snake, constricting his airway. Flashes of that day so long ago flickered in his mind until the alley faded away and was replaced with his old bedroom.

Everett morphed into a fourteen-year-old version of himself, sitting on Ricky's patched and worn bedspread.

"I don't have anyone else." Ricardo gasped. The tears burned his eyes as he fought so hard to keep them in. There was no place for tears anymore. Any softness allowed in the house had disappeared when his mother had passed just weeks ago.

"You've got me." Everett pulled him into his chest and held on tight. He'd always felt so safe when his friend was around. He trusted Ever more than anyone. Loved him almost as much as he loved his mom.

"I'm always here for you, miy lev. Always. No matter what." Everett's words soothed over Ricardo like a warm blanket.

It was the only comfort he'd had since his mom had died. Ever had told him it meant "my lion." That even when he didn't feel so strong and fierce, the inner lion was inside him. Maybe someday he could be stronger, but not today.

"You swear it?" Ricardo asked.

"Promise. And it's okay to cry. My mom says if we hold it in, it just gets bigger and meaner and hurts us. I don't want that for you," Ever said.

The first hot tears fell and then became a deluge. Ricardo let it all out and Ever held him for minutes or hours—Ricardo wasn't sure. Finally, he sniffed. Ever held a dirty towel from the floor to him and Ricardo wiped his snotty nose on it.

"Come on." Ever lay down and patted the bed next to him.

Ricardo lay beside him so they were face to face. His eyes ached and were puffy and swollen from crying like a baby.

Ever worriedly studied him before he leaned in enough for his sweet breath to become Ricardo's inhale. "I'm here for you. You're my best friend. We'll find a way to get through this together, okay?"

Ricardo nodded. It sounded good to let Ever handle things for a little while. The weight wasn't so heavy on his own shoulders.

"Ever?"

"Yeah?"

"You're the bestest friend anyone could ever ask for."

Both boys stared at each other a moment before Ricky inched forward. Everett met him halfway, their lips melding together.

Pain lanced up Ricardo's arm as he was yanked off the bed like a rag doll.

"What the hell, you little faggot?"

Ricardo put his hands up. "No! No, we weren't—"

"Don't lie to me, boy! I saw your perversion with my own eyes." Donald's fist swung and landed on Ricardo's jaw. Pain burst through his head, making his ears ring as he crumpled to the ground.

"What the fuck is this? In my own house? I should have known," his dad yelled. The stench of stale beer and cigarettes filled Ricardo's nose. "Little bitch. Thought you could do this under my roof!"

Ricardo didn't even see the blow coming. He curled up into a ball, trying to protect himself. Pain radiated through his body and made his teeth chatter. He closed his eyes, waiting for more, but it didn't come.

"Leave him alone! You big bully!" Ever pulled his dad's arm.

His dad shoved Ever onto the ground. Ever landed on his arm and winced. Pain streaked across his face.

No! Not Ever. *His dad couldn't hurt Ever.*

His dad kicked Ever in the ribs.

Ever grunted as Ricardo sat frozen in fear. Stop. Stop. Stop. I just want this to end. *Ricardo pressed his hands to his ears, curling in on himself the way he did when his father got like this.*

His dad unbuckled his belt, pulling it from his waist. The jingle of the buckle sent a bolt of fear down Ricardo's spine. He knew what was coming next. He had to save Ever. He wanted to be the lion for Ever so his dad couldn't hurt him.

"Run," Ricardo said, getting to his feet. He looked up at his dad. "I hate you!" He ran with all his might, shoulder tucked in, headed straight into his dad's gut.

His father grunted from the impact and swayed backwards before bringing the belt down over Ricardo's back. Stinging agony lanced up his spine, but Ricardo didn't let go. He turned his head as Ever scrambled to his feet, holding his arm at an odd angle.

"Run!" Ricardo yelled.

His father crashed over him. The weight of the man suffocated him. Ricardo's lungs burned as his father sat on his stomach, alternating beating him with his fists and the belt. Ricky held his arms up, peeking to the spot where Ever had once been, but he was gone.

Despite the pain and the lack of air, Ricardo smiled because even if he was going to die, he'd been the lion for Everett, just this once, and now his best friend would be safe.

. . .

"Ricky!" Everett's voice drew him back to the present. "Are you even listening to me?"

Ricky took a deep breath and let it out. Everett had been in danger back then because of Ricky. And the same thing had just happened. Sure, it was only a shiner—this time. What if the next time he wasn't so lucky? What if Donald came back like he'd threatened?

What if I can't keep him safe?

A Molotov cocktail of feelings exploded inside Ricky, the shrapnel of anxiety tearing at his organs.

Ricky just being with him put Everett at risk.

"I can't do this anymore."

EVERETT

"What do you mean you can't do this anymore?" Everett asked. Sweat dotted his forehead. A sick feeling churned in his guts. "Do what?"

"This." Ricky motioned between them. "Us."

The blood drained from Everett's face, curdling in his stomach. "Please don't do this again."

"I don't have a choice." Ricky's voice cracked, pain bleeding through the space between them in the alley.

"Yes, you fucking do," Everett said. Ricky didn't really want this—he couldn't. "What are you really afraid of?"

"I'm not—"

"Don't you dare lie to me. You owe me that much." Everett stepped closer, his voice leaving no room for argument. He wouldn't be played with. He was done with this back-and-forth.

Ricky's shoulders sunk a fraction.

Everett searched Ricky's face for the truth while he spoke. "You felt vulnerable and this is how you protect yourself—

anger. This is your tough-guy act, where you compare dicks to see who's the bigger man."

"You're right." The confession was scraped from Ricky's lungs.

Everett waited as the hum of city life continued all around them.

"I did feel vulnerable." Ricky's jaw pulsed in the street-light, his voice quieter.

Half his face was cast in shadows. Much like the man, only showing the world the parts he wanted it to see. But Everett saw all of it—every sharp, jagged piece. He stepped to the side, farther into the dim alley.

"Are you embarrassed to be seen with me?" All this time he'd told himself Ricky had a lot of internal battles to work through. Never once had he assumed it might be him that drove these men away. With anyone else, Everett would have walked away. But this was Ricardo, his lion. The man Everett loved.

Ricky's brows drew together. "No. Not at all."

Water dripped from the eaves. Muffled conversations from the sidewalk became background noise with the rumble of engines.

Ricky ran a hand through his dark curly hair and tugged. "You got hurt because of me. And I feel responsible. And now, with my dad possibly out of prison, you said you're finding notes on your car. What if it's him? What if he comes back?"

"Rick—"

Ricky held up his hands. His dark eyes reflected the city lights. "No. I need to get this out. I failed you in the past. Even these last couple months, there's been times where I know I've hurt you simply by keeping us a secret. And that's not some-thing I'd ever want to do. But this fear, it's fucking paralyzing sometimes."

"I knew what I was getting into with you. I signed up for this," Everett reminded him. He sucked in the stale city air, his chest aching as if his very heart was cracking. "We can work this out together. I told you we didn't need an end time on this if it's the pressure—"

"Just stop." Ricky ran a hand through his hair, glancing at the street.

"Was the visit with my parents too much?"

"The thought of someone wanting to hurt you because of me is what's too much!" Ricky yelled, walking towards the sidewalk.

Everett grabbed his hand, pulling him back. "Don't let other people's ignorance get in the way of us—of our happiness."

Rick scrubbed a hand over his face. "I'm trying not to."

Everett cupped Ricky's jaw in his hands and pulled him closer. "And I see that. You're doing so much work."

"You'd be better off with someone else. Someone who doesn't have this baggage."

"But I want you."

Ricky turned to him, conflict between running and staying to fight warring in his gaze. Anguish poured from him in waves. "I want to be the man you deserve."

"You've grown so much in the last couple months. You were scared to be in the same room with me. Now look at you." Everett motioned to the club beside them where music steadily thumped. "You're hitting up a gay bar on a double date with your boyfriend."

Ricky's mouth quirked before he nodded. "I guess you're right."

"I am. And look, old Ricky would have already been tearing off in his truck. Yet you're still here, talking this out with me."

Ricky glanced at the street as if measuring what Everett had said. He sighed, his shoulders lowered as he nodded. "You're right. I have made progress. I never could have done any of this before."

Everett released Ricky's jaw and backed away, extending his hand.

Ricky took it without hesitation. "When we get back to Shattered Cove, I'm going to do it. I'm gonna tell them about us at family dinner. Would you . . . would you be there for me?"

"Of course." Everett pulled Ricky's hand to his lips and pressed his mouth against his split knuckles.

Ricky stepped forward as if to pull Everett into a kiss. Instead, his focus darted to the ground. His brows drew together before he bent and picked up something from the pavement. Even under the dim streetlight, his face was ashen. He stood. With trembling hands, he held out a piece of paper stained with water—no, an envelope.

Everett's lungs froze. Panic seized him. He patted his pocket where the envelope had been. Of all the moments Ricky had to find this, why now?

"What—" Ricky choked, shaking his head and staring at the envelope.

"I—"

"This is my mother's handwriting." Ricky stared at the envelope.

"It is."

"Why?" His voice as raw as the betrayal soaking the alleyway.

"She gave it to my mom before she passed."

"That's what she needed from the attic?" Ricky confirmed. "This is why you were acting weird?"

"Yeah. I just wanted us to get through dinner with my

parents and tonight. I was going to give it to you later. I knew you'd need some time and space to process without other people around."

"I asked you if something was up, and you said no." Ricky's voice was quiet and even.

Everett swallowed. "I didn't want you to feel stressed. I—"

"I never asked you to manage me." Ricky's hand still trembled as his glare leveled on Everett. "Is . . . is that what this is for you?"

Everett shifted on his feet, nerves twisting his guts into knots. "What do you mean?"

"Ever since you came back into my life you've been trying to be there for me, even when I didn't want you to be. Like you're trying to fix me. Save me."

"So now it's my savior complex again?" Everett shook his head, his hackles rising.

"You're always on my case about opening up, but you kept this from me. You treated me like a child, making a decision for me that was not your call to make." Ricky grimaced. "You know how much I—how much she meant to me. To know you had a letter from her in your possession . . ." He motioned to the ground. "And I nearly lost the last possible chance I had to have something of hers. If I hadn't seen it on the pavement getting soaked . . ." Ricky straightened, his shoulders tense. His mouth formed a grim line.

Anxiety swarmed in his rib cage. An alarm blared in Everett's mind. "I—"

"You had a letter from my mother and kept it from me?" he repeated. Betrayal laced every word—an accusation.

"Just for a few hours. I told you I wanted you to have time and—"

"And you just made that choice for me? When you knew— you fucking *knew*—what this would mean to me?"

Everett scrubbed a hand over the back of his neck. "You know me, Ricky. You know I would never do something like this to hurt you."

Ricky chuckled but there was no mirth in it. "I thought I knew you. But maybe I don't. Maybe everything I feel for you is based off what we had when we were two kids with nowhere to go but to each other. Maybe none of it was based on anything but need and survival and sexual chemistry."

"Don't say that——"

"Why not? Maybe that's the real problem here. We're trying to force something that doesn't fit." Ricky nodded like he believed the absurdity he was spewing.

"That isn't true, and you know it. This is just another way for you to run from something that makes you feel, something that makes you face all the parts of you that you keep hidden because you're ashamed. You know I love you; I wouldn't be here if I didn't. Believe in us."

Ricky's face was an emotionless mask and his tone was just as empty. "How can we work when *you* don't trust *me*?" He turned towards the street again.

"That isn't true." Everett followed him.

"Then why hide this from me? Why not tell me you had something to talk about later when I asked earlier instead of lying to me and saying that everything was fine?"

Everett blew out a breath. "I should have, but——"

Ricky held up the water-streaked envelope. "And this is how you take care of something you knew would be so precious to me?"

Everett pressed his lips together. This was spiraling out of control. "I'm sorry. I should have done things differently."

Ricky stared at him as the sound of cars and conversations of people passing drifted around them. He gave a curt nod. "I need some space. I——I can't do this right now."

Everett grabbed his arm, pleading, "Miy lev—"

Ricky yanked his arm away. "Don't touch me!"

Everett stumbled, eyes wide, mouth dropping open. A few people stopped and stared. Ricky shifted uncomfortably under their gaze.

Shock and disbelief warred with his own sense of betrayal. How had Everett ended back up here? Alone and being physically pushed away from the man he cared for?

Ricky didn't even bother looking at Everett when he spoke. "I'll find my own way home."

Everett stayed frozen to the spot as Ricky turned right and headed down the street.

A few pity-filled and curious stares met his as his heart broke. The lurkers moved on, leaving Everett alone. Numbly, he put one foot in front of the other, turning left from the bar towards the direction of the parking garage. He kept walking. Time passed in a blur. Cars beeped. Laughter spilled out from bars as he continued on. It was all too much. He turned down a street, needing to get away from the noise. He sniffed and wiped his cheeks. His frozen hands came away wet with tears. His mind raced with everything he could have done differently. Maybe if he'd given Ricky the letter right away? *How would I feel in his position?*

"Fuck." He'd never meant to hurt Ricky. And in the end, they'd both caused each other pain. *What if he hadn't seen the letter lying there? What if I'd lost it?* Everett never would have forgiven himself.

Maybe Ricky was right. Perhaps what they shared was only because of the connection from their past, and there was no hope for a future.

Everything inside Everett screamed the opposite. That the man he loved was hurting. But was that fair to Everett? To have a partner who ran away when the hard times came instead of coming together? *He said he needed space. But what if this is the end?*

I love him.

Everett should have learned from his parents—love wasn't always enough.

His chest splintered, pain radiating through him. He'd just lost the person who'd quickly become his whole world.

"Look what we have here, boys." A familiar voice from behind him had Everett jerking around.

The hair on the back of his neck stood on end. How had he been so lost in his heartbreak that he hadn't heard the four men following him?

The asshole from the bar wasn't alone anymore.

Everett swallowed, eyeing the weapons in their hands—a beer bottle and a tire iron, and a knife. "Hey, man, I'm not looking for any trouble." Everett searched the empty, quiet street. Nothing but townhomes were lined up on either side. A few lights were on, but not many as it was close to one in the morning.

The asshole and his friends laughed as they moved closer. Everett backed up on the uneven sidewalk, holding out his hands. "How about you go enjoy your night and I'll head home?"

"Hear that, boys? The little bitch wants to run home after his *boyfriend* broke my fucking nose."

Everett turned and sprinted down the street. Feet pounded the pavement behind him. His heart raced, flight taking over. Pain radiated up his leg, causing him to stumble as his chin hit the hard concrete. Blood filled his mouth as another burst of pain was slashed against his back. He screamed in agony. Blows came from all directions. He curled into a ball, trying to protect his head. He couldn't move, pinned down by their weight.

Panic seized his every cell. He kicked and fought and tried everything he could to get away, but he was outnumbered four to one. Pain became background noise as a part of him left his body, floating somewhere above himself. He could see the men hurting him, could feel the echo of an ache. But he turned to look at the sky. If this was how it ended, he wanted the stars to be the last thing he saw.

Ricky's face flashed in his mind—a thirteen-year-old Ricky, when he'd moved next door, the gangly string bean of a boy with eyes as rich as the earth. At fourteen, when they'd kissed for the first time. And all the months they'd shared since Everett had gotten to Shattered Cove. The moments they'd stolen away. Maybe that was all they were meant to be. A moment in time, locked forever in Everett's heart. Memories he'd take with him to his death. He focused on the memory of Ricky's touch, of his deep voice and how it was even more rumbly in the morning.

If this was how it ended, he'd at least have the comfort of heaven for a few brief moments in time before it all went dark.

42

RICKY

The farther Ricky walked from the alley, the more his heart twisted in his chest, like the tie that bound him to Everett cinched tighter and tighter the greater the distance between them.

Someone pushed against his shoulder, knocking him to the side.

"Sorry, man."

Ricky ignored the passerby as his heart raced, familiar anxiety invading his chest. He wandered to the bus stop, taking a seat on the empty bench. The florescent bulbs above him flickered. Ricky pulled out the envelope, running his fingers over the weathered cursive font, and closed his eyes.

Why hadn't Everett or Sandy given this to him earlier? Did Sandy know what it said?

Was my mother ashamed of me? And what if it had been lost? Would Everett have come clean about it?

A sob ripped from his chest. His mother was gone, but if she'd still been here, would she have been proud to call the man he was today her son? Even if he loved another man?

Everett's bruised face flashed in his mind. Ricky had done that. Maybe not directly, but Everett had gotten hurt because of Ricky.

Because I can't control this anger.

He sniffed and wiped his eyes. His mind and heart were at war. Fear overwhelmed him. Invisible claws sank in his skin, dragging him into a spiral of self-pity. The voices in his mind got louder.

It's okay to be vulnerable.

Ricky gasped. A glimpse of calm teased his senses with Everett's voice.

You're not less of a man for having feelings and expressing them.

The chains of expectation he'd been locked in rattled in his subconscious.

I got your back. And you've got mine. That's what we do.

"He wouldn't have kept the letter to hurt me." As soon as he spoke the words aloud, he felt the truth down to the marrow of his bones.

"I did it again. I ran scared, didn't I?"

I love you, miy lev.

Ricky's eyes shot open. He tucked the letter in his pocket, walking back the way he'd come. Moments they'd shared played through his mind like a collage. At every turn, Everett was there. He'd been patient and understanding. He'd been willing to meet Ricky where he was even at great cost to himself.

Everett embodied love in every way.

"And what did I do? I fucked it up."

A man's head turned at the sound of Ricky's voice. He probably looked a little weird, talking to himself at almost one in the morning with tearstains on his cheeks, but he didn't care. The man he loved was out there thinking Ricky was ashamed of him. That he didn't trust him.

Because I let him down.

"Fuck, what have I done?" Ricky raced past the bar. Adrenaline pumping, he searched every square set of shoulders he passed, hoping one would be Everett's. He darted into the parking garage, searching for the space where Everett had parked. The car was still there. Ricky breathed a sigh of relief. He looked around the concrete building.

Where is he?

Ricky pulled out his phone and dialed Everett. It rang and rang and went to voicemail.

"I know you haven't left yet. I'm at the car. I'm so sorry, baby. I fucked up and I said I needed time, but I'm ready to have this conversation. I fucking love you. I know you didn't—"

The voicemail cut off.

Ricky sighed. Where could he be? Ricky put his phone away and tucked his hands in his pockets, walking outside the garage.

Wait.

He stopped, taking out his cell once more and opening a *Friends Finder* app. Hopefully Everett had his turned on.

The green dot appeared. Everett wasn't far at all. Ricky jogged down the dark streets. Closed storefronts became houses. A dog barked somewhere in the not so far distance.

The hair on Ricky's neck stood on end. Voices yelled ahead. Someone yelped. The sound was unmistakable.

Everything inside Ricky switched. An urgency roared. He ran as fast as he could towards the sounds. Four silhouettes stood around a prone body.

No.

He didn't need to look to see.

Everett.

That red fog—it blanketed him. Everything slowed.

One of the men raised a tire iron.

Ricky could call for help, or he could save Everett—most likely to join him.

Four armed men and one of him. He didn't even hesitate.

Ricky sprinted behind them, looped his arm around the man with the tire iron and put him in a choke hold. The man passed out as more arms grabbed Ricky.

"Looks like a two-for-one, boys! This is the fucker that made me bleed," the asshole from the alley said.

This is my fault.

Ricky fought, blocking and swinging, but three against one was still not a fair fight. He got in a couple shots, his sore knuckles splitting deeper with the thud of each contact.

Pain exploded in the back of his head. Shards of glass clanked against the sidewalk as he fell. He turned, holding up his fists to defend himself. The fucker stood above him with the broken bottle that he'd smashed against his head.

Ricky kicked the man's knee, sending him sprawling on the ground as the other two pinned Ricky to the ground.

"HELP! POLICE!" Ricky screamed, praying that the universe and all the gods and goddesses his sister prayed to would hear. That someone would call for help.

A fist connected with his jaw. Ricky grunted as a boot assaulted with his ribs. He fought with everything in him. The longer he lasted, the more he held their attention and kept it off Everett.

Twenty-five years and they'd come full circle. Overpowered. Helpless.

A knife glinted in the streetlight.

The asshole with a bloody face held it out. "Hold him still."

Ricky used every move he could think of, but the tire iron guy woke up with an angry sneer.

"I can't fucking walk. He fucked up my knee," Bottle Guy said.

"Quit your bitching. You sound as pansy-ass as this fucker," Asshole said.

Another flash of light had his attention darting to the ground where Everett's hand was wrapped around his phone. *He's alive!* And he was calling for help. Ricky needed to buy them time. Everett had to make it.

Everett's mouth hovered over the phone, speaking into it. His voice was carrying. Their attackers would surely hear him.

Ricky looked at the men holding his life in their hands—and he laughed—full-on, belly-aching, hysterical laughter.

"What the fuck are you laughing at, you little bitch?" Tire Iron Guy asked.

"Yeah, we're gonna carve you and your pretty boyfriend up." The Asshole's eyes glinted with malice.

"He is pretty, isn't he?" Ricky smirked, warm, slick blood running over his teeth and out of his mouth.

Another blow pounded into his face. His head jerked to the side. The street darkened. *No.* He had to fight to stay awake. They couldn't get to Everett again.

"He's more of a man than you'll ever be." Ricky spat blood.

"What did you say?"

Ricky straightened as much as he could with three men holding him in place. "I said you're the weak one."

A sick smile spread across Asshole's face. "I'm gonna enjoy gutting you like a fish."

"Couldn't come up with something more original? You didn't get brains or beauty, huh? Didn't realize I was dealing with the village idiot."

There was no pain as Asshole's hand shot forward.

Ricky's smile didn't falter as he whispered.

"What?" Asshole sneered, leaning in.

"I said you'll always be a sad, lonely, pathetic fucker." Ricky headbutted the man.

Screams erupted from the asshole.

Ricky was thrown to the ground on his side, next to Everett. A series of kicks and punches slammed into him. He struggled to stay conscious. Everett's swollen eyes remained closed.

Had he passed out? Was he dead?

What if this was the end? What if Everett . . . died?

Ricky's heart ached with an agony that was worse than any injury the men could give him.

Sirens wailed in the distance.

Ricky grunted as the one with the tire iron kicked him in the gut, stealing his air. Pain lanced through his abdomen as the knife in his belly shifted.

Blackness clouded his vision, pulsing like it was connected to his heartbeat.

The assault stopped. Footsteps pounded on the pavement, moving farther away. Blood whooshed in his ears. He looked down at the knife protruding from his abdomen. A dark stain grew on his shirt. *That isn't good.* The adrenaline slowly drained from his body. Pain leached into his every cell.

He crawled across the cement towards Everett. He dragged his finger down Everett's swollen and bruised face.

"Ever?" Ricky winced, pain lancing his ribs with the movement. But it didn't matter. Everett had to be okay.

Everett's chest rose and fell under Ricky's hand, but his breathing was shallow.

Terror gripped Ricky in a vise. "Baby? Please be okay."

One of Everett's eyes blinked open, the other too swollen. "Ric—"

"It's me." Ricky ignored the pain and gritted his teeth to move into Everett's line of vision. "I'm here."

"Came. Back," Everett choked.

Tears freely dripped down Ricky's cheeks as sirens blared, turning onto their street.

Voices shouted in the distance.

"Over here! We need help!" Ricky yelled, his lungs and ribs protesting. He turned back to Everett, carefully taking his hand in his. "I'm so sorry, baby. I never should have left you. You were right; I was scared."

"But you found the lion. You. Came. Back." Everett's voice was soaked in pain as if it hurt him to talk.

"You're gonna be okay." Ricky looked over the love of his life's swollen and bruised face. "Thought I taught you how to block this pretty face?" He forced a smile, even if it only lasted a second.

Everett released a puff of air and winced. "Guess I need a few more lessons."

Police and paramedics ran up to them, immediately assessing.

Ricky turned to them. "Four men. Ran that way." He pointed.

"Can you give me a description?" the officer asked.

"We have a knife wound," one of the paramedics said, giving her partner a rundown of the visible injuries. Another paramedic looked over Everett.

Ricky gently squeezed Everett's hand. "You're gonna be okay."

"You saved me."

"Now we're even," Ricky teased, smiling despite the ache in his split lip.

They stared at each other. Pain faded from Ricky's body as he grew cold.

"Miy lev?"

"I love you," Ricky said. "I think I always did. I was just afraid. And now it seems like I've wasted so much time on stupid shit."

"I love you too." Everett's gaze dropped to the knife, and his eyes widened. "Ricky—"

"It doesn't hurt anymore."

"That's not a good sign." Worry laced Everett's voice.

"I'd do it all over again. Even knowing this is how it ends. Remember that." Ricky choked, more blood dripping from his mouth.

Hands grabbed him, lifting him onto a stretcher. He held on to Everett for as long as he could, but it wasn't enough. They'd never have enough time because of the choices he'd made—choosing to live a life in fear of what other people thought. Choosing to try and fit into this mold of what he thought being a man really meant. But in the end, it had only ended up hurting him and everyone he loved. The same men who'd attacked them were the very epitome of what Ricky had been taught masculinity was—a rejection of everything perceived as feminine. And all it did was cause pain and loneliness.

Red and blue lights flashed, but he kept his attention on Everett.

"Goodbye, Ever."

Everett sat up, pushing away the paramedic. "No! It's not goodbye with us, miy lev. Never goodbye."

Ricky smiled one last time, memorizing the face of the man he loved with every fiber of his being. "I love you."

And then the blackness sucked him under.

43

RICKY

Ricky's head pounded like he'd drunk way too much vodka. He blinked his eyes open and winced. The lights were too bright. *Fuck, everything hurts. What the hell hap—Everett!* His eyes shot open despite the pain. He blinked.

White walls and medical equipment surrounded him as it had the last several times he'd opened them. It was a dream, wasn't it? Wires and tubes were connected to his body. His attention flicked to the three people sleeping against one another in the plastic chairs.

He opened his mouth to speak, but it was as dry as the desert and sore as fuck, like he'd swallowed a tube of acid.

"Hey." His voice scraped against his throat.

Ma's eyes blinked open. She sat up, causing his dad and Nova to stir.

"You're awake!" Ma said, rushing over to his bed. She reached out as if she wanted to touch him and make sure he was really still there. Like she couldn't believe it. But she held back as if afraid to hurt him.

"Oh my God. We thought—" Renita choked up. Tears welled in her eyes and dripping down her cheeks.

"I'm sorry, Ma." Ricky's head swam, his eyelids still heavy from whatever medication was being pumped into his arm.

"You scared us to death," Nova added, her own eyes shining.

"Scared me too. I didn't think I'd ever see you again," Ricky admitted.

"Son, you ever scare your mother and me like that again and I'll bring you back to life just to wring your neck myself," his dad said, emotion thick in his voice.

"I'll try not to repeat it in the future."

Ma grabbed a cup of water and brought it to Ricky's lips. He took a sip. It hurt to swallow, but the water was like nectar from the gods.

Ricky looked around the room again. "Where's Ever?"

"What do you mean?" Ma asked.

"Everett was with you?" Nova asked, her brows drawn together.

A nurse walked through the door. "Oh, good, he's awake."

"I was brought in here with another man, Everett Popova. Is he okay?" Ricky sat up with a wince. His head spun.

The nurse rushed over to his side. "Lie down. You've had surgery to repair the knife wound. You were lucky it didn't hit any major organs or arteries. But you had a lot of blood loss. You need to rest and not open the stitches." Her tone left no room for argument.

"I need to know how he's doing," Ricky insisted.

The nurse's mouth pursed, but her eyes were kind. "Are you family?"

"He's my boyfriend," Ricky said.

Nova gasped, but he ignored her, staring at the nurse. "Please. I need to know he's okay."

She smiled. "He is. He's just down one floor. Now, you rest and I'll go get the doctor."

"Can his brothers come in now that Ricky's awake?" Renita asked.

The nurse eyed his ma. "I suppose just this once. We're already breaking the rules, so what's two more? But only for a minute." She excused herself and left the room.

"What rules are you already breaking?" Ricky asked, blinking slowly.

His ma waved her hand dismissively. "Supposed to only visit you during certain hours and only one at a time. Pshh."

His dad chuckled. "You know how your mother gets when she's determined to protect one of our kids."

Ricky smiled. He was certain the hospital staff hadn't dealt with the force that was Renita Emerson before.

"What did you mean Everett is your boyfriend?" Nova asked.

Ricky turned to her, trying to read her expression. Her full lips formed a straight line, but he didn't sense any anger from her, just curiosity.

"I'm sorry I kept it from you." He glanced at his parents. "From all of you."

"Everett? As in, the man who was dating your sister?" Ma asked.

"I don't think Nova will be too broken up about it," James said, a knowing expression on his face.

"We were just friends, Mom," Nova assured her and turned to Ricky. "But still. You couldn't let me know you wanted to poach?"

Ricky's stomach rolled, nauseous from the mixture of the meds and coming out to his family. "Everett and I knew each other as teens. He was . . . he saved my life. He's the reason I escaped from Donald and came here."

Ma's eyes widened as his dad nodded.

"I'm sorry," Ricky said.

"Why didn't you tell us?" Ma asked, hurt bleeding into her voice.

"The last time someone found out about us, my—Donald —nearly beat me to death."

Nova sucked in a breath. "What?"

His ma's mouth set in a grim line. She and James already knew about the hospitalization and that his father abused him. It would have been in his file. But they'd never known what sparked it.

"You've kept this part of you locked inside since you were fourteen?" Renita asked.

Ricky shrugged.

"But all the girls . . ." Nova wondered aloud.

"I am attracted to women too. But I've never connected with someone the way I have with Ever. He's—" Ricky choked on the rising affection. "He's my person. I love him."

"And you thought we wouldn't accept you?" Ma asked, tears falling down her cheeks.

His dad remained silent, but he put his arm around Ma's shoulders.

"It had nothing to do with you and everything to do with me. I was scared of opening myself up like that again. I got too much in my head. I didn't want anyone to think less of me," Ricky explained, his eyes falling to the thin hospital blanket in his lap.

His dad walked around the other side of the bed and gently touched his shoulder. "Look at me, son."

Ricky forced himself to face the man who'd taken him in and loved him like his own flesh and blood. The man who hadn't had to give him anything but who'd chosen to give Ricky everything he'd given to his biological children.

"You are one of the bravest men I've ever had the privilege of knowing."

Ricky sucked in a breath of surprise.

Soft brown eyes glittered with love and acceptance. "The day you came into our home was one of the best days of my life. I knew from the moment I saw you that you were always meant to be my son."

Ricky didn't even try to stop the tears that dripped down his cheeks.

"There isn't anything to be sorry for. That's the way you were made, son. Love is beautiful and meant to be shared no matter the gender." His dad's words hit Ricky, healing old scars Donald had given him.

His dad continued, "And there is nothing you could do to make me love you any less. Following your heart takes strength. You should be proud of who you are and who you love. You picked a good man. Everett would be lucky to have you."

Ricky snorted. "I think it's the other way around, actually."

"Don't discount yourself. You have a lot of love to give."

"I fucked up. We got in a fight and I walked away, and that's how he got hurt. Those men were after me, not Everett, but they found him first."

"This is no one's fault but those men who attacked you," Ma said, anger lighting her expression. "Thank goodness they were arrested."

He studied his dad. "You don't seem surprised."

His dad shrugged and straightened to his full height. "I had a feeling when he came to dinner. And I saw you two New Year's Eve night. Then his car was at your house, and most nights when it wasn't, yours was gone. Didn't take much to add it all up."

Ricky swallowed, stunned. "All this time, you knew." But his dad hadn't treated Ricky any differently.

"I try to stay out of your business. If you want me to know, you'll tell me, like you are now. I understand sometimes you need to figure things out yourself. From the moment you came into our home, pushing never worked. You always had to come around to things in your own time. You liked to learn things the hard way." His dad rubbed a hand over the back of his neck and chuckled. "Families need boundaries, especially when we all live so close. Just know I love you, and I always will. And I'm here—day or night. No matter what."

Affection bloomed in his chest, straining under just how much love there was to receive from his family. But that was the thing about love—just when you thought you'd found the end, there was always room for more.

"I love you all," Ricky said.

"What about me? Am I chopped liver?" Nash asked, walking into the room with Roman.

Ricky stiffened. Would his brothers look at him differently? He shook his head. It didn't matter. This was who Ricky was.

"Hope you don't mind—Sandy wanted to tag along. Says she's Everett's mom." Roman motioned to the woman pushing past him.

Sandy's brows pulled together as she rushed to Ricky's side. "Oh, thank God. Everett said you were stabbed. We've been worried sick until I ran into your brothers and they told me you were okay."

"How's Everett doing?" Ricky asked.

Sandy nodded and smiled. "He's fine. A few broken bones and a concussion. Nothing that won't heal. You saved my boy, and I will never be able to thank you enough." She gripped his hand, avoiding his split knuckles.

"It was my fault—"

Sandy shook her head. "No. Don't do that. Don't take that on your shoulders."

A throat cleared.

Ricky swept his gaze over his family. "This is Sandy, Everett's mom. They were our neighbors when I lived in Concord as a teen."

"Wait, you already knew Everett?" Nash asked.

"You've missed a lot," Nova supplied.

"I have a feeling I'm gonna owe Elise fifty bucks," Roman added.

Nash turned to Roman. "What bet did you lose?"

Roman looked at Ricky.

Ricky swallowed. "She guessed. And I did what I do best when I'm cornered with facing the truth—I deflected. I think that's why you guys got into that fight that night of our double date. I'm sorry."

"Guessed what?" Nash asked, looking between the brothers.

"That our brother was in love with Everett," Nova answered.

Nash blinked. "You're joking."

"No, she isn't." Ricky braced himself for any reaction. Anger that he'd lied to them all this time would be understandable.

"They say there's at least one gay kid in each family of siblings." Nash looked around the room. "We lucked out with two I guess."

"Technically, we're both bisexual," Nova said.

"So this means we get another brother?" Nash asked.

Ricky blinked away the tears and chuckled. "Yeah, that is, if he can forgive me."

Sandy rubbed her hand over Ricky's. "There is nothing to forgive."

Ricky shook his head. "We had a fight before everything happened. I said things I didn't mean. I accused him of keeping my mom's letter from me." Ricky's eyes widened. *Where is the letter now? Did I lose it in the fight?*

Sandy nodded. "When I found out you were back in his life, I had forgotten about the letter entirely. My daughter was in the attic going through things and she found an old box I'd kept. The letter was in there. That's one of the reasons I wanted Everett to come up for a visit. I wanted to fulfill a promise I made to Marissa all those years ago."

"What promise?" Ricky asked.

"Your mother knew her time was coming. She knew she wouldn't be here for you when you grew older. She was terrified to leave you with Donald. She asked me to give you that letter after she passed. But you were taken away and we couldn't get into contact with you. I held on to it just in case."

"Do you know what it says?" Ricky asked, grasping at any chance to know what it had said. He may never get the chance now.

"I never read it. But I imagine it's about what we talked about the last time we spoke, when she gave it to me."

Ricky cleared his throat. "And what was that?"

Sandy's smile softened. "We saw how you and Everett were together. We knew, even before everything came out, that you two shared a bond that went beyond friendship."

"She knew?" Ricky blinked.

"We suspected."

"And how did she . . . I mean, she was a devout Catholic. And Donald said—"

Sandy's face pinched. "I'm sorry. I don't even like to hear that man's name. Whatever Donald told you was a lie. He was a miserable man and wanted to make everyone as miserable as he was. Don't give him any space in your mind."

"I need to read it." Ricky searched the room as a doctor walked in. "Where's my stuff?"

The doctor switched places with Sandy. "If it's not in here, I would ask someone at the front desk," he said.

Nash raised his hand. "I'll get it."

"Maybe a few of you could leave with him and give us some privacy?" the doctor asked, eyebrows raised. Clearly it was more than a suggestion.

His ma crossed her arms over her chest.

"It's okay, Ma. Go get something to eat and rest. I'll be okay," Ricky insisted.

His ma hesitated, looking him over once more, and then nodded. "Alright. I could use some breakfast."

"Take your time," Ricky called out after his family. "Nova?"

His sister turned.

"Wait. Please?"

She nodded and sat in the chair as the doctor looked him over and gave him the rundown of his injuries. Everything hurt, so the long list wasn't a surprise. Ricky couldn't care less. He just wanted the doctor to leave.

"Do you have any questions?" the doctor asked.

"Nope."

"Okay, well, make sure you rest. The nurse will be in with another round of pain meds soon. The police will be in for a formal statement. And I'll check in tomorrow."

"Thank you," Ricky said before the doctor left. He turned to his sister. "Are you mad at me?"

Nova sighed. "No. I'm not mad. You know Everett and I never really dated. He's gay. I just didn't know my own brother was into one of my best friends."

"I'm sorry I didn't tell you."

"You should have. And I'm still a little upset. But I'll forgive you, eventually," she teased.

He smiled, pain stabbing his lip as his cut reopened. "Do you think you could forgive me enough to help me?"

She narrowed her eyes on him. "Help you what?"

He wiggled his eyebrows up and down. "Why, dear sister, break out of this hospital of course."

A slow smile curved the side of her mouth up. "On one condition."

"Anything." Ricky knew just how steep a price it would be, but it would be worth it.

Her smile grew. "I'll hold you to that, big brother." She reached out her hand to shake his. "A favor to be called in at any time in the future. No questions asked."

"Deal." He shook on it. "Now, let's go. I've got to see the man I love and beg him to take my sorry ass back."

"Calm your tits. I have one more condition."

Ricky rolled his eyes, sitting up and shoving the blankets off his legs. "What?"

She walked forward, pointing in his face. "You'd better not break his heart again. That man was broken on Valentine's Day, and I'm assuming it was something to do with you. He's a good guy. And I don't want either of you hurt. So I'm gonna help you break out of here and you're gonna apologize and do all the groveling you need to in order to make this right. And you'd better not fuck it up again."

Ricky nodded. "Yes, ma'am."

"Good."

"You can be scary sometimes." Ricky looped his arm around her shoulders as she pulled off a few wires from him.

"I'm my mother's daughter." She smiled, but it didn't quite reach her eyes.

"There's someone out there for you too, Nova."

She shook her head. "Don't you start. I'm fine on my own. Trust me, everyone's better off that way."

She helped him stand. Everything inside Ricky screamed at him to get back in the bed and never attempt to move again. Each step pulled at his stitches, but it didn't matter. He had one destination in mind, and nothing could stop him from getting to Everett.

44

EVERETT

Everett stared out the window overlooking the parking lot. It wasn't much of a view, but it was better than the four white walls that had surrounded him for the past several days. He was lucky to be alive—again. It had taken pleading to get his parents to finally leave his room. He'd begged for any news on Ricky.

He's alive. But would he want anything to do with Everett after this? Or was this all one huge sign that they were never meant to be?

The visceral pain that stabbed through his chest like a spear said otherwise. But was it fair to continue this anymore? He loved Ricky with everything in him, but was it enough?

Crash!

Everett jolted upright, immediately regretting the movement. His ribs screamed in protest. And his head throbbed. Nausea rolled in his stomach as the room spun.

"Shit," someone cursed.

Everett squinted through the blurriness as a very fine bare ass came into view. An ass he'd know anywhere.

"Ricky?"

Ricky spun around, one hand on a metal IV pole, the other clutching his stomach over a thin hospital gown.

"Ever?" His voice trembled.

"You're here?" Everett searched behind him, but no one else appeared. "The doctor cleared you to walk around so soon after surgery?"

Ricky bit his bottom lip and tilted his head from side to side as if weighing something. "Not exactly. But I had to see you. Make sure you were okay."

Oh. "I'll make it."

Ricky stared at him in silence for a moment before hobbling closer.

"You should really be in bed. You were stabbed—"

"Then move over." Ricky made his way to the side of the bed and turned, the back flap of his gown wide open.

Everett couldn't help but smile despite the levity of the situation. "You're practically naked and no one stopped you?"

Ricky winced as he sat on the mattress. Everett moved as close to the edge as possible despite the pain every time he breathed.

"Actually, Nova helped me get down here in a wheelchair. I only walked from the door and she thought it would be funny to untie my gown as I got to your room and take off apparently."

Everett chuckled and then hissed, gripping his ribs. "Fuck. Don't make me laugh."

Ricky settled next to him slowly. "We're two of a kind, aren't we?"

Everett's smile dimmed. "Yeah."

A beat of silence passed.

"I—"

"How—"

Everett scratched the skin at the top of his cast. "You go first."

"I thought I lost you." Ricky's voice trembled.

Everett couldn't stop from reaching out with his right hand and taking Ricky's, hoping to provide him with some level of comfort. Even if they couldn't be together, he'd always love the man.

"Ditto." It hurt to talk. Everett's jaw was still swollen and bruised. The men who'd assaulted them had fractured it. "Why did you come back? And how did you find me?"

"That friend app we downloaded. I had some time to cool off and think about everything. I was scared and confused and overwhelmed. I told myself I was protecting you by staying away. But I was really protecting myself."

Everett took a shallow breath. Anything more hurt too much.

"It hurt finding that letter," Ricky confessed.

"I'm so sorry. I should have given it to you and taken better care of it. I never would have forgiven myself if something happened to it."

"I know I overreacted. And as I walked away, I realized that deep down I knew you would never do anything to hurt me. That you were right about everything and I was still running scared. So, I went to the parking lot. Tried calling you. And then I used the app to find you. I heard you before I saw you and I knew—" Ricky snapped his mouth shut. Fat tears shone in his eyes as he turned towards Everett. "I knew there was no going back. Facing the reality that I was going to lose you forever put everything in perspective. I have a million regrets, but the biggest one is not showing you that you are the most important person to me on this earth. That I made you doubt yourself and my love for you. That I let you believe you were the problem for even one second."

"Ricky—"

"No, I need to get this out. I've fucked up so much already. All I've ever brought is trouble and violence to your door." He took a breath and wiped his eyes. "But . . . if you think you could forgive me, I swear to you, you'll never have to doubt my feelings for you again. I'll be the most obnoxious boyfriend you've ever had, but I won't run away. I may need a few minutes to get my head in order, but I'll always come back."

Everett took in Ricky's words. He wanted to say yes. But he couldn't live a life hiding one of the biggest parts of himself. And because a lot of the things Ricky accused him of were true. Everett had tried to manage Ricky like he would a patient of his.

Everett licked his lips. "I fucking love you, miy lev, and I always will."

Ricky's eyes filled with hope, one corner of his lips curving upwards. "I love fucking you—I mean, I fucking love you too . . . Well, both actually." He chuckled. Wincing, he pressed his hand to his stomach. "But I think it might be a while before either of us get to do any fucking."

Everett cleared his throat. "I'm not sure we can continue this way."

The color leached from Ricky's face as he blinked and then nodded, his shoulders drooping. "What are you saying?"

Everett squeezed Ricky's hand. "I can't stay in the closet with you. And that isn't fair of you to ask me. Just as I would not ask you to come out for me."

Something sparked in Ricky's dark eyes. "Is that the only thing holding you back from giving us another chance?"

Everett considered the question, going through everything in his mind once more. Ricky had run, but he'd come right back this time. "That wasn't okay, but I can commit to working on my issues. I think one of the biggest things holding us back is being able to be with you out in public. But I also need to take a deeper look at why I made a unilateral decision without communicating with you."

"You were trying to protect me like always. It seems both of us know how to get in our own way."

Everett nodded.

Ricky's breaths were pained and ragged. "You should probably know, I kinda already came out to my family today."

"What?" Everett asked.

"When the nurse came in, I asked about you. I told her you were my boyfriend. Apparently, my dad knew. Saw us New Year's Eve," Ricky said.

"What about your mom?"

"She was surprised, but they were fully accepting and supportive like you said they'd be. I've been worried all this time for nothing."

"How do you feel about it?" Everett asked.

Ricky was silent a beat before he answered, "I feel like I've been an idiot, wasting so much time hiding that part of my life. I deeply regret the pain I've caused my family by assuming they would not love me the way I am. And I feel lighter—free. And totally drained."

"I'm proud of you."

Ricky's dark eyes slammed into his. "I know my pride got in the way, caused you so much pain. If I hadn't needed to prove I was the bigger man, you wouldn't have gotten hurt."

"But you saved me. You were fucking stabbed. That has to count for something," Everett argued.

"I think we saved each other. Maybe that's how it's supposed to be."

"I thought I lost you too, you know?" Everett asked, emotion clogging his throat. "And all I could think about was how much time I'd wasted living life apart from you. My biggest regret is that I didn't try hard enough to find you earlier."

"How about we leave the regrets in the past where they belong? We learn from them and step into the future?" Ricky suggested.

Everett took as deep a breath as he could with his broken ribs. His next answer would change the trajectory of his life. Could they find their way through this after everything? Their rocky relationship had been a roller coaster, reminding him of his parents.

His mind conjured up the fourteen-year-old version of Ricky who'd told him to run and get help, taking the brunt of the beating. The angry man who'd tried to scare him off. The Ricky who was sarcastic and antagonistic with his family but loved them hard. The loyal man who'd learned from his mistakes and come back—just in the nick of time. The man who'd saved his life not once but twice. The broken human who sat beside him, pouring out his heart.

"Something I learned from my parents is that you can love someone with your whole heart, and sometimes it isn't enough. I think . . ." Everett's throat clenched tight. He was full of heartache. "I love you but I'm not sure we're good for each other."

Ricky flinched and closed his eyes. He cleared his throat and faced the plain white wall with a black TV screen mounted next to a whiteboard in front of them. "I see."

"I want you to be happy—God, I want that for you more than my next breath. I'm just not sure I'm the one to give you that." Everett's eyes stung with unshed tears.

Ricky released a shaky breath and nodded once. Resignation hardened his features, but they couldn't hide the pain in his tear-filled eyes. "For what it's worth, I'm so incredibly sorry for any pain I've caused you. And I want you to find your happiness too."

Ricky moved as if to get out of bed.

Everett tugged gently but firmly on his hand. "Don't go, miy lev. I know it's selfish, but stay with me for a few minutes?"

Ricky relaxed into the hospital bed, slipping his little finger through Everett's peeking out from the cast.

A few moments of silence passed. Everett turned as carefully as he could to look at Ricky. Bruises marred his face, and stitches darkened his swollen lip.

"I just need some time to clear my head without all of this."

Ricky's dark gaze sparked with hope.

"So I agreed to stay with my parents when I leave the hospital until my broken bones heal. I can work remotely for a bit."

"Oh." Twin tears rolled down Ricky's cheeks. He sniffed and wiped his face. "So, this is it?"

"I think it has to be."

They stared at each other, two hearts breaking. A cacophony of confusing emotions swirling inside Everett until he didn't know which way was up or down, left or right. He didn't want to cause the man he loved any more pain. And he had a lot to process.

Selfishly, he wanted one last sweet memory with the man who consumed his heart. Everett leaned forward, ignoring the pain that wrenched through his body. Ricky did the same, their lips meeting for a soft kiss.

"Oh, sorry—I didn't mean to interrupt," a deep voice from the doorway said.

Everett waited for the inevitable—for Ricky to flinch away,

but it never came. Instead, Ricky deepened the kiss, sliding his tongue between Everett's lips.

"Oh, now you're just showing off," Nash grumbled.

Ricky sucked Everett's bottom lip and finally ended the kiss, still staring into Everett's eyes. "I love you."

"I love you too."

Ricky turned to his brother. "Now you know how we all feel when you're sucking face with Bella."

"Worth it." Nash held out a clear bag full of material. "Here's your personal things. They said they had to cut through them so Nova is running to the store."

Ricky took it. "Thanks. Did Nova tell you where I was?"

Nash nodded. "Yeah. And Mom and Sandy have bonded over harassing the medical staff to get you moved in here with Everett."

Everett smiled. "Renita is a force to be reckoned with."

"So is your mom, apparently," Ricky teased and then his smile dimmed. "Is that okay with you? I don't need to be in here—"

"No, I want you to be. I want to know you're okay," Everett said.

"Awww, isn't that sweet," Nash teased.

Ricky smiled, holding his stomach. "Laugh it up while you can, old man. Once this injury heals, when you least expect it, I'm gonna show you who's boss."

"The only thing you're showing anyone anytime soon is how well you follow the doctor's orders and rest, young man," Renita scolded, pushing past Nash, followed by an angry-looking nurse.

Ricky tensed beside Everett.

"I'll take that as my cue to leave." Nash ducked out the door.

They had a long road ahead of them in more ways than

one. Everett couldn't live without Ricky in his life in some capacity. And they couldn't be together—not like this. But how could you move on from someone that shared a piece of your soul?

45

———

EVERETT

Seven weeks later

Everett stared at the TV, flicking through the channels. Sports. Reruns of an old sitcom. Over a hundred options and there was nothing to keep his attention. He turned the screen off and tossed the remote on his mother's couch.

"Nothing good on?" His father's deep voice startled Everett.

"Not really. What are you doing here?"

His dad released a deep sigh as he took the spot next to Everett on the couch. He pointed to the cast on Everett's arm and leg. "I came to check in on you."

"I'm getting the casts removed today and getting checked out for my all clear to get back to work."

"That's great. Have you heard how Ricardo's doing?"

Everett's hand reached instinctively for his phone. "He's . . ." Everett blew out a breath. "Nova said he's doing good."

"Nova said? You haven't spoken to him yourself?" Lines formed between his father's thick brows.

"Not in a little while. He, uh, checked in, but I told him I needed space. I need to figure out how to live without him again." Everett turned to his father. "How did you do it, after you and Mom separated?"

His father blinked, remaining quiet for a few moments, his assessing gaze heavy on Everett. "You and Ricky can't work this out?"

"I mean, we probably could, but then something else would happen and we'd end up back here. I can't do this again. I've been down this road before. I've seen where it leads."

"You've been down this road with Ricardo?" his dad asked. "What really happened between you two?"

"We got together and he wasn't out, like Justin. And I thought I could help him realize that he'd be freer if he let himself be . . . himself. So I agreed to keep things on the low." Everett took a breath. "And then he thought his dad was getting out of jail and that I was in danger, and he lost it. We broke up. We got back together and he agreed he wanted to work on coming out. He made so much progress. Things were going amazing, and then you know what happened the night we visited here. We argued, he said he needed space, and he couldn't talk it out right then. He told me not to touch him." Everett's chest squeezed at the visceral reminder of the rejection. "And then he walked off. I went my way and got jumped."

"Do you hear what you said to me?" his dad asked.

Everett blinked at him in confusion. "Of course I did. I said it all."

"You drew parallels between him and Justin."

Everett's gaze volleyed between his dad and the cream-colored couch. "Because it's a similar situation."

"Are you sure you're not projecting?"

Am I? No. I couldn't be . . . Could I? "Ricky was in the closet like Justin. There's no getting around that."

His dad nodded, relaxing into the couch. "True. But did Justin show you any growth in the time you were with him? Did he ever truly put in the work to be a partner for you?"

Everett searched his memories. How many nights had he waited for a text or call to go out and spend time together just to be disappointed, time and time again. Justin only ever came over for sex. But Ricky—he'd pushed himself at every turn. Even the night everything had happened, he'd shown growth. Everett was alive because of it. He was living proof.

"No, Justin didn't. But it doesn't mean Ricky and me are right for each other."

"He loves you."

"And I love him. But you told me that you can love someone, and it still might not work out—even if they love you back."

A humorless rumble of a laugh left his father as he shook his head and wiped his hand over his beard. "I also said a relationship cannot survive if only one of you is fighting for love."

Everett was silent, taking in his father's words.

"I know you've fought. You have this deep need inside you to serve others. This empathy is both a blessing and a curse sometimes. It is good to be conscious of it. To not overextend yourself in the strive to help others. From what you've told me, it sounds like Ricardo was fighting a lot of battles, and all of them to be a better man. He just went about it in his own way."

"But you and Mom tried everything, and it still didn't work out between you."

His dad frowned. "We certainly fought—just not in the right ways."

Everett remembered the screaming matches, the tears, and the stress of his parents' last years together. Things had been good for spurts of time, and then something would happen and the tension and anger would return.

"I come from a different generation, and I used that as an excuse for a long time. I didn't support your mother the way a husband should. And when she reached out to me for help, I shut down. I thought I was doing all I needed to do as a man by working and paying the bills. But she needed more. She needed me there to help with the mental load, the everyday stresses. She needed a partner who would listen and support her. And I failed, miserably."

Everett had never heard his father's version of his divorce. It was striking to see from his perspective what had gone wrong. "You've been a great dad."

His father chuckled. "I am now. But I know you remember the nights I would come home, and you'd ask to throw the ball outside or do something as a family, and I'd switch on the TV instead. It wasn't until we almost lost you and everything happened with Ricardo that something clicked inside me. It woke me up. I knew I had to make changes and work on myself. I would have regretted everything if we'd lost you, and I never wanted to feel that again." He cleared his throat as if it was clogged with emotion. "It was too late to repair things with your mother. There was too much resentment and hurt built up. But I knew I could be a better co-parent with her. That was the least I could do after all the hurt and loneliness I'd caused both of you."

"I must have blocked a lot of that out. I remember you fighting and being tired after work. But to me, you've been the best dad," Everett said.

His father smiled as he patted Everett's shoulder. "I love you, sonechko. More than anything in this world." He folded his hands over his stomach. "I've had my fair share of experience in this life. Which is why I will tell you to think really hard before shutting this door on Ricardo and you forever. Just take some time and consider everything. After, if you decide he isn't the one for you, then you do what you have to. But if there's a chance you two can work through this, don't waste time like I did."

"I will." Everett laughed. "I think maybe you should have been a therapist too."

Deep, belly laughter reverberated from his father. "Ni. I am who I should be, and that's a father to you and a husband to the love of my life, Lorna."

"Thanks, Tato."

"Always, miy sonechko. Now, how about we get you to this appointment to get these casts off? They have to be driving you crazy by now."

"Oh, you have no idea how itchy they are."

His father stood, extending a hand to Everett, which he took.

As they headed towards the doctor's office, Everett couldn't help but play the conversation he'd had with his father over and over in his head. Everett had been comparing Justin to Ricky, and maybe he had projected after their assault. The two relationships had been similar. But Everett would have to be delusional to believe they were the same. Ricky had protected Everett. He'd put in the work. So what was it Everett truly wanted from Ricky? Hadn't Ricky done everything Everett had wanted and more?

Why doesn't it feel like enough?

46

RICKY

Ricky checked the address in his phone once more before looking at the decrepit building in front of him. He inhaled the scent of rotting garbage and filth. *Ugh.* A car alarm sounded not too far off in the distance as Ricky approached the brown door streaked with what he'd guess was urine, judging by the smell. He lifted his fist to knock and grimaced as his skin touched the sticky door. The rusty metal number four on the door fell and crashed to the creaky wooden porch.

"What do you want?" the scratchy voice from inside yelled.

Ricky froze. His body tensed; he was ready to defend himself. He closed his eyes and breathed through his nose, using the horrible smell to ground himself. "Open the door, Donald."

A moment later the door cracked open, a flimsy chain holding it in place as his biological father peered out.

"Well, look what we have here." Donald snickered before

closing the door. The sound of the chain clanking preluded the door opening wider.

Ricky stood toe to toe with his biological father. Donald was older than he remembered, his brown hair a mix of grey and white. Lines marred his wrinkled face. His eye sockets were sunken and discolored. Ricky had never thought skin could take on both a yellowish and sickly grey sheen, but apparently, that was possible.

He'd imagined this moment a million times. Played over scenarios late at night of what he'd do when he faced the monster that had taken everything from him. All that anger boiled to the surface, heating his blood.

"Told ya I'd see ya soon. You bring me money?" Donald searched the empty street as he took a swig from the bottle of cheap rum in his hand.

"When did you get out?" Ricky's voice remained emotionless despite the riot thrashing inside him.

"A couple months ago."

So after Everett had received the notes on his car. It wasn't him, then.

A slight relief filled Ricky that at least his father wasn't to blame for that. It didn't make it much better that some ignorant fucker was out there leaving notes on cars for people who worked at Hope.

Ricky tuned back into Donald's voice. He was rambling about his shitty situation.

"I didn't come here to catch up," Ricky interrupted.

"You better show me some respect, boy. I see some things never change. You still a fag—"

Ricky's hands were around the man's throat before he could finish his sentence. He shoved him against the wallpaper in the hall behind him.

Donald's eyes bugged out as he gripped Ricky's forearms and then hands, trying to pry them off his throat.

But he couldn't.

Ricky relished that for this moment, he was the one over-powering the man who had abused him. The man who could have fought for his mother, and instead caused her more pain. The man who'd made him—who'd been supposed to love him, but never had. The figure in his life who had always seemed like an unbeatable, scary giant.

But he wasn't.

If Ricky squeezed just a little harder, he could end this man's life. And a part of him still wanted to. To kill the demon that plagued his nightmares.

But he wouldn't.

"You're not worth it," Ricky snarled in his face.

"Stop! I'm your father." Donald coughed, struggling against Ricky. The bottle of rum shattered on the ground and spilled over their feet.

Ricky leaned in, his nose wrinkling at the stench of unwashed body odor and rank alcohol emanating off the man. "Listen to me, and listen good, because I will only say this once. You are not my father. We share nothing but DNA, and that's unfortunate. I have a father, and you are not it. You're not even one-tenth of the man that my dad is."

Ricky took a breath, staring into Donald's reddened, angry face. And all that anger he'd carried all his life—it morphed into apathy. He saw Donald for the pitiful degen-erate he was—a man so miserable and selfish he didn't deserve one more minute of Ricky's energy.

"I'm going to let you go, and I'm going to live my life with the people I love. I'm going to have a family and a million happy memories, and you won't be a part of a single one. You will be forgotten after I walk out this door and left to rot in the filth you've brought upon yourself. You are *nothing* to me."

Donald swung his hand, but Ricky blocked and twisted,

maneuvering them so his father's arm was twisted behind his back, his face shoved into the wall.

"Let me go—"

"No. Not until I'm done," Ricky barked, leaning closer to Donald's ear. "You *ever* try to contact or come after me or someone I love and care about, and I will come for you. The one thing we share—as dismayed as I am to admit it—is that I have a monster inside me too. And if you hurt someone I care about, if you even show up in their vicinity, I will let him out and he will end you without a second thought—and it won't be fast. So get out of this town—out of this fucking state. I don't ever want to see you again. Understood?"

Donald's lips thinned. Ricky twisted his arm.

Donald yelped in pain. "Alright! Okay. I'll go."

Ricky released his hold.

Donald stumbled, gripping his arm and rubbing it. "You little pussy. Got the jump on me. You're nothing, you hear me? Weak fucking runt. I should have killed you the moment your bitch of a mother told me she got knocked up with you—"

Ricky gritted his teeth, his body shaking as if he could shake off the filth of the words the man spewed at him.

"Don't you *ever* talk about my mother. You're not worthy of saying her name." Ricky wiped his hand on his jeans, not wanting any of Donald's stain to come with him. He turned around and walked away.

"You little shit. Come back here and fight me like a real man!"

Ricky shook his head, his father's slurs drowned out by the thudding of his heart. The adrenaline was wearing off. His body trembled and his stomach lurched.

Ricky made his way to his truck and climbed in. He sucked in a breath, but it didn't feel like enough. His chest rose and fell more rapidly as the panic attack sunk its claws into him.

"I'm safe," he repeated. "It's over."

He inhaled for four seconds and out for six over and over, like his therapist had taught him. He named what he could see, what he could hear, smell, taste, and feel, grounding himself. He used the tools he'd learned until his breathing evened out.

Inside, he was still an unstable mess, but he had a handle on it. He knew it would pass. Ricky couldn't run from it—he had to go through it.

Starting the car, he switched on music that helped calm him even more as he drove home, where everyone would be waiting for him. Where his family lived, loved, and learned together.

The drive was just long enough for him to get a better handle on himself. When he arrived, he climbed out of the car and tilted his face towards the sun. *I'm free.*

47

EVERETT

Everett stretched as he climbed out of his car and shut the door. Bright afternoon sunlight glinted off windshields as he walked into Hope Facility. Birds sang and the occasional car rumbled by. The warm summer breeze carried notes of something floral. He opened the first set of doors and then swiped the badge that Aaron had been kind enough to mail him since he'd been away.

He wished this level of security wasn't needed, but there had been an uptick of notes found on cars in the lot, and Aaron wasn't taking any chances with the kids' safety.

Everett made his way through the main room, waving at the kids who looked up.

"Hey, Mr. P. You're back!" Billy said, giving him a fist bump.

"I am. You'll have to come visit me later and catch me up on all the things I missed while I was away."

"Sounds good." Billy turned back towards the couch he'd been sitting on.

"Hey, have you seen Mr. Ridley?"

Billy pointed towards the main hall the offices came off. "I think he was in one of the meeting rooms."

"Thanks." Everett moved in the direction Billy had motioned, taking in the building and the changes that had taken place since he'd been gone. His injuries hadn't kept him away the full two months, but Everett had needed the emotional space. Everything here reminded him of Ricky. He had been avoiding the center and Shattered Cove as he hadn't wanted to fall back into their same pattern. But after Everett's talk with his father, things didn't seem as clear anymore.

Everett passed his office. Colorful cards hung from tape all over the door with *get well* sentiments written on them. He smiled. He'd have to read every single one when he was done checking in with Aaron.

A deep chuckle stopped Everett in his tracks. He froze, his ears perked at the unmistakable voice that came next.

"I don't know about all that." *Ricky.*

What was he doing at Hope? Everett moved towards the cracked meeting door, peeking in. Ricky had his back to him. Bailey and her friends stood around him, cracking up at whatever they were talking about.

"What about you? Have you ever been in love?" Bailey asked Ricky.

Everett's heart thudded in his chest.

"Yeah." Ricky's voice sounded like it scraped against his throat. His pain was palpable.

"Are you still with them?" another girl asked.

Ricky cleared his throat. "No."

Everett's stomach clenched.

"Why not?" Bailey asked.

"That's a hard question to answer. We . . . . Back then, I don't think I was ready to be the man he needed."

"What about now?" another voice asked.

"Now? I think it's too late."

"But you'll find someone else," Bailey encouraged him.

Something violent twisted inside Everett. Jealousy that he had no right to burned in his guts. *Of course he would move on. That was what I wanted, wasn't it?*

"Maybe," Ricky said, but there was no hope in his voice. "So, did you write out that letter we talked about last week in group?"

A handful of yeses echoed through the room. Ricky had been there last week? For a group therapy? Everett's brows drew together. He took a quick glance around the hallway to make sure he was still alone and no one would catch him eavesdropping.

"Awesome. How did writing that letter to your caregivers who rejected you make you feel? Does anyone want to share?"

"Wait, wait. You promised us if we did this, you'd tell us how your visit with your bio dad went," Bailey insisted.

Everett's jaw dropped open. Ricky had visited his dad?

Ricky chuckled but there was no mirth in it. "It went like I expected. I knocked on his door, and it was a shock to see him after so many years. He wasn't the big scary monster of a man I remembered. He seemed . . . small. In a lot of ways. And I think, someday, when you get to a certain point in your healing journey, you'll realize that these people who wronged us, who hurt us to our core, they were just very small people who put others down to make themselves feel better."

"You really think so?" Bailey asked.

"I do."

"What did he say? Is he . . . Does he still think it's wrong for you to love a man?" another kid asked.

"He does. But that wasn't a surprise. I went there to speak to him for myself. I knew nothing he could say would give me any peace. But I needed to speak my mind and set boundaries with him so he would stop trying to contact me and the people I care about."

Everett held back a snort. He was sure that conversation had been a messy one. And with Ricky's temper? Was he okay? Seeing his dad after this long and everything that happened must have brought up a lot of stuff. *I should have been there for him.* But Ricky had not only done it, but he seemed okay. More than okay, if he was talking openly to a small group of teens about it.

A throat cleared behind Everett and he jumped.

"Am I interrupting something?" Aaron asked.

Everett shook his head and moved away from the door to the meeting room. "No, sorry. Is that Ricky in there?"

Aaron nodded and headed back down the hall with Everett following. "Yeah, he's been volunteering. Said it was just until you returned. I guess he didn't want us to be short-staffed."

Ricky had covered for him? That tugged at Everett's heart, his chest expanding with warmth. Ricky knew how important these kids were to Everett. And yet he'd planned to be done when Everett returned. Was that so they didn't have to run into each other? His stomach twisted at the thought.

"He brought the rest of the Emersons a few times too. Mama E helped Marge cook up a soul food feast for us all. We weren't expecting you back for another week. Are you feeling up to the task?" Aaron asked.

"Yeah. I got the official all clear from the doctor yesterday. I'm more than ready to dive back in. I couldn't find Bailey's file in the folder on the Google Drive; I was going to ask you about that. Does she not want to find a family to be placed with anymore?"

Aaron smiled and opened his office door. Everett took a seat across from Aaron's desk.

"Actually, we found her a placement. All the paperwork has gone through, and she's agreed to the match."

Everett smiled, happy for the young girl. She deserved a good home, someone to show her love and acceptance and support.

"She'll be moving in with Ricky once we finalize everything later this week. So we're going to throw a party for all those that have been matched this month."

Everything screeched to a halt in Everett's mind. "Did you just say she was placed with Ricky? Ricky Emerson?"

Aaron nodded. "Yes."

"But it takes months to vet someone. To do the background checks and interviews and inspections."

"Yeah, he approached me earlier this year about it. Do you have reservations about him I should know?"

Earlier this year? Everett's eyes widened. Ricky must have spoken to Aaron one of the days he'd brought him lunch. *Holy shit.* He'd really been making changes, even ones Everett hadn't seen. *Maybe I didn't know him as well as I thought.* And perhaps that was a mistake on Everett's part. Assuming that because of their past, he knew Ricky more than he did, and he'd made assumptions accordingly. *And then projected my baggage with Justin on him too.*

Ricky was going to be raising a teen girl. Everett's chest squeezed as he smiled. Bailey and Ricky seemed like a good fit. They shared a common past. He would be able to understand her situation and relate. That was still a huge undertaking. But he'd have the Emerson family to support him.

But not me. The reminder settled like a lead weight in Everett's gut.

"Everett?" Aaron's voice brought him out of his head.

"I'm sorry. I'm just taking this all in."

"Do you have any reservations about Ricky?" Aaron clarified, always the protector.

"Not at all. He's . . . he's one of the most qualified people to help someone like Bailey, in my opinion."

Aaron sat back in his chair, studying Everett. "He came to me privately and explained he was seeing you when we spoke about Bailey's placement."

"He did?" But that was . . . before the accident. Before he came out to his family. Ricky had started coming out more than three months ago.

"Yes. And then he showed up with stitches and bruises, asking about volunteering after your accident, which I'm assuming included him too?"

Everett nodded. "We're not, uh, together anymore. But that won't affect my duties here. Even if he stays on as a volunteer."

"Okay. If you're sure."

"Positive."

Ricky's ability to care for Bailey was the only thing Everett was sure of anymore.

48

EVERETT

Everett walked down the pathway lined with lanterns to the barn on the Emersons' farm. It had only been a week since he'd been back in Shattered Cove and yet so much had happened—internally at least.

This would be the first time he'd be seeing Ricky face to face. Nerves skittered down his spine, making Everett's stomach flip. God, he was so fucking nervous. He wiped his hands on his suit jacket as the people in front of him filtered inside for Elise and Roman's wedding.

Everett took a moment, stepping to the side to let others pass. He tipped his head towards the sky. Stars glittered above, reminding him just how small he really was in this wide world. It was a good reminder of how insignificant so many things were that he'd spent so much time worrying over. It made a man look inward at what really mattered. At what Everett needed.

He took one more deep breath and rejoined the few stragglers making their way into the venue.

James and Nash stood by the door, taking turns greeting guests and ushering them to their seats.

Everett smiled, wiping his hand one more time on his dress pants before shaking James's hand.

"Good to see you looking so well." James nodded.

"Thank you, sir."

"I got this one, Dad." Ricky's voice was like the rich honey, warm and decadent. It slid through Everett's veins, heating him from the inside out as moths of anticipation tumbled and spun in his guts.

"Ricky."

Their eyes met. Dark, guarded, seemingly endless spheres pulled him into their fathomless depths.

"Hey," Ricky breathed out.

There were so many words bubbling up inside Everett that he wanted to say. But this was not the time nor the place. His focus slid down the dark charcoal suit that hugged Ricky's muscular form. A pink square stuck out of his pocket and a bow tie was fastened snugly around his neck. "You look good."

Ricky smirked and nodded towards the seated guests.

Everett's cheeks heated as he followed beside Ricky. "I mean, you look like you healed well."

"Thanks. You too. I see the casts are off."

"Yeah. Last week."

"Awesome. I'm glad you're doing better." Ricky stopped by an empty seat.

Everett stared at him. "I—"

"You—"

They shared an awkward laugh.

Ricky's pink tongue darted out, leaving a shiny sheen on his lips. "It's good to see you."

Was it? "I'd like to talk at some point."

Ricky blinked, his eyes widening and lighting up before he looked around them.

"I mean, it doesn't have to be tonight," Everett added.

Ricky focused back on him, his shoulders falling a fraction of an inch as his smile dimmed. "Sure. I'll leave you to enjoy the ceremony."

Everett stood frozen as Ricky walked to the front to stand by Roman, who was nervously messing with his bow tie. Ricky patted his brother on the shoulder, leaning into Roman's ear and saying something that had Roman's smile splitting his face and his shoulders relaxing. Everett sat while Ricky adjusted his brother's tie and stood beside him, his hands clasped together as Nash joined them.

Soft music played as Roman ushered his mother and Elise's to their seats. There was a sign language interpreter in the front for the ceremony, as well as a traditional Japanese officiant and a pastor who was a friendly face from Hope.

Ricky's nieces and nephew walked down the aisle first. Alba pulled away from Eli, and her eyes lit up at the sight of her father at the end of the aisle. She ran to him, her little legs stumbling, but her father stepped out of line to catch her just before she fell. A series of laughs drifted from the guests. Lights flashed as pictures were snapped. The rest of the kids made their way down the aisle, followed by a woman in a soft pink dress, holding a bouquet of flowers. Nova was next, and then Elise's two men of honor lined up to the left of the aisle just before the music changed. Everyone stood as Elise made her way down the aisle with her father, her eyes locked with her future husband's.

The wedding continued in a beautiful blur. Everett wished he could have paid more attention, but his focus was locked on the beautiful man beside the groom. They incorporated Elise's

Japanese culture into the ceremony, part of it in Elise's family's native language.

It was beautiful to see two cultures blending together so seamlessly.

Ariel joined Elise and Roman as Elise made her own separate vows to Ariel, promising to be there for her and love her for the rest of her life and beyond.

Ricky's gaze met Everett's as the couple recited their vows. Everett didn't look away—he couldn't. Ricky was the first to break the connection, his cheeks blushing slightly.

The bride and groom kissed, sealing their bond before they held hands and jumped over a broom laid at their feet. Cheers rang up as they smiled and made their way down the aisle, the wedding party following close behind.

Everett stayed in his seat long after they were gone, running through everything in his mind.

"Why did I wait so long?" Everett stood as employees moved chairs around, making room for the tables and the reception.

He swallowed, heading to the outdoor bar set up and getting himself a drink. And that was where he stayed while the wedding party returned from photos.

This was his chance. Everett stepped towards the gift table, but someone else grabbed Ricky's attention first. Person after person pulled Ricky away, chatting, and hugging him.

Anxiety hummed through Everett's veins. He couldn't stand it. Yet he'd done this to himself, hadn't he?

"I'm so glad you came," Nova said, standing in front of him.

"Thanks for the invite."

"You look good."

"And you, my dear, are breathtaking." He admired her gauzy pink dress, flowing to the ground.

"Why, thank you."

"Did you bring a date I should meet?" he asked, partly teasing.

She rolled her eyes. "Unfortunately, my date's flight got canceled. You know, something about an engine problem."

Everett shook his head. "These fake boyfriends are getting even more creative."

She shrugged. "If it isn't broke . . . Have you spoken to Ricky yet?"

Everett straightened and cleared his throat, his attention darting back to the man currently surrounded by a few beautiful women, one of whom kept touching his arm. Acid churned Everett's stomach.

"He seated me."

"Don't let him fool you," Nova said.

Everett turned to her. "What do you mean?"

"He may look put together, but he hasn't been the same since the hospital. He's like a sad puppy, moping around."

He is? Everett's heart squeezed. "I think you're exaggerating."

"He hasn't picked a fight with Nash this whole time."

Everett's eyes widened. "Seriously?"

"Nash has even tried to get a rise out of him." She sighed. "Look, you'll always be my friend no matter what happens between you and my brother. But I'm going to tell you the same thing I told him."

"And what's that?" he asked.

"You better not break his heart again. I don't want either of you hurt. So pull him aside and make this right, whatever that means for both of you."

"You said that to him too?"

She shrugged. "I mean, I might have been a little harsher with him, but you get the idea."

Everett pulled her into a hug and kissed her cheek. "Thanks for being such a good friend."

"Psh. Whatever. Just go kiss and make up with my brother."

"Kiss and make up?"

"We both know you haven't taken your eyes off him more than a handful of minutes since you got here. You look more dopey than the groom." She laughed.

"Do you think he'd forgive me?" A part of him wondered if there was still hope for them. Had he waited too long?

"Only one way to find out. Besides, we've got some time before the reception officially starts. I can stall if you need me to." She gave him one last squeeze and released him.

She was right. Everett couldn't wait another minute for this conversation. He reached for his drink on the bar and downed what was left before he licked his lips.

Each step towards Ricky had waves of anticipation and nervousness rushing through him. His tongue felt thick and his palms grew damp with sweat.

Ricky's shoulders tensed as if he could sense Everett's closeness. He looked up and their eyes met. A million memories crashed into Everett. The first time they'd met. The first time he'd felt something different for his friend. The laughs they'd enjoyed. The first time they'd kissed. The intimate night Ricky had given in and opened up to him. The moments they'd shared, the good, the bad, and everything in between rose like a storm between them. Energy crackled as the air grew thick with tension. The tiny hairs on Everett's neck stood on end.

"Can I steal you away for a few minutes?" God, his mouth was as dry as the desert. His heart thudded so hard against his ribs, he thought for sure they'd be bruised.

"Yeah." Ricky turned to the ladies around him. "Excuse me."

Everett felt the eyes on him as he led Ricky away from the crowd. Ricky's hand brushed Everett's, sending pulsing energy rushing up his arm. Instinctively, he stretched out his fingers, wanting more.

"What's up?" Ricky asked, tucking his hands in his pockets, as if he too felt the same connection but denied himself.

Because of me.

"Can we talk somewhere more private? Unless—"

"Yeah, sure." Ricky surveyed the dark woods. "You want to come to my house, or . . .?"

"Sure."

This was it. Everett was going to put everything on the line one last time.

It's now or never.

49

EVERETT

Everett and Ricky walked in silence with only the moon lighting their way, traveling up the dirt road until it split. They took a left and continued down the path.

"I missed you," Everett confessed.

The wind blew through the trees, carrying the sweet scent of fresh-cut grass and wildflowers. Gravel crunched under their feet. Everett's stomach twisted tighter with each moment that passed without a reply. Had he lost Ricky for good? Had he sabotaged the best thing he'd ever had?

A few more torturous minutes passed as they made their way onto Ricky's porch. The outside light switched on automatically, temporarily blinding him. Everett blinked as he stepped into Ricky's home and shut the door.

Ricky stood stock-still in his foyer, his shoulders ratcheted up to his ears, his hands fisted at his sides. He slipped off his shoes as Everett followed suit.

Everett reached out. "Ricky—"

Ricky spun around, his bloodshot, anguish-filled eyes leaking tears. "I don't know what you want from me."

"I'm sorry."

"You asked me for space, and I've respected that."

"You have," Everett agreed.

"It killed me not to reach out and see how you were doing, but I didn't. Every single time I picked up my phone, I put it back down." Ricky's voice trembled.

Everett stepped closer. "I saw you at Hope."

Ricky blinked and wiped his eyes. "Oh, I—I didn't mean to overstep."

Everett shook his head. "No, you didn't. I was surprised to see you but in a good way."

Ricky nodded. "Well, I won't bother you there. I told Aaron it was only until you got back. I don't want to make you uncomfortable at your place of work."

"I'm really fucking this up." Everett blew out a breath.

"Just tell me what you need from me and I'll do it." Ricky stiffened, like he was bracing himself.

"I need more."

Ricky's brows drew together, his gaze wandering to the coat rack on the wall. "I don't know what that means."

"I need more time with you."

Ricky's attention snapped back to him, confusion warring with hope in his expression.

"I need more cooking lessons that hopefully don't end with a fire. And more date nights."

Hope lit like a golden spark, igniting in Ricky's expression and crashing into the space between them, flooding the room.

"I need more PDA and your cocky jokes. I need more mornings where we get to sleep in and drink coffee together while smoking weed." Everett smiled. "I need more nights of making love with you."

Ricky's chest heaved, more tears running down his cheeks. "What else?"

"I need more tomorrows. More trust. More lessons in the gym, family dinners, holidays—I just need more of you. I want everything."

"I can do that—"

"And what is it you need?" Everett asked honestly.

Ricky swallowed, cupping Everett's face. Lines appeared at the corner of his eyes. "I need your patience and your support. I need you to hold your boundaries and keep communicating with me. I need space to cool down when we argue. But I promise, I'll come back. Give me an hour at most, and I'll return to work it out with you."

"I can do that," Everett promised.

They stared at each other and a part of Everett felt like he was truly seeing Ricky for who he was for the first time. Not the boy he remembered. Not the man he'd met when he'd moved to Shattered Cove. This was Ricky Emerson, the man who'd stolen Everett's heart, who supported him and his dreams. The man who respected him enough to let him go to chase his own happiness. And a huge source of that joy stood in front of Everett, laying his heart bare.

"I need your vulnerability," Everett continued.

"I need . . . I just need you."

With their eyes locked, Ricky leaned in, tilting his forehead to touch Everett's. Ricky's sweet exhale melded with Everett's as they stood there like that, holding each other in the silent home.

"You have me," Everett said a moment before his lips crashed against Ricky's. Everett became swept up in a kiss more powerful than all the kisses they'd shared combined. Ricky grabbed Everett's wrists, lifting them above their heads as he backed him up, pinning him against the smooth wall.

Everett's cock surged with blood as Ricky took control. Everett surrendered, wholly, fully giving in to the energy burning between them. He couldn't stop this even if the house caught on fire and burned down around them. He'd be there in the ash and smoke, streaked with soot and handprints from the man who'd stolen the last piece of his soul.

Sharp teeth nipped at his bottom lip until he tasted his own blood. Ricky held his wrists against the wall with one hand while using the other to untuck Everett's button-up shirt from his dress pants. Nothing about it was gentle. Ricky's blunt nails scraped over Everett's abdomen, making his muscles clench.

"Fuck, I missed you so much." Ricky sounded as if he was seconds away from coming undone.

"Show me." Everett pushed against the hold on his wrists and shoved Ricky's jacket off his shoulders to the ground.

Ricky grabbed the back of Everett's neck, forcing him into the kiss, his tongue sliding between Everett's lips in a tangle of needy licks. Ricky devoured him as his hands wandered to Everett's top button. He yanked Everett's shirt open, buttons scattering over the floor.

Ricky pinched Everett's nipple and twisted. Everett hissed.

"You like that, don't you?"

"I like everything you do to me," Everett confessed.

"Then you're gonna like this a whole lot more." Ricky unbuttoned his shirt, the heat in his gaze only intensifying as one button turned into two, and then three. He must have given up, because he tugged the bottom of the shirt over his head and tossed it on the floor.

Ricky reached for Everett's belt and tugged him forward for a kiss as he undid it. Ricky's hands weren't gentle as he gripped the longer strands of hair on Everett's head, leading him in a kiss of soft yet hungry lips. Want and need burned like a thousand suns inside Everett. Lust and love blended together, hanging heavy in the air, saturating every breath they took.

Cool air hit Everett's legs as Ricky shoved his pants down. Pain on his scalp prickled, adding to the pleasure and need building inside Everett. Ricky tugged his hair, forcing Everett to back up into the kitchen. Ricky spun Everett around, bending him over the counter. The cool wood was a contrast to Everett's flushed skin.

The clank of Ricky's belt had Everett's cock digging into the cupboards.

"Ricky—"

Warm leather wrapped around his neck, the belt cinching tight enough to let him know who was in control but loose enough for him to breathe.

Ricky's bare chest met Everett's back. Skin to skin, Ricky sucked the sensitive spot at the base of Everett's neck.

His eyes rolled up. "Miy lev—"

Ricky's hot breath tickled his ear, making Everett shudder. "That's right. I'm your lion. You woke this up in me. You always believed in me." Ricky bit gently into Everett's shoulder and then dragged his teeth downwards. He smacked Everett's ass.

"Fuck! You're gonna make me come."

"I've only just started, Ever. You need to know, I won't be able to let you go after this." He peppered kisses over the bite mark and tugged the belt so Everett was forced to look at the ceiling, his hands braced on the counter.

"I don't want you to. Make me yours."

Ricky's deep chuckle wound around Everett and sunk into his skin like a drug. "You've always been mine, Ever. And you always will be." His hand wrapped around Everett, grabbing his cock and stroking.

"Unh." Everett gasped, his mind going fuzzy as Ricky took control.

Ricky pinched Everett's nipple once more before his hand disappeared altogether. A moment later, a slick finger glided between Everett's ass cheeks.

"What—"

"When you come, I want you screaming my name. You hear me?"

Something liquid dripped between his ass cheeks as Ricky worked a slick finger around the rim of muscles.

Everett relaxed, trusting Ricky. "Yes."

The tip of Ricky's cock lined up with Everett's ass, slick with something oily.

Ricky pressed a hand to the center of Everett's back. Everett bent farther over the counter as Ricky gripped the belt by the base of his neck and tugged, adding more of that delicious, firm pressure.

Ricky's cock pressed against the ring of tight muscle. Everett relaxed and pushed back against him. Ricky's dick slid in just a little. It was a tight fit. Everett breathed. This was the hardest part, but he knew pleasure was imminent.

More liquid dripped over his ass. Ricky lubed up his hands, setting the bottle of olive oil on the counter.

Resourceful.

Ricky's hand wrapped around Everett's cock, jerking him off slowly, making Everett's balls draw up.

"Give it to me. Let miy lev out. I can take it," Everett said.

Ricky rolled his hips, his cock sinking deeper.

Everett's eyes rolled up in pleasured pain. "Fuck, yes. You feel so good."

"You like when I stretch your hole like this?" Ricky drove his cock deeper, stealing Everett's breath.

"Yes!" He gasped. "But I need you to move."

"As you wish." Ricky pulled almost all the way out and thrust back in. Over and over. Higher and higher, Everett climbed on a cloud of pleasured bliss. Moans and groans filled the dim kitchen. The slap of skin against skin joined in.

"You're so fucking perfect." Ricky tugged the belt, guiding Everett to arch his back.

"Promise me you're mine. That this is real," Ricky gritted out as he fucked Everett harder and harder.

"I—"

Thrust.

"Promise."

Thrust.

"Yours."

"Ever!"

"Please! Ricky!" Ever cried out, his hot cum shooting out of him. His vision went white as ecstasy flooded through his veins. The leather around his neck fell away, replaced with Ricky's hand as he turned Everett's head and bent forward, locking them in a kiss. Ricky's cock pulsed inside Everett, sticky cum dripping from his ass.

Ricky made a move as if to pull out, but Everett gripped his arm. "Hold on to me or I might just fly away."

"Can't have that, can we?" Ricky kissed his shoulder, wrapping his arms around Everett.

With their chests heaving, they stayed like that until Everett's hazy vision cleared. Finally, Ricky pulled out.

"Let's get you cleaned up." He took Everett's hand and led him up the stairs.

"What about the wedding?" Everett searched the floor at the mess they'd made. "And our clothes?"

"You can borrow some of mine. Sorry about ruining your shirt. I just couldn't wait." Ricky smirked.

"You can rip my shirt off anytime. It was pretty damn hot."

"I'll keep that in mind." Ricky turned on the shower and then grabbed a couple fresh towels, setting them on the counter.

"We still have a lot to talk about," Everett said.

"We do. But it can wait. Let me clean you up first. We'll get back to the wedding where I want a dance with my boyfriend. Then, tonight, we can come back here and eat leftovers and talk. Does that sound good to you?"

"I think that sounds perfect."

"I love you, Everett." Ricky leaned forward, tenderly sweeping his lips over Everett's.

"I love you too."

Ricky's smile lit up the whole room. Everett couldn't help but be awed by the man in front of him.

The shower was quick and efficient yet gentle. They dried off and Ricky pulled out a spare shirt for Everett to borrow.

Everett walked over to Ricky and straightened his bow tie. "Good as new."

"You think anyone will know what we've been up to?" Ricky asked.

"Probably, seeing as I left with a light blue button-up and am returning with a black one."

Ricky remained silent as he stared at the nightstand by his bed.

"Is that a problem?" Everett asked. Was Ricky still having trouble being out?

"No." Ricky shook his head. "God, no. I just . . . I've been waiting to do something until—" He blew out a breath through his mouth. "Well, honestly, I was scared. But with you here, I feel like I'm ready."

"What is it?" Everett asked.

Ricky reached to the nightstand and pulled open the drawer, holding up the water-stained envelope.

"You haven't read it?"

Ricky shook his head. "No. But I think I'm ready now. Will you . . . no matter what it says, just know that it won't change anything between us. I loved my mother, and I know she loved me. Even if the version of her back then wouldn't have been open to two men loving each other, I think she'd come around once she saw how much you meant to me."

"Of course I'll be here for you." Everett wrapped his arm around Ricky's waist as they sat on the edge of the bed. "I hope you know that whatever it says, you have a whole chosen family standing behind you."

Ricky took a shaky breath and opened the envelope. He pulled out folded pieces of lined paper with a pretty cursive font written across them.

Ricardo, my sweet boy,

I know you won't want to talk about this, but I don't have much time left. The doctors are not hopeful and have let me know that I won't be here for your next birthday. They said it would be a miracle if I made it through the holidays. I will do my best to hang on as long as possible. I want as much time with you as I can, and maybe that is selfish of me. But I can be selfish this once.

I'm worried for you, mijo. I know I'm leaving you with your father, a man who I regrettably chose when I was young and foolish. He wasn't always the way he is now. Or maybe he was and I didn't see. I was blinded by pretty words and attention.

Don't let him harden you. Protect that soft, sweet side that you have inside you—it's my favorite part of you.

Facing death makes you really think about things in a different way. I know that if I have any say in it, I will not be entering the gates with

Saint Peter. I cannot abandon you when you need me most. Even when you feel the most alone, know that I will always be with you, watching over you. And you will always carry a piece of me within you because you are all the good parts of me.

I won't be there to see you graduate from high school, or college. But you will. I won't be there to see you get married or have children. But I will be there in spirit. Look for the signs, mijo.

So, my advice for when things get hard:

Follow your heart, wherever *that leads.*

Trust in yourself.

Believe that you are good and worthy of love and respect.

Tough times will come, but they will also pass. And you will become stronger for it.

Know that no matter what, *I love you.*

I know you will find your way.

Love, Mom

Ricky inhaled a shaky breath, tears rolling down his cheeks. A sob tore through him.

Everett's heart ached for the man he loved. He held Ricky tighter and kissed his head. "I've got you. It's okay."

A few minutes passed before Ricky wiped his eyes and folded the letter carefully back in with his things.

He sniffed. "I feel so many things right now."

"That's understandable."

"But you know what I feel most?" Ricky asked, turning back to Everett.

"What?"

"Free. I feel like all my life, I've listened to the seed of doubt that my father planted—that she would be disgusted by me if she knew I was also attracted to men. He beat it into me. But a small part of me rejected the notion. And that piece of me was right. It's always been right. My mother did love me unconditionally. She would have supported me and loved you as my boyfriend. And I can't help feeling angry for letting Donald steal that from me." Ricky sighed. "I've wasted so much time trying to fit into this mold of what I thought I should be out of guilt and fear, and for what? It certainly didn't make me happy. It hurt so many people in the process." He shook his head. "I'm done living my life for anyone but myself and those I truly love."

"Good. Because I like who you are—in fact, I kind of love you."

"Kind of?" Ricky released a puff of air from his nose.

"You're growing on me." Everett smiled.

"You know, I've spent a lot of time wishing for yesterday—for the past—a time when I truly felt loved and seen. I thought I had my chance and it would never happen again. But it's been my fault because I've kept myself hidden under this facade of stupid things I thought made me appear strong. I never gave anyone the opportunity to really get to know the real me—at least not all of me." Ricky shook his head. "And then you came in and saw through it all. You called me out on it. So, thank you."

"I'll bulldoze you any day of the week," Everett added playfully.

Ricky waggled his eyebrows up and down. "I like when you talk dirty to me."

"Good. Because I don't plan to stop."

"Ever?"

"Never." He smiled. "Besides, someone wise once told me there's no reward without risk. Sometimes you gotta take a chance. So, I think I'll take his advice."

"Sounds like a very wise person indeed." Ricky ran his hand up and down Everett's back.

They would have a fresh start after this. They could move into a new future, creating the life they wanted to live together. Their past would always be a part of their story. But Ricky was right—there would be no more wishing for yesterday when everything Everett ever wanted was right there in his arms.

EPILOGUE - RICKY

August

Ricky walked out of Poseidon's Treasure with a goofy smile. Excitement spiraled in his chest, making his heart skip. The sun shone on his face, competing with the warm, floaty happiness pressing against his rib cage that was making room for *more*. A floral scent whispered in the wind. Spring flowers brightened the small town that was his home. Shattered Cove had welcomed Ricky almost as quickly as the Emersons had.

I want to raise a family here.

Ricky's grin widened even more than he'd thought possible. A woman passed by on the sidewalk. She did a double take, the corners of her mouth turning up as she passed. His joy was contagious. He wished everyone could feel one tenth of what he was experiencing. It would solve world peace. How could anyone want to cause another harm if everyone felt this happy?

He chuckled and shook his head. What had he turned

into? Ricky took a left, walking towards his car, parked on a side street. He glanced at the storefront window carrying precious gems, and natural crystals in unique settings forged by the owner himself. But that wasn't what caught Ricky's attention—it was his own reflection. The smile that curved his lips might have been a stranger to the Ricky before Everett.

He continued down the sidewalk, patting the velvet box in his pocket, a cacophony of lovesick moths tumbling in his belly. This feeling—nothing could shake it. Ricky had found his happiness.

He climbed into his truck and headed home where a house full of people were preparing to share in the love he'd found.

* * *

"There you are." Everett's deep voice was like a balm to Ricky's growing anxiety as he climbed out of the truck.

"Here I am." Ricky closed the door and walked up to his boyfriend and the mess of potting soil surrounding him where he stood outside Ricky's home. "Looks like you've been busy."

Everett blew out a breath, wiping a drip of sweat from his forehead, leaving a streak of dirt. "I always thought gardening looked relaxing. But it's hard work."

Ricky laughed, shaking his head as he searched for Bailey. "I thought you had a helper."

"Oh, she got too hot. Said she wanted to go see if Nova wanted to hang out. I'm glad she's fitting in here."

"Me too." Ricky glanced around them. "So, we're alone?"

Everett's smile grew. "Yes."

Ricky didn't say a word. He walked up to the man who was his everything and pulled him into his arms.

"I'm sweaty and covered in dirt," Everett said as Ricky held on.

"I need you." Ricky leaned forward and pressed his mouth to his boyfriend's.

Everett's arms immediately went back around him, and he returned the kiss with gentle care. But Ricky didn't want gentle. He wanted hungry, writhing bodies sticky with sweat. He reached for the button on Everett's pants, opening them and shoving his hand inside, gripping his hardening cock.

Everett gasped. "Whoa, what is this?"

"This? This is us." Ricky kissed him harder, pinning him against the truck. He tugged Everett's bottom lip with his teeth and then dropped to his knees.

"Ricardo—unh—" Everett's head tipped back as Ricky's mouth enclosed his cock. Salty pre-cum oozed onto Ricky's tongue. He lapped it up, taking him as deep as his throat would allow. Apparently, that was pretty far because his oxygen was cut off momentarily.

"Fuck, that feels so good, baby," Everett said.

Ricky hummed, bobbing his head up and down on Everett's cock. His own erection pressed against his jeans. It didn't matter. This moment wasn't about him. It was about bringing the man he loved pleasure, because he fucking deserved it—but also because it was a way to show Everett just how much he appreciated him.

Everett thrusted his hips, tangling his fingers in Ricky's hair, gripping the back of Ricky's head. The bite of pain, the control Everett held over Ricky only made it hotter. Urgent need built inside Ricky. He had to make his man come as if the world depended on it.

"I'm gonna come."

Ricky hummed, sucking hard as Everett increased his pace.

"Miy lev!" Everett yelled as spurts of hot cum hit the back of Ricky's throat. He swallowed it down and licked Everett's cock clean.

Everett's chest heaved as Ricky stood back up and wiped his mouth on the back of his arm. "What about you?"

"Ricky! Everett!" Nova interrupted, jogging out of the woods that separated Ricky's house from the rest of the farm.

Everett tucked himself back in his pants and zipped them up discreetly. Thankfully, they had the truck between them and Nova to hide what they'd been up to.

"There you are." She cut Ricky a pointed look. "Mom's been calling you."

"Sorry, I was busy." He didn't bother to hide his satisfied smirk.

Nova looked between them. "Oh, God. Everett's cheeks are about as red as Mom's tomatoes. I think I know exactly what you were doing. Ewwww." She shook her head and held up her hand. "I didn't need to know that. And next time, maybe don't do naughty things where one of your nieces and nephews or Bailey could stumble upon you."

"The truck blocked us from the house, and there's a fucking field and line of trees between us and anyone else," Ricky argued.

"Still."

"Is that thing ready that I asked you to get?" Ricky asked.

Nova rolled her eyes. "Yes, that's why Mom was calling. The kids are getting antsy."

"Don't have to be such a brat, you know."

She crossed her arms under her chest and narrowed her eyes. "You'd better be a little kinder to me, dear brother. Remember, you owe me."

"As you will never let me forget." Ricky chuckled and turned to Everett. "But it's worth it, a million times over."

Everett's eyes sparkled with a mix of satisfaction, love, and happiness. "Wouldn't want to keep your mom waiting. I know how seriously she takes these weekly family gatherings."

"I'm gonna change real quick, and then we'll meet you there." Ricky waved off Nova.

"Okay, but no funny business. Hurry up." Nova turned around and headed back the way she'd come.

"It can't be easy being the only daughter in a house full of boys," Everett mused as they walked into Ricky's house—which had become their home. They hadn't spent a night apart since Roman and Elise's wedding.

"She's feistier than she looks." Ricky laughed.

Everett pulled off his shirt as they went upstairs. He dropped it in the washer and stripped off the rest of his clothes, adding them too. "I know I don't have time for a shower. I'm gonna go wash up quick and then change and we can go."

"Sounds good." Ricky walked into the bedroom and sat on the bed as the water ran in the other room.

Everett came back in a few moments later, naked.

"Your cheeks are still flushed. God, you're so sexy." Ricky admired his lean body as he pulled a pair of shorts on. "No boxers?"

Everett smirked. "I want easy access for my man later."

Ricky grinned. "I like the way you think."

Everett reached into the unfolded laundry bin and pulled out a clean T-shirt.

"Toss me one? I think when I hugged you I got some potting soil on mine." Ricky pulled his shirt over his head and stood.

Warm fingers traced the scar on his abdomen. He clenched his abs as Everett gripped his hips and placed a single kiss on the raised flesh of the mark that would be with him forever—a reminder of everything they'd survived.

"I love you." The depth of Everett's tone made it clear just how much he meant the words.

"I love you more." Ricky leaned down and kissed the corner of his lips.

Everett's laughter poured out of him, filling the room with mirth which wrapped around Ricky and sunk into his skin until he too smiled, pulling the shirt on.

Everett stood, gripping the back of Ricky's neck, and pulled him forward until their foreheads touched. "I love you most, miy lev."

"We'll just have to see about that," Ricky teased, heading back into the bathroom to put his dirty shirt in the washer. He patted his pocket, the blue velvet box still safely tucked inside.

"Let's go before my ma comes to get me herself." Ricky laughed, only half joking.

They walked hand in hand under the bright spring sunshine towards his parents' home where everyone else important in their life had gathered, unbeknown to Everett.

The wooden steps to his parents' porch creaked under their weight. Ricky opened the door and Everett walked in through the mudroom to the entryway. He shut the door behind them and followed Everett into the kitchen where both their families waited, along with Pops from the gym, surrounding a giant cake shaped like two roosters. Instead of fighting, they were touching beaks with hearts in their eyes. It seemed Remy still thought she was funny.

A swell of anxious energy sloshed in his stomach as the man he loved walked into the room, looking around at everyone staring at them.

"Surprise!" they all yelled mostly at once. A few of the kids' voices rose a second later like an echo.

Ricky dropped to his knee.

"Mom? Dad? Bree?" Everett looked at his stepparents. "What are you all doing here? What is this?"

"We were invited by your boyfriend," his dad explained as Ricky retrieved the box from his pocket.

"And it was a great excuse to meet my granddaughter." Sandy wrapped her arm over Bailey's shoulders in a side hug as Bree and Bailey exchanged smiles.

Ricky had so much love to share, and with Everett and all their family behind them—that love was limitless.

Everett turned around, his eyes immediately dropping to Ricky on the floor. His hands covered his mouth as he took another look around at everyone gathered with new understanding.

"Are you—"

Ricky cleared his throat as all eyes fell on him. "Everett Popova, you came into my life when I needed someone most."

Everett lowered his hands, his eyes shining with unshed tears.

"You were my best friend and then my lover. You quickly became my everything." Ricky fought the overwhelming emotion that welled in his chest, moving up his throat, burning his eyes. "Those years without you were lonely. But I didn't know what was missing until you came back into my life. I didn't realize you'd carved a piece of my heart out in an Everett-shaped hole until you brought it back."

Everett knelt in front of him, taking his hand as Ricky continued, "I don't ever want to know what life without you is like. I have your yesterdays. I want your tomorrows—every single one. I want to build a home with you. To raise a family together."

Alba squealed, and everyone laughed.

"Even my niece agrees." Ricky chuckled. "I want everything with you that you're willing to give me. No matter what comes, I promise to be by your side. I won't run when things get hard, and if I do, it will be to your arms. I love you with every thought, every kiss, and every piece of me."

Ricky blinked, trying to keep the tears at bay for this next part. "Will you do me the honor of being my husband and marry me?"

Everett pulled him into a hug, kissing his neck and pulling away to kiss his mouth. A chorus of cheers rang out. The love of their family surrounded them. They were not alone. And when they faced the hatred that some of the world had for them, they would have all these people backing them up. Every single one of them loved and accepted both Ricky and Everett for who they were. Believed in them. Wanted the best for them and their love story. This was family—not by blood, but by choice. And it meant everything.

"Is that a yes?" Ricky asked.

Everett pulled back, cupping his face with one hand. "It's a fuck yes." He kissed him again.

"That's a dollar for the swear jar!" Ricky's niece, Lyra, said.

A few people laughed, including Everett as he pulled away. "Do I get to see the ring now?"

Ricky opened the box and held it out.

Everett took the case and pulled out the thin silver band, narrowing his eyes on the inscription etched inside.

I choose you yesterday, today, and tomorrow. ~ Your lion

"It's perfect." Emotion clogged Everett's voice as Ricky took the ring and slipped it on Everett's finger.

"Almost as much as you."

"Who knew all our baby brother needed was the right man to turn him into such a sap?" Nash teased.

"I knew," Renita said, making everyone crack up again.

"Can someone explain why there are two roosters on the cake?" his dad asked.

"I think my wife has a very unique sense of humor." Mikel rested his hands on Remy's shoulders and smiled down at her.

Remy grinned, shrugging and acting innocent. "What? I was asked to make a cake for two cocks falling in love."

"That doesn't even make sense." Nova shook her head.

"What's a cock?" Ariel asked Elise.

"Ricky!" Roman glared at his brother.

Ricky held up his hands as he and Everett both stood. "Hey, I'm not the one that said it in front of the kids."

"You ordered it to have it in front of the kids," Nova added, not so helpfully.

"What is it?" Ariel asked.

"Another name for a male chicken, also known as a rooster," Eli helpfully explained.

"Right." Elise smiled.

"Can we have cake now?" Eli asked.

"Absolutely." Ricky nodded.

His mother cut the cake, and their families took turns coming up and congratulating Everett and Ricky with hugs and kind words. The kids got their dessert and dragged the teens and tweens out the door into the warm spring day.

"You have quite the amazing family," Pops said next to Ricky's parents.

"Thank you," James said, his arm around Renita as they looked out the window towards the different generations of mixed and blended families playing on the lawn that would be their legacy. "We are blessed. Aren't we, honey?"

"Absolutely." She kissed him. "Only one more kid to go." She turned towards Nova.

Nova stiffened, grabbed her empty plate, and hustled towards the cake. "And that's my cue to leave."

"You don't have to go," Renita said.

"I do actually, because I have a date." Nova's voice rose in pitch.

Ricky moved next to her while she added another piece of cake to her paper plate. "Is this like an actual date? Or another fake one?"

She peeked over her shoulder at her mom and then looked back to him. "Does it matter?"

"You gotta tell her you're happy being single. She can deal with it."

Nova rolled her eyes. "You've fallen in love and turned into one of them."

"Nova—"

"Don't. Okay? It's better this way, for everyone. They didn't have to take me in and adopt me and treat me as their own. This is the least I can do for them." She sighed, glancing at her parents at the window once more. "I just don't want to disappoint them, you know? I don't want to cause them stress."

He understood that kind of gratitude. He felt it, too, for the people who'd taken in a boy with anger issues and showed him love without conditions and expectations. "I get it. Just know I'm here for you."

She smiled. "I know, and I'd hug you if I weren't afraid of dropping my cake."

He looked at her plate. She'd taken a couple pieces.

Nova shrugged. "Hey, the least you can do after stealing my fake boyfriend is give me cake." She walked away, a smile on her face, heading out the back door.

"Is everything okay?" Everett asked, handing Ricky a water bottle.

"Yeah. It is." Ricky took his hand, and they walked towards the front door. Warm spring air blew against his skin.

The scent of flowers and fresh-cut grass filled his nose. He took in the fathers rolling in the grass with their children. Mikel had Lyra on his shoulders. His brother-in-law, Atlas, carried Zoey on his as they raced. The girls squealed with glee as the puppy yipped and ran around them.

Eli sat crisscross-applesauce, his mouth moving in conversation while Ariel stuck flowers in his hair.

Alba nursed from Bella as Bella talked to Elise, lounging on a picnic blanket. Roman and Nash kicked the soccer ball around with the other kids. So many men Ricky looked up to, and every single one had learned to show this softer side. They loved their family fiercely, would punish anyone who tried to hurt them, and yet they could also show tenderness. There was a side of them that only a lucky few would see. They were protectors, but also nurturers. This was real strength. In the end, true masculinity wasn't about physical prowess; it was about being brave enough to live his truth—to be vulnerable. Everything else was just bullshit thrust upon him by society. There was no one way to be a man.

"We should join them. I heard someone mention touch football. You can show me your skills, Mr. Captain of the Football Team." Everett nudged his arm playfully.

"I think I still have my old uniform if you want to know what it's like to fuck a jock." He smirked.

Bently's phone rang. He paused what he was doing to take the call, turning his back to everyone.

"I think that sounds like a great way to celebrate our engagement," Everett said.

Bently turned around, all happiness and relaxation from his expression gone. It was replaced with the professional mask his honorary cousin donned in his job as sheriff.

His gaze swept the yard once, and then once again, like he couldn't find what he was looking for.

As if sensing something was off, his wife, Belle, joined him. Ricky approached, taking Everett's hand to bring him along.

"What's wrong?" Ricky asked.

Bently turned to him. "Where's Nova?"

"She left a few minutes ago," Nash answered as Roman walked up behind him.

Bently's jaw pulsed.

"What is it?" Ricky asked.

"That was my connection in the FBI."

Ricky's shoulders tensed. Everett's hand rested on his lower back in silent support.

"And?" Nash asked.

"The other missing girl was found."

"Hannah?" Ricky asked.

Bently nodded solemnly. "She's dead. Left with a symbol like the others."

Ricky's chest tightened with worry.

"There's more," Bently said.

"What?"

"Another woman has gone missing, and she's from the same foster home Nova was in."

The blood drained from Ricky's face. The brothers looked at each other. Fear and determination lit their eyes.

"Where's the foster dad?" Nash grit.

Bently rubbed a hand over the back of his neck. "I did some digging, and he lives near Boston."

Roman jumped in front of Nash. "Wait, don't do anything stupid."

"Nash, you asked me to keep you in the loop of this investigation. I told you I would but only if you didn't go off half-cocked," Bently snapped. "I know how hard this must be. I'm crossing lines just telling you this. But let the feds do their jobs. They got more resources to nail this fucker."

Nash seemed to lose some of his steam, his shoulders drooping a bit.

Roman let go of him and looked between Ricky, Everett, and Nash. "You know what this means, right?"

"Yeah." Ricky swallowed. "It means Nova could be next."

THE END!

Now, turn the page for a sneak peek of Book 4 in The Emerson Family Series, *Promising Today* (Nova and Jude's story), right away.

Or visit the website below to order book 4 in The Emerson Family of Shattered Cove Series right now.

<u>WWW.AMKUSI.COM/PROMISINGTODAY</u>

SNEAK PEEK OF PROMISING TODAY
CHAPTER 1

Nova

"Where the hell am I?" Nova Emerson turned down the radio as her truck bounced over a pothole in the quickly fading day's light. The headlights glinted off puddles on the dirt path ahead of her. Tall dark trees lined both sides of the road, only clearing when there was a pull off littered with abandoned rusted vehicles and old buildings. This was certainly the scenic route home.

As soon as she'd seen Chad wave in her peripheral in town, she'd been in flight mode. The man couldn't take a hint. You'd think not calling and totally ghosting after a one-night stand would be enough of a message. But Chad was determined. If only he'd been half as determined to find her clit, then maybe they could have had another round. So when he'd waved to her at the crossroads in town, she'd averted her gaze so he'd think she didn't see him. But when he'd turned the same way she drove, the opposite of which his blinker signaled, she'd gone into flight mode. She'd sped up and taken turns to lose him. She'd forgotten how clingy he was.

"If I remembered, I wouldn't be lost in my own goddamned hometown," she grumbled under her breath.

Her shocks creaked as she drove slowly over the deep divots with a wince. She'd driven off fast and taken so many turns, she wasn't quite sure if she was still in Shattered Cove or had crossed the boundary into Dark Cove. It had been twenty minutes since she'd seen another set of headlights coming either direction.

Guess it was time to use her GPS. She picked up her phone, but it rang with the wedding march. She tensed. Only one person had that ringtone. *If I don't answer, she'll just keep calling.* And the last thing Nova wanted to do was worry her mother—the woman who had quite literally saved her life.

She shut the music off and clicked answer. "Hello?"

"Hey, baby girl. I just wanted to check in and see if you had everything ready for the consult tomorrow and the wedding this weekend?"

"Yes, Mom. It's all taken care of."

"Great."

A beat of silence passed before Nova said, "Well, if that's all, I guess I'll—"

"I noticed your car wasn't in your driveway. Are you on a date tonight?"

Nova rolled her eyes. "No. You know the guy I've been seeing doesn't live too close. I made some deliveries to the nursing home and stopped to get some dinner at the diner and a drink by myself at the Shipwreck. I'm headed home now."

As soon as I can find my way out of this place. A large industrial-sized abandoned building appeared in front of her. Her headlights glinted off broken glass in the windows. It had an eerie feel to it. She shivered.

"Nova? Are you even listening to me?" her mother asked, clearly frustrated Nova had zoned out again.

"Yes, of course," she lied.

"When am I going to get to meet this mysterious boyfriend? You are still seeing him, aren't you?"

Nova sighed. The last thing she wanted to do was hurt the woman who'd chosen to be her mother. "I know, you want me married like the rest of your children and popping out grandbabies like it's nineteen fifty. But you know I like to take things slow." *Slow as in never gonna happen.* Why would she let a man in that close again, just to stomp what was left of her heart to bits? No fucking thank you.

"I know. But there is such a thing as too slow. You know… ca-…al-…"

"I think I'm losing service. You cut out. Can you hear me?….Hello?"

She pulled the phone away to look at the screen. Call dropped. "Thank you, universe."

A loud pop sounded. The car jerked to the side. She gripped the steering wheel for dear life, trying to right it. The phone went flying. A metallic grinding noise whined as she pulled to a stop.

"Fuck!" Nova looked around the truck. Just abandoned buildings, and overgrown woods lit only by the dim glow of her truck's headlights.

She exhaled and reached to the ground for her phone.

No signal.

She sighed and took one last glance before climbing out of the truck. She turned on her flashlight on the phone and inspected the tires…or what was left of one. The back one was blown to bits with jagged black rubber bits sticking out. She hadn't even been going that fast. What could—

"Shit." She grabbed the four by four with long sixteen

penny nails sticking out of it. And tugged, but it was embedded too deep in the shredded tire.

"So much for the universe being on my side," she grumbled as she let the board hang from the rubber.

A twig snapped behind her. She whirled around, tense and alert. A few men stared at her, their faces lit with the orange glow of the barrel fire they surrounded in front of a decrepit apartment building.

I certainly picked the worst place to get lost. Wait, that saying didn't make sense. Who chose to get lost? And if they decided where, where they really lost?

A shout pulled her back to her present predicament. One man shoved another before they laughed.

The hair on her skin stood on end. Her heart thudding in her chest. All her senses on alert. Crickets chirped as a bead of sweat dripped down her forehead. The sun might have set ten minutes ago, but it was still summer and today was a humid one. She spun around, taking in her surroundings. A large industrial building sat to the right of her truck with boarded up windows. Maybe an old factory? A few flickers of light bled from behind the rotting boards somewhere inside. The bottom floor windows had fared even worse, boards ripped out in some places and broken glass now littered the ground.

I need to get out of here.

Nova grabbed the tire iron and jack from behind her seat. She set the phone light on the back of the truck for light and got to work cranking the jack until what was left of the tire was off the ground.

"What do we have here?"

Nova's hand instinctively reached for the knife in her boot, keeping it in one hand and the tire iron in the other. She whipped around.

Two men approached her. The missing posters of her friends flashed in her mind. What if these were the killers? What if they abducted her? What if —

"Did you get lost, girly?" the one with the missing tooth asked.

"I don't want any trouble." She was proud of how firm her voice sounded, despite the terror gripping her chest in a vice.

"Looks to me like you've already found yourself some." The other nodded towards her tire.

"Nothing I can't handle."

"You got a few dollars to spare?" the first one asked as they crowded her, one going to her left and the other to her right. She swallowed. She might be able to take one on, but two at the same time?

Why did I turn down this road? I should have just faced Chad and told him I wasn't interested.

Fuck, I didn't even tell Mom where I was.

What if these two kill me and that was the last conversation we had?

No.

Nova was not going down without a fight. She straightened her shoulders, and tipped her chin.

"I don't carry cash. Now, if you two gentlemen would be on your way, I'll return to my business and get out of here."

"No need to be in a hurry, girly. Bruce and I here are just looking for a little fun," the second one took another step forward.

"Back up!" she yelled, raising the tire iron.

Both men looked at each other and laughed.

"No need to get your panties in a bunch," Bruce said, his eyes dropping to her crotch lasciviously.

"Look, buddy, you better back the fuck off or I will break the teeth you have left."

Bruce's eyes widened before he scowled at her.

Nova had been told a time or a hundred that her mouth would catch up to her one day. Didn't stop her though. She had never been good about keeping quiet. Besides, she'd tried to be nice, even called them gentlemen. Everything that happened next was on them.

"Bitch thinks she's so much better than us—"

"I think she made herself clear. Beat it." Another deep voice had the two men glancing past her. Nova didn't dare take her eyes off the two threats in front of her.

Oh, goddess. What if it's going to be three against one?

This isn't happening.

"Come on, we're just having a little fun," Bruce said.

Heavy footsteps sounded closer as the third man rounded the truck. Everything screamed at Nova to run, but she was trapped. She had a weapon in each hand, and some self-defense skills her brother had taught her. Even if this guy scared the other two off, she'd still have to deal with him.

The third man stepped closer, the reflection of her phone light highlighting coal black eyes. His face was all sharp angles and a severe expression. The slope of his nose was a little off center, like he'd broken it in the past. A five o'clock shadow peppered his jaw. He was hot. But Ted Bundy had been an attractive man too. Nova wasn't gonna fall for that.

His deep voice lowered an octave as he faced the two men down. "Get the fuck out of here."

"Or what, pretty boy?" Bruce snarled.

The newcomer tilted his neck to the side and cracked it before staring back at the men, menace lacing his voice. "You lay a hand on her and it will be the last thing you do."

Holy fuck. That was hot. Like the heroes right out of her romance novels. Which meant it was too good to be true. Hottie with the deep voice probably wanted her all to himself.

She swallowed, the idea terrifying. So why were butterflies swirling in her belly?

"Mouthy bitch isn't worth it anyways," Bruce said, scowling before he turned and walked away, his partner spitting on the ground by the newcomer's feet before taking off towards the abandoned factory building.

Nova stared at the new man, her heart racing a million times a minute. Was he going to attack her?

"I'm not going to hurt you," he said, as if reading her thoughts.

"That's probably what all serial killers say." She gripped the tire iron tighter.

The corner of his mouth tipped up before his full lips flattened into a straight line once again. "Get in the car and lock the doors. You can hand me the tire iron and I'll put the donut on."

"And give you my only weapon?" She scoffed.

"You can always stab me with the knife you've got hidden in that other hand if I step out of line."

She sucked in a breath.

"Get in the car," he ordered.

She bristled. She'd never been good when people told her what to do. It only made her want to do the opposite. "I don't need your help."

He sighed and shook his head. "Stubborn, aren't you?"

She tipped her chin up, which still didn't help. She barely stood five foot four and he was taller than her brothers, at least six foot nine. If he really wanted to do her harm, he probably could. *Not that I wouldn't get one good stab in.*

"Listen, it's late and hot as fuck. The mosquitos are biting me and I don't have time for games. Get in the truck. Lock the doors. And give me the tire iron so I can fix your tire and you can get the fuck out of here and back to where you belong."

"I-I don't even know you."

He leaned his head back, hands on his hips like he was counting to ten. This was not abnormal. Nova tended to push people's buttons and get these reactions a lot.

He looked straight at her and held out his hand, palm up. "I'm Jude."

She shifted on her feet, weighing her options as he waited patiently. His heavy gaze not leaving her for a moment. Her gut told her this guy was not going to kill her and rape her, but her gut had been wrong about men before.

"Fine." She backed up, climbing into the driver's seat backwards and shut the door. She rolled down the window a few inches and handed the tire iron out. He took it and got to work. The car jostled as he finished unscrewing the bolts from her tire and tossed it into her truck bed.

Nova glanced around them. No one else was in sight in between the dark abandoned buildings that she could tell. Though that wasn't saying much. Those two other men hadn't exactly just melted from the shadows. Were they watching and waiting?

What if they joined forced with the men around the fire? Would this Jude guy stick around? And if he did, we would still be outnumbered. I need to find a better weapon. Nova searched the front seat of her truck. *I just need —*

A knock sounded against her window.

Nova screamed and jumped in her seat, whirling around.

Jude stood at her window, his eyebrow quirked up. With her cab lights on, she could see him a little more clearly. If she thought he was hot before, that was nothing compared to in the dim light of her interior. *I really need to get a grip.*

Heat bloomed in her core, making her panties wet. *I'm so fucked up.*

He handed her phone to her through the window, his hands covered in black grease and dirt.

"That was fast."

He was good with his hands. *I bet he knows how to find a clit.*

"Get someone to put a tire on tomorrow. You shouldn't go far with the donut. And stick to the main roads. I don't want to see you down this way again." His tone left no room for argument. "You don't belong here." With that parting shot, Jude spun around and walked around the front of her truck, his ass a spectacular sight in his camouflage pants.

She wasn't sure whether or not she wanted to thank him or argue with him for bossing her around like that. By the time she shouted a, "Thank you!" It was too late, he was already too far ahead by the edge of the factory.

She slipped the truck into gear and drove forward slowly. The ride was much bouncier, but he'd put the donut on. Jude walked ahead off to the side of the road veering to the right at the edge of the big building. She passed as he stopped at the rear of a truck with Michigan plates and climbed in the back without one more glance in her direction.

Did he live there? Was he homeless? She kept driving. Her hands trembled, the adrenaline wearing off.

"What the hell just happened?"

She'd almost been in big trouble, that's what.

Her brothers most definitely didn't need to know about this. It would be bad enough when she got home and they realized she'd been gone this late without one of them hounding her.

Nova blew out a breath.

She really did need to be more careful. The last thing she'd want to do is cause more hurt for her family. They'd suffered enough loss.

But the truth was, there was a killer out there who was

taking people from Nova's past. She was obviously going to be on that list. Which is why she'd be ready for that asshole when he came.

She tucked her lucky knife back in her boot. A gift from her brother, Ricky.

Nova pressed on the gas and turned onto a paved road. "You want me, motherfucker? Come and get me."

To continue reading Nova and Jude's story, visit the website below to get your copy of *Promising Today*.

WWW.AMKUSI.COM/PROMISINGTODAY

AUTHOR'S NOTE

Ricky was an interesting character to write. This book was plotted to be the shortest in the series and ended up being the longest (so far).

I (Ash) can relate a lot with Ricky, and I think a lot of our readers will be able to as well. I too was raised in a similar home environment and had to suppress my sexual identity. I denied it until in my early twenties when my roommate, Kasey, came out to me and introduced me to her girlfriend. I wondered why an amazing person like her would have to face punishment simply for loving someone who was the same gender as her. It finally made me face what I had denied and kept hidden for so long.

The next year, I came out as bisexual to my college friends. And the scene in The Queen, the gay bar, was inspired by my own exploration. Going to a gay club was the first time I felt totally accepted and free to be myself without judgment. I knew Ricky needed a piece of that to help show him what he was missing out on.

There is a lot of hate and misguided people in this world

filled with ignorance. Sometimes it can be a life-or-death situation. But that shouldn't stop us from pursuing love and happiness.

Love will win. I have to believe that.

Our hope is that you find your freedom and joy in being who you truly are—even if you have to create a chosen family like we have.

Thank you for reading!

ACKNOWLEDGEMENTS

This book went through a lot of revisions and changes. The first draft was a whole thirteen thousand words less than the final manuscript. Thanks to our very thorough beta readers, Holly, Valina, and Kristina, who pointed out what the first draft was missing, and hopefully, we've done it justice.

We'd like to thank Renita for your unending support as our diversity editor and friend. Your faith in our writing and stories keeps us pushing the boundaries! From the bottom of our hearts, we appreciate you and all you've done for us.

To our sensitivity editor Jon Reyes, thanks so much for your help in making Ricky and Everett's story accurate. Working with you was wonderful, and we look forward to doing so again in our future MM books!

A huge thank-you to Lauren our editor and writing coach. You helped keep us motivated and from losing our minds when we couldn't see the forest through the trees. Your positivity is contagious and we always look forward to our Zooms with you. Thank you for taking our baby and helping us smooth out the rough edges and putting forward our best product.

To Emily Krat, thank you for sharing a little of your Ukrainian language with us. We appreciate your willingness to help another author out and look forward to repaying the favor in the future.

Regina Wamba, goddess of book cover designs and

photography, you are amazing! Thank you so much for taking our story and translating it to a beautiful cover.

To Ash's stepdad, Timothy Mcfarline of *Mcfarline Apiaries*, thanks for letting her interview you about all things bees to freshen up her memory, to enable her to write two beekeepers in this series. Your patience and knowledge is much appreciated.

And to our readers, reviewers, and ARC group, thank you doesn't seem like enough. Your support means everything to us. We hope to keep putting out books you enjoy.

JOIN OUR NEWSLETTER

The best way to get updates about new releases, sneak peeks, pre-orders, giveaways, and more is by joining our newsletter.

You'll also receive a FREE short novel that's not available on any retailer to read.

Visit the website below to join now.

WWW.AMKUSI.COM/NEWSLETTER

THANK YOU

Thank you for reading *Wishing for Yesterday*. We hope you are emotionally satisfied with Ricky and Everett's love story. If you enjoyed this novel, please consider leaving a review on your favorite retailer and sharing it with your friends and family.

If you haven't read Nash and Isabella's story yet, check out **Stepping Into Tomorrow** (Book 1 in The Emerson Family of Shattered Cove Series).

If you haven't read Roman and Elise's story yet, check out **Risking Forever** (Book 2 in The Emerson Family of Shattered Cove Series).

If you haven't read Aaron and Brynn's story yet, check out **Hope Between Us**.

Lastly, if you haven't read all the books in **The Shattered Cove Series**, make sure you get your copy so you don't miss out any of the eight amazing romances.

Thank you again for reading *Wishing for Yesterday!*

Cheers,

Ash and Marcus

ABOUT A. M. KUSI

A. M. Kusi is the pen name of a wife-and-husband team, Ash and Marcus Kusi. We enjoy writing romance novels that are inspired by our experiences as an interracial/multicultural couple.

Our novels are about strong women and the sexy heroes they fall in love with, are emotionally satisfying, and always have a happy ending.

Discover more about us at:

WWW.AMKUSI.COM

To receive updates about new releases, preorders, give-aways, and more, visit the website below to join our newsletter today:

WWW.AMKUSI.COM/NEWSLETTER

After you join the newsletter, we will send you a FREE story to read.

To contact us, use this email address: amkusinovels@gmail.com.

Happy reading!

Ash and Marcus

tiktok.com/@amkusi.romanceauthor

instagram.com/amkusinovels

facebook.com/amkusi

pinterest.com/amkusinovels

ALSO BY A. M. KUSI

Stepping Into Tomorrow

(Book 1 in The Emerson Family of Shattered Cove)

Risking Forever

(Book 2 in The Emerson Family of Shattered Cove)

A Fallen Star (eBook FREE on all retailers)

(Book 1 in The Shattered Cove Series)

Glass Secrets

(Book 2 in The Shattered Cove Series)

Defying Gravity

(Book 3 in The Shattered Cove Series)

The Lighthouse Inn

(Book 4 in The Shattered Cove series)

His True North

(Book 5 in The Shattered Cove series)

In The Grey

(Book 6 in The Shattered Cove series)

Brave Love

(Book 7 in The Shattered Cove series)

<u>Hope Between Us</u>

(Book 8 in The Shattered Cove series)

<u>Beautiful Collision</u>

(A Shattered Cove Novel)

<u>One Holiday Kiss (eBook FREE on all retailers)</u>

(A Shattered Cove Short Story)

<u>The Orchard Inn Series</u>

(Our first complete steamy romance series.)

For a complete list of all our books, visit:

www.amkusi.com/books